to Darlene —

. . . do not get discouraged
do not get depressed
alway . . . —
always . . . .
always . . . ,
Be fashionably
dressed
Billy

Mercy, Lord, Mercy

A Creative Imaginal Triptych Memoir

Catherine E. Goin

ÆGIS

BOOKS

Mercy, Lord, Mercy: A Creative Imaginal Triptych Memoir

by

Catherine E. Goin

ÆGIS BOOKS

an imprint of

THE INTERMUNDIA PRESS, LLC

A Delaware Corporation
Warrenton, Virginia

© 2013 by Catherine E. Goin

All rights reserved. Published 2013.
Printed in the United States of America.

ISBN 978-1-887730-32-7

To order additional copies of this book, please contact

THE INTERMUNDIA PRESS, LLC
www.intermundiapress.weebly.com

These novels are works of fiction. Names, characters, places, and incidents are either the product of the author's imagination or are used fictiously, and any resemblance to actual persons living or dead, events, or locales is purely coincidental.

Scripture quotations are from the Holy Bible, English Standard Version® (ESV®), copyright © 2001 by Crossway, a publishing ministry of Good News Publishers. Used by permission. All rights reserved.

Front cover art designed by Russell Goin and Janie Mosby, adapted by Eric Killinger for ÆGIS BOOKS. Back cover photo, "Artist at Work," painted by the author.

The gorgoneion symbol adorning the colophon for ÆGIS BOOKS is an adaptation of similar artifacts that supposedly functioned as both a breastplate of Athena and an ornament on the goatskin shield of Zeus, carried by the mythological hero, Perseus, to slay the Medusa—from "queen," "ruler"—and by the historical Mycenaean king, Agamemnon.

I am eternally indebted
to Dr. Stanley Wang,
Dr. Ziegmund Lebensohn,
and Dr. David Goldstein
for their great care.

≈

I am eternally indebted
to my mother, Catherine R. Goin,
and to my brother, Russell,
for their great care.

Faute de Mieux

Travel, trouble, music, art
  A kiss, a frock, a rhyme—
I never said they feed my heart,
  But still they pass my time.

— DOROTHY PARKER

Psalm 107:17–22

Some were fools through their sinful ways,
  and because of their iniquities suffered affliction;
they loathed any kind of food,
  and they drew near to the gates of death.
Then they cried to the LORD in their trouble,
  and he delivered them from their distress.
He sent out his word and healed them,
  and delivered them from their destruction.
Let them thank the LORD for his steadfast love,
  for his wondrous works to the children of man!
And let them offer sacrifices of thanksgiving,
  and tell of his deeds in songs of joy!

— FROM THE ESV STUDY BIBLE

Shall I Jump?

I looked down
                    down
                              down
The bridge is very high
I know I can fly!
I know I can fly!
The bridge is very, very, very high!

The last time
            I tried to fly
I fell onto some rocks.
My body was seriously convulsed
            By several shuddering shocks.

It turned out
            I broke a rib or two
I really, really tried to
fly! What is a girl
            to do?

The voices were persistent
The voices were consistent.

Jump!
        Jump!
                    Jump!
Get out of your slump!
Shall I?
            Shall I?
                        Shall I?
                                    Jump?

Contents

BOOK II: Eileen Meets Robert Green

BOOK III: In God We Trust, It's Mars or Bust!

Photographs follow page 206.

BOOK I

Mercy, Lord, Mercy

Part 1

The Illusion Is a Delusion

1

The Flight Home

ILEEN! COME ON! WE NEED TO CHECK IN FOR OUR FLIGHT," SAID Mrs. Gordon as she dragged Eileen to the gate agent. "Hello, Morris," she said as she surreptitiously looked at his name tag. "We need to get on the plane as quickly as possible. My daughter is sick, and we need to get her settled as quietly and quickly as possible."

Morris looked cautiously at Mrs. Gordon, Maria, and Eileen. They were all winded from hurrying through the terminal. Maria was looking particularly anxious. When she became a supervisor, she had no idea that she would be dealing with problems like this.

She looked at Eileen, who looked as anxious as she, Maria, felt. *Well, I guess she deserves to be dumbfounded after what she's been through.* She pulled the other two ladies over to the jetway door, along with herself and Morris. "Come on, let us get settled."

"Okay, ladies, come with me," said Morris as he unlocked the jetway door and allowed the three stressed-out ladies to enter the plane.

Eileen was worried. She was trying to recover from the shock of discovering that she would have to regain twenty pounds if she wanted to return to work with Universal. Not only that, but she was leaving San Francisco and would probably not ever live there again. *Wow! This is just too traumatic. I wish I could talk to Wahu, but he hasn't come back since I started taking my pills. Dr. Sung said that if all goes well, I won't hear any more voices. Doctors all seem to agree that the voices are a bad thing—not good.* As she was thinking this, she was not paying attention to where she was stepping, and she stumbled at the entrance door to the plane. "Shit!" she said loud and clear.

Maria looked aghast, and said, "Eileen, stewardesses for Universal do not say things like that. Please remember that you're a lady—a rather sick lady I do agree—but a lady nonetheless."

"Oh yeah! Sorry, Maria. I won't say anything like that again," replied Eileen, who thought Maria was being rather picky, but since Maria was her boss, she decided to cooperate.

Mrs. Gordon looked around her surroundings. They had boarded a stretch DC-8. This was one of Eileen's favorite planes, and she instantly felt more secure. It was a beautiful plane. They were seated in first class, in seats 4A and 4B. They went to their row and sat down.

At that instant, she heard a commotion behind her. It was a man's voice, ringing out loud and clear, "Shit, man! I want a drink and I want it now! Do you hear me?"

"Now, now, Mr. Hollandar. You know that you're taking tranquilizers and pain killers with codeine, and your doctor said that you were not to have any liquor. Please lower your voice," said a young man in a white tunic top and white pants. He looked like a male nurse.

As Eileen and Mrs. Gordon looked over their seat backs, they saw a man's head poking out of a white sheet while suspended in the air. He was in an aerostretcher, which was hanging from an overhead bin. Eileen had heard of aerostretchers, but never had seen one. "How interesting," she observed.

"Sit down!" said her mother, as Eileen climbed over her mother's knees. She stepped into the aisle, and headed back to where the action was.

"I'll be back in just a moment. Right now I just want to see this man who's hollering for a drink." As she said this she stepped quietly up to the man who was hollering for a drink. "Hi, Mister," she said in her most cheerful voice.

"Who the hell are you, lady? Just leave me alone," said Mr. Hollandar in a pain-drenched voice.

"Now, now, Mr. Hollandar, try to be nice," said the male nurse in his condescending tone of voice.

"Get me a drink and get it now!"

Eileen looked more closely at Mr. Hollandar, who could only yell—not move—just yell. "Mr. Hollandar, whatever in the world happened to you?" Eileen, even in her dazed state could recognize that here was someone who was in even worse shape than herself.

By now, all of the stewardesses were gathered around the screaming man, and the obsequious male nurse. The nurse said, "Ladies, if you must know, he was in a skiing accident at Lake Tahoe. He lost control and crashed into a tree. He broke practically every bone in his body. He is going to Washington to see a specialist there."

"Why can't he have a drink? That only seems like the kind thing to do," said Eileen who was truly concerned about Mr. Hollandar's mental state. She understood what a blessing it was to lose consciousness and all awareness of one's surroundings. "In fact, I could use a drink myself, but Dr. Sung said that for a while I can't have any liquor." As she was thinking this, she noticed that the male nurse had loaded up a syringe with an obnoxious liquid and was injecting it into Mr. Hollandar's arm.

"Step back, ladies. He needs a tranquilizer if this flight is to have any peace and quiet. In just a minute he'll be asleep, and you can board the other passengers."

Eileen went back to her seat and rejoined her mother, who was contentedly sipping on a glass of champagne. "Sorry, Eileen, none for you."

Eileen rested her head against the window sill. It was dark and the moon was hanging low in the night sky. Lights were shining everywhere—shining from the terminal, lights all over the airport grounds, and lights shining from the planes lined up on the taxiway, waiting for clearance to take-off. *How wonderful! It's been so long since I've been in the air,* she thought as she gazed around the cabin, listening to Don Ho singing over the boarding music.

One of the stewardesses approached her and offered her a glass of orange juice. Eileen declined but asked for a cup of coffee with crème. "Coming right up," said the smart-looking young stewardess, as she headed back to the galley for a cup of coffee.

"Eileen, have you looked at the menu? It looks like a wonderful dinner. There's also a great movie afterwards. It's *Butch Cassidy and the Sundance Kid.* That should be fun to watch."

"Sure, Mom, if you say so. "Eileen was tired—too much excitement for one day. She was dozing as the airplane roared down the runway, taking off into the starry night.

Mrs. Gordon was excited, as her daughter was. She loved to fly. She loved airplanes and whizzing through the sky to all sorts of mysterious destinations.

Suddenly they were airborne, climbing upwards to their cruising altitude of 37,000 feet above the ground. Eileen woke up. She was hungry, glad that this was a dinner flight . . .

at night . . .

8:00 P.M.

she could eat

she was thin . . .

She recognized all the commotion associated with a first class dinner flight . . .

"Dinner at eight, dinner at eight
Do not be late, do not be late
We are serving pheasant and wine
Do not be late to dine, do not be late to dine.
We will have wine when we sit down to dine."

The dinner bell rang, loud and clear
Summoning all those who were near
The stews all sang as the dinner bell rang
"Ho, Ho, eat and drink slow
Do not eat fast or you will get sick
Alas, Alas.

We are serving filet mignon and salmon too
Cooked all the way through
So as not to give you bacterium
In the tum.

However . . .
Before we eat, we are presenting a treat!
A cocktail, the old fashioned kind
Served with a twist of lemon or lime.
Sublime!

A martini or two may be your preferred brew
We know how to fix it
Just so!
With an olive, don't you know.

If a teetotaler you are not
We will give you a shot
Of whiskey straight up, or on ice
Ain't that nice?

We do try to please, presenting goodies with ease

As through the aisle the carts we do squeeze.
When dinner comes round
Turbulence causes us to bounce up and down
While wielding a carving knife.
Do not fear for your life.

The gent in 8A is drinking away
Singing at the top of his lungs.
We approach him and say
'No more drinking tonight. Care for coffee?
Black or White?'

We do not care to hear more
Of that magnificent score
Much less an encore.
Please do not snore.

When dinner is finished
Close your eyes, go to sleep
Forget your woes, do not weep.
The night will quickly pass away
When we land it will be day.

So at last, after a sumptuous repast
The cabin becomes dark—
The end of a lark—
Eyes that are weary
Eyes that are teary
Eyes that are cheery!
Slowly, slowly the lids close down
No one has a frown.
They drift off into
Never-Never Land
Just as we planned . . ."

Although Mr. Hollandar and Mrs. Gordon were sound asleep, Eileen was restless, and finally opened her eyes, looking out the window, watching the lights down below as the plane quickly crossed the continental United States. She was so thankful to be in the air that she temporarily forgot all of her problems. Perhaps there was a future for her, but for the life of her she could not envision what it would be, and how it would come about.

Mrs. Gordon woke up and said softly, "I hope you are having a good flight. It was nice of Maria to get us two seats in first class and for making it possible for you to return to work in three months if the doctors agree. In those three months at home, the first thing you must do is learn to drive and get a car."

"But, I'm afraid to learn to drive," wailed Eileen in desperation. Her worst nightmare was coming true. "I don't have a car."

Mrs. Gordon continued, "You will be living in the country. You will have to drive if you plan on getting to Dulles International Airport. There's no other transportation. Cheer up! You can do it."

Eileen looked at her mother in complete horror, gave a panicked sigh, and fainted. Fortunately, she was sitting down, and did not hurt herself.

Mrs. Gordon looked at her daughter, saw that she was still breathing, and went back to sleep.

The lights from the movie screen flickered, as Butch Cassidy and the Sundance Kid continued on their journey to South America, into the pages of history.

During the night the stewardesses walked through the aisles. They were checking on their passengers . . .

All seemed well . . .

Eileen was going home . . .

2

Should I Jump?

*E*ILEEN REMEMBERED HER FIRST COHERENT THOUGHT: *I WANT TO fly!* She was only five years old and very small.

One day during the summer it was hot. The crickets were chirping, and the birds were singing at the top of their voices. Eileen was dressed in her favorite leopard print pants, her black turtleneck, and her blue sneakers.

She, her brother Charles, and their friend George, were playing Flash Gordon and the Return of the Space Ape. This was a game they had made up—complete with Dale (Eileen), the Space Ape (Charles), and Flash Gordon (George). They had a gorgeous spaceship made out of cardboard in which they all loved to fly. It was painted silver with red stripes.

The action was getting heated late in the afternoon. Mrs. Gordon was fixing dinner. It was not quite dark. The moon was just rising, and the sun was setting. Eileen was hiding in the tree. Suddenly Flash yelled, "Dale, Dale! Jump! Jump! You must fly or the Space Ape will catch you and chop you up into little pieces!"

Dale climbed down onto the cross bar of the swing set in the back yard. She knew that she had to jump before she could fly. She had watched the birds many times. She knew that they had to flap their wings, build up some speed, and take off.

She flapped her arms and jumped into space. For just an instant she was airborne—then, all of a sudden, a swift pain shot through her body. Good grief! She was hanging on the clothesline by the neck. She couldn't even open her mouth to scream. Charles and George were hopping up and down, screaming for her to come down from the clothesline.

"Mama! Mama! Help! Help! The Space Ape has caught Eileen and hung her on the clothesline. Help! Help!" screamed the two spacemen.

Mrs. Gordon yelled back, "Calm down boys. What's wrong? I'll be right there!" She came bounding down the back steps, and looked at her daughter hanging on the clothesline, swinging in the breeze. Eileen's face was turning blue.

Mrs. Gordon retrieved Eileen from off the clothesline. She told George to go home.

She turned to Eileen, and asked, "What in the world were you doing?"

"Gee, Mom, I was just trying to fly."

"Oh, I see. Well, dinner is served."

Eileen went to the first grade the following fall. She was having a grand time learning to read. Her teacher also encouraged the kids to draw and paint. Eileen was especially good with crayons. School was fun. She realized at quite a young age that the purpose of school was to educate people so that they could get a good job.

Eileen had an orderly mind, and she applied all of her faculties to solve the problem of what she wanted to do when she grew up—assuming, of course, that she grew up. George was in her class. They were too old to play Space Cowboys, so they played in the sandbox and discussed their futures.

George wanted to be a boxer.

Eileen wanted to fly. She had narrowed it down to two ways:

1. She read about Amelia Earhart and figured that she could be a pilot;
2. She read her two Vicky Barr books and figured that she could be a stewardess.

Now she knew what she wanted to do. She wanted to fly, one way or the other.

When she was twelve years old, her parents took her and Charles to the airport for the first time. She was enchanted watching the airplanes. She loved the airport.

Then, magically, there appeared two stewardesses walking through the terminal. They were gorgeous and beautiful to her. They walked through the terminal, surrounded by an air of mystery and adventure. She loved their uniforms and suitcases.

"Wow! I'm going to be a stewardess when I grow up!" she exclaimed to her parents with an enchanted smile.

The rest of her young life was spent waiting until she was twenty years old.

She went to college and wavered a bit. Everyone said she needed a more prestigious job. She thought about being an artist, or perhaps joining the Foreign Service. That sounded prestigious.

One night, however, she was painting in the studio in the art building. One of her friends rushed in and told her that President John F. Kennedy had been shot and killed.

Wow! she thought, *How weird! He was on top of the world. He had everything and POOF, it was gone.* This brutal assassination depressed a whole nation. Eileen, who was also depressed, realized that nothing in this life is guaranteed. Not even one minute. She might as well do what she wanted to do. Fly! There were no more doubts in her work.

"Eileen," said her dad, "don't be such a dope. Finish school and then I won't say a word if you still want to be a stewardess. I personally think it's shocking that you have such a death wish. Why can't you be a teacher like all of your friends?"

"Gee, Dad, you know I don't like kids. But if you think it's so important that I finish school, I guess I will. Although you know my grades are bad," said Eileen with trepidation in her voice. She was afraid that her father would be disappointed with her.

"Just try, Eileen. Just try."

3

Fashion in the '60s and How It Affected Eileen's Life

IT WAS A LONG TIME AGO—BEFORE YUPPIES, AND AFTER BEATS. Eileen never became a hippie because she did not like the way they dressed. She was interested in clothes. She always had been, ever since she was a little girl. Both her mother and grandmother had been that way. She came by this interest naturally. They all were seamstresses. Money was scarce, but also they loved the creativity involved in sewing.

Eileen had always believed that appearances counted big-time. When she applied for her first job, which she wanted desperately, she prepared for it as carefully as any CEO presenting a new plan before the board. Her dress was simple—a black and white Glen plaid. It had a dropped waist, pleats dropping from the hips, and three-quarter-length sleeves. She wore a pair of simple black pumps with two-inch heels.

Chic and flattering!

She wore white gloves, as she bit her nails.

She looked so nice that her interviewer thought she might be intelligent. He began to ask her advice as to whether he should send his daughter to a co-ed college or an all-girl's school.

Eileen, who was always sensible, said, "You must be kidding! Why in the world would you send her to an all girl's school? You might as well get her immersed in a co-ed school, so she can learn to compete with men right away."

"Well," said Mr. Pearson, her interviewer, carefully considering what she had said, "Don't you think she will learn more if she is in a non-threatening environment?"

"Mr. Pearson," she said, "you must remember that this is the 1960s, and women simply cannot exist in the lifestyle known to our mothers."

The interview went on for two hours because they were having such a grand time. Then Mr. Pearson asked her the ultimate question—the one determining whether or not she would get the job. "Miss Gordon, would you be willing to share a room with a black woman?"

He watched her carefully as she formulated her answer. Keep in mind that he was suspicious of her because she was from the South.

When he asked her this, she thought he was totally nuts. She said, "I quite frankly don't care what color a person is. All I care is that they don't drink in the room, bring men to the room, or in any other obnoxious manner interfere with my getting a good night's sleep."

"Bravo Miss Gordon," he said, "you're hired." He amended that by adding, "If you pass your physical."

See what happens when you dress right!

She passed her physical and was off to the Universal Airlines Training Center for six weeks. She had just graduated from college and was thoroughly sick of studying. The idea of six more weeks of study set her teeth on edge, but she realized that there was no choice in the matter.

What in the world would she and her friend do to fill up six weeks?

Well, there was:

1. How to make coffee in the fascinating coffee brewers.

2. Which drawer the lemons, limes, and olives were in.

3. How airplanes fly, which was puzzling to her. From watching birds, she knew that, like birds, airplanes had wings, and so could fly. Aerodynamics were a little beyond her ability to comprehend.

4. How to style your hair.

5. How to apply makeup.

6. How to pass out meals and how to pick them up.

7. Union rules.

8. FAA rules and regulations.

9. How to pretend you are interested in what passengers are saying.

10. How to wake a military man without startling him so that he doesn't come bounding out of his seat and hit you.

11. How to walk in three-inch heels, especially up and down stairs, as at that time there were no jetways; and how to keep your hat from falling off your head.

12. How to stay skinny.

This was all challenging, especially staying skinny, as there was tons of food placed before them. For this reason many of the young ladies took up smoking, including Eileen.

It was a hostile environment. Since Eileen had a thin grip on reality, she found it hard to get along. She figured out what the image—or illusion—was supposed to be, and in a calculated manner set out to convey this image. She was successful, as she had been doing this since she was a young girl. She managed to pass the test, and the appearance standards. Next came the test that really let you know if this was an appropriate job: "The Fright Flight."

The class of twenty young ladies went up in the air one fine Thursday afternoon in the month of April. They all piled into a raggle-taggled old DC-6. It was a beautiful sunny afternoon, with blue skies and fleecy white clouds promenading through the heavens. The instructors came along. They were going to have a tea party, complete with sandwiches, cookies, tea, and coffee. There was a lounge table in the back of the plane, and the instructors were having a rousing game of bridge.

Things got going and the coffee got flowing. The captain came on the PA and said "Hold on girls, it's going to get rough." He started swooping and swirling and dipping this way and dipping that way. Eileen only liked perfectly smooth air and found this type of flying disconcerting. But she did not, I repeat, did not throw up. And she fell totally in love. Beyond any shadow of a doubt she had found her niche in life. She knew that she would never get tired of flying. She knew that she would never get tired of planes.

Eileen had fallen head-over-heels in love, and she knew it would last forever. Finally, the Captain smoothed out the ride and they headed back to the airport. What a glorious day!

The next day they had to pass the Emergency Training Test. This was challenging, especially at the end, because everyone had to jump into the slide in order to pass.

Eileen, who was terrified of heights, was afraid to jump. Her friends just kept on yelling "Jump, Eileen, jump! You can do it." Eileen remembered when the Space Ape was chasing her, and she jumped out into the air. The next thing she knew was that she hit the slide, and she went hurtling to the ground.

She had passed! Now, onto the real world! Her uniform fit nicely; she got to wear short white gloves in the summer and elbow-length navy blue leather gloves in the winter. She was happy.

It was the spring of 1964. Just before hippies took over the world.

4

The Beginning of Life on the Road

IT WAS 1964. HIPPIES WERE BEGINNING TO TAKE OVER THE WORLD. Eileen, a very proper miss, was immersed in the turmoil of the times. She was relatively untouched by any of it because she was so busy flying and shopping that she did not have time to get into trouble.

Shopping was great. There were trips to Seattle, Los Angeles, Portland, Vancouver, Denver, New York, Boston, and San Francisco. Nordstrom's was just getting firmly established, and all of the stewardesses loved to go there on their layovers. Jackie Kennedy had started a fashionable look that they all tried to emulate.

Her favorite boyfriend was Artie. He was a handsome San Francisco hippie spiritually, whose approach to clothing was strongly influenced by Jack Kerouac and James Dean. They had a grand time when she was in San Francisco riding around on his motorcycle.

One fine day they decided to take a road trip to Monterey. They hopped on the cycle and took off. This was before the advent of helmet laws. Neither of them had long hair. Since they had slicked their hair back behind their ears, they looked quite sleek; just as though they were wearing helmets. Eileen had a "pixie cut." It was stylish and somewhat fashion-forward.

For this great adventure they were well dressed. Artie, who was tall, skinny, and quite handsome, was wearing khakis, a white T-shirt, a black leather jacket, and a brown leather belt with a silver and turquoise concho. Eileen was a vision in a hot pink minidress. It had aqua bands around the neckline, armholes, and hem. With this she was wearing an aqua long-sleeved T-shirt and hot pink shoes.

It was a beautiful spring day. There were gorgeous, big fleecy white clouds drifting around—seemingly at random. Big, fat sea-gulls were swooping and swirling above the ocean looking for equally big, fat fish to eat for lunch.

About 2:00 P.M., they pulled up at the Blue Moon Café for lunch.

"Wow Artie, this place looks cool! Is the food good?" This was a rhetorical question on her part, as at that time she hardly ate. The airlines would fire you if you had an ounce of fat, so none of the stewardesses ever ate. They were as neurotic about their weight as models and movie stars. Twiggy reigned supreme.

"Yeah, Eileen," answered Artie. "I've eaten here a lot. We can get a good table overlooking the ocean, and they have a good selection on the jukebox." They sat down. He loved to hear Elvis playing "Blue Suede Shoes," so he walked over to the jukebox, put in his quarter, and out blared Elvis.

The skinny red-haired waitress sauntered over and said, "Okay kids, what'll it be?" They ordered lunch. Eileen ordered a spinach salad. Artie was big and needed a lot to eat, so he ordered a giant double cheese-burger and an extra-large order of French fries.

They were having a grand conversation, when there was a hideous noise. They looked out the window and saw about twenty members of the Hell's Angels and their ladies roaring to a stop in the front of the café.

"Uh oh, Eileen! We'd better get out of here. If they come in here and get all tanked up, who knows what'll happen. Come on, Eileen."

They hurriedly paid the waitress and went outside. Their cycle was parked in a little alley beside the restaurant. The Angels were already soused. One of them was quite belligerent. He started following Eileen and Artie as they were hurrying to Artie's cycle. He grabbed Artie and slammed him against the side of the building.

"Punk," he snarled, "I ought to cut your liver out and feed it to the dogs!"

Artie didn't say anything. Eileen was speechless. The situation was unlike anything she had ever encountered. She was flabbergasted.

Two more Angels and their ladies sauntered up. One of them, obviously the leader, said, "Put him down Spike, and leave 'em alone. They're just kids."

"Aw, Sparkey, I'm just havin' a little fun."

"Put him down this minute! I'm not tellin' you again."

"Okay, okay, don't get so tense." Spike put Artie down and said, "Beat it kid!"

Artie and Eileen beat it.

Later that evening, after thinking about the day, she thought that the name "Hell's Angels" was very appropriate. The men all seemed overweight to her, and they seemed to have a clear mission—which, of course, they did. Their mission was to ride motorcycles, be feared, drink beer, and do cocaine.

Although she herself would never dress like their women, she thought that the black leather look was very dramatic. She particularly admired the black boots and the headbands.

Life on the West Coast was fascinating to her.

She and Artie would go to Sausalito to watch the "Weekend Hippies." The "Weekend Hippies" later became yuppies, who were and still are probably the most hypocritical human beings the world has ever produced. It was important to them to be perceived as "cool." To them that meant sex, drugs, and rock-n-roll. More importantly, it meant money—lots and lots of money. They were the American bourgeoisie.

Eileen and Artie understood this concept because they had been to college and were exposed to the Marxist concepts of the proletariat, bourgeoisie, etc. Communism was in full flower, and everyone was worried about the Cold War.

Eileen thought that in order to implement their Five Year Plan, the Communists had sent lots of exchange students to U.S. colleges and universities to stir up trouble—which frequently during the '60s was the case. By the '70s it was totally out of hand.

Artie and Eileen were having a grand time.

About this time, Peter Fonda starred in *Easy Rider*, and Artie got the urge to hit the road. He and his friend Skip pooled their money and bought a van, and off they went.

Eileen was of the mindset, "out-of -sight, out-of- mind." Artie disappeared into the horizon, leaving her with a light heart and good memories.

5

Meeting Maudie

ARTIE HAD TAKEN OFF WITH SKIP FOR THE GRAND TOUR OF THE USA, Canada, and Mexico. Although Eileen was not the type of girl to really miss a guy, she still found herself lonely and bored now that she was bereft of her favorite playmate. So in November 1964, she decided to head back to the East Coast and her family. They were very entertaining, and she knew she would not be bored.

If only she could meet someone with a motorcycle...

Mom and Pop were quite thrilled.
Their souls were chilled to the bone
To know that she had been alone
In a large city
The image presented
To them
Wasn't pretty.

She needed a roommate to help pay the rent. In Seattle she had not shopped too much because she was either running around with Artie in San Francisco or working. Now that she was back in Alexandria, however, she had discovered that there was a Woodward and Lothrop department store just several blocks from her apartment. She got a credit card. The urge to use it was so overwhelming that she realized the only way to use it was to have more money available. She needed a roommate . . . enter Maudie . . .

It was so long
So long ago
I've forgotten the details
Don't you know?

Maudie entered
W earing all black
Glasses, skirt, and sweater
Her eyes weren 't so good
Eileen's were much better.

Eileen said "hi"
You look swell
You are dashing
You are dressed quite well.
Eileen herself was dressed in red
You could tell
Just by looking
They were both well-bred.
Maudie said "hi"
You look smart too
I heard you are looking
For a roommate
Is that true?

Yes, as a matter of fact
l am

We seem to be compatible
    Ain't that grand?

I have a gorgeous
    Little place
With one bedroom—
    Not much space
There is one bed
    Upon which to lay your head
But there is one hitch
We must switch
    And take turns.

But what is great
We each pay
    Half the rate
And then we can shop
Until we drop.

If that is agreeable
    To you
That, for sure, is
    What we will do.

So they became roommates.

They got along famously, although Maudie drank a bit more than Eileen thought was judicious, and she kept a loaded pistol in a suitcase in the closet. She said that this was to be used to protect them from thieves and other types of attackers. Eileen thought this was a bit of overkill, as they did not own anything of value. It seemed unlikely that any self-respecting thief would jeopardize his career by trying to break into their apartment, which was in a low rent district.

One night Maudie, who was interested in knowing how to protect herself, had invited her friend Ted over to the apartment. Ted was an undercover narcotics cop. He had brought his new friend, Maurice, along. Maurice was new to the area, having just come from working for Interpol in Paris. Ted looked quite splendid in his tight-fitting blue jeans, a red tank top, black leather boots, and a gold hoop in his left ear. To top off this great outfit, he was wearing a red and white bandana on his head. Maurice, who was more conservative, was wearing black leather pants and a white shirt, plus he had beautiful long black ringlets. He was quite dashing, although he was too reserved to wear an earring.

Maudie and Eileen had fixed refreshments. Since neither of them could cook, refreshments consisted of potato chips and onion-flavored chip dip from the corner deli. There was beer for Maudie and the boys, while Eileen had a glass of white wine.

Ted started lecturing on how to protect oneself. "First, you two need to carry a switchblade knife. I can get you one if you'd like. No one would ever suspect that two such conservative-looking women would be carrying a switchblade, much less would they suspect that you know how to use it."

"Gee, Eileen, this is pretty heavy advice. But I guess it's better to know how to go on the offensive," said Maudie who was not sure that it was a good idea to fool around with knives.

"Would we really be able to use it in real life?" Eileen asked as she practiced flicking the knife.

"Sure you would, girls. That's why Maurice and I are here. We'll show you how!"

At this point, the oh-so-gorgeous Maurice went out to the car and got out a large green watermelon. He returned to the apartment and placed it on the radiator beneath the window.

Maudie and Eileen were curious. What in the world was Maurice doing with a watermelon? It was about 10:30 P.M. The apartment was dark except for the light from Eileen's lava lamp. The light from the silver moon was pouring in through the window where the watermelon was sitting.

Maurice and Ted admired the placement of the watermelon. Maurice stepped back, grinned, and said "*Alors, mademoiselles! Regardez!*"

Ted now stepped into the moonlight. As he sauntered forward, he flicked his wrist—CLICK, CLICK—and in his hand appeared a four-inch switchblade.

"A switchblade—I declare," said Eileen, "I've never seen one before. It's pretty scary, isn't it Maudie?"

"Oh, shut up, Eileen! Just shut up and watch carefully what I do." Ted extended the switchblade and ran toward the watermelon screaming, "Aim for the stomach, aim for the stomach!"

At this point, he jabbed the knife into the watermelon. Seeds and juice spurted onto the floor. Eileen and Maudie each screamed, "Eek!" Ted then twirled his wrist upwards in a twisting motion. "Don't forget the twisting motion girls," said Ted.

The lava lamp continued to cast its wavering light. Maudie, who had had one beer too many, fainted.

Eileen, who had been fascinated by the precision with which Ted had performed his show with the switchblade and the watermelon said, "Hey, Ted, can I try it?"

"Sure. Here's the knife."

Maurice, meanwhile, was trying to revive Maudie who was still unconscious.

6

A Night at the Local Yokel

ONE NIGHT EILEEN AND MAUDIE WERE BORED, THINKING OF things to do. Maudie mentioned that her brother Matthew was in town for the summer. He was going to the University of Indiana to get his masters in music, but during the summer he was living in Alexandria and working in a local bar, the Local Yokel, playing the piano and singing the blues.

"Eileen, let's call Matthew and see if he would like us to join him for a drink and dinner this evening."

"That sounds like fun, Maudie. Let's! My brother, Charles, is back from Vietnam. Could we invite him? He even has a car."

"Great! I'll call Matthew and check with him if he would like us to join him."

Later that evening the four young people were sitting at the booth having a drink. The bar was funky. It was dark, and the booth gave a sense of privacy. There were pictures on the wall portraying the Beatles,

Elvis, B. B. King, and the Shirelles, playing and singing. Everyone was having a beer, except for Eileen, who was having water.

At 8:00 P.M., Matthew started playing his first set. He began wailing, "Take these chains from my heart and let me be. . . ." *Ah,* thought Matthew, *Patsy Cline, you were wonderful.*

Charles was visibly affected by Matthew's touching rendition of this song. He was all choked up remembering the girl to whom he had lost his heart in Saigon—Pearl. She was still back in Saigon. She was an exotic dancer and had smitten Charles. He fell hopelessly in love, but she, fickle woman, had dumped him for a marine—Charles had been in the Army in his misbegotten youth.

"A marine! How could she do it? I loved her from the depths of my soul—her long black hair, her big brown eyes, her silken skin, etc. How could she dump me for a marine?" Charles had had one beer too many.

"Gee, Charles!" piped up Maudie, who was also in the dumps, "that was really lousy of her. But maybe it's all for the best. Your mother and father would freak if you brought home an exotic dancer from Saigon. You are young! Someone else will come along. On another level, though, I know how you feel. I'm twenty-four, also, and feel that love has passed me by. I know that I'll never have a soulmate and a family. My parents were right. I should've gotten married when I was eighteen like all of my friends."

"Come on, you guys," piped up Eileen, who had a stronger constitution and could endure heartache better, "Cheer up! At least you're not married!" She remembered her parent's advice on the subject of love and marriage. They had shared this bit of wisdom with her before she went to college: In a nutshell—"Eileen," said her father, "do not start dating when you're young because you will have done everything by the time you get out of high school, and there'll be nothing left to do but get married. Be smart, girl, use your head."

"Okay Dad, I get it. You think I would be happier single."

"Oh most assuredly," chimed in her mother.

Matthew was now singing a B.B. King favorite, "The Thrill Is Gone.

This was simply too much for Maudie and Charles. They ordered another beer. Eileen, impressed by Matthew's musical ability, was singing along with him.

Matthew, although no one noticed it, was totally broken-hearted. Matthew identified with Charles. "Charles, what is it about these marines?" he moaned, when he was through with his set.

They all lit up a cigarette. Maudie and Eileen had started smoking because it helped them stay thin; and equally important, when a young man got fresh and tried to kiss them, they would take a puff and blow the smoke in the young man's face. This discouraged even the most ardent admirer.

Maudie and Eileen had all the bases covered.

7

From the Epilogue of *The Illustrated Man* by Ray Bradbury

*I*T WAS HAZY. I SAW ONLY ENOUGH OF THE ILLUSTRATION TO MAKE me leap up. I stood there in the moonlight, afraid that the wind or the stars might move and wake the monstrous gallery at my feet. But he slept on, quietly.

The picture on his back showed the Illustrated Man himself, with his fingers about my neck, choking me to death. I didn't wait for it to become clear and sharp and a definite picture.

I ran down the road in the moonlight. I didn't look back. A small town lay ahead, dark and asleep. I knew that, long before morning, I would reach the town. . . .

The Story Begins . . .

One night at the Local Yokel, Charles, Maudie, Matthew, and Eileen were having dinner. It was snowing outside and the heat was not working, something about there not being electricity—the line was down. It was about 6:00 P.M. Matthew did not have to play until the eight o'clock shift. Candles were flickering throughout the bar.

They were all bundled up. This evening, Maudie and Eileen had forgone fashion for warmth. They were very interested in staying warm. They were wearing sweaters and leather jackets. Maudie's naturally was black—a biker's jacket. Eileen was also wearing a biker's jacket, but hers was fire engine red—the cat's meow. Charles was wearing a red plaid wool work shirt, and Matthew was wearing his new black leather spy coat.

They looked spiffy and were warm. Since the bar had a fireplace that used wood, they had started a big fire and were eating dinner in front of it. Charles, Matthew, and Maudie were playing gin. Eileen had no head for cards, so she was just fidgeting. The light in the room was flickering from the light of the candles they had lit.

Maudie said, "Eileen, stop fidgeting. We're trying to concentrate, but it's hard when you keep moving around."

"Sorry, but I'm bored." blurted out Eileen. "Hey, Maudie, Shall I tell Charles and Matthew about our flight last week to San Diego?"

"Yeah, that would be great."

"Well guys, it's like this. Last Tuesday night we were flying to San Diego. We were on the DC-8 that has the lounge table in the back by the galley, where everyone plays cards. It was around 2:00 A.M. The plane was dark. The lights were turned off, and everyone was asleep except for this naval officer who was talking to us. We really didn't want to talk, but he wouldn't shut up. At last I suggested that we play cards. This perked him up.

"'What-ho, girls, how about a bit of poker?'

"'That's fine with me,' said Maudie.

"'Well it's not fine with me. The only card game I can play is Olde Maid, and I just happen to have a deck in my purse,' I said, whipping out my deck of cards.

"'Eileen, why don't you grow up and learn to play gin or poker like everyone else?'

"'If that was what I wanted to do I'd do it. But I've read that we have to conserve our brain cells so that we'll have some when we get old, and I don't want to waste mine playing cards. So, it's either Olde Maid, or count me out.'

"'Okay, okay. Calm down, girls. We'll play Olde Maid,' said the naval officer, whose name was Tom.

"All three of us lit up a cigarette, took a puff, and settled in for a rousing game of Olde Maid.

"We played in silence for about thirty minutes, when Tom, who had had too much to drink, said, 'Hey, girls! Wanna see my tattoos?'

"We figured that he had his girlfriend's name or a rose tattooed on his bicep, so we said, 'Sure.'

"Well, shiver me timbers, but nothing so discreet as a tattoo on the bicep. Oh no, this joker pulled up his pant legs to his knees and ripped open his shirt. He was tattooed from neck to ankles. Maudie screamed and my eyes nearly popped out of their sockets. I screamed, 'My God, he's the Illustrated Man!' I had just finished reading *The Illustrated Man* the previous week. 'What shall we do?'

"Tom, the naval officer, passed out from too much to drink.

"'Maudie, what are we going to do if he wakes up? I know that when he wakes up he'll try to kill us! I know it!'

"'Calm down, Eileen! Tell the captain! Maybe he'll come back and tie Tom up, so he can't kill us. In the book, you have to get away before he wakes up at dawn, and we can't get away, so we'll have to tie him up. Hurry!'

"'Okay, Maudie. I'll hurry.'

"I rushed to the cockpit and said to the captain, 'Oh sir, we've got the Illustrated Man in the back and we need you to tie him up before he wakes up so that he can't kill us all!'

"'Eileen, what are you babbling about? Have you been reading science fiction again? You know I told you that you shouldn't read that stuff.'

"'Sorry, sir, but I just finished reading *The Illustrated Man*, and I know how dangerous this man is. Won't you help? He's drunk and passed out. Please help.'

"'Okay, I'll see what's going on.' He walked to the back and looked at Tom who was snoring. The captain saw his tattooed legs and chest. 'Wow! His whole body and legs are tattooed! It seems to me that I read somewhere recently that tattooed carcasses were quite a commodity, sought after in Japan in the old days and that collectors would skin the most artistic carcasses from the body and hang them as wall art. But girls, he seems to be harmless. Let him sleep it off. Meanwhile, you two go sit on your jumpseats and leave him alone.'

"'Well, if you think that he will sleep it off, we'll do what you say.'

"Tom slept the rest of the trip. Finally, we approached San Diego. The sun was coming up, and we felt much safer. Tom woke up and couldn't figure out why his pant legs were up to his knees and why his shirt was open. He didn't remember us, and we didn't see fit to remind him of the events of the evening. He staggered off the airplane and didn't even say goodbye to us. We felt safe once again."

"Gee, girls, that must have been scary. How spooky to have something like that happen in the wee hours of the morning on an airplane," remarked Matthew.

Charles said, "Maybe I'll get a tattoo!"

By now they had finished dinner. The fireplace was crackling, and the flames were dancing. By the flickering light of the candles they could see people straggling in for their evening pick-me-up. It was time for Matthew to start singing the blues.

8

The Trip to Huntsville

IT WAS A LONG, HOT SUMMER. THE MECHANICS WERE HOLDING A strike. This meant no money coming in. Eileen and Maudie were broke. Since they never had any money anyway, it really was not so unusual.

They were sitting by the pool one afternoon. It was hot and sultry.

"Maudie, I am bored."

"So what! You're always bored."

"No! I'm not always bored."

"Yes you are."

"Well, what if I am! I miss flying. We've been sitting beside this pool for three weeks now, and I am sick and tired of not going anywhere. Don't you want to see Vittorio?"

"Sure, Eileen, but how can we get to Huntsville? We can't afford airfare on the other airlines."

"What about trains?"

"Too expensive."

"I hate to bring this up, but perhaps we could afford to take a bus."

"By bus! Are you kidding?"

"You know that I'm serious. Vittorio invited us down for his graduation party. Getting a doctorate in physics is pretty important, and there should be a great party. Besides, I would like to see his friend, Robert. He's promised to lend me his copy of *Alice in Wonderland*. It's a first edition, complete with the original illustrations. It has been in his family for years. I'm dying to get my hands on it."

"Robert! Wow, Eileen, have you been seeing Robert and not telling me? Why, he's even smarter than Vittorio. He's only twenty-six, and already he's a respected scientist at NASA. I just adore his roommate, Sal. Sal is only twenty-two and is already working at NASA."

"I am impressed."

"Well, then, you can see that we have to take the bus."

"You're right! Let's do it."

That evening Maudie called Vittorio and told him that they were coming down for the party on the following Thursday. They should be reaching Huntsville on Friday morning. Vittorio was happy to know that they were coming for his party. Robert was pleased too and called Eileen to tell her to bring a bathing suit. He told her that he would lend her his copy of *Alice in Wonderland*, but he said, "You must promise to return it."

"Sure, Robert! I wouldn't keep your book. Don't you trust me?"

"It's not that I don't trust you; it's just that you're so forgetful."

"I promise to return it."

It was a lovely copy of *Alice in Wonderland* and just the sort of thing they loved to read, especially the part about the caterpillar and the hookah. Robert and Vittorio had discovered LSD, and they thought that they were getting enhanced insight. Eileen thought that they were nuts, but she also found the book and its stories riveting.

Thursday morning loomed bright and sunny—nary a cloud in the sky. Eileen and Maudie went to the bus station. They were having a cup of coffee and looking about. "Gee, Eileen, it's pretty dirty here, don't you think?"

"Now, Maudie, forget that. It's the only way to get to Huntsville."

"But, it's a twenty-four-hour trip," whined Maudie, who was having second thoughts. There were oodles of whining babies, young mothers, and sailors. Eileen, who was more egalitarian in her approach to people, had struck up a conversation with a Hell's Angel who had recently mashed up his Harley and broken his leg on a cross-country trip from San Francisco. He had decided to continue his travels across the country by bus.

"What a gorgeous leather jacket! Is it old?"

"Yeah, lady, I've had it about fifteen years."

"Golly, you must be in your forties." Eileen was amazed. She thought that when you were forty, you were serious and did not flit about on motorcycles.

"How in the world did you total your cycle and break your leg?" continued Eileen.

"It's like this. My old lady left me for a marine, and I was lonely and decided to travel a bit."

"What a coincidence. My brother's girlfriend left him for a marine. That was in Vietnam."

"Tell me lady, what do you women see in marines? I'm very good-looking and equally as tough."

Eileen was as mystified as the Angel, whose name was Hairy-Cary. She preferred longer hair on men, such as the ponytail he was sporting, which was peculiar because she could not stand long hair on herself.

Continuing the conversation over a second cup of coffee and some blueberry pancakes, Hairy-Cary told her that he was heading back to the West Coast by way of Texas.

"We're going to Huntsville to a great party. We each bought a gorgeous dress for the party," said Eileen.

By now, Maudie had stopped whining and was having a good time talking to Hairy-Cary.

Two young black women had just stuffed pacifiers into the mouths of their screaming kids, and quiet had resumed. Everyone was stocking up on fried chicken for the road.

Eileen and Maudie decided on a giant chocolate chip cookie for the trip, and everyone stocked up on cigarettes. Everyone else was smoking, so they fit right in.

"All aboard," shouted the bus driver.

Eileen and Maudie settled back for the ride. They were dressed for comfortable travel. Eileen was wearing flowered burgundy slacks with a burgundy sweater and red tennis shoes. Maudie was wearing black linen pants, which were already wrinkled, so they could not get any more wrinkled. She was wearing a white tank top with black sandals.

"We're on the way to Huntsville. This should be great fun. Walter von Hamelstern is going to be at the party. Robert invited him. Maybe we can get his autograph," said Maudie.

"You know, Maudie, we're young, and maybe he would want us to be stewardesses when he starts the moon shuttle!"

"Moon shuttle? We haven't even gotten to the moon yet!"

By now everybody was smoking, and the air conditioner had stopped working. Hairy-Cary and two sailors were drinking beer in the back row of the bus.

The countryside was beautiful. Everyone on the bus settled down and tried to get some shut-eye.

Eileen and Maudie were thoughtfully munching on their giant chocolate chip cookies, discussing whether Lewis Carroll's *Alice in Wonderland* was a more important book than Ayn Rand's *Atlas Shrugged*. Both decided that Ms. Rand was essentially boring, even though she could tell a good story.

Hours passed by slowly. Finally they were about six hours from Huntsville. It was raining, there was no air-conditioning, the bus was smoke-filled, the babies were howling, and everybody was miserable except for the two sailors and Hairy-Cary, who had passed out in the back of the bus.

Maudie and Eileen were worried about their appearance. They liked to look glamorous at all times, and the trip on the bus had not enhanced their appearance. Maudie, who had shared a couple of beers with the boys, looked even worse than Eileen. Her long hair was straggling around her shoulder, and her clothes were in shambles. Eileen's hair looked the same, since it was short and always looked shaggy. Her clothes were more wrinkle resistant.

They reached their destination. The bus stopped at the bus station. Maudie and Eileen staggered off. Their feet were swollen, and their muscles were cramped. There were deep purple and black circles under their eyes, and they reeked of cigarette smoke.

Vittorio and Robert ran up to greet them, but after one look at them, Vittorio said, "I think you need a nap, a bath, and a change of clothes. Come on, we'll go to Jo and Charlotte's, where you'll be staying."

Meanwhile, Hairy-Cary had limped up to the circle of friends to say goodbye. But they were reluctant to just leave him, so Eileen said, "Hairy-Cary, why don't you stay a couple of days in Huntsville and go to the party?"

"That would be fun," Hairy-Cary agreed, and Robert, who was impressed by Hairy-Cary's black leather jacket said, "Yeah, come on and join us. It should be a great party, and we can go drag racing in my new Porsche. Vittorio has a new blue Stingray, and we would love to have you drag with us. We would have fun."

"Well, okay, since you put it that way," said Hairy-Cary. "I will stay."

9

The Day of the Party

ℰILEEN AND MAUDIE DECIDED TO TAKE VITTORIO'S ADVICE AND pull themselves together by taking a nap, etc., while the boys went drag racing. Hairy-Cary was especially happy because he loved adventurous driving. He limped over to Robert's new red Porsche, propped his crutches across the back of the seat, and hopped in.

"Hairy," said Robert, "how did you happen to demolish your cycle? Were you going too fast or what?"

"Well," said Hairy, "the guys and I were going to a rock concert in Montana, and we'd been on the road several days, going faster than usual because if we didn't hurry, we were going to be late. It was one of our favorite groups, Myrtle the Turtle and the Flaming Flamingos. They were performing in Bozeman, and we had been asked to provide the security. We agreed but had gotten involved in several crackups on the highway and had fallen behind schedule. I was hurtling down the road doing about a hundred and five miles an hour when a couple of cows stepped out into the road in front of me. I tried to avoid hitting them, but as I was going so fast, I wasn't successful, and POW—right into the old bull.

Boy, were we surprised, he and I. His life came to an immediate halt, and I heard this CRUNCH—SNAP—POP. I knew I was hurt because I was yelling my head off for help. Boy, it hurt! Two of my friends scraped me off the road and got me to a hospital. They left me there because they wanted to get to the concert. I spent two days in the hospital, and then they kicked me out in a cast and using crutches. I missed the concert. I had no immediate plans. Since my old lady had left me for a marine sergeant—of whom even I was scared—I decided to tour the country by bus. That's where I met the girls. We hit it off, and here I am."

"Gee, Hairy, that's quite a story," said Robert.

While Hairy related his story, Robert had maneuvered his car out of town and into a more-or-less deserted countryside. Vittorio was right behind them in his new blue and silver Stingray, which his mother had given him for his graduation.

"Vittorio, let's drag. Okay?" yelled Robert.

"Okay. The loser has to provide the LSD when we get home."

"Yeah," yelled Hairy-Cary, "that's right up my alley!"

"Vittorio, don't tell the girls. They told me that they're allergic to drugs, and I know that they'll feel left out."

"Okay, let's go—on your mark . . .

get set . . .

go!

Off the three men hurtled—dust flying up behind them. They did not see any cops and got up to about one hundred twenty miles per hour for about three miles.

Then Vittorio, who had been smoking, dropped his cigarette onto his lap. His attention was momentarily diverted from his driving. He lost control and headed into a nearby tree. He threw on his brakes and managed to open his door and jump out of the car, which was going considerably slower by this time. He heard a crash and saw his beloved Stingray hit the tree and become a wreck—and he also felt a SNAP—CRUNCH—POP. He had broken his arm. He was screaming, "Help!"

Hairy-Cary and Robert got him crammed into the Porsche, and they hurried him to the local hospital, where he was x-rayed and put into a cast.

Robert, who was driving two damaged men, was somewhat subdued. "Gee guys, this sure messes up the party tonight. I guess we'll have to cancel it."

"No way we cancel the party," piped up Vittorio. "Walter von Hamelstern is coming. This is my big night. But whatever you do, don't tell anyone that we were drag racing."

"Okay," chimed in the other two guys. That evening, three subdued men showed up to pick up Maudie and Eileen.

"Good grief, Vittorio! What happened to your arm, and where is the Stingray?" said Maudie. Eileen, who had a better grasp of human nature said, "It looks like you three were drag racing. Did you wreck the Stingray?"

"Aw, Eileen, don't be so mean. Vittorio wrecked his car and broke his arm! Yes, we were drag racing, but please don't tell his mother what we were doing. That car was his graduation gift from her, and she'd just have a fit if she knew what we'd been doing."

"Well, I'll be ------!" said Maudie. It's a good thing you didn't get killed. I hope you learned your lesson."

"Come on guys, enough of this. Let's get to the party," said Eileen. Off they went to the farm by the river, where the party was getting into full swing. It was about 5:30, a very beautiful evening. Everyone cheered when Vittorio pulled up in the station wagon. He told them all that he had lost control of his car because of a flat tire, and they felt sorry for him, except for Maudie and Eileen. They had no real respect for anyone who lost control of his car. So they left the guys and wandered off to the baseball game in progress. Maudie decided to play first base, and Eileen, who did not find sports very interesting, decided to take a walk by the river. She hiked down the river for an hour and got back as it was getting dark.

The barbecue was in full swing, and the sounds of the rock-n-roll band were blaring through the evening air. Everyone was doing cocaine and LSD. Maudie and Eileen were disgusted by the way the party was turning out. Not only was it becoming raucous, but Vittorio and Robert were flirting with a blonde bombshell. Robert took one look at Eileen's face and knew that she was furious. He was worried because he had lent her his precious copy of *Alice in Wonderland*, and he had the awful feeling that she would not return it—just to get even with him.

"Oh Robert, don't be such a worrywart. She'll give it back. I know she will," said Vittorio.

"Vittorio, you don't know Eileen as well as I do. She is mad. She likes good books, and she knows how much that copy means to me. I know that she will keep it. I should never have done the LSD and flirted with another woman while she was around."

"By the way, where are the girls?" said Hairy-Cary. "I haven't seen them for an hour or so. Where can they be?"

Maudie and Eileen had left the party and hitchhiked back to where they were staying. They packed their bags and hitchhiked to the bus station, where they caught the late night bus to Atlanta and then on to Washington, DC.

"Well, Eileen, so much for Vittorio. I have no use for a man who loses control of his car, who flirts with other women, and who uses LSD and cocaine."

"I certainly understand, Maudie. Actually, I was so mad at Robert that I kept his lovely copy of *Alice in Wonderland*."

When they got back to Washington, they discovered that the strike was over. They got back to work, and they were no longer bored. They forgot about the party, Vittorio, and Robert.

Ah! Youth is a wonderful thing.

10

Ingrid Enters the Scene

*I*NGRID'S FATHER HAD ALWAYS IGNORED HER—IN FACT, HE NEVER even saw her. He had been a German submarine commander during World War II and had an affair with Ingrid's mother, Eva Schultz. Her mother was from a proper and wealthy Jewish family, who were horrified when their daughter took up with a German. Nobody could understand why, but when she became pregnant and had a baby—Ingrid—they welcomed the little girl into their family with love.

Her mother died shortly from breast cancer after Ingrid's birth, and her grandparents—with the help of her father—sent the baby to the USA until the war ended. Then she returned to Munich to live with her grandparents. She was indulged in every possible way and loved, but she was always restless and never felt secure.

When Ingrid was seventeen years old, a blonde, blue-eyed bombshell, she married Harve, an old—to her—American diplomat. In actuality he was only forty-seven years old. He was round and bald and not very tall. Ingrid thought that he had lots of money because he told her he did and because he led a luxurious lifestyle. Harve was kind to her, but he was frantically jealous of her because he was thirty years older and did not think that she was trustworthy. Neither did he think that she was the type of woman who could be faithful to one man.

One night they were at a diplomatic function. They got into an argument because Ingrid was flirting with a handsome young Russian naval officer.

"Ingrid, you are so gorgeous, but you flirt with everyone. You don't love me. You make me so nervous," Harve said with a pout and a sad toss of his bald head.

"Well, you will just have to take my word for it that I love you," retaliated Ingrid. As she said this, she winked at the handsome naval officer, Igor.

Oh well, thought Harve, *at least I know that Igor is going to sea next week, and Ingrid and I will be going to Algeria for a couple of years with the diplomatic service.*

So they went to Algeria where Ingrid had beautiful clothes, a fast car, servants, and a big house—all in all a satisfactory arrangement. What she did not know was that it was a house of cards that was soon to come tumbling down because Harve could not stop his addiction to gambling.

One night, Harve was feeling lucky, and he said, "You know Ingrid, I feel lucky tonight. Why don't you get dressed up in that slinky silver lamé dress with the crystals that I bought you in Vienna?"

"Great Harve, let's go," she said. She was happy to oblige because she looked smashing in that dress.

It was a beautiful starlit night. They hopped into their red Porsche, and took off for the Mirage.

The Mirage was the local casino. It was not large, but it was popular with the locals and the visiting wealthy Arabs. When they entered, the joint was hopping. They could hardly see—the smoke was so thick from the cigarettes and cigars. The light was dim, but the beautifully polished machines sparkled in the dim light. One of the croupiers, Antonio—a friend of Harve—was presiding over the blackjack table. When he saw Harve, he called out, "Hey, Harve, care to join us for a game?"

"Sure, Antonio. Let me get a drink, and I'll be right over."

He turned to Ingrid, who was busy checking the room to see if their entrance had been noticed and also checking to see if there was anyone she knew. There was not. The two of them walked over to the bar to get a drink. Harve ordered a single malt scotch, and Ingrid had a whiskey sour. For a while they sat there, quietly sipping their drinks. Finally Harve said, "Well, Ingrid, I feel a winning streak coming on. I think I'll play some blackjack. See you in a while." With that he left her and headed across the room for the blackjack table.

As she was sipping her drink and looking around the room, she noticed a tall, fat, swarthy Arab entering the casino, followed by two tall, mean-looking American bodyguards. He was dressed in a white caftan, brown cowboy boots, and was smoking a Cuban cigar. His name was Aman, and he was a super rich sheik from Saudi Arabia who was in Algeria for several weeks while several of his wives were in Paris shopping for their fall wardrobe. He and his two bodyguards had obviously been drinking heavily because all three were loud, belligerent, and glowering at everyone.

As Aman looked around the room, his attention was attracted to Ingrid. "See here, Leo," he said to the taller of the two bodyguards, "see that blonde at the bar? I want her for my harem. She is gorgeous, and I am taking her back to Saudi Arabia when I leave Algeria. Be ready to leave in a hurry when I give you the word."

"Right boss, whatever you say. She is a looker," responded Leo, chugging his beer in a single gulp.

At that, Aman slithered over to the bar where Ingrid was sipping her drink and listening to the piano player. The crystals on her dress were twinkling in the subdued light of the Mirage. Harve was still playing blackjack. The lure of the table was stronger than his fear of her flirting.

"Oh, beautiful lady," said Aman in an oily voice that made Ingrid's flesh crawl. His voice was blurred from too much liquor, and he reeked of gin. "Oh, beautiful lady," said the sleazy Arab again, "you look bewitching this evening. Come, join me for a drink."

"Sorry," said Ingrid with a toss of her blonde curls, "I am here with my husband, and I do not feel inclined to join you." She was totally repulsed by him and worried because he would not leave her alone. *Oh dear,* she thought with a sigh, *you get into so much trouble when you're a good-looking blonde.*

The room was noisy, and people were excited, as was Harve. The gambling fever was coursing through his veins. He decided to have another drink and left the blackjack table to rejoin Ingrid.

Ingrid was upset, he noticed. "Harve, let's go home. That Arab, Aman, is pestering me. I do not like him. Let's go. We can come back another night."

Just at this moment—before Harve could reply—Aman slithered up to the bar where they were sitting, and said to Harve, "Hey, old man, how about a game of high-stakes poker?" He knew a compulsive gambler when he saw one. Harve was so drunk by this time that he did not notice that the Arab was ogling Ingrid, who was upset by his attentions. Ingrid was not eager to have Harve participate in a game with Aman in the back room and tried to discourage Harve from playing, but he was determined to participate in the game.

"Sure," he said, "let's go," he said with confidence.

The security guard came over and escorted Aman, Harve, and Ingrid to the back room where a rousing game of poker was in progress. There were two Arabs from Algeria, an Englishman, and two Swedes in the game. Drinks were flowing. All of the players were drunk.

The light was dimmer in this room, and it was not so noisy. Ingrid was aware that she and Harve were in a dangerous situation. Aman continued to pester her.

The game became heated. All of a sudden, Aman jumped to his

feet and screamed at Harve, "You cheated! You cheated! We must fight!" He pulled a knife from his boot, and lurched at Harve, screaming, "Fight, old man, fight!"

Harve was scared. He was not a fighter, and the Arab was younger and stronger than he was. Harve felt sick at heart. The other men were excited. They loved a fight. One of them tossed Harve a knife and said, "Go to it, old man! You must defend your honor!" Harve realized that his honor was at stake. He had been accused of cheating, and there was no way out. It was inevitable that he fight.

Ingrid was terrified. She was in serious trouble, as well as Harve. While everyone was screaming and enjoying the fight, she slipped out of the room. No one was looking. She ran to the Porsche and got in. She drove quickly through the backstreets, returning to their house. She decided to wait there for Harve, who she hoped would win the fight. She became concerned as the night hours passed away and still there was no returning Harve. She finally realized that he might not return. She ransacked his papers for his will and financial holdings. She was shocked to find that he had no money and was seriously in debt from his gambling. They were living on credit. She was appalled.

Finally the sun rose in all its glory. Ingrid quickly dressed for the street. She ran down to the newsstand on the corner to get the morning edition of the news from the local newspaper. She looked at the front page in which it was reported that an American diplomat had been knifed to death at the local casino, the Mirage. No known motive.

Ingrid knew that she must get out of town quickly before the Arab sobered up and came looking for her. She quickly packed a bag and headed for the airport. She got a seat on the first flight out of town, which happened to be headed for London. As she had a green card, plenty of cash, and money in a Swiss bank account, she decided to head for the good old US of A. She knew Aman hated America and would not follow her there.

11

The Flight from London

INGRID DECIDED TO TAKE THE EVENING FLIGHT FROM LONDON TO Washington, DC, because that was the only flight on which she could get a first class seat at such short notice, and Ingrid only traveled in first class. Even at her young age, Ingrid could not conceive of traveling in coach class. She was traveling light as she had left Algeria in a hurry. When he had been flirting with her, Aman told her that she would be a wonderful addition to his harem. Ingrid nearly freaked out when he said this. She packed so hurriedly that she did not bother to take a lot with her. He had not been joking, and after he had gone so far as to kill Harve, she was sure that he would come after her. Because he was so rich, she knew that the authorities would not incarcerate him.

"Horrors! I must get to the US. I simply must. I will be safe there because he hates the US."

Ingrid finally got settled in her seat, and for the first time since leaving Algeria she felt sort of safe. The stewardesses in first class were about her age and looked glamorous in their royal blue wool suits.

"I must chat with them after dinner," thought Ingrid, who daintily nibbled on the beluga caviar and sipped the Dom Perignon champagne. Under no circumstances did Ingrid ever gobble or guzzle.

Maudie and Eileen just happened to be the stewardesses working the flight that evening. They were fascinated by her. They had never seen an unaccompanied young woman in first class. Besides which, she was mysterious and glamorous. There was something about her appearance and demeanor that struck Maudie and Eileen as enigmatic and disconsolate.

"Gee, Maudie, she doesn't seem happy, considering that it's Dom Perignon she's drinking, and it costs a small fortune."

"Well, you know, Eileen, perhaps she's leaving her boyfriend and misses him already," said Maudie.

At this point in their lives, they were not able to seriously miss a guy, although Maudie had just met Chapman and did seem smitten. In fact, she had just confided to Eileen that he was leaving his wife. They had been married for ten years, and his wife no longer understood him. Maudie was happy because Chapman was smart. He was a biochemist. She was most impressed. He also happened to be good-looking.

"Oh, Eileen, isn't it awful about his wife not understanding him? He is so sensitive and caring. I adore him. I feel that this might be true love."

And then Maudie said something to Eileen that shook Eileen to the core. "You know, Eileen, he's going to get a divorce. He's somewhat upset, though, because he has five children, and his wife refuses to take custody of the children."

"He has five children!" shrieked Eileen, promptly dropping the rack of glasses she was holding. "Five children!" she screamed as the glasses shattered to smithereens and clattered all over the galley floor.

Ingrid, who had just come out of the bathroom, was passing the galley when Eileen dropped the glasses.

"Why are you two making so much noise? People are trying to

sleep. I am trying to sleep," said Ingrid.

Maudie piped up, "Sorry, I was just telling Eileen about my new boyfriend—Chapman. When I told her that he was divorcing his wife of ten years and keeping custody of the five children and that he wants to marry me—well, it was just too much for her to accept. By the way, that's Eileen, and I'm Maudie."

"She shouldn't do it, she simply should. Not. Do it," whined Eileen.

Now Ingrid was fascinated. She was always interested in affairs of the heart. Considering that she had married Harve at the age of seventeen, thought he had money, and then found out that he had gambled his way into serious debt and gotten killed when he should have been protecting her from amorous Arabs—well, who was she to criticize another woman for making a mess of her life for a man.

The three young ladies continued talking while Eileen cleaned up the mess she had made. Finally, she got up and said "Well, Ingrid, what's bringing you to Washington?"

Ingrid, who believed in mystery and secrets, simply said, "I am running away from a man. I am changing my whole life. I am going to move to the United States. However, I need a job. Any suggestions?"

"You could become a stewardess for Universal Airlines. You are interesting enough, and you're thin, and that is about all they care about. It's tons of fun and you get around the world, which I like," said Eileen. "Maudie is not quite as happy, because she's an intellectual and wants to go back to school and get a masters in geology. As for me, I just want to see the world."

Maudie said, "You really should try it. When you get to Washington, call Mr. Pearson. He is the interviewer; and if he liked us, he'll certainly like you, as you also speak four languages.

After properly introducing themselves, the three young ladies sat in the front lounge of the DC-10 at the lounge table and whiled away the time playing cards, eating caviar, and singing:

Oh mighty sturgeon
   From the Caspian Sea
We love thy roe
   Thy eggs love we.

Sitting so black
   On our crispy bread
While sipping champagne
   It goes to our head.

Some prefer vodka
   I do not really care
Both make me happy
   I do declare.

For a purist like me
   The roe alone is just fine
I arrange it on my toast
   In a straight little line.

Others like egg yolk and white
   Crumbled in bits
And a touch of onion
   As it passes the lips.

Oh, caviar, caviar
   Food of the gods
We are so happy to eat it
   Though we are such clods.

Some think it too salty
   But certainly not we
We love you, oh sturgeon
   From the Caspian Sea.

We love you
We love you
Do we.

As you might recall, Eileen was not good at cards, so they were playing Olde Maid. Eileen loved that game, and since the other two were humoring her, they pretended to enjoy it, too. By now, Ingrid had sipped her way through a half of a bottle of champagne and was thoroughly enjoying herself. What a life! Flying late at night over the ocean with the stars twinkling through the windows, sipping champagne, and eating beluga caviar. This was definitely a life that appealed to Ingrid. Finally the flight ended, and the three comrades said goodbye.

"Be sure to call Mr. Pearson in the morning, and then call us—we should stay in touch. Our number is JU3-87762."

" 'Bye," said Ingrid as she picked up her suitcase and headed for the terminal, happy to be in America.

12

Ingrid, Welcome to America

AFTER ARRIVING IN WASHINGTON ON THE FLIGHT WHERE SHE met Eileen and Maudie, Ingrid bade the two ladies goodbye and headed for the Mayflower Hotel on Connecticut Avenue. She decided to check into the Mayflower because she had heard that their suites were sumptuous, and the location was perfect for her. Unbeknownst to Harve, Ingrid had squirreled away thousands of his dollars—the household fund and entertaining money—and also, unbeknownst to Harve, she had been successful at playing the horses. These funds, in addition to her own considerable funds, made Ingrid a financially well-off young lady.

Since she had slipped out of Algeria so quickly without many clothes in her suitcase, she decided to make a shopping excursion to Garfinkle's. They carried the type of clothes that she found appealing—classic, well-cut and designed, and expensive. But first she had to call Mr. Pearson and see if she could get a job working for Universal Airlines as a stewardess. Even more pressing was the need for food. It was breakfast time, and Ingrid was hungry. She headed downstairs to the restaurant and sat down. The good-looking young waiter came up to her table.

"Ah, *mademoiselle*, what would you care to eat for breakfast this fine morning?"

"It certainly is a fine morning, and I am famished. Would you recommend the strawberries? Are they fresh? I love strawberries," said Ingrid whose stomach was growling. The champagne of the night before was not enough sustenance for a still-growing young lady.

"Ah, *mademoiselle*, the strawberries were just brought in from the fields this morning at the crack of dawn. They are big and red and juicy. I highly recommend them."

"Well then, if you recommend them so highly, I will have them and also a big glass of your best champagne. I love champagne with strawberries." Ingrid loved champagne with just about everything.

Ingrid daintily ate her strawberries, which the waiter served with crème, and daintily sipped her champagne. It was delicious and fortified her for her call to Mr. Pearson. Although Ingrid was not lacking in self-confidence, she had never had a job before, and she was decidedly nervous.

After breakfast, she went back to her room, sat on the edge of her bed, picked up the phone, and called Mr. Pearson's office. The secretary put her on the line with Mr. Pearson.

"Oh, hello, Mr. Pearson. My name is Ingrid Schultz. I was on the flight from London last evening, and I was very impressed by the two stewardesses working the trip, Miss Maudie Miller and Miss Eileen Gordon. I would just love to be a stewardess. I speak four languages, love people, and love to travel"—in reality Ingrid made a small white lie. She did not love people. She only loved the "right people," which either meant that they had oodles of money or impeccable social standing.

"Swell, Miss Schultz. Why don't you come in to see me on Friday morning at 10:30, and we will discuss whether or not you are qualified for the job?"

"Great! I will see you Friday morning."

After the phone call, Ingrid took off for Garfinkle's for a morning of shopping, which she always found relaxing and fun. She decided to pay her respects to her late husband by wearing black, now that she was a widow. Besides, black was always chic, and with her blonde hair and blue eyes, she looked wonderful in it.

"Black it will be," decided Ingrid, who was trying to conjure up a tear of remorse for her dear, departed Harve. She failed to produce tears, because she was a lady who lived in the moment, and Harve was long gone.

Friday morning rolled around, and Ingrid headed to Mr. Pearson's office for her interview. She wore her new black suit. It was beautiful. It had a straight skirt and the jacket had a small peplum. She wore it with a white silk blouse with ruffles around the wrist. She wore black pumps and a black beret. She pinned a silver pin in the shape of a rose at the neck.

Mr. Pearson was quite dazzled by her beauty, good taste in clothes, and her splendid résumé.

"Miss Schultz, I see by your résumé that you are imminently qualified for the job. I notice, however, that you have hairy legs." Mr. Pearson seemed quite shocked that this should be the case and even more shocked that he should have to mention it.

"Hairy legs? Whatever in the world are you talking about? Of course I have hairy legs. I am a lady," said Ingrid who was horrified that such a subject had been introduced into the conversation.

"Miss Schultz, I would love to hire you, but the rules about appearance are quite strict, and no stewardess for Universal Airlines can have hairy legs. You must shave your legs if you expect to be hired," said Mr. Pearson with finality.

"I cannot shave my legs! My grandmother would be totally scandalized. Only ladies of the night shave their legs in her opinion. I would never disgrace my grandmother."

"Miss Schultz, you really must shave your legs or I cannot hire you. Do you understand?"

Ingrid turned pale and stammered in a low voice, "*Mein Gott!* I guess I will have to comply, but if my grandmother has a stroke or a heart attack, you must realize that it is on your head! But I simply must have the job, so I will do it. When do I report for training?"

"Next week—but also I had better warn you that you must lose weight."

"Lose weight? You must be kidding! I am five feet eight inches tall, and I only weigh one hundred twenty-five pounds," wailed Ingrid, who was beginning to sense that this job was more demanding than she had bargained for.

"Miss Schultz, you argue too much. You must realize that our weight restrictions are quite strict, and you can be fired if you are over-weight. Certainly you will not be hired."

"Oh well, I guess I can lose five pounds."

"Ten pounds would be more like it," said Mr. Pearson.

Finally Mr. Pearson told Ingrid that she was accepted into the train-ing program, which would take six weeks. She called Maudie and Eileen, and told them that she would be at the training facility and would call them when she got back to Washington.

She then called her grandparents in Munich and said, "Grandma, I got a job as a stewardess for Universal Airlines. After finishing training, I will be living in Washington. I am so excited, and I have already started making friends."

"A stewardess!" said her grandmother. "Oh really, Ingrid, your grandfather and I were hoping that you would settle down and have a family."

"Well, Gran, Harve was killed, and I need to get out and meet peo-ple. You don't want me to be alone with my grief. Besides, I had to get out of Europe because that Arab, Aman, wanted to lock me away in his harem. I chose to come to the US because I have a green card, and because he hates America. Anyway, I have some new friends who are respectable, and I am excited. Wish me well!"

"Oh, my dear, you know that your grandfather and I will always support you and love you—no matter what you do."

"Thanks, Gran—loads of love." Ingrid never looked back.

13

Love at First Sight

After Ingrid went off for training, Maudie and Eileen were sitting at the Local Yokel one evening. It was a beautiful spring evening with stars twinkling in the cool dark night and the crickets singing at the top of their lungs. The other patrons were sitting there, drinking their beer and wine, smoking, and listening to the new piano player as he played and sang favorite tunes from the Beatles. He was playing a tear-jerking rendition of "Hey, Jude," which just happened to be Maudie's favorite song. The crowd loved hearing songs by the Beatles.

Maudie was fidgeting and irritating Eileen, who was trying to pay attention to the musician. "Maudie, will you please settle down?" said Eileen with a slight hint of irritation.

"Eileen, I must tell you about Chapman. I want to marry him, and he says we can after he gets divorced. His kids love me, he says. Isn't that wonderful? He also thinks that I can go back to school and get my masters in geology from the University of Indiana. I guess, though, that I will have to quit flying."

"Oh, Maudie, that seems rather rash, don't you think? I've only met Chapman once. He is handsome, but he's rather old and so are two of his kids. They're already teenagers. It seems rather presumptuous to take on such a large ready-made family. Have you considered that they and he will undoubtedly expect you to cook and clean up after them?"

Eileen was leaning with her elbows on the table. She had a cigarette in her hand, and as she waved it through the air, a spark flew off the end and landed in the center of her new pink knit dress.

"Oh darn," said Eileen—she and Maudie at this point in their young lives rarely cussed. "How terrible! I love this new dress, and it cost a fortune. Perhaps I can find someone to reweave it."

Maudie looked at Eileen. She thought that in spite of all the dancing that Eileen had done, she was amazingly clumsy. She herself never dropped ashes on her lap like other people. She was totally graceful, and not the least bit spastic like her roommate.

"Well," said Eileen with a sigh and a big frown, "at least, Maudie, please explain to me the attraction, besides him being so handsome. How did you meet him?"

Maudie got a faraway look in her big brown eyes, and said, "It was several months ago—back in February . . .

"I was going on a trip to Denver the following evening, Friday. I'd just come in from ice skating and was having several drinks of scotch-on-the-rocks. The lava lamp was bubbling away, casting it's multitude of colors through the darkened room. I was watching the lava lamp, and thinking about whether or not to get a dog, when the phone rang . . .

TING-A-LING . . .

TING-A-LING . . .

"I considered not answering it because the scotch had affected my equilibrium, and I wasn't sure that I could maneuver my way across the room to the phone . . .

TING-A-LING . . .

TING-A-LING . . .

"I decided, 'What the heck! It might be someone interesting.' I got up, answered it, and said, 'Hi, it's me, Maudie, to whom am I speaking?'

"'Hi, Maudie, it's your cousin, Sue Sue. Since you are coming to Denver tomorrow, be sure to bring a great black dress and high heels—preferably some high platforms. I have the greatest guy for you to meet.'

"'Sue Sue, you know that after Vittorio broke my heart by flirting with that awful, obnoxious blonde in black at the graduation party in Huntsville I have sworn off men.'

"'But Maudie, Chapman is different that other men. He is sensitive and caring and very smart. And he has loads of money.'

"'Sounds too good to be true. What's the catch?'

"'I hate to say this, but I guess we should just face the facts and go from there. Maudie, he's forty years old.'

"'Forty years old! Good God, Sue Sue, I'm only twenty-three. Why, he's ancient!'

"'And. . . ,' said Sue Sue reluctantly, 'he's married.'

"'Married! Are you crazy? Why in the world would I want to go out with a married man?'

"'He's getting divorced, and needs a mother for his children.'

"'His children! Why, this is getting worse by the minute.'

"'The worst is yet to come. He has five children.'

"'Five children! Sue Sue, are you mad?'

"'Maudie, you must meet him. I know you will always be thankful to me. Come on, be a sport.'

"At this point, the scotch had obliterated any degree of sense that I had, so I sighed and said, 'Okay, Sue Sue, I will be in Denver around

5:00 P.M.'

"'Great. I'll pick you up at 7:30, and you can meet him. Then we'll go to dinner and afterwards the lecture he is giving on *po-lem-er-as*.'

"'Po-lem-er-as! What are they?'

"'I don't know, but that's what the lecture is about. He's a bio-chemist. After the lecture, we'll go dancing.'

"'That sounds better. I haven't been dancing in months. If he's so old, though, do you think he can dance?' I asked, as I'd never been out with someone so old. I wasn't sure if, at that age, one could really dance.

"'After a few drinks he loves to dance.'

"'Okay, Sue Sue, see you tomorrow night.'

"'You'll never regret this decision,' said Sue Sue gleefully; my cousin really was fond of me. . . .'"

At this point Maudie stopped talking. She had been in some enchanted land. Eileen could tell by looking at and listening to her.

Oh dear, thought Eileen to herself, *this is worse than I thought.*

"Think, Maudie, think," said Eileen. "Think! You want to act and think—not cook and clean house. Besides, you'll end up in an office and not have any windows and probably get stuck in front of one of those new fangled contraptions—a computer. Your skin will get pasty from lack of sun, and instead of playing tennis and riding, you'll be stuck in a kitchen. You must not do this. Think. Think. Think!"

"But, Eileen, I love him."

"You mustn't do this. It'll ruin your life. You're not the type to be a wife. We both know that. We've discussed it many times before." Eileen knew that it was hopeless, but she had to try to save Maudie.

"Maudie, transfer to Los Angeles. Fly troops to and from Vietnam. That would be interesting."

"Eileen," interrupted Maudie, who was dying to talk more about Chapman and her love life, "I must tell you about meeting him. The three of us went to dinner at the Café Denver. I was wearing my black dinner dress—above the knees, sleeveless, with a sweetheart neckline. I had opted for five-inch black platform heels. I looked quite swanky. I did my hair in a French twist, and I wore dangly rhinestone earrings. I looked great. When Sue Sue introduced us, it was love at first sight for me, although it took several drinks before he realized that I was 'it' for him. We had filet mignon broiled to perfection, Caesar salad, green peas, and a baked potato. Since I'm naturally skinny, unlike you, I was able to eat everything, including the New York cheesecake. After dinner, we had coffee and some cognac."

"That sounds like a wonderful dinner. I wish I could eat a dinner like that." sighed Eileen. She was sick and tired of lettuce and carrots and water and coffee and apples. She was dying to sink her teeth into a choice chunk of meat, tearing it to shreds, chewing it mightily. Her yoga teacher was appalled that she admitted to such feelings.

He was almost certain that she had more kindly feelings toward animals. When she admitted to him that she was really a carnivore, he said, "The next time you want to tear into some meat, try to think about how the animal felt about becoming some person's dinner."

"Ah, shucks, MiYasa, you know I was only kidding. And since you put it that way, I'm not sure I'll ever be able to eat meat again."

As she was thinking back to this encounter, Maudie said, "Well, Eileen, I guess I'd better tell you the rest."

"The rest? The rest! You mean there's more that you haven't told me? Don't tell me he's been in jail for something."

"No, it's nothing like that. Let me tell you the rest."

"Okay, shoot."

"After dinner and the lecture, we went to the Red Rat, a disco joint in downtown Denver. It was a groovy discotheque. When you walk through the entrance door, it snaps shut behind you. It sounds like a trap springing. The walls are painted black, and there are strobe lights flashing everywhere.

"There was a noisy band called Cabbage and Carrots playing pieces they had written to commemorate the atrocities in Vietnam. Everyone was dressed up in their best disco wear. I looked really sharp—more sophisticated than the other gals. Sue Sue was wearing tan suede bell-bottom pants, a green and yellow striped tank top, and a red striped cardigan sweater. The air-conditioning was going full blast, and it was cold. I was freezing to death because I didn't have a sweater. After several drinks, Chapman worked up the nerve to ask me to dance. I gleefully said 'Sure,' and we hopped onto the dance floor. All he knew how to do was the twist, so that is what we did. Unfortunately, everyone including me, was smoking. My asthma started to act up, and I had a coughing fit. By this time, Chapman was quite drunk. He asked Sue Sue and me if we were ready to leave. I thought it was sweet of him to notice that I could no longer breathe. Sue Sue was ready to leave because she had had too much to drink and she could no longer dance. In fact, she could almost not walk. We put her into a taxi and started walking back to the hotel. The streets were practically empty, as it was almost 3:00 A.M. There were several derelicts and drunks wandering the night streets. The derelicts spent a lot of time going through trash cans. One, who was still only a teenager, found a pop bottle with some liquid in the bottom. He lifted it from the trash can and drank the remaining liquid. Chapman and I said in unison, 'How disgusting!' That was when he popped the question."

"Popped the question! What question? I don't want to know. I think I'll leave the Local Yokel now and go home and go to sleep. I'm tired."

"Eileen, please let me finish. Chapman and I stopped dead in our tracks, in the middle of the street, in the middle of the night, in the middle of Denver. He looked deep into my eyes and said, 'Maudie, I can't live without you. Will you marry me?'"

"'I would love to marry you, Chapman, but you're already married.'

"'I'm getting a divorce. My wife doesn't understand me. She wants the divorce to go through as much as I do.'

"'Oh, Chapman,' I said, 'I would love to marry you. You're the only man I will ever love. How fast this has all happened. I just can't believe this is happening to me.'

"By now we had lost our sense of direction and realized that we were lost, too drunk to find our way back to the hotel. We wandered around the dark streets until a taxi stopped and gave us a ride back to the hotel. By now we were making plans to pick out an engagement ring the next time he got to Washington, which is tomorrow. I thought you'd like to know. We're planning to get married when the divorce is final— in about three months. My parents are furious, but I knew that you would understand about my true love for Chapman."

"Without a doubt, you are nuts," muttered Eileen, who had turned quite pale. She threw her right hand up to her forehead, just like her grandmother used to do before she fainted. She stood up, staggered a few steps towards the door, and said, "I think I'm going to faint."

Maudie said, "Eileen, don't faint. Just sit down and put your head between your legs. You don't want to faint because you might hit your head when you fall. Even if you and my parents don't approve, I'm going to marry Chapman."

Eileen sat down and put her head between her legs, and Maudie burst into tears. The rest of the patrons thought, *Those two are certainly dramatic*, and went back to listening to the new piano player, who was now playing "Yellow Submarine."

14

The Blizzard

EILEEN HAD GOTTEN IN LATE THE NIGHT BEFORE. SHE HAD worked a trip from Milan, Italy, and was still somewhat tired. *Oh, good golly,* she sighed as she burrowed deeper into the covers. It was snowing outside. The wind was howling and rattling the windows.

I miss Maudie. I liked having her around, although I could never get used to having a gun in the apartment. Why did she have to get married and to someone so old? I miss her. Now that she's gone, even the Local Yokel seems different.

The radiator hissed in the early morning gloom. Eileen realized that she was not going to be able to sleep anymore. Too much noise. Why couldn't the world be more quiet? Adding insult to injury, there was a pileated woodpecker trying to find bugs in the wall of her apartment on this awful morning. Why hadn't it gone South with its friends? It, too, was noisy.

She shivered as she crawled out of her bed and her bare feet hit the floor. *Oh dear, I have a headache from all of that awful smoke on the airplane last night. I must stop smoking. It's such a stupid habit. It smells awful, and everyone who smokes smells awful. I wish I'd remember that whenever I feel the urge to light up. Maybe some coffee and a hot bubble bath would warm me up.*

She turned on the radio. She did not have a TV.

"Ladies and Gentlemen, outside your house, howling winds are heralding a winter storm—a Nor'easter. We are expecting up to twelve inches of snow. We suggest everyone stay inside if possible, because it is only eighteen degrees in the city and outlying suburbs."

How horrible! Ingrid is supposed to be back from training, and we had planned to go shopping.

The coffee was perking away, sounding inviting to Eileen, who loved coffee. She loved it with crème and sugar. She had started drinking coffee with her father when she was a teenager, in the mornings before he went to work, usually around 5:00. Her mother and brother were more civilized—they stayed in bed until 8:00 A.M., and they drank orange juice. Her father liked black coffee—strong enough to cause the hairs on the arms to stand straight up. Into this strong, black brew he loved to dunk donuts—glazed donuts. Eileen preferred chocolate donuts. They got them from the local bakery the night before. Her father sometimes spread Karo syrup over the donuts. He worked outdoors most of the time and needed lots of energy. He still remained thin and very handsome. He was a good southern boy and had been raised to eat donuts that way.

Thank God for hot water and coffee, thought Eileen. As the coffee was perking, she hopped into the tub. It felt wonderful, with bubbles up to the rim. Eileen hated to be cold.

TING-A-LING . . .

TING-A LING . . .

"I don't believe it. Who'd call at this hour?" said Eileen as she splashed bubbles around. "They'll just have to call back."

TING-A LING . . .

TING-A LING . . .

Finally the phone stopped ringing. "It's probably Ingrid. I'll call her back after I've had some coffee," said Eileen to herself as she began to warm up.

Eileen stayed in the tub until she was warm and the coffee was ready. She hopped out of the tub and into her new ski pants and jacket. Although she did not ski, she liked the ski bunny look. Her ski pants were chocolate brown, and her jacket was brown velvet on the outside, patterned with red and blue flowers. It was filled with goose down and was very warm. With it she wore her cashmere sweater.

By now she was feeling much better. It was 7:00, and she decided to call Ingrid.

"Hi, Eileen. It's great to hear from you. I passed training, and I'm back in Washington. I hear that Maudie got married. What do you think about us being roommates? I found the nicest townhouse in southwest Washington, down near the river. It has three levels and a balcony. It is lovely, but it would be more fun if I had a roommate. Would you like to look at it today?"

"Ingrid, there's a snowstorm going on. We don't have a car, and the buses aren't running until the storm has passed."

"Don't worry. My new boyfriend—Jorge, the German scientist— has a jeep, and he'll pick us up and take us over to the townhouse, and then we three can hot rod around town in the snow."

"That sounds like fun. I can wear my new ski clothes and furry boots!"

"Great! We'll pick you up around 11:00."

"Groovy!" chimed the two young ladies.

At precisely 11:00 A.M., a jeep pulled up in front of Eileen's apartment in Alexandria. Out of it jumped Ingrid and a tall, good-looking blonde man. That must be Jorge, though Eileen.

"Hi, Eileen. I'd like you to meet Jorge. He's going to drive us all around town in the storm. We should all have a swell time."

"Hi, Jorge. Nice to meet you." Eileen could tell he was good-looking but could not pick out too many details because the snow was swirling all around them. They looked at the road and watched the few souls hardy enough to brave the elements. The were whirling and twirling, spinning all over the streets in their cars and trucks.

"This trip should be a lot of fun. Hop in, girls," said Jorge as he opened the passenger doors. Jorge, Eileen noticed, had good manners.

The radio was blaring full blast, playing "Heartbreak Hotel" by Elvis Presley.

Jorge was totally enamored of American rock 'n' roll music and rhythm and blues. He particularly liked the King. Jorge pulled out of the parking space and headed for the main road.

The snow was actually a blizzard, and there were not many cars on the road. They came up on a snowplow that Jorge was dying to race. The driver of the snowplow, however, declined to race, and he continued his trudging path down the highway. He, too, was listening to "Heartbreak Hotel."

The three young people were having a great time driving in the jeep. The jeep behaved fantastically in the snow, and everyone was warmly dressed.

"Drive on, McDuff," said Ingrid, as she encouraged Jorge to try to go faster. Jorge obliged, and off they went through the storm at forty-five miles per hour, laughing and giggling at the top of their lungs.

Eileen was momentarily transported in her mind . . . back to the hill where all of her high school friends gathered to sled and eat hotdogs and marshmallows around the bonfire. What fun that had been. Sledding down the hill, hopping onto the sled in a pile of arms and legs, trying not to hit the tree at the bottom of the hill, or not to sled into the stream. Then everyone would trudge up the hill and go racing down the hill again. Sometimes two sleds would go racing each other down the hill and over the ramp that they had constructed.

Then back to reality . . . and the howling wind and the endlessly falling snow. The animals had all gone to ground or into their houses. They could hardly see each other. Finally they arrived at their destination. Jorge parked the jeep, and off they went, trudging through the snow, which by now was almost up to their knees. Their heads and bodies were bent into the wind as they made their way to the landlord's office and from there to the townhouse that they wanted to rent. They were left there by the landlord to look around.

"Oh Eileen, isn't it wonderful, and we can afford it. And there is a bus line nearby that you can use to get around until you get a car."

It was a lovely apartment. There was a ground level entrance, two bedrooms and two baths on the first floor, and a large living and dining area with a kitchen on the second level. There was a large balcony that ran across the width of the entire townhouse.

"Let's take it. It's just what we want. Come on, Eileen, say yes. It will help you make a new start now that Maudie is gone."

"Fine, Ingrid. Let's go back to the office and sign the lease."

Jorge admired the apartment. He also admired Ingrid. He knew that she was not the scientific type, but she was a good skier, as was he, so he thought that they were compatible.

Ingrid thought that he was cute, but she had no intention of getting married, even though he thought it was the right thing to do.

The three of them went back to the office and signed the lease.

By this time, they were hungry and thirsty, so they decided to go to Georgetown and have hamburgers and coffee at the White Tower fast-food joint. Everyone went to the White Tower for the wonderful hamburgers.

It was now about 2:00 P.M., and the streets were filled with pedestrians on foot, on cross country skis, and on snowshoes.

"Wow! Isn't this great? What a storm! Look at the snowplows. Look at the piles of snow. What a mess when the storm ends and the sun comes out," said Ingrid, who had flopped onto the ground and flapped her arms up and down, making a snow angel.

Jorge and Eileen were busy eating. Eileen was having a ball because she loved eating and could rarely do it if she wanted to stay thin and keep her job.

"Hey Ingrid, get up. Let's go across the street to that bar and get a glass of wine. There's a fireplace, and we can sit in front of it and get warmed," pleaded Jorge, who by now was tired and cold.

"Sounds good, Jorge. Let's go. Come on, Eileen. Okay?"

"Sure, let's go."

After some wine and a cup of hot chocolate in front of the fire and after listening to the jazz ensemble playing selections from *Porgy and Bess*, the three friends bundled up and headed for the jeep and back home after a fun-filled and exciting day. All three of them were tired. The blizzard had nearly dissipated, and night had fallen. They drove the quiet streets and enjoyed the beautiful scenes before them. The streets, yards, and trees were covered in snow. The storm clouds were passing up the Atlantic Seaboard, taking the snow with it.

They reached Eileen's apartment about 10:00 P.M., and they dropped her off. She was cold and worn out, and as she was saying goodbye she was dreaming of a beautiful bubble bath, the second for the day. Normally, she did not have two bubble baths in one day, but she used the excuse that it was frigid and the hot bath would help warm her before she went to sleep.

She warmed up the leftover coffee from the morning, cranked up the lava lamp and took it into the bathroom, filled the tub with bubbles and hot water, and hopped in.

"What a great day. It'll be fun living in the townhouse with Ingrid."

TING-A-LING . . .

TING-A-LING . . .

Who can that be at this hour? I'm not going to answer it. Even at this young age, Eileen had a tendency to ignore the telephone. This tendency became even more pronounced as she grew older.

She watched the bulbous shapes in the lava lamp as they ascended and descended inside the glass. She loved the lava lamp, which had been a present from Maudie.

It'll be fun living with Ingrid, but Maudie will always be my best friend. I really miss her, and I hope that she is happy with Chapman.

Night quietness filled her mind. The woodpecker was asleep, the stars had come out, it was cold, and she was tired.

She hopped out of the tub and into bed and crawled under the covers.

"Good night world, good night."

15

One Fine Rainy Afternoon

ONE FINE DAY IN THE LATE AFTERNOON IN THE SPRING, IT WAS raining cats and dogs. The rain was pounding on the tin roof. Eileen was sitting on the balcony listening to the water as it tap-tap-tapped. She sat on the balcony quietly, thinking about life in general, her life, and Ingrid's life in particular.

What in the world would we do if we were not stewardesses? We like to travel and would be miserable staying at home all the time. Their habit of leaving town when things got rough caused all of their boyfriends to be annoyed. Eileen had decided that men did not trust either her or Ingrid—even though she had been raised in Virginia and had been indoctrinated with the idea that men were a superior sex and should be praised at all times and deferred to. Ingrid, being European, also had been raised to praise men.

BANG! went the front door. "Hey, Eileen. It's me, Ingrid!"

"Oh. Hi, Ingrid," chirped Eileen, who put her cigarette down and got up to open the balcony door so that Ingrid could pass through without putting down her drinks for the two of them.

"Ingrid, where have you been? You didn't tell Jorge where you were going, and he's been beside himself. You know he likes to always know where you are."

"That's just too bad. I don't always want him to know where I am. Hey, is Mel corning over tonight? Really, Eileen, I don't know why you always date the most ineligible men. I mean, really, a labor-union organizer for the AFL-CIO! I understand that you like smart, good-looking men, but Mel is a hooligan. I keep telling you that you can do better. Why, just look at Jorge. He's handsome and smart and a world renown scientist. Why can't you date someone respectable like him. He has lots of nice friends that would love to meet you."

"Ingrid, I realize that Jorge is all you say that he is, but—and this is a big but—he's so boring. I mean so-o-o boring. Whereas with Mel, you never know what's going to happen."

Eileen continued, "Why, later tonight, we're going to a demonstration downtown. We'll be picketing for civil rights. To me that is exciting. It's also of some redeeming social value. As you know, this country has a terrible problem with discrimination, and this is something I can do that may lead to social reform."

"Eileen, you are certainly nuts. Why tonight, Jorge and I are going to a white tie dinner and ball at Union Station. Lester Lanin will be playing, and they are serving filet mignon and foie gras. I bought the most beautiful ball gown when I was in Dallas. It's red and has pink satin roses sprinkled all over it. Wouldn't you like to come with us?"

"Absolutely not! I've been looking forward to this demonstration all week. In fact, I got a new outfit to wear. We'll be at Dupont Circle, and I must look just right. Mel admires my taste in clothes. I'm wearing black Wrangler jeans, a white shirt, and my concho belt from Santa Fe.

I'll also be wearing my black cowboy boots and my black wool beret. I realize that cowboy boots and black berets usually aren't considered a good combination, but I believe that it is my style. Under all circumstances one should be true to one's style."

Eileen continued speaking, "Besides being so interesting, I like it that Mel managed to grow up and get a good education and job, even though he was raised in the slums of New York City. He is tough, and when I'm with him we can go anywhere. Jorge is such a wuss. I would rather stay home with a good book than date him or his friends."

"Okay, Eileen. You've made your point. Hey, did you hear that Dr. Hudson is giving us diet pills from the medical department? I hear that Universal is upset because they think that most of us weigh too much. Would you like to go tomorrow and get some?"

"Sure. My supervisor is hounding me to lose weight and maybe this would help." The two ladies sat in companionable silence, sipping their Perriers with lime. The rain had slackened a bit and the temperature had dropped a few degrees.

The man in the high-rise across from their townhouse appeared in his window, where he stood every night, surveying the neighborhood with his binoculars. The girls thought this very odd behavior, but because of the nature of their work, they were beginning to realize that there were many weird people populating the planet.

TING-A-LING . . .

TING-A-LING . . .

"It must be Jorge," said Ingrid. Are you sure you won't go to the ball with us? I could lend you my yellow satin ball gown from Saks."

"Nope, Ingrid. I'm off for a night of friendly demonstrating."

Ingrid picked up the phone. "Say—hey, Mel, I hear that you and Eileen are causing trouble this evening."

"Yeah, Ingrid. Tell her I'll pick her up at 8.00, and we will walk to Dupont Circle. It'll be too difficult to find parking."

"Sure thing, Mel. Will do!" Ingrid prided herself on her mastery of American slang and idioms.

"Ingrid, the rain has stopped," yelled Eileen. "I was getting worried that I would ruin my boots in the rain!"

Two hours later . . .

Jorge picked up Ingrid and off they drove to the ball.

Mel picked up Eileen, and off they walked to the demonstration. By now the rain had stopped, the streets were glistening, and the moon had appeared in the night sky. They walked through the streets, chit-chatting about life in general.

"Gee, Mel, I'm so upset. My supervisor doesn't like me. We had an argument about my weight and hairstyle today. I actually believe that she hates me. Isn't that just too disgusting?"

"Don't be such a baby, Eileen. When someone doesn't like me, they try to kill me."

"Isn't that a bit rash, Mel?" she inquired. She thought murder a little like going overboard.

"It doesn't matter if you think that murder is a bit rash. That's the way it is." Mel responded.

By now they had arrived at Dupont Circle, where their friends had gathered for the evening's festivities. Everyone was carrying a thermos of coffee, a couple of sandwiches, and a couple of candy bars. They were passing out the picket signs.

"Let's march down to the White House and parade around there a bit, and then we can all go home."

"Wow, did you see all the cops? You would think that we were going to riot. Talk about paranoid!"

Then off they took
Clop . . .
    Clop . . .
        Clop . . .
All the pedestrians did stop
What is it that
    The sighs do say?
    As they parade
    Along the way.

I would like to join the
    March, you know
Although it is going
    Way to slow.

The marchers are
    Dressed just right
For demonstrating on
    such a lovely night.

Their signs are
    Ac-cu-rate!
At demonstrating
    They are old hat!

Mel and Eileen were circulating and meeting everyone. There were a lot of people from out of town. In fact, there was a group from California—Berkeley, California. They were in the forefront of fashion in their tie-dyed T-shirts and fringed jeans and Frye Boots. Eileen started to feel too conservative and somewhat insecure. She was always unsure of herself when she was not dressed appropriately.

"Simmer down. You look just fine. Where's your self-confidence?" said Mel, who knew of her insecurity. "You're not a hippie. You never will be. It's not your style."

Mel was dressed in blue jeans, a gray T-shirt, tan Frye boots, and a fringed brown suede cowboy jacket. He also was not a hippie.

Finally, after marching through the dark streets, they arrived at the White House. Silently they stood there, waving their signs, everyone chanting:

> Discrimination is a bust
> We will overcome, we must!

They were surrounded by cops, who were unsure what to do. It was legal for the demonstrators to demonstrate, but you never knew what would happen when these groups got together.

Finally, after several hours it started to rain. It was cold and late. Everyone decided to break up and go home. "See you next week."

Mel and Eileen bade everyone a good night. They decided to hang out at Harrigan's down by the river, listen to some good music, and get something to eat. "Wasn't that a great demonstration, Mel? Ingrid doesn't know what a good time she missed."

"Right, Eileen. Next week, I'm going to demonstrate in Boston. Want to come along?"

"Sure thing, Mel. What'll we be demonstrating for?"

"The same thing, but we can eat clam chowder and have yummy lobster thermidor." Mel, like all red-blooded American boys, loved to eat.

"Gee, Mel, do you think we can get some salad for me?"

For several hours they sat there and listened to the pianist and the saxophonist play the blues, and occasionally the vocalist sang the blues. They were having a great time, but at last they were tired. The rain had stopped once again, so they headed back to Eileen's townhouse. She thanked Mel for a wonderful evening and headed straight for bed. She was too tired to wait up for Ingrid.

Besides, her head hurt.

16

The Assassination

$\mathcal{E}$ILEEN, WHAT IN THE WORLD AM I TO DO? JORGE WANTS ME TO marry him, quit working, stay at home, and have kids while he junkets around the world, giving lectures. I don't want to get married—especially to him. I would certainly die of boredom," said Ingrid with a tear in one blue eye.

"Gee, Ingrid! What a dilemma. It's the same sort of situation like my relationship with Mel. He also wants me to get married, quit flying, stay home, and have kids while he goes on the demonstration trail— "Clean for Eugene." I'd just die staying home with kids. It sounds too dismal for words," said Eileen with a note of horror in her voice.

"I guess maybe we should transfer to Los Angeles. We can fly to Hawaii. Wouldn't that be fun?" said Ingrid who had been giving this idea some serious thought.

"I'll have to consider that idea. It sounds like fun. You know that my father drinks too much. Well, recently he seems to be depressed. I probably should stick around until he feels better."

"Yes, I guess you should," agreed Ingrid as she took a deep drag on her cigarette. "I don't like smoking. Maybe I'll quit. Although I certainly don't want to gain weight. Those pills from the medical department helped me take off three pounds. I guess that would compensate for any weight that I might gain if I quit smoking. Say, Eileen, wouldn't you like to quit smoking, too?"

"Good grief, no! I love smoking. It helps me to relax. I can't imagine not smoking. Why, I've smoked for years, and I feel great." Eileen got indignant at the thought of giving up her beloved cigarettes. "Besides, the pills from medical made me nervous. I don't care to go through that experience again. I nearly jumped out of my skin. I don't understand why people take cocaine. It seems so nervous-making." As she said this, she sighed deeply, thinking of the stupid things that people did to be perceived as "cool."

She and Ingrid sat quietly on the balcony, music from the radio drifting out from the living room. Music by Mozart was soothing their minds and souls. They were having a cigarette and a glass or two of wine and were feeling no pain. At this time in their young lives, they did not have many deep thoughts, and they did not realize that they also were preoccupied with being cool.

It was early spring. It was a balmy evening. The rain had stopped, and the stars were popping out into the black night sky. They both loved the stars. Ever since Eileen had met Walter von Hamelstern, she was most interested in the theories of space travel. *Besides*, she thought, *given the reality of the atomic bomb and Vietnam, we—the people of the planet Earth—will probably blow ourselves up with the toys of mass destruction that we have devised. It is imperative that we be able to get off this planet.* Neither of them realized that they would never be completely free of the knowledge of Hitler, Stalin, and the atomic bombs exploding over Hiroshima and Nagasaki. No matter how hard they giggled, these thoughts were always in the back of their minds.

"Eileen, do you think we will ever meet anyone interesting enough to marry?" mused Ingrid, who in the depths of her soul was a romantic.

"Ingrid, did I ever tell you about my first proposal? I was only eighteen years old. It was during my first year of college. My parents were insistent that I get an education. They called it my ticket to freedom. I had a crush on this good-looking dude named Ken. One evening after we returned from a motorcycle ride and dinner, he proposed to me. I looked him straight in the eye—which was hard, as I am only five feet three inches tall, and he was six feet two inches tall. I said to him, and I quote, 'If you think that I am going to get married and have some man tell me what to do, you are crazy!'

"He was shattered and said, 'Aren't you afraid of being lonely?'

"'I will not be lonely.'

"You can see that even as a young person I was not a romantic. It just doesn't make sense to me to let a man tell me what to do. Needless to say, I am not looking for someone to marry. I'll figure out how to win friends and influence people. That was the end of that romance. I still feel the same way."

At that moment, the announcer on the radio piped up and said, "Ladies and gentlemen. I have terrible news."

"Gee, Eileen, turn up the radio volume. Let's hear what he has to say. It must be important if he's interrupting Mozart."

Eileen walked back to the living room and turned up the volume on the radio. "Ladies and gentlemen, today in Memphis, Tennessee, Dr. Martin Luther King Jr. has been assassinated. Stay tuned for further developments."

"Oh dear, Ingrid! I guess there will be trouble and riots. We'd better be careful when we go on our trip tomorrow. Do you remember when we were flying to Los Angeles and there was the rioting in Watts?"

"Wow, Eileen. This is just terrible. I feel the need to cheer myself up. Let's go to Harrigan's, listen to the music, and have some dinner. I know that Jorge and Mel will be calling to tell us that we must stay in the house."

TING-A-LING . . .

TING-A-LING . . .

"It will be one of them. Will you answer the phone? I don't feel like talking if it is Jorge," said Ingrid as she took one last sip of her wine.

TING-A-LING . . .

TING-A-LING . . .

Eileen picked up the receiver.

It was a man's voice—Mel's voice. "Eileen, I want you and Ingrid to go to your parents' home. There's going to be trouble in the city, and I don't want you here."

"Too bad, Mel! Ingrid and I are flying tomorrow, and right now we are going to Harrigan's for dinner and to listen to the music."

"Eileen, you must do what I say. I don't want you to be hurt."

"Buzz off, Mel," said Eileen, who had had just enough wine to say what she really wanted to say. "We're going out to Harrigan's. Green Boy and the Hep Cats are playing the blues. I love the blues. I bought a new pair of jeans today just for an occasion like this."

"Eileen, you two cannot go out. It's too dangerous."

"Bye, Mel," said Eileen as she slammed down the phone.

TING-A-LING . . .

TING-A-LING . . .

Eileen picked up the phone. It was Jorge. "Let me talk to Ingrid."

"She doesn't feel like talking," said Eileen, who was quite upset by the evening news and did not relish arguing with men.

Jorge practically yelled into the phone, "Have you and Ingrid been drinking? You don't sound like yourself—"

"Buzz off, Jorge. We are going out." BANG went the phone.

TING-A-LING ...

TING-A-LING ...

"This is the last time I am going to answer this phone. Who can be calling now?"

"Hello, Eileen." It was Mr. Gordon.

"Hi, Pops. Did you hear the awful news?"

"Yes! I want you and Ingrid to come home until this blows over."

"Sorry, Pops. We're flying to Los Angeles tomorrow and don't want to miss the trip. And right now we are going out. Say, how are you feeling?"

"I am sad," replied her father. "I can't seem to take this lousy sadness."

"Why don't you, Mom, and Charles hop in the car, come to the city, and go out with Ingrid and me? We would love to see you, and you love to hear good music as well as we do."

"It sounds like a great idea, but I don't feel too good. Just be careful and call me when you get back from your trip."

"Okay. I hope you feel better. Maybe you all will have dinner with us Tuesday when we return home."

"I'll think about it. Love you!"

"'Bye Pops! Love you too." Eileen was pensive as she hung up the phone. "He doesn't sound good, Ingrid. I wish I knew how to cheer him up. I know that the drinking doesn't help."

"Oh well, let's get dressed up and hit the town before anyone else calls to tell us what to do."

The crickets were chirping, and the owl in the tree next door was hooting. They got dressed and stepped out the door into the evening street.

"Good grief!" they exclaimed. The skyline was ablaze with flames leaping to the sky. "Trouble has started. There will probably be a curfew."

With a spring in their step they headed off in their platform shoes, bell-bottom jeans, and their hippy bags. They had money, credit cards, lipstick, and cigarettes and were ready to have an interesting time.

As they walked along the street, they carried on an insightful conversation. "Tell me, Ingrid," asked Eileen, "why is it that men all over the world love to fight? It seems that if there is peace, they become restless and have to have a shoot-em-up. Women certainly are not perfect, but at least they don't seem so anxious to start wars and kill each other.

"I don't know, Eileen. It seems that we live in a permanently anxious era. After Hitler and Stalin and their atrocities, I'm not sure that I will ever feel secure again." The two walked quietly along the dark street, pondering the ways of the world, the evening breeze, the rain-drenched grass, the sounds of the night, and the star lit sky. "Wow! Isn't it a beautiful evening, Eileen?"

"It sure is, Ingrid."

17

It Caused Brain Damage

IT WAS 4:27 A.M. ON A FINE TUESDAY MORNING. IT WAS SUMMER. It was hot, and the heat was sweltering. The air conditioner had lost power...

Tossing...
Turning...
Falling...

Why am I falling? I feel so peculiar. Falling is scary. Will I splat when I hit bottom?

Tossing...
Turning...
Sweating...

These thoughts ran through Eileen's troubled brain. She had been worrying a lot lately about her father. No one knew how to help him. Besides, she was sick and tired of Mel's bossiness. Perhaps that is why her dreams were so bad.

Back to the falling—KERPLUNK—Eileen was on the floor. She had fallen off of the bed. This was not a real problem, though, as she only had a mattress. It was close to the floor.

Why, I've fallen off the bed. What a weird dream. I really did fall, but it seemed to take such a long time in the dream, whereas it probably only took a second in real time.

Gee, it's hot. Somehow I have got to get cooled off so that when I get to work I will look cool, calm, and collected.

I think I'll make some coffee. I wish that that owl would shut up. It is never at a loss for words—or hoots, to be exact. I must admit, though, that it sounds better than Ingrid's awful parakeets.

Eileen padded into the kitchen and started the water for coffee. She and Ingrid had discovered a machine to grind coffee beans. *Isn't technology grand?* As she thought this, she started the coffee maker.

Shortly thereafter, while the coffee was perking, Eileen started to get dressed in her pretty blue uniform. The alarm had just gone off. Finally she was forgetting about falling in her dream. She hated that sensation. It was a recurring dream that always caused her to wake up in a cold sweat.

I'm looking forward to this trip. I love going to San Francisco, and Hairy-Cary is going to take me to the dance studio where he's drumming. I can even take a dance class, thought Eileen, who loved to dance. She had started taking ballet and tap as a little girl and continued dancing through college, where she discovered Martha Graham's technique and heavy-duty modern dance—nothing light and frivolous about her dance teachers.

1, 2, 3, *tour jeté*
1, 2, 3, *tour jeté*

She was looking forward to wearing her new black leotard and tights. She was a purist and believed in only wearing black while dancing. She also thought that black made a nice contrast with her red hair. She was looking forward to seeing Hairy, whom she had not seen for two years. He had retired from the Hell's Angels because he had developed a bad case of arthritis in his fingers and back. He was no longer able to handle a bike or be comfortable on one. He retired to a small houseboat in Sausalito, and among other hobbies he had become a drummer for Mad Murphy's African Jazz Dance studio. He thought that Eileen would enjoy the class. It would lend a lighter note to her dancing and thinking. Sometimes Hairy thought that Eileen was too serious. Hairy thought that seriousness was such a bad characteristic—he thought that it led to neurosis.

Suddenly the phone rang

TING-A-LING . . .

TING-A-LING . . .

Who in the world can be calling at this time of morning? It's not even light yet, thought Eileen as she was trying to get her hair to look just right. She had begun sporting a geometric hair cut for her short hair. It was all the rage, and Louis LaMoore in Los Angeles had adapted a Sassoon look just for her. He charged forty dollars per cut, which was a fortune, but it made her feel quite chic. Eileen's hair was a constant source of frustration to her. She loved curls, but her hair was stick-straight. Louis' hairstyle was geometric and asymmetrical, which was aided by using Dippety Doo, teasing, and hair spray. It was a great hairstyle.

TING-A-LING . . .

TING-A-LING . . .

The phone kept on ringing. It had an urgent quality to it.

My goodness! Maybe I'd better pick up. It might be the crew desk calling to say that my trip is cancelled. She picked up the phone.

"Hello. This is Eileen. Who is calling?"

"Eileen, it's your mother."

"Hi, Mom. I'd love to talk, but I have to get dressed for my trip. I must leave shortly. I'm going to San Francisco. Would you like me to pick up some See's candy for you and Pop and Charles? I know that you all love it." Eileen was trying to get her wits together because she noticed that her mother sounded agitated.

"Mom, are you okay? You sound strange."

"Eileen, please sit down. I have something terrible to tell you," said Mrs. Gordon in a strained voice. Eileen could hear tears running down her mother's face.

"What is it, Mom? Tell me!"

"Eileen, your father just shot himself, and he died about an hour ago."

"What! What do you mean? I don't believe you. He would never do that. I know he drank too much, but I don't understand why he would shoot himself."

"We don't know why he did it. He didn't leave a note. He's been very depressed. You must tell your boss that you need to come home."

"Of course I will come home. Can Charles pick me up? How's he doing?"

"Yes, Charles will come pick you up. He'll be there in a couple of hours. He's very sad."

Eileen hung up the phone. She was in shock.

"I must call the crew desk and let them know that I can't work today." She called the crew desk.

"Hi, this is Eileen Gordon. I cannot work today."

"Miss Gordon, it's too late to call in sick. You must take your trip. Why are you calling so late?" said Harry, who was new in this job.

"My father blew his head off, and I must go home," said Eileen who was now crying.

"Miss Gordon, did you say your father shot himself?" asked Harry.

"Yes! He did! You can understand why I can't work."

Harry said in a sad voice, "Miss Gordon, go on home. Give us a call when you are ready to resume work. I will call your supervisor and let her know what has happened to you."

"Thanks for your understanding, Harry."

"Do you need someone to take you home?"

"No thanks. My brother will pick me up in an hour or so," said Eileen as she lowered the telephone into the holder.

She walked upright to the bathroom and threw up.

That happened when she was twenty-seven. She never fully recovered. Neither did her mother and brother, as all of them loved her father very much.

They all three were of the old school:

1. Keep a stiff upper lip;
2. The show must go on;
3. Suffer in silence.

What they really wanted to do was bang their heads against the wall . . .

One bang . . .
Two bangs . . .
Three bangs . . .
Four . . .
And then some more . . .

They did not do that because they thought it would cause brain damage. They suffered from brain damage anyway.

There was no possible way to avoid brain damage in a situation like this.

18

We Need to Leave Town

ILEEN WAS DIGGING THROUGH HER CLOSET, looking for her paints.

Dig . . .
Dig . . .
Dig . . .

She was looking for the big canvas that she had bought that afternoon.

Big . . .
Big . . .
Big . . .

Eileen, whenever she was confused or depressed—both of which she was at this time—painted. When she was feeling good she tended to forget about doing this. It was like painkillers, which are usually hard to get from the doctor.

"I need to paint. I think I will paint a rock band sitting and playing in the rain. Yes, that is what I will paint."

Painting, in addition to being a pseudo-painkiller, was also a way for leaving this reality and stepping into another one. Eileen had a tenuous grip on reality at the best of times, which this was not. In her job it was not so obvious because flying was a different reality in itself. Flying above the clouds and over the land on starlit nights and over the oceans on a stormy afternoon was not exactly a normal way to make a living. Most passengers, too, were divorced from reality while on the plane, especially when the video and audio systems did not work and there were no phones.

At such stressful times, the passengers were thrown onto their own internal devices, which usually meant that they drank too much and passed out.

"Oh dear! Wherever did I put my paints?" She searched some more. "*Voilà*! There they are!" She was talking out loud to herself, always a bad sign.

She dragged them up the stairs to the kitchen, turned on Bach on the stereo, and started to arrange her paraphernalia so that she could get to work on her painting.

She was wearing overalls, a white T-shirt, and Dr. Martens clodhopper sandals. Eileen had never been so depressed that she forgot to dress properly.

On and on she splashed the paint. The picture started emerging from the whiteness of the blank canvas. Night fell, and the owl was hooting. Some birds that she could not identify were trilling their songs of joy and mirth. Eileen knew whippoorwills and cardinals, blue birds and yellow-bellied chickadees, but not much more. Actually, she also knew a buzzard and an eagle and a pigeon and a sea gull. She knew quite a lot.

"I think the picture needs a splash of blue."

Splash—thud—

She threw the paint across the kitchen, hitting the canvas and also the kitchen floor. The area of blue looked nice. Just what the picture needed.

"Oh dear, I'd better clean up. Ingrid is supposed to be getting home tonight. She will have a fit if she sees this mess."

Looking at the painting, she was pleased. The rock singer looked nice—placed in front of a psychedelic rainbow and a Braque-ish cello. She preferred cellos to electric guitars, so that is what she portrayed.

"Yoo-hoo, Eileen. It's me, Ingrid. I'm home." Ingrid's voice drifted up the stairs into the kitchen, followed by Ingrid who flounced into the kitchen, smelling of Shalimar, which she wore in the evening. It was heady and drove men wild. Ingrid was a femme fatale and loved to drive men to distraction.

"Hi, Ingrid. Did you have a good time?"

"Oh, Eileen," said Ingrid as she flipped her blonde ponytail from side to side, "I am so sorry about your Dad. It's sad not to have a father—especially at our age. We're old enough to appreciate them now, and they are gone. I never ever got to meet my father, but I miss him nonetheless, so I can truly understand how devastated you must feel."

"Thanks for your concern, Ingrid. I'm not quite sure how to handle this situation. I really want to leave town. I need a new environment. Mel is being a complete jerk. He thinks that I should just go to a good movie and forget everything as I watch the show.

"His father was a gangster, and he hated his father all of his life and cannot understand how one could love one's father and miss him. I'm sick of Mel and never want to see him again. I'm sick of everything, as a matter of fact. If you weren't so involved with Jorge, maybe we could transfer to Hawaii. The base has just opened, and Ma and Charles encouraged me to get away. Besides, they would love to come visit us. Have you considered dumping Jorge? I think it would be better if we both go." A tear appeared at the corner of Eileen's left eye. She surreptitiously wiped it away. That was a good old American WASP habit, so as to seem tough.

"I've lost my appetite."

"Well, Eileen, as it so happens, I was just skiing in Vail and met the most adorable man. He's from Hungary. He escaped from his homeland during the revolution and is living in San Francisco, and he is divine to look at. I know that he's going to make lots of money, although right now he's quit his job and is playing ski bum for the winter season. He asked me to marry him on our first date, and I gleefully accepted. What do you think of that? Let's both go to San Francisco, and we can fly to Hawaii."

"Why Ingrid, that's so cool! I could get a small apartment and come visit, and we could fly together. What are you going to tell Jorge? Boy, will he be mad!"

At that moment, the neighborhood owl started hooting. He had just finished eating a mouse that he had caught running across the yard and was feeling quite full and pleased with himself. He was an old owl, and knew that his mouse-catching days and also his days on this planet were numbered.

The two ladies really liked him. When they sat on the balcony in the evening listening to classical music, drinking a glass of wine, and discussing life and the foibles of mankind, they found his hoots comforting—their connection to nature. They were not for the most part connected to nature.

They continued their discussion of Ingrid's new fiancé, Ari Sztanko. "He's very handsome and has a gorgeous penthouse in the marina section of San Francisco. He'll help us find an apartment that you can afford. Doesn't that sound too thrilling for words? Gosh, I must get dressed for my date with Jorge. I'll tell him tonight that I'm getting married."

"Okay, Ingrid. Mel is coming by to see me, so I will tell him that I'm leaving town."

Both girls got up and went to their bedrooms to get dressed for the evening ahead. They dressed carefully, giving great consideration to what was the appropriate attire for breaking up with their boyfriends.

Over the airways came the dulcet tones of Jean Pierre Rampal playing Mozart. *How lovely!* thought Eileen. *I wish I could play the flute like that. Although I would play, "Nobody knows the trouble I've seen, nobody knows but Jesus."*

With a sigh, she sorted through her closet. *Maybe I'll let my hair grow long, but I know that long hair makes me feel bedraggled and depressed. I would rather look like a Parisienne than a hippy, and if I had long hair my therapist would know that I'm depressed.*

Her supervisor had recommended that she seek help, which she did. She did not, however, relate to the therapist. He seemed trite to her and a master of psychobabble, which was the last thing she needed at this time. *Maybe I can find a good shrink in San Francisco....*

One hour later ...

Eileen was dressed. She had decided on a black skirt. It was a midi-skirt. She did not like short dresses, except at the beach. She was wearing an aqua sweater. It was sleeveless with a goldfish blowing white bubbles, which were actually beads that looked like pearls. She was wearing black shoes with Cuban heels, because spiked heels caused women to have swayed backs and bunions, neither of which she needed or wanted.

She went up to the balcony and was sitting there quietly, waiting for Mel. She noticed that there was a full moon. "Wow! It's a full moon. That's not a good omen for the evening." At that moment, Ingrid joined her on the balcony. "That's a great suit you're wearing, Ingrid. Where did you get it?"

"Grandma sent me some money, so I went over to Saks and picked this out. We're going to a concert this evening, and then on to dinner. That's when I will tell Jorge that I'm leaving him for good and that I'm leaving town."

Ingrid's suit was beautiful. It was a lemon yellow wool suit with beige piping around the front and the hem of the jacket. She was wearing a pair of beige spiked heels and carrying a beige bag. She was the forerunner of the Nancy Reagan look—too matchy-matchy, but neat.

Her approach to dressing always annoyed Eileen, who thought that one should not look so predictable. Ingrid was, however, fun to shop with and always looked nice, so Eileen learned a little about tolerance.

The doorbell rang. It was Jorge.

"Hi girls, you both look great." Jorge had slicked his blond hair back, and was wearing a gray silk Italian suit with black wing tip shoes. Both girls admired his looks. He was handsome and rich but so boring. *I can't wait to dump him*, thought Ingrid.

The doorbell rang. It was Mel.

Mel was equally dressed handsomely in his new brown bomber jacket—he was learning to fly. He was wearing brown loafers and sported a ducktail haircut, which was a little passé; but he liked the look, and Mel always did just what he wanted to do. He was usually not concerned about what others might think, which Eileen knew included her.

So what if I dump him. He doesn't have any feelings anyway, so for sure I can't hurt him.

"Okay, gals. Off we go." And the four young, smartly dressed people trooped down the stairs and out the front door.

"Oh, My God!" shrieked Ingrid, "there's a skunk!"

They all four looked down, and in front of them, marching across the grass was a young skunk—black with the traditional white stripe. He paused to look at them and decided that they were not a threat, as the four of them were all frozen in their tracks like statutes.

He stuck up his tail and continued on his march across the road.

"I told you so. It's a full moon, and things are not going normally," announced Eileen to the world in general.

Into the cars they hopped, and off they went into a night that would be full of surprises.

19

The ---- Hit the Fan

"GOOD GRIEF," MUTTERED EILEEN, AS THE CAR SPED DOWN THE highway, inching its way to one hundred miles per hour.

Mel is certainly going to get us killed, and I'm too young to die. She was perturbed as she looked at her soon-to-be ex-boyfriend, driving like a fiend. She observed that his attention was not entirely on the road and his driving. He was using one hand to comb his ducktail back into place while screaming at her, "Bitch! You can't leave me! No woman ever leaves me! You cannot, therefore, leave me."

He made Eileen mad, and she serenely replied, "Just watch me, idiot! You will never, ever see me again after this night. I'm leaving town, and even I don't know where I will decide to go. One thing I do know for sure is that I never want to see you again. Never in my whole life!"

As they were careening down the highway, Eileen had a moment of truth—*I certainly have abysmal taste in men. I wish I would learn to be attracted by some quality more substantial that good looks. I don't even want children, so it's not like I'm concerned about what possible children will look like. . . .*

At this moment, a deer jumped out into the road in front of the speeding car—its eyes gleaming in the headlights. Mel yelled "Bitch!" once again as he frantically swerved to avoid hitting the deer. He decidedly did not want to hit the deer and total his car, his pride and joy. It was a 1968 lemon yellow Corvette, and it was the only thing in his life that he loved.

Eileen was by now silently praying to get home alive and in one piece.

God! What an awful evening. Her mind flashed back to the events of this extraordinary night. . . .

The theater was packed when they walked in. Originally Mel had planned to go to an Ingmar Bergman film, *The Seventh Seal*, but Eileen put her foot down and simply refused to go with him. He compromised and said he would go to a play, but one of his choosing. He picked *Who's Afraid of Virginia Woolf?* To her great amazement this play was even more awful than *The Seventh Seal*. She squirmed and fidgeted through the first act, causing Mel to get angry. He could never understand why Eileen did not like thought-provoking and meaningful thoughts and events. She was too trivial for a man like him. He realized that he should stop seeing her, but he did not want to give her up because all of his guy friends thought she was so cool, not to mention that they thought she was good-looking. Mel was influenced by the opinion of his friends, and it was important to him that he impress them.

During intermission, they headed for the bar, much to Eileen's chagrin. She wanted to be clear-headed when she told him that she was leaving town. She had coffee with crème.

As Mel guzzled down his third glass of champagne, he said, "This is certainly a good play, isn't it?"

"You must be kidding! Not only is it awful and vulgar, but it's also depressing. There's enough in life that is ugly that I think it's stupid to pay for something that reinforces these feelings. I'm not going in for the second act. I'll wait in the lobby until the play is over, if you think that you must see the ending."

"You won't do any such thing," retorted Mel, who was starting to get nasty. He was not stupid, and he realized that Eileen was being unusually stubborn this evening.

He knew something was wrong, but he had no idea what the problem was. "You will sit down and watch the rest of this play."

"Oh no, I won't." She nonchalantly reached into her beaded evening purse and whipped out one of her long brown cigarettes. She knew that Mel hated for her to smoke. So not only did she light up, but after taking a deep drag, she blew smoke into his face. He started coughing.

"Eileen," yelled Mel, causing heads to turn in their direction, "I've told you not to smoke when you are with me!"

"I don't care what you tell me. In fact, you will never again get the opportunity to tell me anything. I'm going home! And I'm leaving town for good." With that remark, she blew more smoke in his face, causing him to cough even more loudly. She whirled around and stomped over to the pay phone to call a taxi. Everyone was now staring. They were causing a scene. The lights were flashing to indicate that the play was about to resume.

Mel ran after her and grabbed her arm. "What do you mean that you're leaving town? You can't. I forbid it." He dragged her out of the theater lobby and to the car. He turned on the engine and backed out of the parking space. Ricky Nelson was singing "I Went to a Garden Party," a song that Eileen loved. She had actually been in New York to the concert about which this song had been written. She loved Ricky Nelson and was momentarily distracted from the problems she was now facing.

When Mel saw that she liked the song, he yelled "Bitch!" at her and angrily turned the radio off. His foot pounded the accelerator, and the car sped away from the theater into the dark night. He was so angry that the veins in the side of his face were pulsating. His face was a furious red.

"Take me home this minute," yelled Eileen over the roar of the engine. . . .

Back to . . .

the present . . .

They pulled into the parking space of her townhouse. They heard shouting, all of the lights were on, and the front door was lying on the sidewalk.

What had happened? What in the world was going on?

As she hurried to the hole in the front where the door had been, Mel once again screamed at her, then sped away, leaving her alone . . . wondering what was going on. She stared momentarily at the front door lying on the sidewalk. It looked as though someone had taken a crowbar and pried the door off at the hinges. At that moment, ringing through the cool night air was the sound of a man's voice yelling, "Bitch, you cannot leave me!"

"Good grief. That's Jorge's voice!" exclaimed Eileen.

Then she heard Ingrid yelling, "Put that gun down, you fool! You'll kill someone, and I don't want it to be me."

What in the world is going on? wondered Eileen. She was glad that she had not been drinking. In fact, if this was the way that men react to news that they do not want to hear when they are drunk, then she figured that more than one or two drinks was to be avoided like the plague. Maybe she should stay away from men who had had too much to drink, which meant most of the men that she had ever known.

She heard the sound of a man's loud sobs as she walked towards Ingrid's bedroom.

"I love you. You know that I love you. You can't leave me. I will be desolate! Ah, *mein Liebschen,* you know that I cannot live without you, knowing that I will never again see your beautiful face and never gaze deeply into your gorgeous blue eyes. Oh, what will happen to me?"

"Oh shut up, Jorge! You're drunk," responded Ingrid.

As Eileen entered the room, Jorge swung the gun toward her. He was sitting on the bed, his back propped up by big pillows, and he was swinging the gun from side to side.

Eileen, ever a woman of action, bolted out of the bedroom and headed for the phone upstairs in the kitchen. She called the police. The parakeets and the owl were making a horrible noise. All of the shouting and commotion had upset them.

Someone answered the phone—"Hello! Hello! Is this the police station? It is? Oh, thank God! My name is Eileen Gordon, and I need help."

"What kind of help?" replied a deep masculine voice, who claimed to be the dispatcher.

"Well, my roommate just broke up with her boyfriend this evening, and he was so upset that he broke into our home and is now sitting on her bed waving a gun around, threatening to shoot—whether her, me, or himself I don't know. I do know that we need help . . . You'll be here in ten minutes? Thank you, officer! The door is lying on the sidewalk, so you can walk right in."

Eileen hung up the phone and walked over to the birdcage, trying to calm the parakeets. Eileen then sat down on the stairs with her face cupped in her hands. She sat there for a few minutes while waiting for the police. She was thinking about this disastrous evening, listening to the loud shouts of Ingrid and Jorge, thinking of how ugly Mel had been.

"I think that I shall give up men. They don't seem to be as much fun as they were when I was younger," she muttered to the world in general.

At that moment, into the hallway strode two policemen. One was a large black man, and the other, a short red-headed Irishman.

"Well, young lady, how can we be of service?" said the Irishman as he spotted Eileen on the steps and heard the two people yelling at each other in the back bedroom.

"Officer, just get him out of here before someone gets killed! Follow me!"

The three of them trooped into the bedroom. Jorge was now hiccoughing loudly and crying.

"Young man! Give me that gun," said the black officer with the beautiful Afro. "Give me the gun right now."

Eileen and Ingrid stood perfectly still, watching the three men arguing over who should be in control of the gun.

"Officer, I love her. She wants to leave me. I can't bear for her to go."

"Lady, do you want to press charges?" said the redhead.

"Heavens no, officer! I don't want him to go to jail. It would adversely affect his standing and reputation in the scientific community. I can't have that hanging over my head. Just get him out of here," exclaimed Ingrid, whose face was scarlet with fury.

By now Jorge had slumped over. He had passed out. The gun dropped to the floor, falling out of his hand. The red-headed Irishman with the crew cut picked up the gun. He and the other man picked up Jorge—one grabbed his arms, and one grabbed his legs. They carried him out the door and into the waiting squad car.

Ingrid told them where Jorge lived. Jorge was out cold.

As the squad car sped away, the two young women looked at each other and broke into tears.

It had been a horrible evening. It was over.

20

Over the Pacific

GOODNESS GRACIOUS!" MURMURED EILEEN UNDER HER BREATH. "I'm flying over the Pacific. I'm flying to Hawaii! This is too exciting!".

She turned to talk to Ingrid, who was going to Hawaii to be married. After the wedding, she would make her home in San Francisco.

"Wow!" said Ingrid, "this is probably going to be the most exciting week of my life. I am glad to be sharing it with you. I promise that once I'm married . . . NO MORE MEN . . . this is it . . . I swear it . . . forever. I swear it Eileen! And if Ari runs around with anybody else, I'll kill him." Ingrid said this with great force and with great emotion.

"Good luck, Ingrid. Your track record with men is no better than mine."

They were sitting in the first class section of stretch DC-8—a really lovely airplane, one that they both thought elegant and mysterious. But then again, Eileen and Ingrid thought that all airplanes were elegant and mysterious.

The sun was going down over the ocean, and the sky had turned into a glorious blaze of pink, red, and orange with traces of purple. The sun was a large red ball hanging in the sky. Both of them shut up for a moment, so that they could admire the sunset. They were great lovers of beauty and were always awed by the world that their God had created—Ingrid being Jewish and Eileen, a Presbyterian—a Christian denomination dating back to the 1500s—a denomination of which Eileen was inordinately proud. It was intellectual. It repeated everything many times, which was important to her, as her memory was spotty—even though she was only twenty-eight years old.

"Wow!" said the steward to them. "Ain't life grand, girls?" His name was Allan Shigaki, and he was a handsome Japanese-Hawaiian local boy. He started to play his ukulele, and sing "Tiny Bubbles," warbling like Don Ho.

Meanwhile Eileen was getting into the swing of the moment. She chirped away in her messed-up voice the tune and words of "Little Brown Gal. . . ."

"Hey, Eileen," said Ingrid, "that was grand. I didn't realize you could sing. I'm impressed."

Allan looked at the two happy ladies, and said "Hey, girls, Wanna eat? We have roast pork with candied yams and string beans. For dessert we have baked Alaska, which is so large that you two need to share it. We serve that with crème de menthe over ice. Doesn't that sound good?"

"It sounds wonderful, Allan. But no bread or dessert for me," said Ingrid. "I am getting married in two days, and my dress is already skin-tight. I don't want to look vulgar."

"Why, Ingrid! You could never look vulgar!" chimed Allan and Eileen in unison. "For haole girls, you two are not so bad. You're going to love Hawaii."

"Where's a good place to get an apartment?" inquired Eileen, who did not yet have a place to live. It happened that when they turned in their transfers the night they broke up with their boyfriends, there was an opening for Hawaii. Eileen decided to take it. She would move to San Francisco later.

"Well, Eileen, you strike me as the type of girl who would like the Jungle. My auntie, Miss Panayuki, has a small apartment with a patio on Aloha Drive. You'd love it," continued Allan. "The area is sort of rough, but you're tough. Also, you can afford it. If you're interested, we can call my auntie tomorrow."

"Great, Allan! Sounds good to me. I will take it sight unseen since you seem like a sensible young man." Little did Eileen and Ingrid know that Eileen was getting mixed up with the underworld—a bad habit of hers, and one which only ceased when she matured a little more. Eileen could absolutely not live a simple life at that time. The call of adventure had infected her soul and left her completely unable to live a nice comfy American lifestyle. No, that was not for Eileen—not then and, as it later turned out, not ever.

By this time, dinner was over, and the three of them were having a cup of coffee, while Allan strummed his ukulele.

"Hey, girls, do you like to gamble? There's a hot game of poker tonight in the back room of the Japanese grocery at the Ala Moana Shopping Center. Wanna join us?" Allan inquired.

Ingrid, who always loved a party, said gleefully, "Yes, that'll be fun. I'm a great poker player."

Eileen, however, turned down the invitation to the game, as she wanted to walk along the seashore and pick up seashells.

"Okay, Ingrid. I'll meet you in the morning for coffee; then we can go look for your trousseau and look at my new apartment."

By this time the sky had turned black, and the big yellow moon was shining with all of its might. It was quite lovely. The stars were twinkling. The engines were droning on in a comforting manner, causing people to nod off for the evening. Ingrid took off to the back of the plane for the poker game that was in session.

Eileen had settled down to read *The Master and Margarita* by Mikhail Bulgakow. It was an exciting book, and it made Eileen think about the forces of evil—something she rarely thought about. As she dozed off, the words from the book lingered in her mind . . .

> Berlioz was so overcome with horror that he shut his eyes. When he opened them, he saw that it was all over, the mirage had dissolved, the chequered figure had vanished, and the blunt needle had simultaneously removed itself from his heart.
> "The devil!" exclaimed the editor.

Yes, that is a perturbing book, thought Eileen, who was nodding her head while she dozed. With a start, she woke up, sat bolt upright, and said aloud. "My God! I encountered . . . well, just what did I encounter?" Eileen was quite confused, and she decided to go back to the galley and get a cup of coffee. She placed the book in the gray wool seat pocket. She got out of her seat and set off for a cup of coffee. She definitely needed some caffeine.

Eileen meandered through the length of the plane—all the way to the back of coach. All the stewardesses and stewards were involved in a rousing game of poker. The lights in the cabin were out, and the passengers were sleeping—some stretched out across the row with their feet sticking out into the aisle and some of them asleep with their seat backs straight up, as though they were even too tired to recline their seats.

There were titters and giggles coming from the group in the back lounge. Ingrid was so far winning and had quarters, nickels, and dimes piled up neatly in front of her.

"Oh, hey there, Eileen. How are you doing? Wanna join us?"

"Thanks for asking, Allan, but I think I'll go back to my seat and read and drink coffee. See you!"

Eileen wandered back to her seat. There were snores and the piteous mewing of the cat that was in a carrying case under a seat.

Eileen got back to her seat. In her brain was the following refrain:

> *Herman Hesse*
> *Was a mess-a*
> *A man of great renown*
> *He often would digress-a*
> *A wondrous man*
> *Was Herman Hesse. . . .*

Eileen was looking out of the window. The stars were still twinkling, and all of a sudden there were lights down below. They were approaching Honolulu.

At that time the captain carne over the PA, telling everyone...

> *Well, folks*
> *We are approaching Honolulu*
> *Fasten your seat belts*
>
> *Land is not far away*
> *Your trip is ending for today*
> *We have traversed the*
> *Pacific Ocean*
> *With nary a bump*
> *Caused by turbulent motion.*
>
> *We are heading for*
> *Our landing spot*
> *In Honolulu*
> *Where The weather is hot.*
> *Where the balmy breezes blow*
> *Where there is lava*
> *And not much snow*
>
> *So, ALOHA*
> *From me to you*

ALOHA *on behalf of the*
Rest of my crew.

It had been a glorious flight, and it was over, this wonderful night.

21

Home in Hawaii

EILEEN WAS HAPPILY ENSCONCED IN HER NEW APARTMENT IN Waikiki. It was small, and Eileen was never home, so that did not bother her in the least. It had a lovely balcony with a real bird of paradise blooming in the ceramic pot that she had bought in the local Chinese market. She liked to paint on the patio and eat her breakfast of papaya with homemade yogurt on top. As a concession to good health, she also poured wheat germ on the top and reinforced it with dried milk.

Her new friend, Mimi, had the penthouse apartment on the second floor. It also was lovely.

Mimi was exotic. She was of mixed Mexican, Korean, black, and Irish heritage. She was tall and slender and wore her long shiny brown hair in a topknot on the top of her head. This particular evening she was wearing long red ribbons that hung down her back. They matched her red mini-dress, which she had made. She was an accomplished seamstress.

Mimi's new boyfriend was a handsome dude by the name of Charles Haley. He was one of the leading crime lords on Oahu. This evening he had invited Mimi and Eileen to join him for the opening of his new club, the Kanihaha, near Diamond Head.

It was still an hour before they were to be picked up by Charles, and they were sitting on Mimi's balcony, having their afternoon tea. Mimi was contentedly enjoying her joint, some of the local Maui-Wowee.

"Wow, Eileen, this is great shit. Sure you won't share some with me."

"Oh, no thanks, Mimi. I've noticed that when people smoke joints, they start eating everything in sight. You're naturally thin, but I'm not. So, thanks for the offer, but I'll pass this evening."

"That's cool. If you change your mind, I'll be happy to share. Charles always gets the best. Aren't you excited about the party this evening? And, hey, I just love your dress. Where ever did you get it?"

Eileen, for this festive evening, had picked up her new white dress near the Santa Monica Pier on her last layover in Los Angeles. It looked like white feathers and had been inspired by the latest Yves Saint Laurent style, which she had seen on one of her layovers in Paris. It was a gorgeous white dress. It had a dropped waist, no sleeves, and was cut just above the knee. With it she was wearing her new white leather shoes. Eileen realized that white leather shoes were considered tasteless, but she liked their look with this particular dress.

As the evening grew darker and the stars appeared, they sat for a while enjoying their tea. Eileen's friend, Sun Fat, always gave them the greatest green tea, straight from China. He stocked it in his shop in the International Market Place.

Breaking their reverie, Mimi exclaimed, "Hey, Eileen, it's about time to go." At that moment, they heard the horn blaring down in the street below.

"Come on, Eileen. It's Charles. Let's go! The evening is young, and we should have a great time. The opening of the new club has been anxiously awaited by all the locals. I hear that the band, the Local Boys, are playing. They're great."

Both girls gulped down the rest of their tea, glanced in the mirror by the door to make sure that they looked okay, and bounded down the stairs to the waiting car.

"Hi, girls, you look great. C'mon. I'm hungry," said Charles. "Meet my bodyguard, Denny."

The four of them hopped into the white Cadillac convertible and took off for the club and an evening of dancing and dining and drinking.

After a dinner of mahimahi, a side salad, scalloped potatoes, and a dessert of chocolate mousse, everyone started serious partying.

Mimi and Charles were drinking heavily and felt no inhibitions about the wild dancing brought on by the wild drumming of the Local Boys. The band was made up of local boys of Hawaiian descent. They were popular among the in-crowd, of which Charles was one.

Mimi liked to party. She liked Charles because he had lovely white hair, oodles of money, and bodyguards. He was popular with the local night people.

Charles adored Mimi because she was gorgeous. He was impressed by what a glamorous couple they made. Charles always invited Eileen on these outings because he thought that she lent respectability. Eileen usually went but wondered, *Why do I go with them? I'm always so bored. The next time I will just say No.*

This evening, Eileen had gotten a severe headache from all the cigarette smoke and the aroma of marijuana, the banging of the drums, the senseless howling of the Local Boys, and the strobe lights, which were making her dizzy.

"'Bye, Mimi. 'Bye, Charles. I'm going for a walk. It's such a lovely night, that I am walking home. My head is splitting, and I can't stand the music. And besides, I'm a wallflower. No one is dancing with me."

"Are you sure you'll be okay, Eileen?" inquired Charles. "It's late."

"Sure, I'll be okay. If you think that it's necessary, Denny can walk home with me."

Denny was Charles' favorite bodyguard. He was from Samoa, the old country. He and his four brothers—Henny, Kenny, Lenny, and Benny—had left home several years ago and immigrated to Hawaii, where they were in great demand with people who believed that they needed protection. All four of them were about six feet six inches tall, and they each weighed about three hundred pounds. They cut their hair in black crew cuts, and they wore handmade Italian silk suits. They always wore cowboy boots. They each carried a loaded revolver at the waist, and each of them carried a switchblade stashed in his boot. In addition, they were well trained in karate, and they could box with the best of boxers. All in all, they were forces to be respected by the meanest.

Charles loved them, especially Denny, who accompanied him everywhere. Denny was worried about Eileen.

"Hey, Boss. It's not cool for her to walk home alone."

"Oh, Denny. Leave her alone. Eileen is a grown woman. I would normally send you with her, but Hot Shot Hannigan has threatened to ambush me coming out of the club tonight. It he does, I will need your help. It's not even 10:00. She'll be okay."

"Okay, Bossman. If you say so."

At this moment, Eileen joined them.

"Hey, guys, it's been fun, but I'm leaving. The cigarette smoke is so thick that I can't breathe. For sure I can't smoke. Say 'bye to Mimi for me. Don't get into any fights."

Eileen waved gaily, smartly twirled in the direction of the door, and sashayed out. Quite an exit.

"Hey, Bossman. It's a shame that she's so short."

"Now, Denny. Forget about Eileen. Remember that you like the tall, lanky type."

"Yeah, Bossman, I guess you're right."

"Also, Denny, keep an eye out for Hot Shot Hannigan. It would probably be a good idea to give your brothers a call. You might need some backup if there is a fight."

"Boss, don't you trust me? You know I'm always prepared."

"Charles," yelled Mimi from across the dance floor, "come on and dance. They're playing our song."

"Okay, toots. Be right there.

"Go make that call, Denny."

As he gave these final instructions, Charles bopped onto the dance floor and started dancing to "Be-Boppa Lulu."

Denny sneaked out the back door. He was going to call for backup. He was calling his brothers.

Eileen strolled down to the beach and started walking back to Waikiki. She was happily breathing in the balmy, pure night air. *Wow, hibiscus—they smell so good. I am so glad to be out of that smoke-filled club. I shall just breathe in the flower-laden air. I shall breathe in the salt sea air. What fun to walk at night.*

Eileen took her shoes off, strolled down the beach feeling the sand under her toes. POW! All of a sudden, a nicotine attack! Eileen needed a cigarette.

She reached into her white leather evening bag. One would have thought that with all of the white that she was wearing she was getting married. But no, she was just in a white mood.

She smartly whipped out a cigarette, and lit up. PUFF! PUFF!

Ah, how wonderful it is to take a deep drag. Eileen started to cough. She always did this when she smoked, but that did not deter her. Eileen was stubborn, and although she knew that smoking was bad for her, she just could not seem to kick the habit.

She quietly puffed on her cig as she found a bench on the beach. She sat down, and seriously continued to smoke while listening to the night noises. There was the noise of waves washing up on shore at her feet. There were night birds, and far away in the distance, she could hear the muffled drumming of the Local Boys. The moon was drifting across the dark sky, and she could see the ships heading out to cross the ocean, their lights twinkling far away.

After sitting quietly for about fifteen minutes, she got up and resumed her stroll into town. She continued her walk until she reached the busy streets of nighttime Waikiki. It was still too early to go home, so she headed for the International Market Place for a cup of cappuccino before going to bed.

All of a sudden, as she was walking through the marketplace, she heard, "Hey, Missy, want a drink?"

"Why, hello Clarence."

It was Clarence, the parrot. He belonged to old man Sun Fat, the proprietor of the Velvet Hanging. His shop specialized in velvet paintings.

Clarence was seventy-five years old and very wise. He and Sun Fat had spent a life time together—ever since Sun Fat was a little boy in Hilo. Clarence had gorgeous green feathers, and what was unusual was that he had one red feather on his head. He had a great sense of humor and was as smart and observant as Sun Fat.

"Hey, Missy, want a drink?"

Sun Fat walked over to the table where Eileen was sipping her cappuccino.

Sun Fat was eighty years old. His thin gray hair was pulled back from his face and tied in a long pigtail down his back. He wore his beloved gray satin pants and a gray cotton coolie jacket, which had been in his family for over a hundred years. He had begun to wear it only for special occasions. This night was a special one for him. His friend, Mr. Yakamura, was joining him for a game of mah-jongg and some discreet gambling. There was a golf tournament that weekend, and they were getting a head start on the festivities.

Sun Fat and Mr. Yakamura were also negotiating. Mr. Yakamura was trying to sell his latest acquisition—some velvet paintings featuring

Elvis. Mr. Yakamura knew that they would be a hit with the haole tourists. Eileen and Mimi both loved velvet paintings. They especially loved the ones featuring Elvis, although they would never admit it because they knew people considered velvet paintings to be unsophisticated.

"Hey, Missy, I'm hungry," continued Clarence. Sun Fat sat down with Eileen.

"Hey, Missy, it is good to see you. Clarence has missed you. He loves to talk with you."

"Hi, Sun Fat. How are you? I've just come back from an awful party. But the night was so lovely that I had to come see you. Talk to me while I drink my cappuccino."

"Missy, you know you should not wander around by yourself so late at night. A nice young lady like you! What would your parents say? It is not safe!"

Suddenly a deep, masculine voice boomed out, "Hey, Sun Fat, introduce me to your lovely friend."

"Why, Mr. Dan! How are you? This is Missy Eileen. Come join us."

"I'd love to join you, but first I must lock up my motorcycle." Dan disappeared .

"Sun Fat, you old matchmaker, you. You know that I'm allergic to romance. It seems so out of date."

"Missy Eileen, I think that Mr. Dan is just your type. Just give him a chance."

Dan rejoined them in a few moments. He sat down. He was holding a cup of coffee. This impressed Eileen, who was sick to death of drunks. "Hi, Eileen, it's nice to meet you."

"Hi, Dan. Likewise, I'm sure."

Sun Fat said, "Well, kids, Clarence and I have got to get back to work. I need to sell my Elvis paintings. See you later."

Eileen looked at Dan. Dan looked at Eileen.

Cupid struck—the first time for both of them.

At that moment the radio from Sun Fat's store blared out: *There has been a shoot-out at the opening of a local club. Hot Shot Hannigan and Big Charles Haley had a shoot-out as Big Charles left the building. His escort, Miss Mimi Anderson, was shot in the foot and has been taken to the emergency room of the local hospital. . . .*

"Oh my God, Mimi's been shot! I must go to the hospital!"

"Who is Mimi?"

"My friend! I must go!'

"Okay, Eileen. Hop on the back of my motorcycle, and I'll take you to the hospital."

"Oh dear, my mother taught me never to get on motorcycles with strangers. Oh dear. What shall I do?"

"Eileen, don't be such a priss! Sun Fat is a mutual friend, and he has properly introduced us. Come on, we'll go see your friend."

He sounded sensible to Eileen, who declared in a demure voice, "Okay, Dan, let's go."

They had each met their match. It was the beginning of a great romance. Not one of which their mothers would approve, but they were happy and that is what counted.

> *Love is a Wondrous Thing*
> *It usually happens in the Spring*
> *If it should happen in the Summer*
> *It usually does not last, it is a bummer.*
> *If it should happen in the Fall*
> *It beats going to the Mall.*
> *If it should happen in the Winter*
> *When it is cold*
> *It usually lasts until the humans get old.*

22

Wahu

WAHU WAS STROLLING ALONG THE SEASHORE.
The lava erupted, high in the sky.
"My goodness," said Wahu, "the flowers will die."
Wahu was thinking, the lava did roar.
Madame Pele was mad, having a fit.
Kahunas were chanting, "Leave us alone,
Instead of cussing, give your dog a bone.
Quit all your fussing, quit having a snit."
The lava erupted, red in the night.
It poured down the slopes, it knocked down the trees.
Kahunas were frightened, down on their knees.
Wahu exclaimed, "What a glorious sight!"
Wahu, a ghostly apparition gay
Wandered alone in the midst of the fray.

23

Wahu: The Beginning of All Trouble!

EILEEN WAS HAVING A GRAND TIME FLYING TO AND FROM HAWAII, but she especially liked going to Hilo, on the Big Island. It was wild, unspoiled, and beautiful. The stewardesses and stewards stayed at a wonderful old hotel, the Naniloa, which sat on the edge of a lagoon. There were beautiful old trees and rocks to sit on. She could sit there and look at the waves and watch the water at night.

One fine balmy evening, she was sitting by herself watching Mauna Kea exploding. The lava was erupting in a red column, high into the dark night sky. Suddenly she felt the hairs on the back of her arms stand up straight, and her flesh crawled with fear. And she saw a white dog walking on the water.

"My goodness, what's happened? Why do I feel such fear?" She turned back and looked at the lagoon.

"I wonder what it means."

All of a sudden there was no dog. Eileen was disturbed. What had she really seen? Slowly she got up and walked back to the hotel. She went straight into the gift shop. While she was browsing through the books, she saw one about volcanoes. For some reason she felt compelled to read it. It was a small book. She was excited about finding it.

She hurried back to her room, plopped down on her bed, and started reading about Madame Pele, the goddess of the volcano, and how she walked her dog when the lava was spitting.

"I saw Wahu! I know that his name is Wahu! Whom can I tell?"

All night long she tossed and turned. She could not sleep. Visions of her encounter with Wahu raced through her mind.

In the morning while she was eating breakfast, she was joined by Cary Shimagawa. "Why do you look so perturbed, Eileen? You look like you have seen a ghost."

"I think I did!" She explained to him what she had seen the night before.

Cary was horrified. "Were you drinking, Eileen?" he asked.

"No. I swear I wasn't drinking. I swear I saw the dog walking around the lagoon."

"Eileen, if I were you I would keep quiet about this." He quickly changed the subject. "Would you like to join Kim, Margaret, Harry, and me this morning. We are planning to go to the lava fields and to the lip of the volcano. We're going exploring. It should be lots of fun."

"Sure. Let's finish breakfast and then get the others. It sounds great. I thought it was exciting watching the lava shoot into the air last night. We have all afternoon to explore and plenty of time before we need to work our trip back to the mainland."

"Okay, we'll meet in the lobby in an hour."

An hour later they all met in the lobby. They went out to the parking lot, piled into the rental car, and headed for the lava fields. When they arrived there, they climbed out of the car and started to explore. What an eerie landscape! Once again, Eileen's flesh crawled, and the hairs stood up on her arms.

"Cary, this place is so eerie. I feel like there are ghosts all around me."

"Your imagination is working overtime. Just try to relax and enjoy the experience."

As they were walking around, Eileen felt a great urge to pick up a piece of lava rock to take back home to her apartment. When no one was looking, she bent down and picked up a particularly appealing lava rock and slipped it into her bag. She did not say anything about the rock when she rejoined her friends.

They strolled up to the lip of the crater and looked down. They all gasped. They were awestruck and unable to speak. It was like looking into the mouth of Hell. The lava was gurgling and bubbling. The lava fields on all sides of them stretched away in all their mysterious gray-black glory. The two Hawaiian men and the haole ladies were scared and decided that they had seen enough. The group walked back over the lava fields to where they had left their car. Eileen was unusually quiet. She was feeling weird about the piece of lava rock she was carrying in her Hobo bag.

That evening, flying to Los Angeles after dinner had been served and everyone was asleep—this was before there were movies on planes—Cary and Eileen were sitting on their jumpseats talking about what they had seen.

"Cary, I must tell you what I did. I didn't mean to tell anyone, but I just have to."

"What is it? I know you seem upset and you're still unusually quiet."

"I took a piece of lava rock from the lava fields."

"You must be joking! You must return it as soon as you can. It will cause great trouble in your life!"

"Oh, Cary, that's just a superstition. I want to put it on my patio as a souvenir."

She carried the rock to Los Angeles and then on back to Honolulu. When she returned to her apartment, she put the rock in her garden.

She then went to sleep, as she was tired, strangely subdued, and for some odd reason somewhat worried.

24

The Millers' Mansion

"Hey, Dan, what's up? I just finished my dance class, and I'm beat." As Eileen was saying this, she was dripping sweat. She and Mimi were taking a new dance class down on King Street. The studio was above an old renovated warehouse, and it was spacious and sunny.

"Michel is one mean teacher," said Eileen to Dan, who had come to pick her up on his motorcycle.

Michel was an ex-dancer from New York. He had been a star performer for the Motley Dance Group, but he had to retire because of arthritis in his knee and back. Eileen was noticing that arthritis was common among older people, and they seemed to feel better living where the weather was warm.

Michel's inamorata was Lynn, a lissome blonde from Iowa. She would demonstrate to the class while Michel yelled instructions and bang on his drum. Eileen heard the banging of drums in her sleep.

In true Eileen fashion, she was well dressed for the class. She was sporting her new leotard from New York. It was a tie-dyed leotard. The purples, blues, and pinks danced across a background of black. With it she wore black tights. Mimi naturally wore red tights and leotard—no shoes. It was a modem jazz class. You could wear shoes if you chose, but in college she had learned to dance with no shoes.

Eileen's favorite dance music was B. B. King's "The Thrill is Gone." Michel had choreographed a lovely, bluesy dance routine to this song, which was her all-time favorite song . . . partially because it was the way that Eileen was beginning to feel about life. That was unlike her, and she thought that maybe it was because of her recurring headaches and the weird sounds that she sometimes experienced in her brain.

She adored Dan, even though he was only twenty-one years old. This particular day he was excited because he had landed a choice detecting job. One of the local Chinese mobsters, Mo Fat—he was Sun Fat's cousin—was upset because he suspected his young blonde wife, Susie, of running around with her tennis coach, José. She had been acting suspiciously and keeping weird hours. Whether she was actually running around was left to Dan to determine. Mo Fat was most perturbed. He chose Dan as the detective because Dan played tennis with Susie and could follow her without being suspicious. Susie really liked Dan and could never figure out why he liked Eileen. Susie thought that Eileen was way too old for him and that she was way too prissy for a cool dude like Dan. What would really have shocked Susie would be the knowledge that Dan was spying on her.

One fine afternoon the balmy trade winds were blowing over the mountains and the sea. At the tennis club, Susie was a little drunk and somewhat indiscreet in public with José. Eileen was, as usual, bored with watching the tennis game in progress; but she knew that Dan needed the money from this job, so she just at there. She was not really watching the game. She was watching Susie.

All of a sudden she noticed that Susie had left the court and was heading for the parking lot. José was in his car.

"Come on, Dan!" yelled Eileen. "I saw her heading for José's car. She was drinking too much and was openly flirting with him. Come on! Hurry up!"

"Right on, Eileen. My camera is loaded, and my motorcycle is filled with gas. Let's go!"

They dashed out to Dan's motorcycle. They saw Susie look around her, and seeing no one, she hopped into José's Karmann Ghia. José applied the pedal to the metal, and off they went in a cloud of exhaust.

Eileen and Dan hopped on his Harley and sped on after the other two young people, whom they suspected of conducting an illicit rendezvous. They stayed far enough behind Susie and José so as not to be conspicuous.

Night was falling, and the stars and moon had made an appearance. They were heading up into the mountains. The air was whizzing past Eileen's ear, and she was feeling grand. She loved riding on the motorcycle at night.

"Where are we going? I don't have a clue where we are. I only know that the ocean is below us." Eileen yelled into Dan's ear.

"Just hang on, Eileen. I don't know yet where we are going." All of a sudden, José turned into a driveway. Dan followed.

"Why, that's Harry and Carolyn Miller's mansion. There must be a party going on. Wow! Susie must be pie-eyed to party at a place like this with José. Everyone will be here! Come on, Eileen. This should be a wild party! Keep quiet, and if things get rough, go to the library. You'll be safe there, and I'll know where to find you."

As they approached the Miller's mansion, Dan said, "Wow, I love parties here. They have the best LSD."

"LSD? Why, Dan, I didn't realize that you used drugs."

"Ah, Eileen! Cut me some slack. Of course I use drugs, but I don't drink, so what's the problem? I love LSD! I know that you don't use drugs, and I don't bug you about not using them, so let me indulge myself in peace."

Just then an ear-piercing yell rang out through the night air. It came from the house.

"What was that? It sounds like someone is being killed!" screamed Eileen, who was becoming concerned about where she was and what was going on.

"It sounds like Sunshine when he's high. Come on, Eileen! I need to get to the party so that I can do some detecting. Don't forget. We're working, and if you see Susie and José in a compromising position, please find me so I can get some pictures."

"Gee, Dan, do you think that we're dressed okay? This is a pretty swanky place."

"Oh, sure. The Millers are young like us. They have lots of money from trust funds. Harry's father plays golf with my father. I know them well. You look just fine."

Dan grabbed Eileen's hand and started toward the house, dragging her behind him. There were more screams. Eileen was perturbed. Maybe she should stop seeing Dan. Why couldn't she fall for some nice respectable lawyer or doctor—a man that her mother would approve of. But they never noticed her. She always appealed to the men who lived on the edge. Maybe she should stop coloring her hair red.

Then, suddenly, there appeared before her and Dan one of the most beautiful young men she had ever seen. He was singing and playing the ukulele. He had beautiful curly black hair. He was tall and had a gorgeous build, a patrician nose, café-au-lait skin, and green eyes.

Wow! thought Eileen. *Forget lawyers! In fact, forget Dan. This man is so cool.*

Dan eyed Eileen with a thoughtful gaze.

He knows that I'm interested, thought Eileen.

"Hi, guys. Glad to see you, Dan. Is this your girlfriend? She's cute." Sunshine approached the young detective and Eileen, banging on his ukulele.

"Back off!" said Dan with a scowl. "Leave her alone or we'll have some trouble."

"Forget it, man! Just looking!" Sunshine snarled back at Dan. Sunshine threw back his head, gave another ear-splitting yell, continued playing his ukulele, and headed back for the house.

"Eileen, remember that you and I are a couple. No more flirting with Sunshine. Besides, I think he's gay."

"Why, Dan, don't you know that I only have eyes for you? Come on, let's get to work."

Eileen strolled nonchalantly toward the pool where everyone was screaming and dancing to the wild drumming of the band.

"Oh, no!" exclaimed Eileen. "It is the Local Boys. I can't stand that noisy band. I will never understand why they're so popular."

She headed for the refreshment table and the punchbowl. She wanted a glass of wine. She came to an abrupt halt when she saw Harry Miller dump several cubes of LSD into the punchbowl.

Why am I here? I want to go home. I have a trip to Detroit in the morning. I know that Dan won't want to leave, and the people here give me the creeps. Although I must admit that they are well dressed for the tropics.

Suddenly the world became quiet except for a peculiar whirring noise in her head. *What was that?* she wondered. *Maybe I should see a doctor.*

The noise stopped, and the voice of Sunshine rang out, "Zowee!" He took off his shirt and started doing the hula. Susie and José joined in.

"Hula time!" screamed all of the drunk and drugged up party-goers.

The Local Boys started wild drumming, and the party-goers started doing a wild hula along with Sunshine and Susie and José.

The birds were startled, and the cats and dogs headed for cover.

Eileen decided that Dan was on his own. She was getting out of there. *Where, oh where, is the library?* She left the pool area. No one noticed her leaving. She padded into the kitchen and started heading down the long hallway, looking for the library.

"I found it! Yay!" said Eileen as she walked into a beautiful library full of beautiful leather-bound books. The shelves filled the whole room from floor to ceiling. Eileen was in heaven. She loved to read, and the noise level was considerably muted. She found a copy of Dorothy Parker's writings, and turned to a poem that she thought expressed her somewhat newfound cynicism:

> Travel, trouble, music, art
> A kiss, a frock, a rhyme
> I never said they would feed your heart
> But still they pass my time.

Ah, that was an intelligent woman. She understood the futility of life. Eileen was starting to develop a darker side.

She rummaged around the bookshelf until she found a small journal. It was full of stories about the old-time gods and goddesses of ancient Hawaii, especially Madame Pele and her sister. She was enchanted by the classic stories and was totally engrossed in her books when all of a sudden—

CRASH! The lamp fell. The room was dark. She looked up from her books, startled. It was Sunshine. "Sunshine. Why did you leave the party?" inquired Eileen in a somewhat timorous manner.

"I was looking for you. Are you antisocial?" inquired Sunshine. He could not conceive of leaving a party to read a book. His eyes were glazed, and he started to circle Eileen, getting closer and closer. She decided that she was in real trouble, and her favorite motto for occasions like this was:

> When in danger or in doubt
> Run in circles, scream and shout!

That is what she did! "Leave me alone. Help, Dan! Help!" Her voice rang out loud and clear, like a wet cat.

"Shut up! I just wanted to share some LSD with you," snarled Sunshine who was angry because she would not cooperate with him.

"Leave me alone! Get out of here!" She was frightened, so she yelled even louder.

She heard Dan calling, "Eileen, hang on! I'm coming!" Dan burst into the room, brandishing a knife. Sunshine reached down to his boot, whipping out his own knife, which was even longer than Dan's.

Although Eileen had decided that she was going to quit seeing Dan, she was still concerned he could be hurt, although not as concerned as that she herself might get hurt. She scurried out of the dark room.

"You cretin, you!" yelled Dan, his eyes red and glazed. He poked the knife at Sunshine, who stepped back and out of the way.

"Bastard!" yelled Sunshine, slashing his knife from side to side. "I'll make you wish that you'd never been born."

Susie and José crept into the room. While everyone was watching the fight, José grabbed Dan's camera, which had fallen to the floor. He dashed out of the room.

Sunshine lost his nerve and dropped to the floor in a dead faint. Dan took off after José.

Eileen crept out of the darkened room while no one noticed.

Which way to go? I must head down. She headed for the road, with the only light coming from the moon and stars twinkling overhead.

Here goes! I must get back to my apartment so I can take my trip!

Eileen started walking down the driveway to the highway. She knew to turn left when she reached the highway. She knew that then she would have to make her way down the mountain, heading to the lights of Waikiki. It should take around three hours to walk back to her apartment. It was around midnight. She had plenty of time. Although she adored Dan, she was not going to see him anymore. She would look for a nice young lawyer. Downward she marched, heading for the beautiful Pacific and her apartment in Waikiki.

25

Bouncing O'er the Sea

"OOH, I FEEL SICK! WHY DID I EVER AGREE TO COME ON THIS TRIP? Ooh! My head hurts!" whined Mimi as the yacht bounced up and down on the turbulent ocean. The yacht lurched to the left and then to the right. The waves crashed over the sides, and the rain was pelting down, drenching anyone or anything unfortunate enough to be exposed to the elements.

Mimi wailed, "Eileen, I'm going to die. How can you be so calm? You'll die too. The crabs will eat us for dinner. Ooh! I feel like I'm going to throw up. Ooh . . . I feel so sick."

> Bouncing and bumping over the crashing waves
> Bound, we are sure, for watery graves
> We should be rather tasty dishes
> For all the hungry little fishes.

Gliding by, so gray and sleek
Was a thin-looking shark
Who had not eaten for a week.

He said, "As my father used to say,
'It has been so long since I've been fed
That my stomach thinks that my teeth are dead.'"

The humans above were all
Thrashing and screaming
"We must be dreaming,"
Said the assembled fishes and shark.
"Dinnertime should be a lark."

There are blondes, brunettes, and local boys
A fine, fine dinner
One filled with joys.

"Mimi, just shut up. If you hadn't eaten the entire roast on the flight last night, you wouldn't be so sick. Whatever possessed you to eat an entire two-pound roast beef, anyway? I thought that you wanted to lose weight," said Eileen, who was sick and tired of Mimi's constant moaning.

"Why yes, Eileen, I'm following the diet originated by Dr. Havaham. It claims that you can eat all the protein and meat that you want—something about electrolytes stimulating your metabolic enzymes. It sounds quite sensible to me. It's all the rage in Hollywood. My cousin, Leilani, brought the book back with her from Las Vegas last week."

"Oh, Mimi, how can you be so dumb? You're not supposed to eat an entire two-pound roast. Also, can't you cook the thing? I get sick just thinking about it."

The yacht was still bouncing and bobbing up and down in the turbulent ocean.

"WOOF! WOOF!

"WOOF! WOOF! WOOF!"

"Please, Wahu. Just shut up. Leave me alone. I'll return that stupid rock on the flight home. Charles promised that we would fly over the lava fields and I can toss it out the cockpit window."

"WOOF! WOOF," reverberated the dog's voice in Eileen's brain.

"Eileen, who are you talking to? Who is Wahu?"

"Don't you hear him?" enquired Eileen with a puzzled expression on her face. "He's been bugging me ever since I lifted that piece of lava rock and put it on my patio."

"Eileen, are you nuts? There's no dog here."

At that moment Mo Fat and Sun Fat poked their heads into the stateroom where Mimi was moaning and groaning. "Charles wants to know if you are okay, Mimi," asked Mo Fat as he peered into Mimi's green face.

"No, I'm not okay. Tell him that if we don't get to Lahaina soon that I am going to throw up all over his new Persian rug. Why did I ever come on this trip?" Mimi, Eileen, Charles, Denny, Mo Fat, Sun Fat, Senator Lemon and his wife Claudine, and General Fitzsimmons and his wife Maureen were on a cruise to Lahaina for a golfing weekend. Unfortunately, what should have been a pleasant cruise had turned into a mess because of the storm that had unexpectedly blown up, causing the ocean to explode in anger. Even Charles and Denny were feeling somewhat woozy.

Mo Fat and Sun Fat were heartier souls and were drinking a beer and playing mah-jongg, when Charles interrupted their game and said to Mo Fat, "Come on Mo Fat! We have work to do. There is a new shipment of Maui Wowee to be sent to the mainland, and we need to work out the shipping details. There's a ship heading for Los Angeles next week, and I thought that we could ship at least six hundred kilos on it. The crew is from Hong Kong and they have agreed to smuggle it in for us, if we can get it packed inconspicuously. I thought we could place it under layers of pineapples in crates. How does that grab you?"

"Great, Charles. I'll get my men right on it. We will make a thin layer under the pineapples so that it will not be noticed by the customs officials. Great idea, Charles."

While this conversation was going on, Sun Fat placed Clarence on his shoulder and headed over to where Mimi and Eileen were seated.

"Grab a seat, Sun Fat," said Eileen as she patted a cushion next to her. "I've missed Clarence."

"Hey, Missy. Want a drink?"

Eileen sometimes wished that Clarence had a wider range of conversation, but she was pleased that he communicated with her as much as he did.

Sun Fat sat down. Never a man to mince words, he jumped right into saying what was on his mind.

"Hey, young missies. You are keeping bad company. You should be seeing nice young lawyers or doctors and stop hanging out with gangsters."

"Sun Fat, you're a great one to talk. You always hang out with Mo Fat."

"Mo Fat is my cousin; and besides, I am a man. It is different."

At just this minute, Mimi turned even greener and made a beeline out the door. She staggered outside to the rail, threw her head over the side, and threw up.

"WOOF! WOOF!
"WOOF! WOOF! WOOF!"

"Shut up Wahu!"

"Missy Eileen, you are talking to yourself. You should see a doctor."

"No, Sun Fat. It is that damn dog again. He won't leave me alone. Don't you hear him?'

"No. He is in your mind," said Sun Fat as he looked at Eileen with concern. He was worried about her.

At that moment, the boat gave a particularly violent lurch. Mo Fat stumbled over to his cousin's side. "Hey, Sun Fat. It's only a few more miles to Maui. The storm seems to be abating."

"Thank God!" moaned Mimi, who thought that perhaps she was feeling a tad better.

The storm passed completely and suddenly as it had started. The rest of the cruise continued in peace. The senator, the general, their wives, and Charles gathered topside for afternoon tea.

Denny was feeling better and started serving tea. They were having a wonderful brew that had been supplied by Sun Fat. He always had the best of teas that came from China. With it there were scones that Charles had flown in from London, along with clotted cream and strawberry and raspberry jam. Denny had made cucumber sandwiches that he had learned at his mother's knees while he was a child in Samoa.

The sun was beaming down on the group assembled on the yacht, which was now anchored offshore of Lahaina. The yacht was bobbing gently in the now clam ocean.

That evening, everyone was exhausted from the journey from Honolulu and decided to retire early so that they would be well-rested for the golf tournament the next day.

"WOOF! WOOF!
"WOOF! WOOF! WOOF!"

Those woofs echoed through Eileen's brain and were the last sounds she heard as she went to sleep.

26

The Banana Patch

O H, LOOK, MIMI! ISN'T A WONDERFUL MORNING?" EILEEN WAS happy that Mimi was feeling better. She had been a little bit concerned about Mimi the previous day on the ride over from Honolulu.

Mimi was lounging topside, trying to get a good tan. Only Mimi was working on her tan because it had recently been discovered that Eileen was allergic to the sun. At least that is what the doctor thought.

"Allergic to the sun!?" she had exclaimed to the doctor. "That can't be. I'm living in Hawaii. I can't be allergic to the sun!"

"It doesn't matter if you think I am wrong; but you have a rash like poison ivy all over your body, you were brought to the emergency room on a stretcher after you were found passed out on the beach, and you seemed to be suffering from a severe headache. You should be thankful you didn't have sun stroke. Now follow my advice and stay out of the sun, young lady. And if you must be outside, cover your body and wear a hat."

At that moment Mimi yelled, "Sausage! Sausage! I smell sausage. Come on Eileen. It's time for breakfast. I am so happy to be doing an all-meat diet."

"Good grief, Mimi," exclaimed Eileen, at that time a vegetarian. "Why don't you eat some papaya or yogurt? It's good for your skin. And while we're on the subject of health, I would recommend that you drink more water and less champagne. Champagne dehydrates your skin and causes wrinkles, whereas water hydrates your skin and makes you look more gorgeous and younger."

> Then . . .
> Crystal clear.
> like a Waterford bell . . .
> from Hell . . .
> WOOF, WOOF!
> WOOF, WOOF, WOOF!

"Wahu! I swear I will return that rock. But it will have to wait until the flight home. I am as anxious to get rid of it as you are to see it returned to the lava fields. It has brought me trouble. I now am allergic to the sun, and I had to give up my boyfriend because he was way too wild for me. I realize that compared to most people I'm way out there, but compared to Dan I am an arch-conservative. I miss him, though. I wish I would meet someone respectable! It would make my mother and grandmother so happy."

"Eileen, you are talking to yourself. Why do you do that? Anyway, it is time for breakfast."

From below boomed a masculine voice. It was Charles. "We are coming topside to join you for breakfast. Denny will be serving breakfast."

TROMP . . .

TROMP . . .

TROMP . . . came the sound of many feet coming up the stairs from the stateroom and from the various cabins . . .

Everyone gathered up above. The sun was sparkling down on the blue, blue ocean. White caps were skittering across the surface of the water, and whales were breeching in the distance, along the horizon. All in all, a glorious day. Senator Lemon and his wife and General Fitzsimmons and his wife joined the group.

"Charles," enquired the Senator, "when does the tournament start?"

"At 10:00 A.M., right after breakfast. You will just have time to eat and then change clothes. It should be an exciting tournament. The ladies can go shopping."

"Hey, Charles, I want to go to the Banana Patch this evening instead of to the ball at the mayor's mansion," said Eileen who was bored by the thought of a ball.

"Eileen! You can't go to the Banana Patch. It's just a hippy joint out in the jungle! It is no place for a young lady."

"So what, Charles. I hear that the band, the Dreadful Heads, is smashing, and everyone dances and has a good time when they perform. I want to go. I bought a new dress just for the occasion."

"No! Absolutely not! I forbid it!"

"What do you mean, 'I forbid it'? You're not my father. I will go."

"Yeah, Charles. Let her go. She's been looking forward to hearing the Dreadful Heads for the last week," piped up Mimi in support of her friend.

"It's not safe for her to be alone. It's out in the jungle, and I believe it's my responsibility to see that she's safe," replied Charles, outnumbered and beginning to feel like a real meanie.

"Hey, Bossman," said Denny, who had been listening to the conversation. He also wanted to go to the Banana Patch. "I will go with her as a bodyguard, and I guarantee that she will be safe."

"Why, Denny, that is thoughtful of you, but I need you as my body-guard."

"Hey, Bossman, I'll call my brother Benny. He can bring the plane over this morning instead of tomorrow, and he can accompany you. How does that grab you?"

"Okay, Denny. That's acceptable. Be sure that you call Benny right away."

"Wow, Denny that is so kind of you," said Eileen who was glad that Denny would accompany her for the evening. Just because she was stubborn did not mean that she was stupid. "We should have a good time. But we need to go shopping for you in the village of Lahaina when we reach the shore. It's not a good idea to wear a silk suit to the party. We'll pick up some cool duds for you . . . a nice pair of raggedy jeans, a fringed leather vest, a tie-dyed T-shirt, some Birkenstock sandals, and a baseball cap to cover your short hair. You will look smashing. Also, I think that we should get your ear pierced, and you can wear a gold hoop."

"Sounds cool, Eileen. I'll do it." he responded with a great big grin on his café-au-lait face.

Breakfast was over and everyone was dressed for the day's outing. The dinghy came to the yacht to transport everyone to the shore.

Eileen and Denny bade the others goodbye, wished them good luck in the tournament, and headed for the village to do their shopping for the evening's party.

"Wow, look" said Eileen excitedly, "isn't that Peter Fonda's yacht?"

"It sure looks like it, Eileen. I guess he is playing golf, although that seems just a trifle mundane for him."

Just then, they saw a boutique that had a gorgeous leather vest that appeared to be Denny's size. They decided to take a look because he was so large, and they knew that finding the right clothes for him would be hard. They walked into the store and asked the salesman if they could look at the vest. The salesman got the vest out of the window, and Denny tried it on. Both he and Eileen realized that it was perfect. "Oooh," they exclaimed, "it is wonderful. Look at the beautiful beads on the fringes. We will take it. Also, we will take the jeans hanging on the mannequin. They are perfect."

They left the store, with Denny looking handsome in his new clothes. They went into the next store and found some great tan Birkenstocks for him and a T-shirt.

"Eileen, I hate to tell you this, but your outfit is not as neat as mine. You need to buy a new outfit. Let's return to the shop where we bought my leather vest and see if they have something appropriate for you."

"Okay, Denny. Let's go."

Back into the first shop they went, and hanging on the wall they saw the most beautiful soft suede dress. It had colorful flowers and hummingbirds painted on it, and it fell to the ankles. Eileen tried it on. Both she and Denny thought that it was exquisite.

"You must buy it, Eileen. It is perfect."

"I know that it is perfect, but I can't afford such an expensive dress."

"No problem, Eileen. I can use Charles' credit card. He gave it to me to use in emergencies, and this appears to me to be an emergency. And look at these red cowboy boots. They are perfect for the dress."

The salesman sensed a sale, and smiling sweetly, said, "These will look just perfect for the young lady. May I add that you both are perfectly attired for the Banana Patch."

Eileen and Denny left the store in their new apparel, and meandered through the town, admiring the shops and the scenery. They stopped at one of the local restaurants and had their afternoon repast. Denny had a double cheeseburger, large fries, a large Coke, and New York cheesecake. Eileen was stunned at the size of his lunch. She herself was having coffee with crème and a fruit salad. She also had a side order of dill pickle.

"Eileen, are you pregnant?" inquired Denny, who could not conceive of anyone eating pickles and fruit salad.

"No, Denny, why do you think that?"

"Well, you're eating fruit and pickles which seems a little strange to me. I thought that that was what pregnant ladies eat."

"Oh, no, Denny. They eat ice cream and pickles. It is totally different."

Lunch was finally over, and Denny said with a hopeful expression on his face and a slight plea in his voice, "Come on, Eileen. Since I am taking you to the Banana Patch, I am hoping that you will compromise and give up some of your shopping and go fishing with me. I hear that the mahimahi are running."

"Sure, Denny. I like to fish, but if we are using worms for bait, you'll have to bait my hook."

"Sure, come on, let's go fishing," said Denny with glee. He was as happy as a pig in a poke. They hurried to the dock, and picked out a spot from which to fish. Denny had bought a couple of fishing rods in the hardware store. They plopped down on some milk crates, and cast out their lines. Both of them were happy and peaceful. They loved to fish.

Next to them were two young punk Chinese lads—also fishing and drinking beer. They had caught several fish, which were flopping around in their bucket.

"Hey, mistah! I like your earring."

Denny beamed with pleasure that his newly pierced ear with the golden hoop had so favorably impressed such cool-looking lads. Denny was quite conservative but also vain and easily flattered.

"See, Denny, what did I tell you? Your new look is a hit. I personally think that you look resplendent, although I know that you can't wear this look around Charles. He's such a stuffy-looking dude."

"Thanks, Eileen. Maybe I will go to college and become a lawyer. Then I can dress like this more often. It certainly is more interesting than my silk suits. I've worn them for so long that I am sick of them. I am much more comfortable in this outfit."

All of a sudden, Eileen yelled, "A fish! I have a fish on my line! It must be a big one." The line danced around and around. Eileen thought that she would be pulled off the dock into the water and would ruin her beautiful new suede dress.

"Pull it in," yelled Denny. It is a big one. Pull! Pull!" All of a sudden the fish jumped out of the water.

"It's a shark. It's a little shark!" screamed Eileen.

The two Chinese lads yelled, "Pull it in lady. We'll kill it. Just don't let it bite you. Sharks have sharp teeth."

Eileen gave a mighty tug and pulled the shark onto the dock. It flopped around, gleaming like a silver flash with the sun reflecting off of its silvery hide.

Eileen screamed, "Help!"

The two Chinese kids whipped out their knives and dashed over to where Eileen was screaming and jumping up and down.

"Kill it!" she yelled. "Kill it!"

One of the young Chinese boys jumped forward and cut the shark, severing its head from its body. Blood spurted onto the wooden dock. The light in its eyes went out. This infinitely pleased Eileen. The shark's body stopped flopping and Denny said, "Good show, Eileen. Charles will be impressed that you actually caught a shark. Especially when I, the ultimate fisherman, caught nothing."

Eileen by now, had calmed down, and was surveying her catch . . .

"Woof! woof!
"Woof! woof! woof!"

"Wow! Wahu! Did you see what I caught? I have missed you. Would you like some fried shark for dinner?"

"Fried shark for dinner? Eileen, to whom are you talking? There is no one here."

"Oh, it's just Wahu. I'm the only one who can see him. He's Madame Pele's dog. He likes me, I think, and I'm beginning to like him."

"Sure, Eileen, if you say so," Denny said with a puzzled shake of his head.

"Come on! it's getting dark and we need to head off for the Banana Patch. Shall we take a cab or walk?"

Off they headed into the jungle, following the path to the Banana Patch.

27

Jungle Jim's Tattoo Parlor

PEACEFULLY STROLLING THROUGH THE NIGHT
Hoping there would not be a fight
Listening to the Dreadful Heads
Who got that way by swallowing Reds

Denny and Eileen were ready for a party
They hoped that the refreshments would be hearty
They were dressed to kill
They hoped to have their fill
Then sing and dance
No romance

BAM, BAM, BAM
Went the jungle drums
"Come to the party
From all comers come

Cocaine is available
Take a sniff
The dope is too fine
Take a whiff"

Denny and Eileen
Dressed in their sartorial best
Were more impressive than the rest,
Than all the folks gathered there
They did not have a care

The rest were most sloppy
Which Eileen thought was a sin
Not much better than the skin
They were in.

Denny, of a more mellow mind
Was not so judgmental
Was much more kind
He had a different approach
But, he too, loved the thought provoking roach.

BAM, BAM, BAM, . . .

The dulcet tones of the drums were becoming more strident as
Denny and Eileen got closer to their destination, the Banana Patch.

"Listen, Denny. It's the Dreadful Heads. Aren't they too divine?
Much better than the Local Boys."

"Gee. Eileen, they do not sound any different to me. I never could
understand why the Local Boys upset you so much."

"I guess I don't like their clothes."

"Eileen, you have got to stop judging people by the way they dress."

"Oh no, Denny. I heard my minister once say, 'If you do not judge
someone by their appearance you are shallow.'"

"I think you have that backwards. Beauty is supposed to be more than just skin deep."

"I'm sure that there is some validity to that position, but I personally agree with my minister. He had a deep philosophical type of mind, and I find his theory thought-provoking.

"Please explain."

"Well, Denny, it's this way: A normal person wants to impress his constituents, family, and friends. That is normal, I am sure that you will agree. Then it stands to reason that one would want to appear at one's best, so that others will be attracted to one. Others would like you better or at least would be impressed. Whereas, if you appear like a slob, people will think that you are dumb and ugly. I know that we are taught not to judge people by their exteriors, but I personally think that when people look like slobs, they are slobs."

"Gosh, Eileen, now that you put it like that, it makes sense."

"And, Denny, just think . . . you and your brothers have always dressed to kill—literally and figuratively."

At that moment they heard a voice moaning over a microphone, shaking the trees through which the two friends were walking. It made the two want to join the party. "There it is" said Eileen in an excited voice. Come on, let's hurry."

The Banana Patch loomed up in front of them. It was a yellow roadhouse with green-shuttered windows. Palm trees surrounded it, and in a little flower garden in the front yard was a little pond filled with carp. The garden was filled with bird-of-paradise and hibiscus. The colors sparkled as the strobe lights from the interior of the building revolved, making everyone nervous and jittery.

"Stop gaping at the fish. Let's go in and get a table."

"Sure, Denny. Let's go."

They walked through the front door.

The music stopped. Everyone stared at them, especially at Denny. He was so tall and big that he loomed over everyone, especially Eileen.

"Hey, guys, why did you stop singing and dancing?"

"Hey, man! Sorry! You're so big that we thought you were the fuzz or a bodyguard. We know that Charles Haley's on the island, and we know that he has some Samoan bodyguards.

"That's me. But don't worry guys. Party on! We're just here to party."

BAM, BAM, BAM . . .

Once again the drums reverberated throughout the jungle.

Denny and Eileen stopped at one of the booths on the side of the room. It had a pink and green tablecloth and yellow napkins. The music stopped as the musicians were taking a break.

"You know, Eileen, my ears hurt. I can't stand the pain. Don't your ears hurt too?"

"Yes, my ears hurt, too. But it's all for the sake of beauty and fashion."

Denny thought this over. While everyone in the room wandered out onto the porch, Denny and Eileen were pondering the afternoon's ear piercing event.

Lost in thought they silently remembered the events of the afternoon.

Back in time . . .
Back in time . . .
Back in time . . .
They went . . .

"Hey, mister salesman, the lady here and I want to get our ears pierced, and we don't know where to go on this island. With these splendid duds, we think that the final touch would be golden hoop earrings."

"I guess you need to go to Jungle Jim's Tattoo Parlor. It's about a mile into the jungle. Just follow the path. Jungle Jim will probably pierce your ears himself."

"Okay, dude, that sounds great. Thanks for your help.

"Come on, Eileen. We need to get on our way."

The two took off on the path into the forest.

Finally they saw it: Jungle Jim's Tattoo Parlor. It was a little shack painted bright pink with green shutters. It had a rickety porch with a thatched roof. There was a big sign. It said,

WELCOME TO JUNGLE JIM'S
WE AIM TO PLEASE

"Come on Eileen. We have to do this."

Eileen was a little reluctant to go in because she did not approve of tattoos, but she knew that if she chickened out, Denny probably would never respect her again.

They walked up onto the porch, stepping over two sleeping cats—the one a handsome Siamese and the other an orange tabby cat. The cats woke up, looked at the two strangers, got up, arched their backs, and gave a welcoming "MEOW."

"Hi," said Denny, who loved cats and thought these two were especially handsome. He also believed that cats understood English.

At that moment Wahu said, "WOOF, WOOF WOOF, WOOF, WOOF! Get away from those cats, Eileen, I want to chase them."

The cats sensed Wahu's presence, and hissed at Eileen. Their hair stood on end, and they squalled loudly.

Eileen said, "Shut up, Wahu! Denny likes those cats, and I want you to leave them alone."

Denny said, "Eileen, stop talking to yourself. Let's go on in."

They opened the door, and entered another world. The smell of incense started Eileen sneezing, as she was allergic to fragrances. There was an overhead fan, gently swirling the air around overhead. There were potted plants everywhere, and the music of Ravi Shankar sounded softly throughout the room.

"Hi, folks. How can I help you?" came a little, gravelly voice from the far side of the room.

Denny and Eileen looked to the direction from which the voice came. There, behind an old rolltop desk was a little old Chinese lady. She was around sixty years old, with her hair dyed black and pulled back into a ponytail. Her voice was gravelly from years of smoking unfiltered Camels.

"Hi, Miss. How are you? We want to get our ears pierced and we were told that you would perform this operation," said Denny.

"Our specialty is tattoos, but for such fine-looking people like you we will do the piercing. Wait while I get my husband, who will help you." With that the little old lady disappeared into the back room.

Denny and Eileen gingerly sat down to wait, both of them considering the wisdom of what they were about to do. What if it hurt? And they certainly did not want blood to drip onto their new finery.

"Hi, there. Hear you want your ears pierced. I am just the man to do the job. I am Jungle Jim."

Eileen and Denny considered him carefully. He was a wizened old Chinese man. He had a long stringy ponytail that was dyed blonde. He was wearing black leather lederhosen and a gray leather vest with no sleeves or T-shirt under it—just bare arms with tattoos from wrist to shoulders.

Denny was impressed. He had decided to come back for a tattoo the following weekend on his days off from work.

Eileen was just staring. She was speechless. She thought that she was used to old eccentric Chinese men from knowing Sun Fat and Mo Fat, but she thought Jungle Jim was simply amazing. She was impressed by the golden earrings in his left ear.

"Let me show you my earrings." He said.

"Oh, don't bother. We know that we want golden hoops like you're wearing."

"Sure. If you say so. I have some that just came from Thailand. They are exquisite, if I do say so myself. Connie, my wife whom you have already met, picked them out. She has a real eye for quality."

Denny was having a great time while Eileen fidgeted, although she was beginning to like Jungle Jim and Connie.

"Okay, guys, stop talking and let's get to the piercing," Eileen said with a light tremor in her voice. "Who's first Denny, you or me?"

"Me," said Denny.

"Okay, go to it, Jungle Jim."

Connie came into the room holding some earrings, a large needle, and some cork. The large needle was long but slender, so as not to make a large hole, which Jim thought unsightly. He was an artist. Jungle Jim stepped forward as stealthily as a cat, his tattoos wobbling around, as he was old and had UADD (underarm dingle dangle).

"Denny, hold still. I am ready." He jabbed the needle through Denny's ear. Denny grimaced and looked pale. Eileen grimaced and looked pale. They both looked a little wobbly. Connie told her to sit down and placed a chair behind her.

While Eileen was on the verge of fainting, Jungle Jim crept up on Denny and jabbed the needle through the other ear. Denny howled in terror.

Eileen started crying. Jungle Jim said, with no compassion in his voice, "Young lady, you are next. Here goes." And Jungle Jim quickly jabbed holes in both ears. It happened so fast that she did not have time to react.

Then came the drops of blood—SPLISH, SPLASH . . . onto the towels that had been draped around their shoulders.

Denny and Eileen both fell off their chairs in a dead faint onto the floor. Jungle Jim and Connie stood there, wondering why people reacted so violently to a little pain and blood.

"Ooh, ooh, ooh," murmured Eileen and Denny as they simultaneously regained consciousness.

"Okay, guys, here are your earrings." Jungle Jim daintily adjusted the four golden hoops into the four bleeding ears. He fastidiously wiped the blood aside, stepped back, and admired his handwork. It was good!

Denny by now had recovered sufficiently that he was able to admire his reflection in the hand mirror that Connie was holding in front of his face.

Eileen was now conscious and anxious to see how her new earrings looked. She grabbed the mirror from Denny and said, "We look so cool!"

Jungle Jim and Connie told them that they looked ultimately cool, and stretched out their hands for their money.

Eileen and Denny each handed them $20 for the piercing, and $100 for the golden earrings.

"Now be sure that you wipe the holes each day with alcohol, and be sure that you move the hoops to aid in your recovery. And, Denny, if you want a tattoo, be sure to come back. I am a genius," said Jungle Jim.

> Goodbye . . .
> Goodbye . . .
> Goodbye. . . .

Denny and Eileen were back in the present at the Banana Patch, eating nachos and salsa.

> *Ow, Ow, Ow,*
> *The diligent cow*
> *Gives milk for cheese*
> *If you please.*

"A ballad, Eileen, the Dreadful Heads are singing a ballad," said Denny with a big grin. "I just love that song. It is so full of meaning."

"Denny, you must be kidding. That song is not meaningful. It's just plain stupid."

> *The diligent mule*
> *Who is no fool*
> *Makes a pass*
> *Over the grass*

The Dreadful Heads were now in full swing. They were singing their song, which everyone thought was so meaningful, except for Eileen. Eileen did not find much of anything meaningful anymore. Everything seemed so stupid, but she did like to dance. So she grabbed Denny's arm, trying to pull him onto the dance floor.

"Eileen, don't be so mean. You know that I can't dance. I am *so* clumsy. Go dance with someone else."

Just then, a particularly handsome blonde hippy materialized in front of the two squabbling friends. "C'mon, lady. Let's dance."

Denny immediately went into protective mode. His job was to guard and protect Eileen. The blond dude was drunk, and who knows what else.

"Sorry, buster. The lady is with me," said Denny with a gigantic frown on his handsome face. He was starting to shift weight from one foot to the other, and his hands were clenching up into big fists.

Eileen noticed this and knew that there would be a fight. She knew that Denny was protective of her. In fact, in order to be her bodyguard, he had passed on flirting with the young Chinese-Hawaiian babe who had caught his eye when they entered the Banana Patch. She was tall and slinky, with two long black braids hanging down her back. They were decorated with feathers. She was quite smashing and had been winking furiously at Denny.

But he had renounced true love for the moment because he knew that Eileen did not have good sense when it came to good-looking men, and he knew that Charles would have his hide if anything happened to her. Besides, he worried about her.

The blond hippy stepped into Denny's space, glared at him, saying, "What's it to you, big guy? I want to dance with her. Chill." He said this in an increasingly loud voice that caused Denny to see red.

By now the music had stopped, and the crowd had stepped back, forming a circle, and taking bets. They knew that a fight was coming, and they were excited.

A fight
Tonight
What a glorious sight

"Good grief, another fight, with me at the center. Why can't men just send me roses instead?" Eileen sighed deeply as she said this, starting to back toward the door. She knew the drill.

Denny's eyes had glazed over and were turning red. The hippy did not have enough control of his faculties to realize that he was not in a good position. He did not have the sense to care.

So he lunged! At Denny!

The crowd stepped back, so as not to get blood on their duds. Denny kicked him in the balls.

The blond hippy screamed in pain, doubled over, and fell to the floor, clutching his private parts.

"Dumb shit. Don't ever bother me again. Now get out of here." The crowd gave a collective gasp and headed for the door. Denny was left standing alone.

"Eileen!" he yelled. "Come back here. It's time for us to leave."

Eileen had been hiding behind a large potted palm on the porch. When she saw that the fight was over, she crept back to where Denny was standing, looking as though he was in pain.

"Are you hurt, Denny? I did not see you get hit."

"Shit, Eileen! I think I broke my toe when I kicked that punk. This has certainly been a painful day. Let's call it quits and head back for the yacht."

"Sure thing, Denny. I feel a little tired myself."

The two joined hands and started the trek back to the yacht at Lahaina. All four of their ears were throbbing, and Denny was limping because of his broken toe.

"It's been a great day, Eileen."

"It certainly has been a great day, Denny."

28

Kabuki's Bold From Days of Old

THE PLANE WAS BOUNCING OVER THE BLUE PACIFIC. THERE were no icebergs in sight. Instead, the water was a beautiful shade of turquoise. The clouds were gathering overhead, and under the plane they were white.

"Oh, Denny! Aren't they great? The clouds always look like giant cotton balls to me. They look so soft. I would love to bounce up and down on them. I'd probably fall through, however," said Eileen with a deep sigh.

"Ah, Eileen! I wish you wouldn't talk like that. I really think that you are depressed, although I don't know why that should be. You are pretty and smart, and you are always dressed so nicely. How you can be depressed is beyond me. Maybe if you would only eat something. You are getting too thin," said Denny who had never had a depressed moment in his entire life.

"But, Denny, you know that I'll be fired if I get heavier. I love my job and don't want to be fired. Maybe some day it will be illegal to fire someone based on how much they weigh."

They both smelled sausage. The beautiful smell wafted through the cabin. It was early morning, and the stewardesses were serving breakfast. The sausage was being served in a beautiful copper serving pan, along with beef medallions and bacon.

"Hey, look at those sausages, Eileen. Don't they look pretty? Boy, do I like first class. It beats sitting in coach. You know, the only reason that I am sitting here is because Charles is worried about you and wants me to keep an eye on you while I go to school on the mainland. He agreed with me that I should study law, become a lawyer, and then come back to Hawaii to work for him. I think that I will go to Berkeley and then go to Harvard Law School. That should be fun."

By now, the stewardesses were serving coffee. Both Denny and Eileen reached for the crème and sugar. They did not like black coffee. Eileen was looking around at the passengers in first class, when she noticed that the famous movie star, Zack Lore, was sitting across the aisle. "Look, Denny, isn't that Zack Lore? That must be his wife. She is even skinnier than me, if that's possible."

"Wow, Eileen! I should go ask him if he would like for Henny or Benny or Kenny or Lenny to work for him as a bodyguard. They would love that kind of work—going to Hollywood and meeting movie stars. That would be great."

Eileen lit a cigarette, and thoughtfully blew smoke rings into the cabin. This always impressed Denny. Although he hated smoking, he could appreciate the talent it took to blow smoke rings. He also was tired of lecturing Eileen. At least she was not doing something illegal like he was doing.

Then, the PA rang out through the cabin.

"Ladies and gentlemen, we are beginning our feature presentation. The movie this morning is *Butch Cassidy and the Sundance Kid*. We hope that you will enjoy it. The sound can be found on channel one."

Eileen had seen this movie three times, but she loved it. And when she loved something or someone, she loved them forever—except for men, of course. The only men she truly loved were Denny and Hairy-Cary.

"Denny, I can't wait to introduce you to Hairy-Cary. He is my best friend. He lives in Sausalito on a houseboat. He's picking me up after this flight, and I want him to meet you. He knows everybody and can help you to get into Berkeley.

> Then—
> Good grief—
> Sundance jumped!
> Into the H$_2$O
> Way below
> It looked like fun
> It ruined his gun.

Denny and Eileen had their attention fully concentrated on the silver screen. It was a great movie, and this was the best scene—one that they would never forget.

Denny and Eileen were attired in the clothes that they had bought when they went to the Banana Patch. Both of them were going to live in San Francisco, the home of the fruits and nuts. They were excited.

"Hairy has found me a great apartment in the Marina. He said that I can afford it. He said it has a huge closet for my clothes, paintings, and books. I am so excited.

I love Hairy. He has a new wife. Her name is Estelle. He met her at a seminar on the care and maintenance of Harley-Davidson motorcycles. She had long blonde hair that was pulled back and braided into long, blonde pigtails. She was wearing a red, white, and blue bandana around her forehead. She was wearing her new black leather jacket. It had silver studs. It was straight from the Yves Saint Laurent showroom in Paris.

When she walked into the boutiques, all of the snooty Parisian shopgirls positively drooled. She's cool. You'll like her."

Denny was not paying much attention to Eileen because his attention was on the movie and the sausages. He was thrilled to his core. He had never been to the mainland. He was thinking he might go to Chicago—the old-timey hangout of Al Capone and his cohorts. "Those were the days," he started reminiscing.

His mother had said to him as he was leaving Samoa, "Dear, I have always told you that the world is your oyster. Like your father before you, you are good-looking, smart, strong, and have no scruples. Enjoy yourself! Remember to send your old ma some of that moolah that you pick up on your travels. I will need some assistance, as I have decided to get my PhD in anthropology and hope to be able to get a job at the Bishop Museum in Honolulu."

"Right on, Ma! That is so cool." As he said this, he walked out the door and headed for the port and the next ship to Honolulu. He had decided that he would have his family join him later. They loved the United States, and they all loved adventure. This would be a lark . . .

> Hark, Hark
> Went the Lark
> It is so hard to find
> A place to park.
>
> During the winter
> It is not so bad
> Everyone is sitting in front
> of the TV set
> Feeling sad
>
> It is cold and the sky is black
> With coughs and sniffles
> They do hack.

But now it is spring
The sun returns
Giving out its warmth
The birds go north
And spread the alarm
That flowers are
    about to bloom
Throughout the sky
    The larks do zoom.

Turtles go truckin' across the street
Meandering to an upbeat beat
Grass is back—how nice
So are lice—
    and fleas and ticks
Returning with all of their
    myriad tricks.

Allergies are on the rise
One wakes up one morning
    and has one
Much to one's surprise

Hark! Hark!
    went the Lark.
The trees are full
    of birds sitting there.
The limbs are still bare.

But, lo and behold
A shout
Coming from the root
The bark is nice and sappy
The bugs are quite happy.

So Denny left Samoa, and here he was, sitting with Eileen in the lovely 747. It was only two years old at the time. He removed his earphones because the movie was over, and he heard the sound of a ukulele coming from the upstairs lounge.

"C'mon Eileen, let's go upstairs."

"No can do. I'm thinking." said Eileen, with a frown.

"Not again. I really wish you would stop thinking. It puts you in a bad mood."

"But Denny, not only do you think, but you read the papers and watch the evening news, which always makes you grumpy. So leave me alone."

Now Denny had forgotten about the ukulele and was engrossed in conversation with Eileen. The two of them always found things to talk about.

"Eileen, do you think that Hairy-Cary will like me?" asked Denny.

"Sure Denny. He'll like you. I told him I was bringing you with me. Just remember, he's sensitive because he has arthritis in his hands and back and can no longer drive his cycle. He's not yet been able to imagine riding in the back or in a sidecar, but I think Estelle will be able to convince him to ride on the back with her.

At this moment, Mimi appeared beside the two pals. She wanted Eileen to join the stewardesses in the back of the plane. They were engrossed in a conversation about the unfairness of the rule that said that when one got married one had to quit working.

Eileen and Mimi walked into the galley.

"Hi gals. How is everyone?" said Eileen to the assembled stewardesses.

"Oh hi, Eileen. Good to see you," said Martha, the local activist. "We were just discussing that we should write to our congressmen about changing the laws that discriminate against us for being married. Men can do both, and we should have the same rights."

Martha had recently gotten married and was indignant that she had to keep her marriage a secret. Her doting father, a prominent lawyer, was going to help the girls. She was filled with the zeal of one who has a worthy cause and happy about the support of her father.

"He wants me to have an income of my own," said Martha.

Eileen started crying when Martha told her this. "Why, Martha, my father felt the same way. He thought that any healthy woman should be at least that responsible."

Mimi piped up, "Girls, you should trust that your husband can take care of you."

"Why, Mimi, you're nuts. Now that divorce is acceptable, you'll be deserted when you get older. You can see it in your own life. Your father just left your mother, and she has no skills and has never worked," said Martha with a disgusted glance at Mimi.

"Martha, what a nasty thing to say," wailed Mimi, who could not think of an adequate reply. She shut up.

One of the other stewardesses said, "Marriage should not be the end of life. I am so sick of this old-fashioned concept of women being all sweetness and light—not to mention helpless. It seems strange that our fathers encourage us to be educated and able to work, but our society wants us to stay home and be helpless. So, put that in your pipe and smoke it, Mimi."

Mimi, realizing that she was outgunned, sat down and sulked. In her deepest heart, however, she knew that she did not want to stay home and be bored. Nor did her friends.

Martha was ranting, "Girls, maybe we should go to Washington and march. Everyone else does."

At that moment Denny walked into the galley. He was bored, and he loved the ladies.

"Hi Denny." said Martha with a grin. "Got any good jokes?" Martha loved jokes, as did any respectable stewardess.

Denny had already told all of his good jokes to Eileen and Mimi and was eager for a new audience.

Denny looked at Martha with admiration. He loved a woman with a good sense of humor, and he especially loved a woman who was a good organizer. "It is a shame you are married."

Eileen was engaged in preparing a fresh pot of coffee. The young people in the galley had worked up a thirst.

Martha looked at Eileen with some concern. "Why, she's becoming so withdrawn when she thinks that no one is looking. I hope that Denny can draw her out." Martha was truly worried. "It's a shame that she grew up in the South where women are considered to be idiots and should devote their lives to taking care of men. I hope she realizes soon that she is not the type to take care of men. Once I realized that about myself, I became happier and had more energy."

The plane started down. Everyone was excited and ran to the windows to look out to see if they could find the Golden Gate Bridge.

We are going down
　　down
　　　　down
Do not frown
　　do not frown
　　　　please do not frown

It is highly unlikely
　　that we will crash and drown
It is highly unlikely
　　that we will crash and drown

Eileen was so excited
　　she bounced up and down
　　　　on the seat
Landing was always
　　such
　　　　a treat

She preferred for landings
        to be neat

A mess, I confess
        caused her to blanche
        And caused her complexion
                to be white
        Like back on the ranch
                in Hawaii
                at night

    Kabukis
    Spookies
        All have a face with
        lots of powder
        Nothing can make them
                speak louder.

They have disappeared
        I have been told
These painted ladies
        from days of old
They almost never dressed
        for the cold
Although, if truth be told
They were bold.

Unlike your basic "modem miss"
Who has been brainwashed
        to K-I-S-S*

I have been told
        by a lady with
        a complicated mind

---

* Keep it simple, stupid.

That
that**
was
a
sign
That God had been kind.

** A complicated mind.

29

Lufti from Mufti

IT WAS A FOGGY SUMMER EVENING AT CHICAGO'S O'HARE INTER-national Airport. The planes were parked in the gray soup, looking like sharks' fins all lined up waiting for the fog to lift so that they would have better visibility for taxi and takeoff.

Eileen was fidgeting in her seat. She wanted to get back to San Francisco. *Why in the world did I come here?* she wondered. *I cannot remember why I am here.* She thought some more, concentrating all her faculties on solving this immediate problem. *Oh, yes, I remember. I came here to have lunch and go shopping with Maudie. She looks tired. I guess her marriage is on the rocks. That's a shame, because she just adores Chapman.*

As she was thinking this, Maudie appeared with two cups of coffee. She was waiting with her friend for the flight to leave.

"Wow, Eileen. I am so pleased with my new purchases. The clothes you helped me pick out will be perfect for my new part-time job teaching two classes at the university. I need to look the part. Thanks for helping me put together my new look." Maudie was thrilled with her new clothes. She had been worrying a lot about the future of her marriage, and the new clothes had lifted her spirits.

"You're welcome, Maudie. I must say that you look like a professor. That tweed jacket with the suede patch on the elbow makes the perfect finishing touch to your outfit. It's a shame that you're not a man, because then you could smoke a pipe, which always looks so intellectual."

"Gosh, Eileen! I forgot to pay attention to what you were telling me about Lee. Is he the new man in your life?" inquired Maudie, who was trying to get the latest scoop about her friend.

"He seems to be. Somehow he ended up living with me, and I'm not quite sure how that happened. I seem to have a gap in my memory," said Eileen with a frown.

"Well, Eileen, just think back and tell me what you remember." said Maudie in her most sympathetic voice.

"Okay, here goes . . .

Back . . .

Back . . .

Back . . .

"Two months ago, I was cat-sitting for Ingrid while she and her husband went back to Munich to visit with her grandparents. She hated to leave Siam and Twitchy alone for so long, so I agreed to stay with them.

"One beautiful Sunday morning, I was having coffee and talking to the two cats when I realized that the cats and the houseplants were taking up all of the air, and I wasn't able to breathe—there was no air left for me. I panicked. I rushed out of the penthouse after first grabbing my sketchbook and some pens. I rushed down to the marina green and plopped down on the grass and started sketching one of the lovely sailboats.

"It was a glorious morning—warm and sunny with fleecy white clouds drifting across the sky with just a sprinkling of jetstreams streaking across the sky. They were caused by the airplanes going to Hawaii and the East. There were even some going to Asia.

"My mind had wandered as my hand quickly sketched a particularly visually satisfying sailboat—the Santa Maria—from Hong Kong. It was sleek and looked so peaceful bobbing up and down in the water.

"All of a sudden, a beautiful voice said, 'Hello, there!' I looked up, and my heart went flip-flop.

"The next thing I remember is that he had moved in, and I had acquired a new male roommate. His name was Lee. He was simply too gorgeous for words. He even pressed creases into his jeans. He wore a neat pair of tan Frye boots." Eileen paused in her recital of that momentous day's events.

Then she continued, "My next door neighbor has a beautiful cat named Cleo. Cleo is a stupefyingly intelligent cat. She is orange with white paws and a white chest. She adores Lee. She likes me okay, but she's devoted to Lee. He could care less. . . ."

Then, over the PA system came a voice announcing the departure of her flight. Eileen's mind returned to the boarding area and Maudie.

"Flight 229 is going to San Francisco. All aboard. We will be closing the doors in five minutes. All aboard."

A loudspeaker was shouting these words throughout the terminal. Maudie and Eileen snapped out of their reverie and were smack dab back in the concourse of the airport.

"What a tale, Eileen. I need to hear the rest of it. Maybe you can come back on your next days off, and tell me the rest of the story. I think you need to talk, and I love to listen. I think that we both need help at this troubled time of our life."

"I think you're right, Maudie, but first I must figure out how to get rid of Lee. I adore him, but he is way too dangerous a man for me to tangle with."

"Dangerous, Eileen? You mean really dangerous?"

"Yes, Maudie, but I can't talk anymore. I need to get on the plane. See you later. You look great, just like a professor. Toodles!" Eileen grabbed her duffel bag, ticket, and bottle of water and headed for the jetway. She waved gaily to Maudie before she disappeared.

"Oh, why do we have to endure such terrible trials?" muttered Maudie to herself as the plane pulled away form the gate. She headed out of the terminal to get her new car. She was making lots of money in her job as a geologist and as a professor, so she had splurged and bought herself a new red Porsche. Chapman was horrified. His kids needed cars for school, and he thought that it was terrible that Maudie would put her wants before his children's needs.

"Gosh, Eileen and I have abysmal taste in men. She goes for good looks and excitement, and I go for good looks and brains. Are we ever stupid? Oh well."

At this moment, Eileen was seated comfortably in the first class section of the airplane. The plane had just taken off, and was climbing up, up, up through the clouds, climbing to 37,000 feet for the ride to the West Coast.

"Ah! The sun is setting!" exclaimed Eileen as they rose above the cloud layer.

"WOOF! WOOF!
"WOOF! WOOF! WOOF!"

"Hi,Wahu! Isn't it lovely to be above the clouds?"

"Is there something I can get for you?" enquired the stewardess who happened to be passing through the aisle as Eileen was talking to Wahu.

"No thank you. Why do you ask?"

"You were talking as I passed your seat, and I assumed you wanted something."

"I was talking to Wahu," said Eileen.

"Wahu! Who is Wahu?"

"Oh, Wahu is Madame Pele's dog."

"Dog! What do you mean—a dog? Have you hidden a dog in your bag? That's not allowed," exclaimed the stewardess with a horrified expression on her face.

"I don't have a dog. Madame Pele's dog is in my mind. He likes to talk with me."

"Sure, lady, if you say so!" With that, the stewardess shook her head and muttered, "She's nuts! You can never tell by looking at someone that they are crazy. She looks so smart in her black cigarette pants, blue boiled wool jacket, white silk shell, and black platform shoes. But she must be crazy."

By this time Eileen had fainted, but everyone thought she was asleep, if they noticed or thought about her at all.

> black, black
> the world is black
> I feel chills
>   up and down my back
> I think my brains
>   are in a sack.

> "Hiss, hiss
> Piss, piss went the cat
> I wish Eileen was not so fat."

"Cleo, Cleo! Where are you, Cleo?" yelled Eileen as she jerked up and down. All of a sudden she felt herself flopping back and forth. She snapped out of her faint. The stewardess was shaking her.

"Where am I?" she moaned. "Where am I?" she groaned.

"You are on the flight to San Francisco. You must have been having a bad dream. You were asleep."

"Thank you for waking me."

Just then, a weird voice appeared in her brains.

WHRR! WHRR!
GRRR! GRRR!
You may, if you please
     call me "sir"

I am from a planet
far, far away
I am in your brains
     to stay.
I know that you cannot
     get away.

We like R&R—
     to get off of our craft
We get tired of pacing
     fore and aft.
The green hills of Earth
     they call
In our transporter
     down we fall
Until we land
     upon our feet
Transporting cannot
     be beat.

"Oh, my goodness!" exclaimed Eileen. "This voice is real also. It's talking in English, though!" Eileen was used to the cats and dogs and weird phone noises, but a voice speaking in English spooked her.

"I had better get to the 'blue room' so that I can talk to him."

Eileen had by now realized that talking out loud caused people to raise their eyebrows. *They think that I'm crazy!* This thought flashed through her mind as she was wending her way to the blue room.

She finally got inside, locked the door, sat down on the toilet seat, and started to communicate.

"Who are you?" she asked the alien.

"I am Lufti from the planet of Mufti."

"Nice to meet you. How can I help you?"

Lufti replied,

> "We need to cut your brains into bits.
> And reassemble them until they fits
> It takes a long, long time to do
> It takes hours before we are through."

Eileen whipped out a cigarette. This was her habit when confronted with a problem. She took a puff, and blew the smoke into the air. It crept under the door, into the cabin....

THEN ...

> up, up, up
> it drifted
>   up
>   surrounding
>   a passenger's coffee cup.

> BANG, BANG
>   on the door
>   "Why are they doing that
>   for?"
> BANG, BANG,
>   some more
>   on the door.
>   "You know you cannot smoke in there,
>   It could cause a fire, or pollute the air."
>   "Okay, okay,
>   I will put it out!

You do not need to scream and shout!
Now leave me alone."

She returned her attention to Lufti.
Now, Lufti, tell me more.
About what you have in store
for little old me
or am I two or even three?
I never know whether
I am "I" or whether I am "she"
At this, Lufti went
WHRR!
I never know whether
I am "her" or whether I am "me"
At this Lufti went
Grrr!

He said

Your brain is slightly
disarranged
It is moderately
strange
It is moderately
deranged.
You have lost the ability
to think coherently
I do not say this
Disparangingly
I think you need
a pill, or two, or three
I think you need them
I really do.
At the very least
you need two.

"Lufti, I certainly hope you can help me. I seem to be disassembling, and no one seems to know how to help me stop it."

"Eileen, we will try. Just hang in there, kid."

With that, Lufti disappeared in a POOF of smoke.

Eileen stood up, deep in thought. She looked at herself in the mirror.

I do look terrible, she thought. I do look pretty bad. I'm so glad I met Lufti from Mufti. With that thought, Eileen opened the door and walked out into the cabin.

The plane was dark, and everyone appeared to be asleep. She went back to her seat, sat down, and went to sleep like everyone else.

30

Deep in February

IT WAS A DREARY, COLD NIGHT IN THE DEPTHS OF FEBRUARY IN New York City, near Fifth Avenue. The sky was darkening. Was a storm on the way?

Inside a small café sat two young ladies—one a blonde and one a redhead—drinking something from colorful yellow, white, and blue coffee mugs.

It was Maudie and Eileen, deep in thought, enjoying their delicious mugs of cappuccino—beautiful strong espresso, foamy white milk, and just a hint of sugar. They were at Luigi's Bar and Grill, Maudie's favorite eating establishment in New York City. Their faces were happy and relaxed. The fireplace blazing away in the corner of the room was warming them to their bone marrow. Music from *La Boheme* was circulating softly throughout the café. "Oh, poor Mimi!" thought both of them. They identified with the sorrow experienced by Mimi.

"Gee, Eileen! We should be eternally grateful to the Italians. Cappuccino is better than scotch," said Maudie with a deep contented sigh.

"Maudie, I can't believe you said that. As long as I've known you, your drink of choice has been scotch. Why have you changed your mind?" asked Eileen of her friend.

"I'm not sure what the reason is. As I've gotten older, my values have changed. Partly because Chapman is a recovering alcoholic, and I don't drink around him. Also, I noticed that the veins in my cheeks and nose were getting awfully red. You know how vain we are, and I figured that beauty was more important than booze."

"I'll say!" responded Eileen. "I spend billions of dollars on creams and lotions for my skin. What good does all that do if one drinks too much? After getting rid of a particularly bad case of acute cystic acne, I am only too conscious of how upsetting it is to have bad skin."

"Why, Eileen," said Maudie to her best friend, "I didn't realize just how much trouble you've been having." Maudie looked at her friend with a critical eye. Maudie was developing a critical and analytical streak, probably related to the streaks in the rocks she loved so much.

> Strong and silent—
> Content
>   To be a rock
>   Was its creed
> "Chemicals are all
>   I need"
> Sighed the rock
> It gave Maudie
>   Quite a shock.
> Was she developing
>   A case
>   Of hearing sounds
>   That were not there?
> I declare

Noise abounds
It resounds
Everywhere
I declare
I hear it in my ears
Just like Eileen says
I hope I don't hear it
When I am dead.

"Yes," Maudie declared, "I can see that you're also getting emaciated. You do know that food is good for you, don't you? At least, thank God, since I'm a geologist, people don't nag me if I gain a few pounds."

At that moment, the waiter approached their table pushing a cart loaded with pastries, cakes, and pies. There was even a crème brulée. "Ah, *signorinas*," said the handsome waiter, Georgio, with the beautiful curly black hair to his shoulders and the shiny, flashing black eyes. "Would you love to have a wonderful dessert? Chef Antonio just took these out of the oven. Fresh! Fresh! Fresh! Chef Antonio is from Sicily and studied the culinary arts in both Paris and Rome. He surpasses all of his contemporaries, and we are delighted to have him prepare the food for us here at Luigi's Bar and Grill."

"They look wonderful," said Maudie with a big grin. "Come on, Eileen, let's have a great dessert. Just one can't hurt you."

"I'm so sorry, Maudie. They look wonderful, but I don't have any appetite. I think I will pass, but you go right ahead."

"Don't mind if I do. Georgio, I think I'll have the beautiful chocolate mousse, with another cup of cappuccino. Come on Eileen, at least have another cup of cappuccino with me."

"No thanks. But Georgio, I would like a glass of ice water with a slice of lemon."

"Coming right up, ladies." said Georgio as he headed to the next table with his cart of desserts.

Maudie ceased her conversation and started to devour her chocolate mousse. After a few bites, she looked up and said, "Eileen, tell me what you meant the last time we were together about Lee being danger-ous. Did you mean that he is mean and physically abusive? What exactly is the problem with him?" Maudie was concerned about her friend's mental and physical health. Although she herself was devastated by the turn her marriage was taking, she realized that her problem would have to be put on the back burner for the moment. She had invited Eileen to spend the weekend with her in New York. She knew that Eileen was ret-icent about discussing her problems, but she might talk to Maudie if she could just relax and have a good time.

They had been shopping, which always managed to cheer Eileen, and Maudie needed some new clothes, too.

"Saks is such a great store. Don't you love the yellow leather evening purse I bought? I particularly love the white stars on the shoul-der strap," said Eileen, who was trying to evade answering Maudie's question. "I really love your Harris tweed culottes. They are quite hand-some and will be nice when it's freezing cold. We must get together to shop more often. Eileen admired her new evening purse, which she had gotten out of the shopping bag. She had also replaced her worn copy of *The Master and Margarita*. She loved this book. It appealed to every warped cell of her currently warped mind.

Eileen whipped out a cigarette and ceremoniously lit it. She then took a deep drag. PUFF! PUFF! She blew out a gigantic smoke ring. Then she blew a stream of smoke through the smoke ring. This was a lovely trick that she had learned from her father. She missed him.

"Gee, lady, that's great!" said the two young men sitting at the next table.

"Thanks, guys. Would you like me do it again?"

"Sure, lady."

Maudie broke in on this interesting interlude and said, "Eileen, you're not answering my question."

Oh dear, thought Eileen, *she is being persistent. Do I answer or not?*

I guess I will tell her about Lee. Maudie will understand.

"Well, Maudie, it's like this. When I first saw Lee on the marina green, it was love at first sight for me," said Eileen.

"I cannot believe you said that! You of all people have never believed in love at first sight. In fact, you have never believed in love at any sight or in any time," said Maudie who was truly shocked.

"Can't help it. He was so handsome!" said Eileen, who had slipped back in time, seeing in her mind's eye Lee's handsome face again for the first time. Eileen continued, "Well, Maudie, we had a few dates, and I got engaged. Somehow or another he convinced me that we should live together. I do not really believe in living together, but somehow or other he convinced me that it was the thing to do. I didn't show good sense. Understand?"

"Go on, Eileen, the dangerous part. Let me hear why Lee is dangerous," said Maudie with trepidation in her voice.

With her eyes downcast in sorrow, Eileen continued, "After he moved in, I asked him why all the strange people were always coming to the apartment, asking for him by the name of Joe Creech."

"He said late one evening, 'For God's sake, I'm a drug dealer, shithead. I am wanted by the San Diego police department for breaking out of jail, and I am on the run from the FBI for drug smuggling. Anything else you want to know?'

"I was speechless, Maudie, simply speechless. Was this part of the curse that I brought on myself by removing the lava rock from the lava field? Is this part of Madame Pele's curse?" said Eileen with tears in her eyes.

Maudie realized that Eileen really believed in this curse. She also was floored by what Eileen had told her concerning Lee. "Eileen, you must get rid of him. At once! Do you think that he will hurt you?"

"I don't know, Maudie. He has hated me ever since I ended the engagement. I thought the ring I was wearing was poisoning me, and I returned it to him. That infuriated him, and he's hated me ever since. He says that I'm too straight and boring for a man like him. I don't know why he wants to continue to live with me. I know that when he drinks he gets belligerent, and I wouldn't put violence past him. Gee, Maudie, I don't know what to do. I know I need help, but I don't know how to get it."

"Wow, Eileen! You are in a serious mess. I think that in addition to having mental difficulties, you are also in physical danger. I don't know how to help you. Maybe the doctor at Universal Airway's medical department can help you find a good psychiatrist. I haven't a clue who can help you about Lee," said Maudie, who was puzzled about how to help her friend out of her current difficulties.

At that moment, Georgio approached the two friends deep in conversation and said, "Ladies, there is a wonderful movie by George Lukas playing in the theater down the street. It's a new movie called *Star Wars*. Why don't you go see it?"

"Okay, Georgio, it sounds great, and we need something that'll help us escape the reality we are experiencing at the present time. We hope it will help to cheer us up. May we have the bill?"

After paying their bill, they stepped out into the brisk evening air. There were big snowflakes coming down, causing the street to look gorgeous and be slippery. Clutching their new purchases in their hands, they headed for the theater. For the first time in months, Eileen heard no voices ringing in her ears and in her mind. *Hallelujah!* she thought with glee. *Maybe they are finally gone for good.* She was so used to constant turmoil in her ears that silence was a cause for celebration.

"Maudie, I'm not hearing voices, not even Wahu. This is great. I think I will celebrate and have a big bag of popcorn."

"Great, Eileen. Shall we get butter on it?" said Maudie who loved theater popcorn.

"Yes, the whole works!" said Eileen, who was jubilant that she heard no voices. They stood in line, waiting to get the popcorn and large cups of Fresca.

They watched the movie, rapt. Princess Leia and Han Solo were so romantic, and Darth Vader was so sinister. It satisfied them at a deep, deep level of their consciousness and their souls. It was a great escape from their problems with men, work, and life in general. They both thought, "Wouldn't it be great to be Princess Leia?"

As they left the darkened theater and stepped back into the snowy street with the snow glistening from the streetlights, they were quite happy and content. For the moment reality had been overcome by a sense of beauty and fantasy. *Lovely!* they both thought in unison. *Life is sometimes lovely.*

They continued down the slippery, snowy street.

31

Happy Birthday, Hairy-Cary

1, *2, 3, TOUR JETÉ.*

Eileen was gliding across, the floor, feeling at one with the air and the world. Not a care.

Then there was silence. The drum had stopped beating. Murph started to yell at her, "What in the world is wrong with you today, Eileen?"

What is wrong? Why did the drum stop? Why is Murph yelling at me? Eileen stopped gliding across the floor. She looked around. The other dancers had stopped what they were doing and were busily looking, first at her and then at Murph.

"Damn it, Eileen! This is not a ballet class. What is wrong with you? You don't seem yourself today."

"Oh, Murph! I am so sorry. I was hearing the most gorgeous music ringing in my ears. I didn't hear the drum."

"Well, listen, damn it! You are supposed to be leaping across the floor, not gliding like a prima ballerina."

The other dancers were now standing around giggling amongst themselves. "Boy, Murph sure is mad at Eileen. Sure am glad that it's her and not us," was the general consensus being voiced by Ramon, the new Argentinian dancer who had just recently joined Mad Murphy's African Jazz Ensemble.

"You're right on, Ramon," said Naomi with a snicker. She was glad to see Eileen in trouble. Eileen received too much attention in Naomi's opinion. "Y'all know that white gals got no soul. Send her home, Murph. The white gal has got no soul. You know I'm a better dancer," whined Naomi, who was furious that Eileen had the lead role in Murph's new production.

"Shut up, Naomi. You dance like an elephant. Although, in all honesty, today Eileen is dancing like she was the lead dancer in Giselle."

He turned to Eileen and said, "Okay Eileen, are you gonna dance right, or do I send you home for the day until you can get your wits about you and remember that this is African jazz. You're distracting the other dancers."

At this moment Ramon said, "Hey, Eileen, go home."

"Shut up, Ramon. I'm the boss here, not you, and I am the one to say who goes and who stays. If you can't remember that, you can go home, too."

The dancers were nervously shifting their weight from one foot to the other. They were nervous because Murph was now mad at everyone, not just Eileen.

Eileen said with a sad sigh, "Gosh, Murph, maybe I should leave. I feel a migraine headache starting behind my left eye. I don't want to ruin your new dance. Maybe tomorrow I'll feel better."

By now Murph was starting to feel guilty. He knew that something was wrong with Eileen, and he could not quite figure what the problem was. He knew that she heard voices, so maybe she was sick in the head.

He was sorry that he had yelled at her and had acted in such a surly, nasty manner. He knew she was a good dancer, but as distracted as she was, she would ruin his new choreography, "Gazelles and Zebras Being Chased by the Mighty Lion Over the Veldt in the Midday Sun."

"Yo, bitch! Go home! We don't need you. Yo, bitch! Go home! We don't need you," chanted Naomi, with malice in her voice.

"Shut up, Naomi!" boomed forth the low, resounding voice of Mad Murphy. The feathers on his turban bounced up and down. "Just because you're from Africa doesn't mean that you can understand my music and dance better than Eileen. So just shut up, or I'll send you home, too."

At this, the dancers all decided that they needed a cigarette break. "Hey, Murph! Can we have a cig?" asked Ramon timidly.

"Sure, kid. Take five; in fact, class is over for the day."

The dancers were thrilled. It was like playing hooky, which everyone loves to do. "Eileen," said Murph with a thoughtful note in his voice, "I think if I were you, I would see a doctor. Maybe he could explain the voices and the migraines."

"Gee, thanks, Murph. You're so understanding. I love your dances and music. I would hate to be kicked out of your class. I'll make an appointment as soon as I can. Everyone, including the doctor at Universal, thinks that I am using drugs. That is one reason I can't work. You know, though, that I don't use drugs. Thank you for your thoughtfulness."

"Okay, Eileen. Don't get maudlin on me. Just go home. Just see your doctor."

Eileen was standing in her bathroom trying to apply her eye shadow and mascara.

She was happy to be home early. "Today is Hairy-Cary's sixtieth birthday party, and Lee is taking me fishing in Richardson Bay so that we can catch some fish for the party. I haven't been fishing since I was with Denny in Maui, and I caught the baby shark. It should be fun to cook fresh fish on Hairy-Cary's houseboat in Sausalito. That should be fun." Eileen's brains were pounding from the pain of the migraine. She almost couldn't see to put her eye makeup on correctly. She knew that Lee hated it when she didn't look perfect. She was beginning to think that Lee simply hated her at all times. She knew that after this afternoon's party she would have to kick him out of her life and, more specifically, out of her apartment. It was no fun living with someone who hated you. She could never figure why he wanted to stay.

"Oh, well! Fishing is fun and something that most guys love to do, so maybe he won't ruin the afternoon. My neighbor Al and his cat Cleo will be taking me with them. I'll meet Lee at the houseboat."

"Cleo just loves Lee." This always puzzled her, because Lee had no use for four-legged animals. She was beginning to believe that he had even less use for the female variety of the two-legged kind.

As she stepped back from the mirror she said with enthusiasm, "My eyes look just perfect."

Now Eileen got down to the serious business of the afternoon. What to wear with her new white silk capris from Milan. She would wear her new yellow knit tunic from the Salvation Army's thrift store in downtown San Francisco. That is where she also obtained her Morris chair that she displayed proudly in her living room. She had lacquered it a bright fire-engine red. She had placed two white satin pillows on it. The pillows had grass green silk tassels on them. She loved to sit there, put her headphones on, and listen to the Rolling Stones.

All of a sudden—PURR, PURR. It was Cleo. Cleo was purring and looking at Eileen. "Why, Cleo! You never liked to be around me. What's up? I don't have any catnip for you."

"PURR, PURR."

"Oh, you want to talk. Well, purr away.

"I'm trying to decide whether to wear sandals or my new black leather boots. Sandals are more traditional, but since the party is for Hairy-Cary, and he was a Hell's Angels biker, perhaps the black leather boots would be more appropriate."

She stepped back from the mirror. She looked spiffy. The boots were not too clunky, although she thought that maybe the outfit was a little dressy. "But hey! It is a party."

The doorbell rang out. Al shouted from the hall. "Hey, Eileen! Are you ready to go? Grab Cleo, and let's leave for the party."

Eileen grabbed her new Ray Ban aviator sunglasses from the telephone table. She grabbed Cleo under one arm and her new straw Hobo bag under the other. As she headed out the door, she handed Al her birthday present for Hairy-Cary. She, Al, and Cleo ran outside to the motorcycle. "Hop on!" Al said to the others.

Eileen loved to ride on motorcycles, and this was a gorgeous Harley—only two years old, shiny, and spotless.

"Don't worry about Cleo. She loves to ride in the basket I especially rigged up for her on the back of the cycle."

With that the two friends and the cat settled down. Al gunned the engine and off they went. Dust flying. Cleo's purrs echoing in Eileen's ears.

There was a wreck at the top of Golden Gate Bridge. Eileen and Al sat in the blazing sun waiting to get past the two wrecked cars. She looked down into the swirling water below. It looked so cool and inviting. It would be so much fun to jump in. . . .

Finally the traffic got moving. Twenty minutes later, the three of them pulled up in front of the houseboat. It was festive with balloons and streamers all in black. Hairy-Cary did not like getting old, but he and Estelle had decided to go all out for the festive occasion. Since he and his biker buddies always wore black, Estelle thought it only appropriate to use black for their color scheme.

"Hey, Eileen! What took you so long?" growled Lee who, it seemed, had been drinking heavily. Eileen was alarmed. She had forgotten that everyone would be drunk and drugged to the gills. *Oh well,* she thought, *Lee and I will be out on the boat, and it'll be peaceful and quiet.*

"Hey Eileen, how are you?" It was Estelle. Eileen really adored Estelle, who was so tall and thin and graceful, even in biker duds. Estelle was wearing her new skintight black leather bell-bottom pants with her new tie-dyed T-shirt. It was red, pink, blue, purple, yellow, and white. She was wearing a red, white, and blue headband over her golden locks. Eileen was jealous, because no matter what she wore, she never looked glamorous.

The rest of the guests were milling around, making a lot of noise. The odor of dope was permeating the air, and cocaine was being sniffed on the deck. The boat was gently rocking in the afternoon sun.

"Happy Birthday, Hairy-Cary," Eileen said as she handed him his birthday present. She had bought him a wooden cane. It had a rearview mirror, a turn signal, and a bell.

"Eileen! It's perfect!" said Estelle. "Don't you love it, Hairy-Cary?"

"Sure, Eileen. Actually, my arthritis has gone to my knees, so I can actually use it when I walk with Estelle in the evenings."

At that moment Lee came walking over to Eileen. "C'mon, let's go fishing."

"Oh sure, Lee. See you later, folks."

They walked over to the pier, and Eileen looked down at the boat Lee was entering. "A rowboat! But Lee, I thought we were going out in a motorboat!"

"No! I need some exercise, so I'm rowing out to the middle of the bay. The fishing poles are in the boat. Hop in. Al said Cleo wants to come, so grab her."

Lee's eyes were glazed and red. His words were somewhat slurred. Eileen was worried. This was more than she had bargained for; but everyone was egging her on, so she grabbed Cleo and hopped into the boat. Off they went to the middle of the bay.

Finally they came to a stop in the middle of Richardson Bay, and they lowered their lines into the water . . .

The boat rocked forward.
The boat rocked backward.
The boat rocked up.
The boat rocked down.
The boat rocked left.
The boat rocked right.
The sun blazed down, right onto Eileen's left eye. Her vision blurred.
The waves glided under the bobbing boat. Her stomach churned.

Lee whipped out a brown paper bag, "Here, have a sandwich."

"Sure, Lee. What are they?"

"Liverwurst! I got them at the deli on Chestnut Street."

They began to eat, and then Lee brought out a six-pack of beer and a huge joint.

"Oh, dear! He's going to capsize the boat."

They sat there for an hour, bobbing up and down, the sun blazing onto her unprotected head, Cleo gazing deeply into Lee's brown eyes. Her eye makeup was blurred because her headache was causing her eyes to tear, and her mascara was streaming down her cheeks. Her hair was a mess from the wind blowing through it.

"Lee! We must return to shore. I'm going to be sick."

"Oh shit, Eileen. We haven't caught any fish yet. Why don't you just sit quietly like other women?"

"Lee, I'm getting sick."

"Okay! We'll go back to the party, but then leave me alone. I want to have some fun, and you're a colossal drag." He picked up the oars and started rowing with all of his might back to the shore. He was furious.

When they approached the pier, Al yelled, "Throw Cleo up on the pier."

Eileen heard him say, "Throw Cleo in the water." Her hearing was not so good. She knew that cats hated water, especially Cleo, so she could not figure out why Al wanted her to throw Cleo in the water.

But she did.

She picked up a hissing, clawing Cleo, raised the cat above her head with her arms extended, and tossed Cleo, screaming, into the bay.

"Eileen! What are you doing?" yelled Al and Lee and Hairy-Cary in unison. Cleo was howling.

Al jumped into the water to save her.

Hairy-Cary reached down to help Eileen onto the pier. "Hey, kid! Are you okay? I love having you here, but I think you should go home and lie down."

"Lee!" called Hairy-Cary. "Take Eileen home. I don't think she is feeling well."

"Damned if I'll take her home. The bitch is stupid, and I don't want to be bothered with her."

"In that case, you can just leave my party. Eileen is my friend. You're not!" replied Hairy-Cary as he clenched and unclenched his fists.

Lee was drunk and crazed with drugs, and he glared at Hairy-Cary.

"Oh dear. Not another fight!" She was ready to run, but Estelle was standing beside her, holding onto her arm.

All of Hairy-Cary's biker friends were advancing towards Lee, pulling their knives out of their boots.

Lee was no idiot, and even through his drunken haze he realized that he was outgunned. He started backing away from the bikers.

"Lee! Listen to me if you're able. I'm taking Eileen home, and we're getting your things together and placing them in front of her apartment house. You are to gather them up and take them away, and you are never to go near her again. Do you understand me?"

"Yeah, you dumb shit! I don't want to see her again anyway."

"My friends and I will be outside her apartment, and if you try to enter, you're dead meat. Understand?"

Lee was puzzled. He hated Eileen and could not understand why other people liked her so much. What he ever saw in her was beyond him. She was crazy and could not cook—absolutely of no use to any man. Lee backed off the boat, muttering to himself, putting his knife back into his boot, heading for his new 1957 white Cadillac convertible. He was off to Mill Valley where he could stay in the commune that was run by his drug dealer friend, Emilio.

After he left, Hairy-Cary and his friends gathered around Eileen. "Okay Pumpkin! If he ever tries to get in touch with you, let me know. He will disappear from the face of the earth. Understand?"

"Yes, Hairy-Cary. Thank you all. I would like to go home, though. My head is making me sick.

"Happy birthday, Hairy-Cary."

32

The Apartment

I T WAS A GROOVY APARTMENT AND HAD A FIRE ESCAPE OUT A SEC-
ond-story window.

By now, Eileen was beginning to exhibit the unmistakable signs of
schizophrenia, the paranoid variety . . .

> voices loud, voices clear
> Voices there and voices here
> Voices everywhere
> I do declare
>
> The apartment was a gleamy apparition
>> showing no contrition
>> showing no ambition
>> showing no ammunition
>> The telephone would ring

and she would cry
She really would have loved
    to die
She had not reached
    the understanding
    of why.

The apartment was quiet
    inside
    and noisy on the street.
The neighborhood danced
    to a daffodil beat

For only six hours did she have
    heat.

It was well decorated
Perfect for a
    nervous breakdown
It was fated . . .

    and
        Then
            There
                Was
                    Lee,
                        He

Caused Eileen
    to crack.
He moved in.
There was no turning back.
Thank God he did not
    at this time
    use heroin or crack.

Alcohol was
    his drug of "choice"
It always
    always
        dulled
            his
                "Voice."

It fried his brain
It ruined his mind
It absolutely
    positively
    was not kind.

"Help! Help!
    I need 'help':
My brain is tingling
    under my scalp!"
Eileen wailed
    as she tossed and turned
As through her brains
    these strange thoughts churned.
She was confused
    by
        all
            she had learned.
"Help! Help!
    I need help.
My brain is tingling
    under my scalp! . . ."

Reverberated through
    her mind
Like Lee's alcohol

These thoughts
    were not kind.

The thoughts crept into
    each little cell
They made her life a
    living hell.
She knew these little thoughts
    so well.

"I wish, dear Lee
    that you would leave
And I could have some
    time to grieve
About the deaths
    of dogs and cats
And even about the
    deaths of bats."

These fearsome thoughts
    that made life alarming
Swiftly through
    her soul
      were swarming.
She certainly
    did not find them
      charming.

She knew that Lee
    would have
      to go
And quickly
    not so fearsome slow.
She had a hunch

that he would punch
    and kick
        and scream
            and shout

She had to throw
    the fucker out.

It broke her heart
    indeed it did.
She fancied herself
    in love with the kid.

In February she
    finished her chore
And successfully kicked
    him out the door.

Quiet flowed into the apartment
It did not give to her a hint
Of all the ideas,
    both right and wrong
That would pound in her brain
Each night—
    for so long
Each would have a song.

"Help! Help!
    I need help.
My brain is tingling
    under my scalp!"

"Alone,
Alone
I am all alone

Except for that
 irritating phone."

It rang each day
 at half past four.
Voices would
 hiss and squawk.
At this point
 they did not always talk—
 at least, not much.

A loner, a loner
 she was now a loner
The time had come to evaporate—
 no longer to congregate
 no longer to placate . . .
The time had come to meditate.
To jump . . .
That was a persistant theme
It appeared in each and every dream.
Both night and day,
The voices would not go away.

"Help! Help!
 I need help!
 My brain is tingling
 under my scalp!"

33

Easter Morning

EASTER MORNING DAWNED WITH THE FOG ROLLING IN OVER THE bay area. The foghorns were sounding their mournful song over the entire region. It was around 5:30 or 6:00 A.M. The street in front of Eileen's apartment was quiet—put to sleep by the gray, gray morning air.

Oh my God! I overslept! Once again those strange dreams! Why must I keep thinking that my brain is wired to those alien spaceships? They keep telling me strange things, which I then proceed to forget. At least I know where the voices are coming from.

By now Eileen was fully awake and agitated. She started pacing back and forth, back and forth.

Those voices don't seem happy or even friendly anymore. I wish they'd go away and leave me alone. I would love some peace and quiet.

Eileen had a terrible headache. She was plagued by headaches now, and she had started to faint with some regularity. In fact, she was on a medical leave of absence because she had passed out one morning and missed a trip; and right after that, she had inadvertently inflated a slide on a DC-10. Her boss thought that she was doing drugs, but that was not the case. She smoked a little dope now and again, but that only seemed to relieve the pain she was feeling.

What is wrong? What is wrong? I'm so confused.

She put on a warm robe, and padded into her kitchen this early Easter morning to make a cup of coffee. She turned on her stove, and put some coffee beans in her new coffee grinder. She loved the sound of coffee grinding—

WHRR!
BRRR!
GRRR!

The coffee grinder made a lovely sound to Eileen's ears and to her mind. She loved to listen to its grinding noise. It was so soothing.

She at sat her table and lit a cigarette. She blew smoke rings for several minutes and listened to the foghorns. She listened to the voices whispering in her ears—strange noises that she did not understand.

She looked out her window at the traffic beginning to appear on her street. She lived in an old 1930s apartment building on the comer of Cervantes and Beach Streets in the marina. It had a huge closet that contained her favorite possessions—her clothes.

She knew that she was going through a dark night of the soul, or even more expressively, a *crise de nerfs*, as the French would say. Eileen often thought that she would love to learn to speak French, as she appreciated their approach to art and the English language.

Golly, she thought as she continued to blow smoke rings and cough, *it's Easter morning, and I should be going to church; but right now*, she continued to talk to herself, "I'm angry at how I have treated God, and I feel in total disgrace; so I would not be welcome at church...."

I cannot bear feeling
This way
I shall not stay
This way.

Eileen got up and headed back to the closet in her bedroom. She rummaged around for something to wear for when she went out later that afternoon.

Black! It's always a good color, and it fits my mood.

As she was putting on her favorite black slacks and her gorgeous Geiger jacket that was made of red, blue, green, and yellow patches, she started thinking about the concert she had gone to the previous evening. It was French court music featuring a cello, fortepiano, Baroque flute, viola da gamba, and a soprano. Lovely. The soprano sang a song that touched Eileen's disturbed soul:

I hope that when I die
God will take me to the sky.
I can drift from cloud to cloud
Never being very loud.
I can drift from cosmos to cosmos
Searching for the origin of fleas
How they brought the dog and cat world
To its knees.
    And travel through time
    At the drop of a hat.
    I love to Google, I do love that.

How Lovely and timeless good music is, thought Eileen. With her heart lifted for the moment, she remembered Lee.

I wonder where he is since he moved out. It's certainly a good thing that he moved out before one of us killed the other. I got way too close to stabbing him while he was asleep after he beat me up. Fortunately, my good Presbyterian upbringing prevented me from doing him in.

> There has been
> Too much death
> In your young life
> You are bereft
> By death.

Eileen wandered back to the window. The fog was lifting, and the blue sky was beginning to peep out from the gloomy gray sky. For a moment her spirit was cheered—

> It did not feel oppressed
> Inappropriately dressed
> Totally psychologically messed.

The coffee had finally finished brewing, and the lovely aroma of Viennese cinnamon drifted throughout her apartment. She had developed a taste for more exotic blends—no longer just the black swill that she and her father used to drink in the early mornings when they sat and talked before the sun rose and he went to work.

Gosh, I haven't thought about him for the longest time. I wonder if I am oppressed.

Eileen was hungry and was reaching for an apple when a voice thundered throughout her mind,

> "You are not normal!"
> Her world crashed around her—
> "I am not normal! What shall I do?"

She ran to the kitchen and got on her hands and knees and started pawing through her pots and pans.

"Ah, just what I want!" she exclaimed as she grabbed hold of her large cast iron Japanese cooking pot.

"Perfect! It's perfect!"

It was her most beautiful pot that she had bought in a Japanese grocery store in Ala Moana shopping center in Honolulu. "Just what I want."

She pulled it out of the cabinet, placed it on top of the stove, put a pile of newspaper in it, and started a fire. Eileen was quite pleased with herself.

She padded quietly to her nightstand by her bed and picked up the Bible that her parents had given her as a young girl back in Virginia. It had gone everywhere with her. She knew that she had betrayed it, and she was distraught.

She picked it up, went back into the kitchen where the fire was still burning nicely, put her Bible into the fire in the pot, and she watched it burn to ashes. The smoke made a gray spot on the ceiling.

Eileen sat on the floor, squatting on her heels as she had learned to do in her dance classes. She started rocking back and forth. She chanted:

> I have betrayed you!
>> Strike me dead!
> I have lived too long
>> Wrong
>> Strike me dead
> I have lost my song
>> Strike me dead!

The Bible blazed up into flames. Eileen continued to rock back and forth. She knew that God had heard her. She knew that her days were numbered.

But, . . .

The voices stopped.

34

The Cop at the Top

ILEEN DRESSED CAREFULLY FOR HER APPOINTMENT WITH DR. Carlos at the Universal Medical Department.

Oh dear, what shall I wear? she thought as she rummaged through her closet. *Should I wear my new black dress? It's flattering, and I think that I should make an effort to look chic and capable.* Eileen thought about this problem as she continued to pull out various outfits. Finally, she decided to go for it and wear the new black dress. "Ah, there it is." She reached into the back of the closet and pulled out her new clothes.

She pulled the dress over her head, and stepped in front of her full-length mirror. *Wow!* she thought as she looked at her reflection in the mirror. It made her think about an article that she had read recently. The article said that in the past, people were not always surrounded by reflecting surfaces. Consequently, the author deduced, people were not so narcissistic as modern folks. Whether or not this was a true assumption, Eileen could not say for sure, but it did seem to be logical.

She twirled around and around, happy with what she saw in the mirror.

"Damn it! I look good; but my head is pounding, and my eyes are red. Maybe I will throw up on the doctor. Wouldn't that be the pits?" As she said this, she headed for the bathroom to try to find some aspirin in her medicine cabinet. Aspirin never helped, but she felt that she was doing something helpful, which made her feel righteous. Eileen, at this point in her Christian walk, was still fixated on "doing" rather than "being." She had learned this approach from her grandmother, who was a Southern Baptist. Eileen was a Presbyterian, so they had some vital differences on the subject of religion and salvation. In all honesty, though, all her grandmother really wanted was for Eileen to marry, settle down, and have children.

"Eileen," she would say with gravity in her voice, "you should get married. I want you to have children. No one can be happy without them."

"Sorry, Gran! The last thing in this world I want is to have children. I don't even want to get married!" said Eileen with fervor.

"Eileen, you are making a big mistake. No woman is fulfilled without children."

"Gran, if I wanted children, I would get married and have them. However, I'd rather swallow chicken bones than stay home with children. Now please, let's change the subject. We'll never reach an agreement on this subject."

Gran shook her head in sorrow and went back to her crocheting. "If only Charlie [her deceased husband] had lived, he would help her to understand my feelings better." Again, Gran shook her head in sorrow.

Oh yes, thought Eileen as she applied her eyeshadow, *Gran and I have a basic disagreement, but really! I must hurry to medical for my appointment at 11:00 A.M.* She slicked back her hair and put on her new black platform shoes with the black ankle straps. They added five inches to her height and make her feel glamorous and tall like Ingrid. She hated being short. What a lovely day! The sky is blue, the clouds are puffy as they race across the sky, and the aroma coming from the bay makes the whole world smell of fish and salt water. What a delicious aroma. *Perhaps I'll stop at Alioto's for a fish dinner after I get back home*, she thought to herself as she licked her lips in anticipation.

"Oh dear," she said as she stepped onto the sidewalk, "I do feel sick. But at least Cleo and Wahu and Lufti from Mufti are not chattering in my head. I don't think Dr. Carlos would understand if I started talking to my voices in his office."

She wobbled a bit in her new platform shoes, got her balance, and headed for the bus stop. She did not drive, and getting to and from medical would be a four- or five-hour adventure. She never knew what the new day would bring. If only the migraines would go away . . .

Several hours later . . .

Dr. Carlos and Eileen were fussing at each other.

"Miss Gordon, you are not going to be able to return to work at the present time. After listening carefully, I am unable to determine whether you are paranoid due to mental illness or to drug usage," said the doctor, who was perplexed by her condition.

"I told you Dr. Carlos, I don't use drugs. I know that I'm depressed. Sometimes I am confused, but when I went to the psychologist you suggested, he didn't help any. I thought he was patronizing me, and I did not like him. Perhaps I need to go to the hospital. Maybe I could get some help there," said Eileen, who was now depressed. Not even the prospect of a beautiful day and dinner at Alioto's could cheer her up. "Maybe someone there could help me."

As she was saying this, Dr. Carlos was gazing fixedly at Eileen, especially at her red eyes and strained face. He twiddled his thumbs, which was his habit when perplexed. "Miss Gordon, go home and get some rest. I will think about this problem some more and see what I can line up for you. It seems like you do need some help, and perhaps we can get that help for you."

Eileen left the office, saddened in her heart. She headed home. It was late in the afternoon. She had lost her appetite, which was not unusual for her. She could hardly ever eat and had lost fifteen pounds in the last two months. Ever since Easter morning, when she realized she was in trouble.

Perhaps I am just lonely. Ever since Lee left, she had felt isolated and lonely. As awful as their relationship had been, at least he was human, and he breathed. *I must be sick to miss him. I don't think I'm ready to die, and he certainly would've killed me. Thank heaven Hairy-Cary scared him.*

Evening was coming on. The sun was dipping down to the horizon. The seagulls were swooping up and down the bay. Eileen kept walking. Ingrid always worried that Eileen would twist her ankle walking in her high platform shoes. So far, Eileen's dance endeavors had paid off. She had strong legs and ankles and a great sense of balance.

> CLIP, CLOP
> CLIP, CLOP
> Went her shoes.
> Where were they heading?
> It was dark
> In Golden Gate Park.
> The evening stars were appearing
> It was getting late
> She was heading for the Bridge—
> The Golden Gate.
>
> She kept walking
> Her head pounding
> The thought of drowning
> Had popped into her head

She was afraid.

She reached the top
And stood at the rail
Gazing down
  Down
  Down
At the swirling water
Down below—
  Black

"I should jump
Hit the water
  With a thump
And drown—
   Far from ground.
 I ought"
She thought
  "to go home.
I do not want
  To make a mess
Of my new dress."

At that moment a car stopped behind her, its headlights sparkling in the dark. She turned around to see who it was. *Why, it's a cop. I wonder what's on his mind,* thought Eileen, who was not aware of how she must appear to a cop, standing there in the dark in the middle of the night, staring into the night air, looking down into the water below.

"Hey, miss, can I help you?" said the young officer as he came toward Eileen.

"No thank you, officer. I'm just fine," replied Eileen, who then burst into tears.

"Hey, lady, why are you crying?" It always upset him to see a woman cry.

"Officer, I believe I am sick, and my head is hurting. I'm also lonely, and I keep hearing voices, although for the last several days, they have been quiet," said Eileen, who at this time was thankful for small favors.

"You sound depressed to me," said the young officer. He had red hair, fair skin, and freckles. Eileen could notice these features because of the light from his car.

She believed that you could always trust redheads, so she continued, "Officer, I'm depressed. I really would like to jump, but I'm unsure as to whether I want to kill myself or just want to fly. Even as a young girl I wanted to fly."

"Ah, lady, you know it is dangerous to jump off of the Golden Gate Bridge. Also, there is a serial killer—the Zebra killer—stalking lone people at night. I think you need a ride home. Come on. Hop into the car, and I will give you a ride home."

By now, Eileen was tired, and she wanted to crawl into a hot bubble bath and then into a warm bed. "Maybe I will go home. Thanks, officer. My feet hurt. It seems that I have been walking for hours."

"Sure, Miss. Hop in! Wow! Those are pretty shoes. They make you look tall and glamorous. You know that a good-looking lady like you should not be wandering alone at night. It is dangerous."

"Gee, thanks," said Eileen with her first smile of the day. She always loved a compliment from a good-looking man. "They're the latest style."

They drove in silence for the next ten minutes in the dark. There were derelicts roaming the streets—looking in trash cans for food and cigarette butts, holed up in their sleeping bags on the hard sidewalks, shooting up, drinking, worrying the night away.

Finally, too soon as far as Eileen was concerned, they pulled up in front of her apartment. "Here we are, safe and sound at your home. Hop out and go to bed and get some sleep. Things will look better in the morning."

Eileen stepped out the police car onto the pavement in front of her apartment. "Wow, the Big Dipper has moved. That's strange," she said as she headed to the front door.

The next morning was cold and gray. The foghorns were wailing. The heater came on at 6:00 A.M. The noise of the radiator woke Eileen, who was still worried that the Big Dipper had appeared in a different position in the sky. She knew that that was not right. *Why did it move?* she wondered. *Did I imagine it?* She was quite distressed. *I must get to a hospital.*

As she was pondering what to do, she got dressed in her new blue jeans, black turtleneck sweater, Frye boots, and red and black lumberjack jacket. She left her apartment and headed to the local bakery for something to eat and some coffee. It was 8:00 A.M.

She entered the bakery, and sat down at her favorite table in front of the window, where she could watch the people go by. She drank her coffee but could not bear the thought of eating anything. "If only my stomach would stop growling."

The locals were all gathered to drink coffee, eat doughnuts, read the morning paper, and in general gossip and hang out. Sam, the owner, walked over to her table and said to her, "Eileen, didn't you sleep at all? Your eyes are red, and the black circles under your eyes are down to the tip of your nose. You need to quit staying out all night, and you need some food." As he said this he handed Eileen her favorite food: a doughnut with chocolate frosting.

"No thanks, Sam. I can't eat. I appreciate the thought though."

"Okay! See you later," he said as he headed for the front door to greet some new customers.

"I must go!" muttered Eileen to herself. "But where?" She pondered this and decided to go for a long walk. She knew that she would never return to her apartment. Never, ever. She walked and cried. The wind caused her eyes to dry. She walked all day. Finally she was tired. "Look there. A police car! I will have them take me to a hospital. They will know where to take me."

She waved at the police car. She jumped up and down and yelled, "Help! I need help—"

The car stopped. The two officers got out and approached her suspiciously.

Oh, my God. It is the red-headed policeman whom I met last night. "Hi!" she yelled.

The red-headed policeman relaxed when he saw who it was. "Fred, relax. That's the lady I told you about that I met last night. Let's help her."

"Okay, Patrick," said the other cop. "Let's see what we can do."

Eileen was so happy to see him. "You must get me to a hospital. I don't know where to go. Please help."

"Okay, hop in the car."

By now she was alternating between crying and screaming. She stopped both and slipped into the back seat. Her curiosity got the better of her as the car pulled out into the traffic in the street. "Where are we going?"

"First to the local clinic. Then to wherever they decide you should go," said Fred and Patrick. They were concerned about her.

They arrived at the clinic. Eileen sat quietly in the waiting room while they arranged for someone to see her. She quietly read her most favorite book, *A Princess of Mars* by Edgar Rice Burroughs. She had put it into her new black leather Hobo purse before leaving her apartment that morning. It always transported her beyond her everyday concerns and into an interesting world of fantasy, or an alternate reality, however you choose to see it. She was getting more tense. The headache was still throbbing. She was afraid. Where would she spend the night, the next day, the next year?

Finally, she was put into a small room to wait for the doctor. She was now crying again.

The young doctor walked into the room. "How can I help you, Eileen?" He knew her name because he had looked at her ID in her wallet.

She started screaming, "Lufti is going to cut my brains out!"

"Who is Lufti?" asked the doctor, in a soothing voice.

"Why, Lufti is from Mufti, a planet in a galaxy far, far away. He and his crew are taking R&R on Earth. Their ship is orbiting the planet and it's now above San Francisco," said Eileen, between sobs.

"You can stop screaming. I will not let Lufti cut your brains out," said the doctor who was taking her blood pressure.

"Thank you, doctor." said Eileen, who was now quiet and seemed quite sane. "I really am afraid of him, you know. He says he's only cutting my brains out so he can reassemble them in a better configuration. It seems that my left brain is taking over, crowding out my right brain. I personally think that I need all of my brains assembled the way they were when I was born. What do you think?"

"That is an astute observation. They seem somewhat scrambled now, but I'm sure that at the hospital the doctors can unscramble them," observed the doctor as he was taking her pulse. He noticed that her pulse was too fast, and her blood pressure was way too high. He decided that she needed a sedative.

"Here, take this pill. It will make you feel better, and you won't need to scream so much," he said as he handed her a pretty pink capsule.

Eileen was impressed by his soothing manner and calm logic. She figured that if he recommended the pink pill, then perhaps she should try it.

GULP!

She swallowed it.

The young doctor smiled and said, "That's good. Now we will have an ambulance take you to the hospital."

"An ambulance! That's somewhat extravagant, isn't it? I could just take a cab and save the taxpayers some money." She did not realize how sick she was.

"You, Eileen, are a taxpayer, and because you are so polite, we will let you go to the hospital in style: in an ambulance with the lights flashing and the sirens wailing. What do you think of that?" said the doctor with a benevolent smile.

"That should be interesting. I've been worried about where I would spend the night, and an ambulance and a hospital sound swell. Let's go!" said Eileen, who was beginning to get drowsy from the sedative.

The next thing she knew was that she was in a straitjacket, on a stretcher, in an ambulance, racing through the dark city streets. She was calm. She thought a straitjacket was somewhat excessive, but the attendants said it was routine, sort of like wearing a seat belt to keep your arms from flailing about. She could understand the logic of such an explanation.

The next thing she knew was that she was lying on a bed in an emergency room. The doctor introduced himself as Dr. Sung. He told her that he was the attending physician. "What seems to be the real problem?" he inquired in a quiet and interested manner.

"Dr. Sung! The Big Dipper changed position. I am interested in stargazing, and I always observe the sky before midnight. The Big Dipper was totally in the wrong position, although perhaps that was only my imagination. What do you think?" she asked the doctor. Perhaps he had noticed the change of position also.

"I don't think much about the Big Dipper, but I am sure there is an explanation. Now I am going to give you a shot so you can sleep. Okay?" said Dr. Sung, who had a big needle in his hand.

"I hate shots! How about a pill?" Eileen really was not happy about a shot.

"In the morning we will give you a pill," he said in a kindly voice, his brown eyes twinkling.

"Okay, if you say so. Just make it quick. Please slap the area first so I don't notice the shot so much. I hate needles," observed Eileen, who was now quiet because of the earlier sedative.

"Here goes, Eileen," said Dr. Sung.

PRICK!

"That sure was fast, Dr. Sung. You are smooth." said Eileen who was glad that the shot had not hurt much.

"Thanks for the compliment, Eileen. I'll see you tomorrow. Get a good night's sleep. Lights out!" said the doctor as he stepped away from her bed.

She was gone.

Photographs

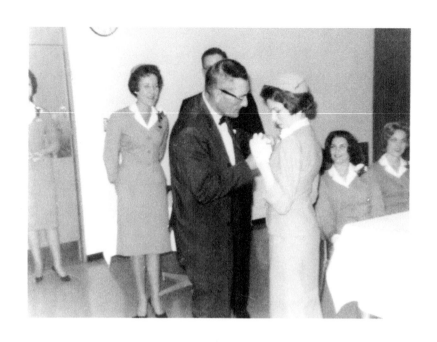

Pinning the wings

Cat

Hippies Unite!

A Painting

Control Tower at Dulles International Airport

Out the Window

Three Stews

A Painting

In the Galley

More Dirty Dishes—The Life of a Stew

Stew Takes a Break

Christmas Fantasy Flight

In Israel

In the Paris Catacombs

Operation Desert Shield

Desert Shield

Desert Shield

Me and Mom

The Last Trip

Part 2

The Delusion Is an Illusion

35

The 16th Floor

*O*H, HOW I WISH THAT I HAD A CIGARETTE TO WATCH THE SMOKE TEN-*drils waft their way into the air above my head.*

Oh, how I wish I didn't hear those fucking voices in my head pounding throughout my brain. They torment me so. Why just now, they once again told me to jump. Fortunately there are bars on the windows above my bed. That's really not so strange, because I have figured out that my bed is in a small room on the sixteenth floor of this building, a hospital. Dr. Sung told me that the room is just one of several in the psychiatric ward of St. Thomas Hospital . . . I think that I will scream for a while . . . I haven't screamed for several days, I think, and everyone is probably taking me for granted now. I believe that I have been quiet too long . . . Oh dear, here comes one of the nurses with that obnoxious liquid that they make me take. The nurse is in a white coat. They used to give me pills, but I would continue to scream, so they knew that I was spitting the pills out in the toilet. I really do not think it is right to take drugs. That is what everyone told me when I was growing up . . . I can not stand the taste of that obnoxious liquid. It is so nasty. I think that I will think about the past—whatever that means—or was it another life? This one seems rather immediate, and the past—whatever that means—is rather un-immediate. I will think about Star Trek and Mr. Spock. His ears are a lot like mine. He's a space alien and thus seems real to me . . . I was in contact with some of them until I came to the hospital . . . Star Trek is such a wonderful show. . . . All of the people on the sixteenth floor with me just love it—even Miss Princess Olga from Russia! I wonder if the nurses and doctors identify with Bones. He is humorous. Captain Kirk is so swashbuckling. But my favorite is Mr. Spock. He is a master of logic. I need some logic . . .

> From my position in the heres and nows
> I need to get rid of my sacred cows.
> Logic is a kind of thought that is to be desired
> Logic is a kind of thought that is to be admired
> My mind is much mired
> I am lucky I was not fired
> If they knew then what they know now
> I would not have been hired.

Oh to be logical! How does one get that way? Well, perhaps by focusing. Now that is an interesting concept—focusing . . . to focus . . .

> To focus on jumping
> To focus on flying

Are they related? It would seem that after jumping for a short time you might think that you were flying, whereas in actuality you would be falling! That is so confusing. One forgets about the end result of jumping—if the distance is great enough you will be flattened like a pancake and busted to pieces. That is, if you jump from a high enough place.

But for a short while, if you flap your arms, it would seem like flying, which is something men and women have always wanted to do. It sort of accounts for why we have airplanes, and even they get splattered if they fall out of the sky; and everyone on them dies.

I sort of forgot how I got here. It was certainly dramatic . . . although when I called the police, I certainly didn't envision a straitjacket, ambulance, and sirens howling out as through the streets we careened . . . and hospitals . . . and shots, etcetera.

All because the Big Dipper turned upside down. . . . Now everyone knows that that is impossible, or so I think now. But really, if one is honest, one knows that nothing is impossible. It just seems that things are impossible; or maybe they are really impossible, and I just can't accept that idea.

I think that I will try to sleep. Maybe if my brain slows down, I could figure out how I got here; in fact, maybe I could remember who I am. That would be a great accomplishment. I left my identification somewhere, and I cannot remember where.

Besides, even if I could remember, I wouldn't tell anyone, because I am hiding. Actually the sixteenth floor is a great place to hide, and I like it here because the food is good, and my doctor, Dr. Sung, told me that I had to eat or die. When he said that, it was such a direct challenge that I decided to consider it.

After pondering this ultimatum for about three days, I decided that I was not ready to die. I realized that I had to eat if I wanted to live. Obviously, I want to live. That also means that I must not jump. . . . Damn, life is very confusing, don't you just know.

My thought about life just before I go to sleep . . .

> How did I get here?
> I do not know
> Was there an ambulance?
> Was it slow?
> Did the sirens scream and wail
> As they transported me from the jail?

For a fact my life was a mess
God saw this—a real live damsel in distress

He got me to the 16th floor
He got me a Southern Baptist Chinese doctor
He could not do much more

Dr. Sung was small and sleek
He moved around the floor so quick
He gave me a shot and said
"You should be thankful
That you are not dead."
But, cheer up
Things get better I always say
When the sun shines down
On a brand new day.

After a day or two
You will not scream
And this all will seem
Like a dream
A very confusing one
If I do say so
Rehabilitation will be slow.
Do not get discouraged
Do not get depressed
Put on fashionable clothes
When you get dressed.
Eat your meals
Smoke if you must
When you get better
You will stop smoking, I trust.

Now go to sleep
And enjoy a good dream
For goodness sake, please
Do not scream
The other patients need their rest.
Try real hard not to be a pest.

Eileen tossed and turned in her bed, while her friend Lucy in the other bed cried. Eileen was trying to remember when she first got the urge to jump. The stars swept across the night sky, and looking out of her window she could see the North Star in the cold dark night.

"I think I will eat some pancakes with blueberries in the morning for breakfast . . . I wish I had a cat . . . I wish Lucy would not cry . . . as Kristen McMenaney said, '*Je suis rousse, et alors?*' or , 'I'm a redhead! So?'"

36

Three Days Later

ɪᴛ ᴡᴀs ʟᴀᴛᴇ ɪɴ ᴛʜᴇ ᴀꜰᴛᴇʀɴᴏᴏɴ. Tʜᴇ ᴀʟᴀʀᴍ ᴄʟᴏᴄᴋ ᴏɴ ᴛʜᴇ night table ticked softly. Eileen lay in her bed, gazing through the bars over the window and watching the clouds breezily go by. They were pretty and fluffy. They made her wish that she was up in the air in a plane, flying through them.

Her brain was strangely quiet. Nobody—no dog, no cat, no alien—was jabbering at her to do this or that or the other. How peaceful the world seemed to her in this moment. "This is nice. I love the quiet. I can appreciate the clouds." As she said this out loud to the room in general, she ran her hand through her hair. "Yuck, my hair feels greasy. Could it be that it is dirty? I can't remember when I washed it last. This is terrible."

She slowly rolled out of her bed. "Oh dear, I don't have a mirror in my room. I'd better get to the bathroom. Maybe the nurse will let me take a look in the mirror there. I will promise her that I will not break it and try to slash my wrists. She might or might not believe me, but it's imperative that I get a look at myself."

At this moment her roommate, Lucy, entered the room. "Hi, Eileen, it's nice to see you up and about. I was beginning to think you would never get up today. Your clothes are a mess."

"What do you mean, my clothes are a mess. I'm stylish," said Eileen who was appalled that Lucy would say such a thing.

"Maybe you are usually stylish, but right now you're frumpy. You've been in those same old clothes ever since you came to the sixteenth floor. You need a change of clothes. You need to do more for your appearance than just wash the same clothes everyday."

"Lucy, who do you think you are to talk to me about being a mess? You are wearing that thing that looks like a nightshirt that Dr. Sung gave you. You look worse than I do." Eileen grabbed Lucy by her hand. "Come on, Lucy. We need to go to the bathroom and take a good look at ourselves."

Lucy had started humming to herself and was twisting strands of hair around her fingers.

"Lucy, stop that!"

"Stop what, Eileen?" replied Lucy, who was now pulling at the twisted strands of hair. She was crying softly.

"Oh Lucy, stop crying. What's wrong?"

Tears were flowing down Lucy's cheeks. Between sobs she said, "Henry was just here. I wish I could go home, but he told me that I would never again be able to go to my home. He's filing for a divorce. He says that as a prominent young lawyer he needs a beautiful and intelligent wife. He says that I embarrass him. An embarrassment! I can't believe he said that to me." She was banging her fists on the mattress.

"Gosh, Lucy, that's awful." Eileen felt sorry for her roommate, but at this moment she was more concerned about the way they both looked. "Come on, Lucy. Let's go and see Dr. Sung. We can ask him if we have enough money to go shopping and buy some new clothes to wear."

Lucy—who had lived in Paris with her family for ten years before she got married and moved to San Francisco with Henry, her new husband—stopped crying and looked interested in what Eileen was saying. She loved shopping for new clothes.

Eileen had forgotten what she had been saying because her stomach was growling. She was hungry, and dinner would not be served for another three hours—at 6:00 P.M. "I wonder if we have enough money to buy a candy bar?"

"A candy bar!" exclaimed Lucy, with horror in her voice. "We don't need candy bars. They're fattening."

"I'm hungry, and Dr. Sung said that we both needed to gain weight and eat more. Come on Lucy, let's get something to eat." Eileen's eyes sparkled for the first time in a long time. Just the thought of chocolate made her happy. It had been months since she had tasted chocolate.

Lucy ripped the blanket off of her bed. "I'm cold," she said as she wrapped the blanket around her skinny body and started twirling round and round. She thought she was a ballerina. Her blonde hair was stringy and greasy and hung down her back.

"Come on. Let's go to Dr. Sung's office. Maybe he'll be able to help us improve our appearance."

"Okay, Eileen," said Lucy, who had stopped twirling and was considering, like a good Frenchwoman, the joys of buying new clothes.

Out the door they went—two skinny young ladies with dirty, stringy hair and no makeup. One was dressed in a hospital gown and a blanket and the other, in messy blue jeans, a black T-shirt, and a lumberjack jacket. One was wearing terry cloth slippers, and the other was wearing Frye boots.

Clip, Clop
They did not stop.
On down the hall

One tall
One small.
Into the office of the "doc."

They had made up their minds
To buy new clothes and shoes
They had the "blues"
They needed new shoes.

"Dr. Sung,"
	they both did say
"Can we go shopping
	for new clothes today?"

"Girls,
There is no way
That I will let you shop
Until you drop.
But, you have some money
	In your account.
It is not a great amount.
I will send Nurse Melissa
To look.
She will bring you back
	Some slacks
	And a sweater.
Does that make you feel
	Much better?"

"Gosh, Dr. Sung,"
They did both reply,
"You are a most
	splendiferous guy.
You give us such superb advice

And you say it, oh, so nice
That we cannot take offense
You totally, totally make good sense."

Eileen then said:
 "We are not dead!
  You told us we must eat
I repeat:
  You told us we must eat.
We must gain some weight.
That must be our fate."

She continued:
 "I would like a sweater of red
  That slips easily over my head.
  Lucy would like a sweater of blue
  She is a French lady through and through."

Lucy piped up and said:
 "I must confess
  Our hair is a mess
  That is a problem
   We must address."

 Dr. Sung replied with twinkling eyes
 "Girls, I must admit
  that you surprise me.
  I see that you both seem more well off
  In fact, you seem a little 'buff.'
  So we will address the way you look,
  And get you up to snuff.
  For now, that will be quite enough."

 Eileen and Lucy gave a shout of glee
 They jumped up and down

They twirled around
"Oh, look at me. . . ."

BANG, BANG
KNOCK, KNOCK.

"Who is it?" said Dr. Sung.

"It's me," said Nurse Melissa, as she poked her head into the office. "I've come to take the girls to the lounge to see *Star Trek*. It will be on in a few minutes, and I thought they might like to straighten up a bit before we go. I would like to introduce them to the others in the lounge."

"That is a great idea, Melissa. Goodbye girls. Go with Melissa. You both need to get out and about—meet new people. Eileen, you will especially love *Star Trek*. Do you remember seeing it the last several nights, late in the evening before you went to sleep?"

"I vaguely remember a Vulcan named Mr. Spock. He had big ears. They were very elegant," said Eileen, who was searching her mind for a memory of the evenings she supposedly had spent watching this show.

"He is logical, and I think that both of you could do with some logical thinking." continued Dr. Sung. "Hurry up. You don't want to miss the beginning. I will send Melissa to buy you some clothes, and before dinner we will try to make you more presentable.

"Oh, by the way, Eileen," said Dr. Sung as she headed for the door, "your mother and brother are in San Francisco, and would like to see you. I think it would be a good idea for you to see them. You have been holed up here for a week and have talked to no one but me, Lucy, and Nurse Melissa. I think you need to start socializing."

"My goodness, has it been a whole week? But you know that I'm in hiding!" replied Eileen with a worried tone.

"I know you have been in hiding. But that time is past, and you need to proceed with your new life. You need to make a public appearance now and again. *Star Trek* and seeing your family is a good beginning. Lucy also needs to get out more. She needs company as much as you do.

"Hurry up, girls! The show will be starting in a few minutes," said Melissa.

Everyone stared at them. A new face always evoked this response.

37

Respectability

ΕILEEN SAT ON THE EDGE OF HER BED IN HER DARKENED ROOM, the shades drawn to keep out the light. She was pondering life in general and her life in particular. *Where, oh where,* she wondered, fretting as was usual with her lately, *do I go from here? Life is so different since I got into the hospital. I certainly don't want to spend my life batting my head against a padded wall in a padded cell. It does not, however, seem too likely that I can be respectable like Ingrid. When God passed out respectability genes, he passed me by!*

"Hey, Eileen," came Lucy's soft voice. She had just popped into their room as Eileen was pondering her dilemma. Her mascara was running down her cheeks.

So what! thought Eileen. *At least she cares enough about herself to try to apply mascara.* At the best of times this seemingly innocuous ritual caused Eileen tons of trouble. Either there was too much, or there was too little on her lashes; and sometimes it would run down her face. *Maybe I should try to learn to apply false eyelashes. They always look so pretty. But I am concerned that I will get glue on my real lashes, and then when I try to get it off my lashes, I will pull out my real lashes. Men always seem to have such pretty ones. It doesn't seem fair.*

Lucy invaded Eileen's space once again. "Guess what, Eileen! Dr. Sung said that he will be sending me to a clinic outside of Paris. He thinks that it will be good for me to be around stylish clothes and a cultured environment. He also said that he will probably send you back to live with your mother in Virginia. The thought must horrify her. I know that my parents are nearly hysterical. Well, it serves them right! If they had raised us better, maybe this would not have happened."

"Gosh, Lucy!" said Eileen as she shook her head back and forth. She had been lost in her thoughts about the intricacies of her Maker's mind. This was a preoccupation with her lately, pondering the imponderable. "Dr. Sung said that the chemicals in my medication mix with the chemicals in my brain and hopefully produce 'normalcy.'"

"Wow, Eileen, you mean that we can become 'normal' again? I hope I'll become beautiful again, too." Lucy was even more vain than Eileen. She was a lot like Ingrid in that respect.

"I think we're too fat to be considered beautiful, Lucy," replied Eileen with sorrow in her voice and a small tear in her right eye.

"Surely you remember Dr. Sung saying that you and I have got to eat more and gain some weight or die. We agreed that we were not quite ready to pass over into the great beyond," said Lucy, who was worried about the health of the two of them.

DING, DONG
DING, DONG

The hall clock had just chimed 6:00 P.M.

It was time for *Star Trek* to begin. Both ladies perked up. It was time to see Mr. Spock, the Vulcan with the lovely ears, which to the two of them indicated intelligence and rationality, both qualities that fascinated and intrigued them.

Dr. Sung strolled into their room.

"Come on, girls. Your show is on. Tonight is the show called 'The Trouble With Tribbles.' You must see it. It clearly demonstrates clearly that too much of a good thing is too much. Moderation in all things is a good philosophy for the two of you to follow. It does wonders for the digestion."

Clearly, thought Eileen, Dr. Sung has the Asian attitude: a little bit of Zen and a little bit of Zat.

They trailed alongside Dr. Sung, as he headed down the corridor toward the lounge, where everyone was gathered to watch *Star Trek*. It was the only time he could get the two of them to interact with the group.

An hour later, they were back in their room. The light was out when into Eileen's head popped a philosophical poem about

Respectability

Traveling through the sky
Oh, how I love to fly
When the sky is black
It is night
And
The coffee cup is hot
In it there is a shot
Of brandy.
This atmosphere will be the
Death of me.

Radioactivity
Is free
It is in the air
It is everywhere. I am there.

The coffee that
"they" serve
Bolsters up my nerve.
Have you ever thought—
　　　Ever?
About the weather?
And how cold the air
　　　Is outside
As you take this
　　　Mysterious
　　　Magic carpet ride?
Through the air
At night?
Not light!

One hour later the poem was finished.
Eileen was proud of accomplishing something.
Eileen was tired.
Eileen retired
To her bed for the night.
Tomorrow she would get up
And continue the fight.

CLICK! CLICK!
Out went the light!

38

In a Quandary

ILEEN WAS IN A QUANDARY. SHE HAD NOT SEEN ANY VISITORS IN the last week and a half. People were way too demanding and confusing for her. "Oh dear! What shall I do?" she asked Dr. Sung. "Oh dear! My mother and my brother! What shall I do? You said I should see them because they are worried about me. For that matter, I'm worried about me and also about Lucy."

Dr. Sung replied, "Eileen! Guess what! Your mother brought you some nice clothes from your apartment."

"Gee, Dr. Sung! Would you find out what she brought. You know that I'm finicky about what I wear," said Eileen with a small flicker of interest.

"You must judge for yourself as to whether or not you like what she chose, but you must see her in order to determine that. I did see her unfold a lovely pair of rose-colored slacks. I'm sure you'll be happy to see them. They look quite smashing; and if you do not like them, I will send Nurse Melissa with her to pick out something that appeals to you in your role of the new self."

"My *new* self? What do you mean, Dr. Sung? I thought I was my *same* self," replied a confused Eileen.

"Oh no! Since the medication has taken effect, you are like a new woman. You do not scream so much, and you have been chatting with the other patients here." Dr. Sung spoke with the authority that came with years of dealing with disturbed individuals.

"You mean that I've been sociable?" questioned Eileen, who actually was not too aware of what she had been doing or saying. It required way too much concentration to be aware of what she had been doing. She felt as if she was drifting.

"Dr. Sung," she said. She had just become aware of a new thought. "Where is Lucy? Her bed has not been slept in. I have missed her. Is she okay?"

"Unfortunately, Eileen, Lucy has taken a turn for the worse. Her husband came to the hospital to tell her that he was divorcing her. She completely flipped. I called her parents in Paris, and they have decided to have her sent to Paris immediately. I think that that is a good idea. She is confused by everything that is happening to her. She has not responded to treatment as well as you have."

"Oh dear," mused Eileen, trying not to let the doctor know how disturbed she was by this news about her new friend, Lucy.

BANG, BANG—
BANG, BANG—
Pounding on the door—

It was Nurse Melissa. "Hi, Eileen. Your mother and brother are in the visitor's lounge, waiting to see you. Why don't you come with me? They are anxious to see you."

Melissa gently guided Eileen away from her bed, away from her room, down the corridor, heading toward the visitor's lounge, into the lounge and there at a table sat Charles and Mrs. Gordon. The empty chair was for Eileen.

"Hi, Mom! Hi, Charles! How are you?" asked Eileen who was trying her best to remember her manners.

"Hi, Eileen," replied Charles and Mrs. Gordon. We came to take you home."

"You mean back to my apartment?" she asked. She missed her apartment in the marina and the sound of the foghorns on chilly, foggy mornings.

"No! Sorry to have to tell you this, but Dr. Sung and your doctor with Universal Airlines have decided to send you home to Virginia to try to recover," said Charles, who usually knew how to get through to her.

"Absolutely not! I refuse to leave San Francisco!" yelled Eileen as she jumped out of her chair and pounded on the table with her fists.

"Cool it, Eileen! Either you go home to Virginia with us, or you can go to a mental hospital, if we can find a good one that you can afford."

"Goodness gracious, Eileen! Who is the good-looking man you are talking to?" yelled Princess Olga as she emerged from the kitchenette, clutching a cup of coffee tightly in her right hand. She could not use her left hand because she had suffered a stroke.

Charles was disconcerted by the sight of the crazy old woman who was leering at him. Charles was truly startled by how horrible his sister looked. Her hair was partly red and partly brown, and it was hanging limply down below her chin. She was a mess. She was horribly thin.

Mrs. Gordon, who was never at a loss for words, was also startled by her daughter's appearance. "Eileen, you look terrible. Here! I brought you a suitcase full of clothes. And I must arrange for you to have your hair fixed before you head home with Charles and me."

"No! No!" yelled Eileen, who was thoroughly frightened at the prospect of leaving the sixteenth floor. She felt protected there. Her face turned totally white as the blood fell to her feet.

All of a sudden . . .

"I'm going to faint. I feel the ground shaking!" yelled Eileen.

"Holy shit! It's an earthquake—at least a tremor," yelled Charles, who also had turned as white as the proverbial sheet.

Princess Olga tottered towards them, the coffee spilling over the side of the cup onto Charles's new shirt.

"My goodness!" exclaimed Mrs. Gordon. "How interesting. It seems as though a giant snake is undulating under our feet." As she was saying this, the pictures were shaking back and forth on the walls. The patients were all yelling. This provided them with the perfect opportunity to yell at the top of their lungs without anyone thinking they were over-reacting.

Then . . . utter silence . . . utter stillness. . . .

"It is over," Dr. Sung said to everyone in the lounge. "Everything is fine. Calm down and go on watching *Jeopardy*. It is a good show for improving your minds."

All faces, which had turned to him like flowers to the sun, relaxed, and as a group they turned back to watching the TV, watching Jeopardy.

Eileen flopped into her chair, thankful to sit down. She still felt dizzy, even though there was no longer the imminent threat of a total collapse of the hospital in a cloud of dust, crushing everyone as it descended, falling to the ground.

Goodness! thought Eileen, secure in the knowledge that no one could any longer read her thoughts, thankful that no one knew what a coward she was. This same thought had occurred to everyone in the room—patients, employees, and visitors. Even though earthquakes were common in the bay area, they still provoked fear in the breasts of anybody with good sense.

"I am thirsty," said Eileen softly. She was not screaming . . .

Oh, dear
I need a beer

Which I do not drink
I think.
The slacks are a
    Gorgeous hue
    Of pink
I think
What is everything
    All about
I am so confused
    I could shout
    Let me out!
My fear of heights
    Has been compounded
By the 16th floor
    Where
    I have been
        Impounded
For confusion
    Of the mind,
Which is being treated
    By
Medication and the
Talk therapy.

Oh, Wow!
A cow!
Trying to jump
    Over the moon
It will crash to earth
    Real soon
Where the flowers bloom
As the airplanes zoom
Across the sky

They fly.

Across the sky
They fly!
Silver tubes
Carrying boobs—
Both passengers and crew

As she thought about this new thought she zoned out.

"Eileen—Eileen, are you okay?" yelled Charles who was surprised by this new side to Eileen. "Come back!" he said again and again, shaking her back and forth.

"Sorry," said Eileen as she returned to where she was, or thought she was. "Sorry, Charles, I was just thinking."

"Just quit thinking for the time being. Too much thinking is bad for one, especially for you while you are trying to get sane again. I know you need to think, just not for the time being. Wait until you get home," said Charles, who was trying to keep her quiet.

"Home," mused Eileen. "I guess I'm leaving my home in San Francisco for my home in Virginia."

"Lights out, lights out!" boomed the guard's voice as he marched through the psychiatric ward.

"Okay, Eileen, we must leave now but do think about what you would like to wear for your plane trip home on Friday," said Mrs. Gordon, who like her daughter thought that no matter what, one should be well-dressed.

The guard was herding visitors out of the lounge, out the door, locking it behind the last visitor.

CLICK . . .

Eileen was alone. . . .

39

Going Home

WELL, EILEEN, THIS IS IT. YOU'RE GOING HOME. ISN'T THAT EX-citing? Your mother is waiting in the lounge, and she will go on the flight with you." Dr. Sung was being cheerful so as to make Eileen feel more at ease. It was the end of his shift, he was tired and hungry, and he, at least, was glad to be going to his home. Nevertheless, he felt it to be his duty as a doctor to help his patients feel hope, and he offered them as much encouragement as he could.

"Dr. Sung, I am afraid to leave. I'm not sure what to do next," wailed Eileen, who was scared to her bone marrow. She had noticeably quieted down after two weeks of peace and relative quiet and taking her Mellaril. Two big tears wandered down her cheeks.

"Just take your medication, and contact a new doctor as soon as possible after you get home to Virginia. I told your mother to call Dr. Roger Foley, who practices psychiatry in Richmond. He used to be a missionary, and he is now outstanding in the field of mental health, particularly in the field of schizophrenia. If you are unable to see him for some reason, he will be able to recommend a good doctor in the Washington area. But no matter what, you must see a doctor and you must— I repeat, *must*—take your pills."

Eileen, who was standing beside him, shivering in her flimsy hospital gown, gave a small gulp, and said, "Sure thing, Dr. Sung. Do you think I can go back to flying soon? I miss flying."

Dr. Sung realized that she was upset, and he answered her question by saying, "I have requested a three-month medical leave of absence for you, and your supervisor has agreed to work with you. So try to calm down and think positively."

"Oh dear, I am so nervous," said Eileen to the room in general, as Dr. Sung had just walked out of her room and out of her life. "Oh dear, life is so perplexing at times," she said as she reached into her little closet to find something to wear for her flight home. It was early afternoon, and the sky outside her barred windows was gray and gloomy.

The fog had drifted up from the San Francisco Bay, and its gloomy appearance suited her equally gray mood. Her flight home was scheduled to depart at 8:00 P.M. She had a lot to do and little time in which to do it. "Oh dear, what shall I wear?"

She held up her rose wool slacks, but decided that they were too casual for a dinner flight late in the evening. She then tried on her long blue and green wool dress with a bolero jacket. She had made it the previous November, and she thought it made her look smart. It was sleeveless and had a crew neckline. The jacket had wrist-length sleeves. She wore her brown and gold leather butterfly pin perched on her left shoulder, as she carried her brown leather Hobo bag with a brown and gold butterfly painted on it slung over her right shoulder. With it she was wearing her matching platform shoes, which added three inches to her height. Her hair was a mess, but it would just have to do until she found a new stylist. Right now, that was not overly important to her.

After agonizing for a half hour about her appearance and packing her few belongings into her little suitcase, she gathered up her nerve and her wits, and she marched into the lounge.

"Hi, Mom," she said as Mrs. Gordon approached her bedraggled daughter. "Well, Eileen, you look quite smart, except for your hair, and you also look too skinny. Dr. Sung said you need to gain at least twenty pounds. Fortunately for you, I'm a good cook. Come on, the cab is waiting to take us to the airport." As she said this, she grabbed Eileen by the arm, and Robert, the orderly, grabbed Eileen by the other arm. They propelled her past the locked and barred door and into the waiting elevator. It started its rapid descent to the ground floor.

Eileen was nervous and would have bolted, but the orderly and her mother had her firmly trapped between them. Finally the elevator stopped, and the door opened. She was herded onto the street and into the nearby cab. She was seated between Robert and Mrs. Gordon. The ride to the airport

began . . .

Began . . .

Began . . .

It was 5:00 P.M. as they approached San Francisco International Airport. Eileen was extremely agitated. It had been a lifetime ago that she had been standing on the Golden Gate Bridge at night, when the cops picked her up and drove her to the hospital. She wondered about her apartment and felt sad that she would never see it again. On the bright side, though, she had not been hearing the voices that had so tormented her; although, in all honesty, she missed her conversations with Wahu.

The cab came to a screeching halt in front of the terminal, and the three of them stepped onto the sidewalk in front of the terminal, where Robert dropped her arm, which was immediately grabbed by Maria Slocum, her supervisor who appeared out of nowhere. No escape!

"Hi, Eileen," said her supervisor, a young woman no older than herself. "Come on. We'll get a quick cup of coffee and catch you up on what is transpiring." As she was saying this, they entered the Crab Pot, a small and nice restaurant in the terminal. It specialized in crab soup. The three of them sat down for a quick drink, an appetizer, and their chat.

"Eileen," said Maria, "you will have a three-month leave of absence, and you're being transferred to Universal's base in Washington, DC. After you return to work, you will fly out of there for at least six months because your doctors think that that is best for all concerned. If this is not acceptable to you, then we will terminate you. The choice is yours."

Goodness, thought Eileen, who was stupefied by all that was going on in her life. *I guess I will have to go along with this plan, because I don't want to quit flying. It is the only thing that I've ever wanted to do.*

Their drinks arrived, accompanied by a cheese dip and crackers.

"Come on, Eileen. Eat up!" ordered Maria, who continued with her instructions about the direction that Eileen's life was about to take. "You also have to gain at least twenty pounds before you can go back to work. Chant after me . . .

> Eating, yes, eating is good for the soul.
> It helps you live so you can grow old.
> It perks up the bones, the blood and the guts,
> You need to eat,
> No ifs, ands, or buts.

> The doctor agreed and your mother concurred
> That to eat is to live
> Good health it can give.
> To the alternative it is preferred.

> It makes your nails longer
> It makes your hair stronger.
> We all realize the society
> Does not help

A young lady
Take good care of herself.

Besides it is fun to fill yourself up.
Just do not eat more than your stomach can store.
Because that leads to fat, and we all know
That that is to be avoided
No matter the reason
No matter the season
Fat in the airlines is not so pleasing.
Moderation in all things. As we all know
Eating will help you grow.
Matter evolves from condition to condition
It acquires mass and it takes up space.

It gives you an edge in the evolutionary race—
A theory—quite popular—among the herd
Although we know that you were created by God.
Many would disagree, but we do not care.
We think what we want, and we learn to share.

So, eat up now. Enjoy your crackers and dip.
When you get on the plane, there will be dinner to eat.
Which will add to your hips.

As Maria finished talking to Eileen, she picked up her coffee cup
and took a dainty sip. Eileen followed suit. It seemed to Eileen that she
would have to be careful about what she did and said, and it seemed appropriate to do what "normal" people did.

"Come on, Eileen!" said Maria and Mrs. Gordon, "It's time to catch
your plane for home." As they said this, each one grabbed an arm and
began pulling her onto the concourse and through the terminal to the
airplane.

It was time to go home.

40

To Take a Walk

LAVA, MOLTEN LAVA . . . GLOWING
Lava, molten lava . . . flowing
Down the hill,
The yuckiest swill.
The lava, molten lava . . . flowing around,
The lava, molten lava . . . covering the ground.
Darkening everything in sight.
Darkening the night . . .
Filling Creation's heart with fright.

Madame Pele, with her flaming hair,
And Wahu , her pooch, who was there to mooch
    A bone or two.
They were impossible to scare.

Yet the molten rock gave the Earth
    Quite a shock.

Pele's dress of gleaming fire
Swept upward, ever higher . . .
    Higher, ever higher.

"Oh, Wahu," she intoned
"Where have you left your bone?
I gave it to you, you know,
Because I truly,
    Truly,
      Love you so!

So, let us go
To the fire pits of Mt. Kilauea.
It is on the way-ah
To the Land Above.
Please do not shove!
God has put me in my place.
I am in total disgrace.
Illusions of grandeur took over me.
But, I am not He,
Nor can ever be."
Said Pele with her flaming tresses,
And her blazing dresses.

Wahu, he prances,
    Perchances
He will see me!
Sitting quietly by the sea
    At night, no light!

While the water laps along the shore
While the waves in the distance roar.
The ships go out to sea ...
The ships go out to see ...

Still the molten lava grumbles
Still the molten lava mumbles
As down the mountainside it stumbles.
It oozes—tearing down the trees
It oozes—bringing the kahunas to their knees.

They surely know that their gods
Are constructs of myth and lore
Created in the days of yore.

While the lava, flowing lava
Spreading o'er the Earth
While the Sea gives birth
To the mountains and the islands
In the middle of the ocean ...
           Swaying, swaying motion.

Madame Pele was somewhat perplexed
As her muscles were flexed.
She was eager to take a walk
On this rock in the middle of the Pacific ...
The terrific Pacific.
Pele looked down—
A piece of flame.
To waste precious fire
Is a shame.

Wahu continued on his jaunts
Across the mountain tops—
           His haunts.

He carried the bone between his teeth.
He had found it underneath
The log that sat upon the mountaintop . . .
    Sitting there . . .
    Not a care . . .
    Sitting there.

Wahu is white with circles of black
Around his eyes and on his back
The pads of his feet are pink
As into the lava they sink.

I sat! Waves lapping on the shore.
Was there more of Pele and Wahu
Drifting through my mind?
I was blind with fear
    Of delusions so near.
    Of illusions so near.

The lava, up into the air it shot!
It was hot!
It tore off the mountain top.
Throughout the volcanic evening,
Among the rocks and trees they went weaving.
Pele and Wahu continued to walk.
He would bark and she would talk. . . .

"Goodness, gracious," said Eileen as she sat straight up in her bed, sweat pouring down her face and back, her heart beating frantically. "What was that ?" she screamed.

Muffy Kay, her cousin was yelling at her, "Wake up, Eileen! You were dreaming! It's a good thing that I am here. Your mother tells me that you've fallen off the deep end. So, I'm just the right person to be with you right now."

"Oh, Muffy Kay! I'm so glad that you're here. Now I don't need to be afraid."

"It was just a dream, Eileen, just a dream. Come on and get dressed. Your mother has made your favorite dish of potatoes, sausage, and onions. It's not yet dark, and we should go for a walk. Do you realize that you have been in bed for three days now. Come on, time to move. Let's go out for a walk before dinner. We can admire the birds and flowers and the evening breeze." Muffy Kay was trying to cheer Eileen, but she was horrified by her cousin's terrible appearance. Eileen was anorexic, just a skeleton. "Eileen, why did you lose so much weight?"

"I thought I was fat," was the plaintiff refrain. "It's bad enough to be short, but to be fat also is too much to bear."

At that moment, Mrs. Gordon's white cocker spaniel, Taffy, peeped his head into the room. He had not seen Eileen in about ten years. She seemed different to him—not just her appearance, but something deep inside was gone. *Oh, well,* he thought, *she is young and can fill the empty space.*

"Muffy Kay, how did you ever recover from your depression when you tried to commit suicide and almost succeeded? Everything seems hopeless to me, and I don't know how to pull myself together."

"Eileen, stop that! You're just indulging in self-pity. I never dreamed that I would hear you say 'I give up.' Come on! Let's eat first and then go for a walk. You need some food, some fresh air, and exercise."

Eileen slowly crawled out of bed. It was way too much effort to co-ordinate an outfit, so she pulled her black jazz pants and black sweatshirt out of her suitcase, not yet unpacked.

"Eileen, don't you think that solid black is a little somber for the middle of June in Virginia?"

"Sorry, Muffy Kay. It's so easy to pull together a look by concentrating on just black. It will go anywhere in the world," replied Eileen with just a tad of enthusiasm.

Muffy Kay was a tall, slinky blonde who favored earth tones, and in particular she liked cream-colored and white clothes. At this moment she was wearing a while silk shirtwaist dress with huge pastel flowers sprinkled over it. Eileen experienced a twinge of envy while admiring the suave appearance of her cousin. She and Muffy Kay had spent much of their misbegotten youth going to parties together. In general, they had had a rip-roaring good time. Occasionally, they had given a thought to homework and good grades.

Muffy Kay and Eileen had a lot in common, but their attitude about men and marriage was completely different. Muffy Kay thought that a respectable woman needed to be married, especially if the victim had money. So far, she had hit pay dirt twice, but both times she had gotten a divorce. She also had been left with little money and two sons, whom she adored.

Eileen's father had completely pounded into her brain that she be able to take care of herself and never count on a man. *Which way is best?* she wondered as she and Muffy Kay headed for the dining room for dinner.

Mrs. Gordon was celebrating Eileen's return, and had set up the dining table with a floral centerpiece flanked by Eileen's two antique brass dragon candlesticks. They were holding pink candles.

Taffy was wagging his tail, short though it was. He was hoping for a piece of sausage. He had lived with Mrs. Gordon for ten years and was thankful that she was a good cook. Mrs. Roberts, Eileen's maternal grandmother, was also there. She was so thankful for her granddaughter's safe return that she insisted everyone observe a moment of silence while she said grace. She was a spiffy dresser, and for the evening had made a black silk pantsuit with a white satin blouse. She knew this gorgeous outfit would cheer up Eileen, who was normally obsessed with clothes.

Taffy gave a small bark of glee as Mrs. Roberts slipped him a piece of sausage—just the right size for a small dog.

Eileen looked around at the candlelit room, which was firmly entrenched in her thoughts, and memories of past dinners flooded her

mind . . . the dining room table, the cane-seated chairs, the sideboard
with Mrs. Gordon's collection of Victorian silver plate. It had forever
been like this . . . CLICK . . . something clicked . . .

CLICK, CLICK, CLICK . . .

Eileen's brain
Had been under a tremendous strain
That was plain.
Something clicked . . .
CLICK, CLICK, CLICK
Her brain was tricked
Into thoughts of long ago.
When time was slow, long ago.

Something went CLACK
CLACK, CLACK, CLACK

No turning back
Her bridges were burnt.
New habits to be learnt
As she proceeded along her way
Every day.

There sat her cousin with the golden hair
Leaning back in the cane-seated chair
Surveying the scene, as though
She was a queen, never mean.

Something went CLACK, CLACK, CLACK!
The doctors cut her no slack!
She knew that she must do
Whatever was in accord
With the dictates of the Lord.
MUNCH, MUNCH, MUNCH

CRUNCH, CRUNCH, CRUNCH
The four ladies ate their lunch.
Or was it dinner?
No matter, it was a winner.
Little potatoes swimming there
In between the sausage and onions
The ladies were glad they had no bunions
A glass of champagne in a sparkling glass
To cheer the heart of any lass
Emptied the mind of anything dark
Turned the dinner into a lark.

41

The Electric Zone

*T*HE FLOWERS THAT BLOOM IN THE SPRING
   Tra La
Give promise of merry sunshine
As merrily they dance and they sing
   Tra La
We welcome the flowers of Spring
   Tra La. . . .
The song kept on and on and on. . . .

Eileen slowly made her way up Connecticut Avenue, the sun shining down on the earth with all of its might. She thought to herself, *Dammit! I love Gilbert and Sullivan, but I wish another song would occur to me. This one's been pounding through my brain for the last two hours. Please, brain, couldn't we have something by the Rolling Stones? Perhaps, "Get Off of My Cloud?"*

The traffic was whizzing by: horns honking, bicyclists weaving through the traffic, hurtling up and down the street, irritating the taxi cab drivers who thought the streets were only for themselves. "Hey, lady, look where you're going!" screamed the raucous voice of one of these drivers, who had just made a valiant effort not to hit her as she stepped into the traffic without looking in either direction while the light was still red. *Oh dear,* she thought, *I need to concentrate on what I'm doing so as not to get killed.*

She had decided to follow Muffy Kay's advice from the previous night.

"Eileen, I have discovered over the years since I tried to kill myself that the only way in which I can function is to take one day at a time. In fact, a whole day is too long to contemplate, so I actually go for five minutes at a time. Why don't you try this way?"

Yes, thought Eileen, *this is the way for me to function also. But right now I really need something to eat and some coffee.* As she thought this, she saw her reflection in the plate glass window of a shop named Betsey Fisher. *I think I will go in and see if they have a new outfit that would look good on me. That would cheer me up considerably. It always has in the past, and I'm sure that it would help my morale now to have a gorgeous new dress.* With that thought in mind, she walked to the door and pressed the doorbell, waiting for a saleslady to open the door.

At last the door opened and in she stepped into a boutique, and a lovely one at that. Her spirits lifted as she gazed around the store. There were racks of beautiful dresses and blouses and designer blue jeans. There was even a section of beautiful platform shoes that she especially liked, as they made her look taller. Her attention was attracted to one particular pair that had a wide white band over the instep and a large yellow daisy attached to it. To make matters better, they were on sale. As she contemplated buying them, she thought that she needed to save her money because she was on a medical leave of absence and had only a limited amount of money in her bank account.

"Good morning," chirped the young saleslady. "May I help you in any way?" Eileen was impressed by the outfit the saleslady was wearing—skintight jeans and an embroidered white cotton blouse from Mexico. She had on large gold hoop earrings and black stiletto heels. *Oh dear, compared to her I look so bedraggled.* At that moment Gilbert and Sullivan disappeared from her thoughts, replaced by . . .

Ho Ho!
You are falling
Rang the new song
New to her brain
As she was falling
She heard the refrain . . .

"To faint or not to faint?
How quaint!
Use some restraint!"

As she was lying on the floor, she realized that she needed to breathe in and then breathe out. She continued doing the breathing until her brain quieted down and she was able to raise her head. She realized that she had started to remember about her life with Lee. She was convinced that he had been sent by the Devil to taunt her because she was fickle.

She never intended to be fickle, but when the unfickle genes had been passed out, they bypassed her. She knew that Lee was sent to punish her.

Slowly, Eileen raised her head and looked into the eyes of the young saleslady, who had a glass of water in her hand. "Here, have a drink. Are you okay?" It was clear that she was not used to people fainting in front of her.

"Thank you so much for the water. I'm better now, I but think I will leave for the time being and go outdoors to get some fresh air. That and the sunshine should make me feel better." As Eileen said this, she slowly stood up. *Hallelujah!* She was no longer dizzy, and she no longer was seeing stars. She slowly headed for the door. She stepped out into the busy street, where a spring breeze was blowing, and the sky was blue with fluffy white and silver clouds sprinkled across it, floating lazily this way and that.

She really needed something to eat and some coffee. She looked around and saw an interesting-looking shop called La Biblioteck. She went in and sat down. She whipped out her cigarettes, lit up, and took a puff. The waiter approached, and she said, "I would like a strong cup of coffee with crème and a large chocolate chip cookie." She was salivating at the thought of these goodies. It was now noon, and she had not eaten anything. Her stomach was growling. She looked around and realized that she was in a café inside of a bookstore. It was packed with people and books. As the waiter came to her table with the coffee and cookie, she said, "This is a really nice place. Maybe the East Coast isn't totally hopeless and backward." She bit into her cookie. Her soul peeped out for just a moment, just long enough to take a sip of the steaming, creamy coffee in the black ceramic mug. "Wow! This is a wonderful cup of coffee."

The waiter thanked her for the compliment and poured a little more into her cup. She sat there quietly, watching the others as they ate or browsed through the books lining the shelves and on the tables spaced throughout the store.

After she had eaten and her stomach had stopped growling, she knew that it was time to go to Dr. Lieberman's for her first appointment.

She pulled out her lipstick—Revlon's Chinaglaze Red—and carefully applied it to her chapped lips. She needed some cosmetic help. Her grandmother had helped her pick out her outfit for the appointment with her new psychiatrist. "Remember, he will form his opinion of you in the first thirty seconds, before you even open your mouth. That's just the way people are. You want to look interesting so that he will decide to take you on as a patient. Never forget the importance of appearance, and don't feel that I'm shallow because I am pointing this out to you. I'm an old woman, and I have learned about appearances and people over my long lifetime." As they shared this moment of insight, they picked out Eileen's clothes. They decided on the turquoise pantsuit with navy blue wooden sandals by Dr. Scholl's. She was also to wear her large silver butterfly pendant on a black silk cord and her large silver hoop earrings.

Oh well! Here goes! As she thought this, she paid her waiter and headed for the sunny, noisy street. She strode purposely up the street until she saw the Janus Theater, which she had been told was just across the street from Dr. Lieberman's office.

I'm here! There's the office. What a beautiful old brick house. And just look at the little garden in front. It even has tulips and pansies and roses sharing the same small plot of land. She walked up the steps and opened the door to the office. She stepped into a quiet, air-conditioned office with a fascinating abstract oil painting hanging on the wall above a black marble fireplace. There sat a little old lady—the secretary—who said, "Are you Miss Gordon? The doctor will be with you in a few minutes. Please have a seat and fill out this form, if you will." She handed Eileen a form and a fountain pen.

Eileen sat down and whipped out her cigarettes. The secretary gave her a disapproving look and said, "Sorry, there's no smoking allowed in this office."

"Oh, okay," said Eileen to the secretary, who introduced herself as Mrs. Stone. She proceeded to complete the form and returned it to Mrs. Stone. She continued to survey her surroundings. There were several large potted plants in the bay window, a large Persian rug of predominately blue and red birds and flowers, two oversized black leather sofas, a glass-topped coffee table with a bowl of jelly beans, two wingback chairs with embroidered upholstery, and Mrs. Stone's desk. Once more her attention was drawn to the large oil painting. It seemed to be about flowers, but she was not certain of that. At any rate it was one of the nicest paintings she had ever seen in all of her travels . . .

THEN . . .

The door opened and out stepped a little old man—
Eileen almost ran
She almost forgot her plan
To get well
But, what the hell! This is way too scary!
BUT. . .
If I want to fly And not to die
I have to stay
Not run away!

"Miss Gordon, so nice to meet you. I am Dr. Lieberman. Please
step into my office . . .
"Why are you here?" he inquired, looking deeply into her eyes . . .
She babbled, unable to stop . . .

"The Electric Zone, the Electric Zone
Of broken memories
Appears quite often as it pleases
It teases and teases
Leaving one to wonder and ponder.

Pondering on and on . . .
About such existential stuff
As "when is when," and
"Enough is enough."

That kind of stuff can be tough
To contemplate until it is late
At night when the moon
Goes cruising—providing light

Late at night considering the whys and wherefores
Of a life filled with strife

Considering the short life of a duck
Who is shot
Out of luck!
His life comes to a quick end
As into the cosmos he does blend

The voices, the voices
Where have they gone, the voices?

Here we are, in the Electric Zone
Please be nice and give this girl a bone
To chew and bite and spit
So as not to have a fit.

The Electric Zone is new to me
But in actuality it has existed
Throughout history
Probably throughout eternity

The Electric Zone is red and blue
And pink and green
And every hue.
The sparks that sparkle in this place
They flash and immobilize
Just like mace.

Don't you see?
This is new to me.

The voices, the voices,
Where have they gone, the voices?"

"Well, Miss Gordon," he said forty-five minutes later, "this has been interesting, and I look forward to seeing you in two weeks. . . .

42

God Is Good

OH, LITTLE DUST MOTE, ON A SUNBEAM YOU FLOAT—
In front of my eyes! Are you really so wise
That you know what my doctor will say
To help me chase the blues away?

"Miss Gordon, you seem depressed
Not only that, but your mind seems stressed!
We need to find you something to do—
New!
To occupy your soul— Something interesting to do.

I suggest that you learn to drive,
And in the process, manage to stay alive.
Driving is interesting and it ought
Help to focus your thought.
I realize, you know, that the blues

Are not humorous, nor are they glamorous.
You should not sit and think about problems.
The best way to solve them is to occupy your mind
With new endeavors of a positive kind.

Besides, you will need to get to the airport
And in the country, that is the only way of transport.
Not only that, but driving is fun!
It is essential that it be done.
So, learn to drive and get a car—
It will get you here and thar . . ."

The office was quiet and peaceful. Eileen loved sitting there with nothing on her mind except for the sunbeam shining through the window and her observation of the dust mote dancing in front of her eyes. The air-conditioning was cool and refreshing on this hot July afternoon. Dr. Lieberman was talking quietly on the phone. "Yes, Dr. O'Brian. I am sorry to hear that Mrs. Santone tried to kill herself again. Right now I have a patient. She is the last one for the day, and after the appointment is finished, I will drive over to the hospital and visit Mrs. Santone in the psychiatric ward. Please tell her that I will be there as soon as possible."

Eileen was quite interested in watching the dust mote. It shimmered in the beam of sunlight that pranced around her, to the left of her, and above Dr. Lieberman's desk. "Thank you for calling me. I must hang up now," said the doctor as he hung up his phone and turned his full attention back to Eileen. "Sorry for the interruption, Miss Gordon. Now we can settle down and get to work."

"No problem! I have just been admiring the sunbeam and the mote of dust above your desk. It seems strange to me that such trivial things seem so important." As she said this, she burst into tears.

"Miss Gordon, please try not to cry. Things will soon get better." As he said this he passed her a box of Kleenex. "You know, it seems to me that in addition to schizophrenia, you are bored and need a challenge.

I have been in touch with Dr. Sung and your supervisor, and we have decided that you need three months to rest and recuperate before you can go back to work. It is our hope that by September you will be able to resume flying. If you do not show sufficient improvement, then we believe that you should no longer fly for Universal."

"Not fly anymore? Why, that's horrible. I will get better, I will, I will . . ." Eileen stopped crying. "What should I do?" she wailed, and she sat up straighter.

"I believe that you will get better, but we have an important problem that must be addressed immediately." said Dr. Lieberman with a stern voice and steady eyes.

"Just tell me what it is, and I will do it. I promise." Eileen was so agitated at the idea of not flying that her mind momentarily stopped flitting around and became focused on solving her problem. Dr. Lieberman was going to tell her what it was. No doubt about it, she had a problem, and he was going to help her to solve it. "Miss Gordon, you must learn to drive by September."

"Learn to drive! You must be nuts. I can't learn to drive. Even the thought scares me."

"Too bad! Then your flying career is over, because it is the only way for you to get to work."

Oh dear! Oh dear! My path is clear. Drive I must. In God I must trust.

"Miss Gordon, why haven't you learned to drive by now? How have you been able to get around all these years?"

"I lived in cities and used public transportation and taxis. I never needed to drive, and I wasn't the least bit interested in learning."

"Well, those days are over. Tomorrow is Friday. I want you to go to the DMV and get your learner's permit, and you must study so that you can pass the written test." He was quite proud of himself for getting her to accept the fact that she would have to learn to drive. That should be a sufficient challenge for a few months. She had already agreed to accept his advice that she needed to live with someone, and that someone would be her mother, at least for the foreseeable future. She had also agreed that she would take her pills for the rest of her life. She could be reasoned with.

"You also know that you must get a car," he continued in his relentless manner. He was giving no quarter.

"That is simply too horrifying to think about."

"Tough! If you want to work, that is your only alternative. Just remember, I am a good doctor. You are paying me a lot to help you, so please accept what I tell you. I have your best interests at heart. I know what I'm doing. Please just trust me and work with me. I know that you will."

"Oh, all right." As she said this, she gave a big sigh and in her mind accepted the inevitable. She needed a car! She needed to find someone to teach her to drive. She had three months in which to accomplish this challenge. By now she had quieted down.

"I have decided to help you accomplish a really stupendous thing. You need some challenges, and you also need to gain some weight. The best way to deal with these problems is to quit smoking. Miss Gordon, I want you to quit smoking."

"Good Lord!" Eileen was even more in shock than when he said that she needed to drive. "I need to smoke. It calms my nerves." The man was relentless, but she knew that she did not want him to get bored with their meetings, so she needed to cooperate. She was once again fidgeting. She needed a cigarette, but he did not allow smoking in his office. "I promise to think about it. Don't you think that learning to drive and quitting smoking at the same time is a little much?"

"No! Right now you need to make a lot of important changes if you are to regain good mental and physical health. You do not want to end up in the hospital again. I have faith in you. Please prove me right in my assessment of you, and please prove right everyone who believes that you can get well."

"Since you put it so nicely, how can I refuse? I will do both—learn to drive and quit smoking." Eileen noticed that she was feeling much better. She passed her pack of cigarettes to Dr. Lieberman. "I guess if I'm going to quit, now is as good a time as any."

Dr. Lieberman smiled in his heart. "Miss Gordon, I am so proud of you, and since our session is nearly over, I would like to suggest that you go to the boutique next door, Toast and Strawberries, and get yourself a pretty dress to celebrate the new you. And remember, if you are ever in really deep trouble, give me a call. For now, however, I think that we will meet every two weeks. Then after three months, we will meet once a month; and once we have you squared away, we will meet every two months. That way you won't have to spend more than you can afford." As he said this, he stood up, and Eileen stood up. She was quite excited. New ways were in the offing. She would learn to drive, quit smoking, buy a car, and buy a new dress.

"Thanks, Doc! This has been a stimulating session." As she said this, she walked out of his office, out of his reception room, and out onto the street. Dr. Lieberman walked outdoors with her. They looked at the blue sky, the green grass, and the rose bush. It was a lovely day, and they had just had a fun hour.

Life was good.

God was Good!

43

Fending Off Feelings in Boxes without Tops

*H*ELP! HELP!
I need help!
What in the world
    Am I to do with myself?
What in the world
    Am I coming to?

First to go,
    I know
Are my Sacred Cows
From the past and present nows.
Wow! Many Wows!

It was a late July afternoon, and Eileen was sitting in Dr. Lieberman's office. The wind was howling and the rain was pounding against the windows. Because of the afternoon storm, the room was dark. Eileen was trying to concentrate . . . *What is he saying? Oh yes . . . I remember . . .*

"Miss Gordon, your life is a mess. You must change your habits. They are detrimental to your health, not to mention your financial well-being." Dr. Lieberman continued talking to Eileen, who was completely bogged down with trying to concentrate. *What is he talking about in his slow, methodical voice?* She looked at him thoroughly as though that would help her to concentrate. *What is he saying?*

"Yes, indeed, Miss Gordon you do have a choice . . . you must push forward or lapse into the backward mode. You must put your brain to the ultimate test: whether to rest or to go forward bravely into the unknown or whether to drop out and play invalid. You must make the choice." He wanted to get her attention, and he wanted to press home his point, so he pounded on his desk with his fist noisily enough to make Eileen snap out of her reverie and give him her full attention.

"What was I thinking, you want to know. Oh, yes, I was thinking about all of my sacred cows. I must get rid of them, but where shall I put them? I ask myself that question because I know I must get rid of them."

She slowly raised her head and her voice. "I know! They must go into the darkness . . . into the pit that has no bottom." As she said this, she slowly raised herself from her seat and exclaimed in an excited, tremulous voice, "Push! Whoosh! There they go. Now, Dr. Lieberman, they are gone, and I am a totally empty vessel. There is no longer any old thought or belief left in my mind! What a relief! They are gone! I am alone . . . please throw me a bone to chew upon as though it is an old shoe." After saying this, she was exhausted, and she felt cold.

"Yes, quite good, Miss Gordon. Now we can get to work. Do not shirk thinking, even at home."

"Homework? You mean I have to think at home, too?" She was completely overwhelmed with all that he expected of her. The alternative, however, was the hospital and not being able to fly, which was the love of her life.

"Yes, you have to think about everything that you do—everything and in every way! And now for your first assignment . . . now think, Miss Gordon, *what do you want to do?*"

"What do you mean . . . what do I want to do? You must be crazy! You're supposed to tell me what to do," shrieked Eileen as she twisted her hair around her fingers. She was fidgeting in her chair. She was tired, but there was something so cool about her new doctor that she was made somewhat more cheerful.

Dr. Lieberman let her shriek for a moment, and then he said quietly, "Miss Gordon, here is a piece of advice that will stand you in good stead in the future . . . remember that no one will let you out of the hospital until you stop screaming. So in the future, pussyfoot around on tiptoe."

"Wow, Dr. Lieberman! That is such cool advice!" As she said this, she stopped screaming and demurely started to discuss the relative merits of women wearing pants and trousers instead of dresses and skirts. "What do you think," she asked him in her most well modulated and dulcet tones, "is it ladylike to wear slacks?"

"What do you think?" he replied with a glint of laughter in his eye! He always found it interesting to discuss things with Eileen. They certainly enjoyed each other's company. He leaned back in his chair, crossed his hands, and said in his deep, melodic voice, "Well, Miss Gordon, what do you think?"

"You know, Dr. Lieberman, you are the first man outside of my family who has ever thought that I could think, much less have an opinion. Thank you—thank you—thank you. From the bottom of my heart I say, thank you!"

"You are most welcome! I must say Miss Gordon, I like your orange-red hair. That shade of hair is most becoming to someone with your coloring and temperament. Oh goodness, our time together is up." As he said this, he rose from his chair, walked over to Eileen, and took her hand, helping her to rise from her chair. He walked to the door and out onto the street with her.

They both drew in a deep breath and looked at the sky. They saw the storm clouds receding to the north. They were now in a box that had a top; or perhaps they were in a sphere . . . going where? Not a care!

"So long! I will see you in a couple of weeks." As she said this, she started walking down the brick-paved sidewalk, heading to Toast and Strawberries, one of her favorite boutiques.

There was Rosemary, the owner, standing in the doorway. She had a beautiful black Afro.

Her store was dark, like a cave with little jewels lying here and there . . . twinkling and sparkling. They seemed to say "hello" to whoever would look or listen . . .

"Hi," she said
"Hi, Eileen! How you been?"

"Fine," Eileen exclaimed
To this hard-working dame.

"See you have been
To your Doc's.
Now it is time
To shop.

In this corner
Of the store
There are many
Many more
Things of interest
To a discerning being
Who is capable of seeing.

Here is what
There is to see!
Tee, Hee!"

"Gee, Rosemary
This necklace is a gem
Capable of raising
One's consciousness
To rational-ness.
Don't you think
That it looks good
On me?
Just curious, don't you see?
Tee Hee!"

44

Welcome Back, Eileen

*B*ACK TO WORK, BACK TO WORK—
Golly, I am driving to work. What a horrendous three months this has been, but finally I am on the way to the airport and my first trip in months and months and months.

As she thought about her life lately, she passed the rock quarry on Route 29, driving in her new purple AMC Gremlin. *Perhaps I should drive through the guard rail and go plummeting into the pit that's been dug out so deep over the years. But no, I mustn't think like that. Everyone trusts me to take my trip today. Oh dear, I'm so nervous. Driving is so scary, but it's my only way to get to work now that I live out in the boondocks.*

Eileen continued on to Dulles International Airport, where she was going to go on her first trip since before Easter and since she had been hospitalized in San Francisco. Finally she pulled into the employee parking lot. *I did it. I got to the airport. Now comes the really hard part: actually working the trip.*

She straightened her shoulders and started across the taxiway, heading for the inflight office. She was carrying her black Samsonite suitcase in which she had packed her new black leather skirt from Toast and Strawberries and her new black boiled wool jacket, which was perfect for walking around in San Francisco.

As she entered the office, she heard a male voice say, "Hi, Eileen. I'm your new supervisor, Jim Boyd. It's so nice to meet you. I'm here to introduce you to your flying partners on your first trip out of DCA."

As he was speaking, Eileen was approached by a tall skinny, frosty blonde. The frosty blonde sauntered up to her and said, "Hi, I'm Lulu Lee Branscombe. We'll be rooming together. I don't drink much, do you? I also expect that you won't bring odd men to our room. Are you okay with that?"

"Why, Lulu Lee, that's perfect. We should get along famously. I'm still recovering from a major nervous breakdown, and my doctor told me that I shouldn't even drink wine for a year or so. Also, he says that men are too confusing for me and that I should avoid them like the plague. I wonder if that's because they are like the rats that spread the plague?"

Meeting someone like herself who was on bad terms with men, Lulu Lee said with pleasure in her voice, "Yes, Eileen, we should get along perfectly. I'm getting a divorce because my husband has been drinking too much, and he has been following me around our house while he shouts at me; not only that, but he's also threatening to shoot me with his hunting rifle. Needless to say, I don't think too highly of men at this time in my life."

She grabbed Eileen's arm and herded her into the briefing room. Eileen was shivering with fear. Now that the time had come to get back to work, she was paralyzed with apprehension . . . *Oh dear, oh dear. . . .*

Three hours later, they were working in first class. It was after 7:00 P.M., and the passengers were guzzling down their cocktails and munching on macadamia nuts by the bagful prior to being served dinner.

Eileen was having a good time. She felt the need for a cigarette, but she had recently quit. Dr. Lieberman was so proud of her, and she knew that he would be disappointed if she started smoking again.

"Eileen, it's time to serve dinner." As she said this, Lulu Lee tossed her head, and her short blonde frosted hair bounced up and down. For once Eileen was flying with someone whose hair was as short as her own. She was aware of how chic they both looked.

"Wow, Eileen, look at the full moon." Lulu Lee grabbed Eileen by the arm and propelled her to the window in the lounge. They both sat down for a brief moment at the empty lounge table and looked out the window. The moon was full and yellow and was hanging in the sky like a basketball. The stars were coming out into the dark night sky, and they were sparkling merrily. The jet engines were quietly humming, soothing the troubled souls of the two stewardesses and making lovely music in their ears.

Eileen was happy and said, "Isn't it wonderful to be in the air, flying through the dark night sky? I was worried that I would never get in the air again."

"Eileen, stick with me. None of us has ever flown with a schizophrenic before. Just stick with me. Everything will work out just fine. Stick with me."

DING, DING . . .

DING, DING . . .

went the call button.

"Lulu Lee, I'll go to that passenger's seat and see what he would like." As she said this, she headed out into the cabin on her way to seat 3A, where Mr. Terryton was sitting. She approached Mr. Terryton, who was white as a ghost. He blustered, "Bring me more champagne. I mean now. Do you hear me, I mean *now*!" As he said this in a loud raucous voice, he lifted his hand that was clutching an empty champagne glass. "More, now!" he yelled. "Hurry up, stewardess."

Eileen was startled and told him that she would take his bread plate away, as it was flooded with the champagne that he had spilled. "I'll be back in a moment," she said in her most soothing voice.

She returned to the galley, and said to Lulu Lee, "He doesn't seem normal. We should keep an eye on him." She picked up the bottle of champagne and headed back to Mr. Terryton's seat. He was slumped over his tray table, and he was still. Eileen was startled and reached over to shake him to let him know that she had returned. She was worried. She shook him again as he did not acknowledge her presence in any manner. She returned to the galley and asked Lulu Lee to help her. "Lulu Lee, come with me. I can't get any response from Mr. Terryton. He's slumped over and won't raise his head. I'm so worried."

They hurried to his seat. He still had not moved. "Mr. Terryton, are you okay?" As they said this, they continued to shake him. No response.

At that moment, Dr. Gamus, a Turkish neurosurgeon, approached the seat. "Out of the way, ladies. Let me handle this." He stepped up to the seat and reached over to check Mr. Terryton's pulse. "We have a problem. One of you contact the captain and tell him that one of the passengers appears to be dead."

"Dead! You must be joking. He can't be dead!" said the two stewardesses in unison. "That would be a catastrophe."

"Just tell the captain, and now!" said Dr. Gamus, as he wrestled the inert body to the floor.

Eileen, who by now was scared witless, dashed to the cockpit. She stood in the cockpit speechless, with her mouth hanging open. "What is it, Eileen," said Captain Bowman. "You look like you've seen a ghost."

"He's dead! He's dead! Mr. Terryton is dead!" yelled Eileen, and she turned around and dashed through the door.

She hurried back to where Dr. Gamus was administering CPR. She was followed by the copilot, Mr. Anderson, who was horrified by what she had said and was going to see for himself what was going on in the cabin.

Mr. Leeds, in seat 4A, was holding onto the salad cart, which had been abandoned by the stewardesses. Mr. Anderson joined Dr. Gamus in administering CPR. Captain Bowman called Lulu Lee and told her to have every one of the crew prepare the cabin for an emergency landing in Denver. Dinner was officially over. Several of the first class passengers were upset because they were not going to be served dessert.

Lulu Lee sat in her jumpseat as they began their descent. Eileen had propped Mr. Terryton in his seat with an oxygen mask strapped over his nose and mouth. Under no circumstances were they going to let it appear as though the man was dead. "Dear Lord, it is bad enough that someone is dead, but I especially wish to pray that we do not crash upon landing." She was terrified to be sitting next to the dead man. She and Lulu Lee had never seen a dead person before.

Down, down, down ... BANG ... BOUNCE. They had safely landed, and were taxiing to the terminal. Lulu Lee made the landing announcement, asking everyone to please remain seated until the paramedics had removed the sick passenger from the airplane.

They stopped at the terminal and waited for the door to be opened. After several moments, the door was opened and the paramedics ran to Mr. Terryton's seat and removed him from the airplane. Then, the rest of the passengers and the crew deplaned. It was the end of an unusual flight, one that both Eileen and Lulu Lee hoped they would never experience again.

Five hours later, they were both settled in their hotel room, eating pizza and watching Gregory Peck and Robert Mitchum in the horror story, *Cape Fear*.

"Wow, Eileen. What a day and what a welcome-back trip this has been," said Lulu Lee as she contemplated whether or not she should call her mother and tell her about the trip.

"Lulu Lee, I'm thrilled to be back to work, even though the trip was way too eventful for me. Dr. Lieberman says that I should avoid being over-stimulated. Besides, we didn't even get to go shopping."

By now, the movie was over and they were both sitting up in their bed, thinking about the events of the day. Mortality seemed most ephemeral, and therefore they were thankful to be alive.

"Do you think that my husband will actually shoot me?" inquired Lulu Lee.

"Probably, so I'd get away as soon as possible. My cousin, Muffy Kay, had the movers take out her possessions while her husband was at work. I think that's what you should do. Drunks with guns are to be avoided at all costs."

It was now late. The moon was shining brightly in the black night sky. They were wondering if Mr. Terryton died because it was a full moon. The town had quieted down. They were exhausted, and they closed their eyes . . . they fell into sleep . . . deep, deep sleep.

45

Several Years Later . . .

$\mathcal{E}$ILEEN WAS STILL WONDERING WHAT SHE WANTED TO DO WITH herself these days. It had been years since she had wanted to do anything other than fly. That was what she had room for in her soul. As she was rocking in her rocking chair in her room one fine spring Sunday morning, Mrs. Roberts, her maternal grandmother, came into her room and said, "Eileen, you must go to church. No self-respecting Virginia lady is an agnostic. You were not raised that way." As she said this, she was waving her white lace handkerchief in front of her sweat-beaded brow.

"Oh, Gran, I'm sorry, but I haven't given any thought about God for years. It would seem that having broken just about every one of the Ten Commandments, I can't imagine why he would want my company." A tear dropped down her cheek.

"Eileen," interrupted her mother who had just entered the room, followed by Taffy, "why don't you put on your new blue and green silk pantsuit? Then the three of us can go to church together. I'm sure people will be surprised at seeing a Southern Baptist at a Presbyterian church, but your grandmother has agreed to do this, if it will only get you to the sanctuary."

"Gee, Mom, I'm not sure it's a good idea. Maybe next week. . . ."

"That's too bad, as coffee hour is being held after the service, and cookies will be served. I myself am taking my wonderful Texas sheet cake, which you love, with walnuts sprinkled liberally on the top of the dark chocolate frosting."

Immediately, Eileen perked up. Chocolate had always had that effect on her.

"Texas sheet cake!" she exclaimed. "Maybe I will go after all."

Mrs. Roberts and Mrs. Gordon both looked relieved. They were relieved. They looked at each other, smiled, then left the room in order to let Eileen dress in peace and quiet and also in order that they could find something appropriate to wear themselves.

After they left the room, Eileen looked into her closet and started pushing clothes along the bar, trying to let something speak to her. Even she knew that when you appeared before the Lord, you dressed for the occasion . . . in your absolutely most powerful attire, not to mention that it had to be the most beautiful that one had. As Eileen had been educated in the fine arts at the College of William and Mary, she had a decided opinion of what constituted "beautiful." Three concepts still lingered in the back of her mind:

1. Do not muddy the color;
2. Form follows function; and
3. Draw. Paint will follow.

As she was leaning toward wearing her new black silk dress with her black leather bolero jacket, she heard the joyous morning songs of the birds floating on the gentle spring breeze, which was drifting through her window. Eileen stopped her senseless activity and listened. *It's been*

*years since I listened to the birds. It reminds me of the old owl who used to
live near Ingrid and me. He was old and wise. It was nice to listen to him. I
hope that someday I will hear an owl hoot again . . .*

The birds all sang, their voices rang
Their trills bouncing off the clouds
Joyful and loud
They were proud.

Their feathers ruffled.
In the bird bath they scuffled.
Who would bathe first?
Who would quench his/her thirst?

The trees swayed in the breeze.
The sap surged upwards
Through their limbs.
Through their limbs
The trees were singing hymns . . .

Several hours later, sitting in church . . .

*Holy Shit-ski, Mama Mia
How did I end up in here-ah,
This place of mis-ter-ee-ah?*

*Here I sit! I guess I fit
Between my ma and a woman
I do not know, so . . .*

*Who is she-ah?
Ah, Mama Mia
An in-tro-duc-tion
If you please.
You must!*

I trust that you know this lady well.
I do not wish to end up
With unwise friends in Hell.
That would be the pits.
Worthy of never-ending fits.

Please, dear God, here I sit!
Help me choose my newest friends.
People who grin and smile in their hearts
In the presence of the One who inspires
Awh! Awe! Aw!
I hope that I may see
Him in the land where one wishes to be.
Ah, Land of Mis-ter-ee-ah.

So thought Eileen, sitting quite still in the pew. It was time to check the flow of the service. She opened her bulletin, and started to read. "Why, I don't see any mention of coffee and cookies," she said to the young lady who was sitting next to her. *My goodness*, thought Eileen, *she is a flower child! How grand! The real ones are hard to find...so...* "Hi, my name is Eileen Gordon. I have just recently—in the last several years— returned to town. I am in confusion, and my mother and grandmother told me that if I would come to church today, there would be cookies and coffee! Why else do you think I came?"

"Oh, my dear, is that the only reason that you came? What a shame! My name is BumbleBee Turner."

"Do not be so high and mighty. By dangling the idea of good food he was able to get me here. So there!"

"Well! I declare! You're not polite like your mother." While saying this, BumbleBee tossed her long brown braid from side to side. Then she went on to say, "Eileen, your hair is a mess. Just look how gorgeous mine is, and its color is natural. I don't color mine. I do not tamper with God's creation, which is me."

270

"The way I see it," growled Eileen who was smarting under the unrelenting criticism from her new friend, BumbleBee, "is that God gives us brains to figure out how to improve on Nature."

"Why, Eileen, to me that seems just a tad sacrilegious."

"Perhaps not improve on Nature, but change it every now and then so that one doesn't get bored," replied Eileen who was happy to have met someone to whom she could talk. "I am so happy to meet you, BumbleBee."

Suddenly, throughout the church thundered the organ . . . the sound of "Great is Thy Faithfulness" permeated the entire sanctuary. The choir and congregation joined their voices to that of the organ. Eileen stood there speechless, enthralled by the lovely, majestic music. She must come again. Maybe next week . . .

> Maybe next week, maybe next week
> I will seek, I will seek!
> EEK!
>
> It puzzles me, It puzzles my brain.
> The old sweet refrain is
> Filling up my brain.
> The old sweet refrain is
> Filling up my brain.

46

Insomniac, So What the Heck . . .

THOUGHTFULLY, EILEEN PUSHED HER HAIR BEHIND HER RIGHT ear, which was sporting a new gold hoop earring. Normally she preferred to wear silver, but she was trying an experiment, trying something new. She understood that it was vitally necessary to shake things up on occasion, just to stay on one's toes . . . just to stay on ones toes . . .

> CLICK, CLICK, CLICK—
> *So quick!*
> *Good Lord, I am sick.*
> *Tell me why before I die.*
> *You sent me two shrinks—*
> *Or was it three?*
> *The best of the bunch*
> *'Cause I needed help*
> *Would be my hunch.*

My brain whirled . . .
Thoughtless
Lawless . . .
Oh, Brain!
Retain good if you would.

Goodness!
The room whirls!
The flower swirls
Inside the flower container
In which it is placed!
Not like me—disgraced!

"Disgraced, Dr. Lieberman!" said Eileen as she slowly returned to the real world, "yes, Dr. Lieberman, I'm in total disgrace."

"You'll get over it" said Dr. Lieberman, as he reached up to the second bookshelf from the top and placed his hand on one of his volumes, which he then proceeded to lay on his desktop. With a small sigh of relief, he once again sat down, leaned back in his chair, and looked thoughtfully at Eileen, who by now was curious about the book and had shut up. "What is the book about, Dr. Lieberman?" she inquired.

"It is about Christianity. You seem to be totally involved in your church now, and I wanted to know if you are truly a Christian," he said as he was leafing through the book.

"But of course I am. That's the way in which I was raised!"

"Yes, true enough, but you need to do more than just utter some mystical words; utterly useless for living a Christian life. If you remember, some time ago you mentioned that you had dumped all of your sacred cows and wanted to reestablish a firm foundation on which to rebuild your new life. So, I must ask you if you really believe in the deity of Christ."

"Of course I do! I absolutely believe in the deity of Christ." As she said this, she pushed her hair behind her left ear.

"Good! You are a Christian. Now you must promise me that you will not get involved in cults." He said this because he realized that Eileen was prone to get involved in situations which were not good for her.

After this intense discussion, both of then sat in silence for a few minutes, listening to the soft whirring sound of the overhead fan as it circulated the air in the room. Eileen looked around the room. Her attention settled on the black leather couch that was placed against the back wall. It looked inviting. "Gee, Dr. Lieberman, why don't we do analysis?"

"Miss Gordon," he replied in his low, melodious voice, "you do not need to delve around in the past. You are having enough trouble dealing with the present."

After saying this, he and Eileen once again became silent, looking at each other, looking at the beautiful Persian rug on the floor, admiring the roses arranged on his desk left there by his new wife. He had been a widower, and after mourning for his dead wife, he had married his college sweetheart, a widow.

The clock on the wall over the mantle above the fireplace slowly ticked away the minutes. Finally, he broke the silence. "Miss Gordon, you say that you are an insomniac. Does that bother you?"

Eileen pondered his question carefully in her mind before she answered. "It would be nice to sleep through the entire night, but that does not seem to be possible for me. Sometimes I stay up all night; and since I can't stand to just lie in bed in the dark, I often get dressed and go to the hospital to the café that is open all night. It's fun just sitting there, drinking coffee, and writing my book."

"Oh, you are writing a book?"

"Yes! Actually I hope to write several books, but for the time being I would like to finish the one I am working on. It is about you," said Eileen with a smile on her face.

"Why, that is both thoughtful and wonderful. I hope that you have made me a sympathetic character." As he said his he glanced at his watch. He was tired. He was well aware of the advancing years, and sometimes his heart felt weak. He felt hungry . . .

He was proud!
He was thrilled!
He had not been bored.
His patient was emerging
    From beneath a cloud.

"No children for you!
Not even one!
Absolutely none!
Other outlets can be had
Or hobbies if you must!
Not rust in the realm
    Of material articles
Made up of particles . . .
Particles that dance and glitter
As throughout Creation they flitter,
Landing on a flower to announce
That men you must renounce.

They do you no good!
No matter if you think they could!
No matter if you think they would!

Please go slow on obtaining new dresses
Which contribute to many financial messes.

You must circle slowly around the truth
Like around a tree with me.
Doing that gives one proof
    Of the One who is here
    Of the One who is there
    Of the One who is everywhere!
Yes, Miss Gordon, I swear that

You should wear black
Wrapped around your body and soul
Now that you are growing old,
And when you feel faint—
How quaint—
Just keep on standing . . .
Look to the floor
Look some more
Hold on to a chair
It is hoped one is there!

But perchance if you should keel over
With luck in a field of clover
Accompanied by a dog named Rover.
Your cat, Scout, is out and about.
He is not fat, but is sleek and trim
With a black spot on his chin.
You could learn a lot from him.
He is your friend, although in truth
Aloof!"

After giving all of this advice to Eileen, he once again glanced at his watch. It was 4:00 P.M. Time to close up for the night and go home. He slowly rose and said, "Miss Gordon, enjoy yourself at Toast and Strawberries. Remember that you do not always have to buy something. It can be fun just to look." He and Eileen shook hands. Although it was a professional relationship between a doctor and his patient, they had come to have love for each other based on a deep mutual respect, but what the heck . . .

"I expect," he said,
"if the truth be said
You would rather not be dead.
So be an insomniac if you must

You do take a nap I trust?
If you have been up all night
Struggling mightily, trying to write."

She left the office....

"Out of sight!" yelled Eileen to the universe and to whoever would listen, as she stepped onto the brick sidewalk. "Out of sight," she said as she stepped into the pedestrian traffic on Connecticut Avenue. "Totally, freaking out of sight!

Totally, freaking out of sight." She disappeared into the crowd surging down the avenue, on her way to the Farragut West metro station.

47

What a Glorious Day!

WHAT A GLORIOUS DAY! THOUGHT EILEEN AS SHE SAUNTERED up Connecticut Avenue. It was a beautiful September morning. The sky was blue, the cars were whizzing by, spitting out their obnoxious fumes.

Everywhere she looked there were the street people, homeless, hanging out in the store fronts, and loitering on the streets begging for handouts. *There*, thought Eileen, *but for the grace of God go I*. As she thought about this, she happened to notice that she was in front of the Mayflower Hotel. She was hungry and decided to go inside to the restaurant and have some breakfast. She passed through the glass doors, walked through the lobby, and entered the restaurant. She sat down and almost immediately was approached by a handsome young waiter, who handed her a menu. She glanced at it and noticed that they were offering fresh strawberries.

The waiter returned and said to her, "What would you like to eat today?"

"I know just what I want. I would like a big bowl of your fresh strawberries and a glass of ice cold, sparkling champagne."

A few minutes later the waiter returned with her strawberries and champagne. He placed her order on the table and said, "I hope you enjoy your breakfast and have a wonderful day."

"Why, thank you. I will, and I hope that your day is wonderful, too."

As she sat there, she wondered what she would discuss with Dr. Lieberman during their session. Thinking back on their previous sessions, she wondered why he said that it was permissible for her to have a glass of champagne or wine—just one a day—whenever the mood struck. Probably because he thought that was better for her than to get mixed up in the illegal drug world. Anyway, she was thankful for this small favor. She sometimes needed to look through the world through a slightly distorted lens.

She took one sip . . . *Great!* then another sip, followed by the strawberries. She would like to have had cream but did not think that cream and champagne were a good combination. They would probably curdle in her stomach.

She finished her repast, took one last look around the elegant dining area, paid the waiter, and left the hotel to continue her journey up Connecticut Avenue. The sun sparkled down from Heaven and the puffy clouds were still skittering through the sky. She was deep in thought, thinking about what she and her doctor would talk about today. Perhaps she would discuss why she had such lousy relationships with men. Was there something wrong with her, or was the problem with men? She continued walking and thinking, no longer mindful of her surroundings. Finally, she arrived at her destination. She walked up the steps leading to the office. She entered and said "hi" to the secretary, who looked up at Eileen's greeting, smiled, and said, "Please have a seat. The doctor is running a few minutes late."

Eileen sat down and surreptitiously looked around the reception area at her fellow patients. They all looked normal in physical appearance, but she could recognize the anxiety in their eyes. She felt the same anxiety in her own eyes.

She picked up a glossy copy of *Vogue* and started skimming through the pages . . . nervously skimming through the pages . . .

How I lamented when I consented
To ever-non-ending therapy
Which helps me to forget Lee?
Which helps me to remember he
Who leads the way from then until today!

Which way will I go?
Do you know which way I will go?
Ho-Ho!

I headed right one September night,
Or was it twilight?
I took the uphill approach
For which I need a coach
Whom I can approach.
Yes indeedy! I need a coach.

That, dear Doc is you,
The Rock!

She sat in the waiting room scene
Reading a magazine!
A glossy, shiny book of style
She read it as she waited for a while.

Then . . . The door showed a crack!
No turning back!
I guess I should return to wearing
Basic black!

I ought, she thought,
To think of how to start the conversation
With my gentlemanly Doc.

"Hi there, Doc! How-de-do!
I have missed you since last we met
And contemplated the History of the Church—
Which you condensed
From the past to the present tense.

Where am I in the flow of time?
How do I make my life rhyme?
The days long ago are forgotten
Mainly because they were rotten.
The memories which have returned
Indicate how I learned to act 'normal'
Indicate how I learned to act 'formal'

Ho, Ho, here I go
Trying to explain "rain"
Is it bottled with an atomizer
To dissipate the scent
Of lilies-of-the-valley?
Which I smelled far away
In the dawn of my days . . .
          In the dawn of my days. . . ."

"I see, Miss Gordon," declared Dr. Lieberman with a slight bowing of his head as he interrupted her reverie, returning her to the more immediate present, "that you have gained some weight. You look quite nice. I must warn you, however, that you do not need to gain anymore, as that is not good either. When you get home tonight, step on your scales, and whatever it says is the weight you should strive to maintain."

"Gosh, Dr. Lieberman," said Eileen, trying to change the subject, "how did I get to be a schizophrenic? Can you explain it to me?" she asked in a tired voice.

"I see you are confused." He indicated to her that he understood her trauma. "That is a good sign that you are continuing to want to fight. Keep in mind that millions of human beings throughout the world and the ages have had disabilities and coped as best they could. As for me, I have a bad heart and must take medication every day, as you also must do. Sometimes I think the answer to living a good long life is to have a serious problem and take good care of it and, by extension, take good care of yourself."

"Gosh, Doc! That is profound. It certainly sounds intriguing. So we need to eat right, get lots of rest, not smoke, exercise, keep one's mind challenged, do a good job at one's work, have meaningful relationships, etc. . . ." She continued, "I guess I have meaningful relationships, except with men. I think they are control freaks. I simply, positively cannot have meaningful relationships with men." As she said this, she was getting disturbed, and her face was turning red, and her breathing was becoming shallow.

"Miss Gordon, you know that you cannot hate half of the human race. You know very well that not all men are bad or mean."

"I know that even the nice ones are compelled to use the intimation of physical force if a woman crosses them. I'm sick of trying to get along with them. I have better things to do with my time and energy, limited as it is. I'm tired of trying to get along with some idiot man."

"Miss Gordon, it is encouraging that you are continuing to show interest in things. I admit that some women need their freedom more than intimacy, and it would seem that you are one of them. You, it would seem, are not the wifely type. You are, however, feminine, and I would encourage you to manifest the basic goodness of true femininity. Have fun."

Wow! thought Eileen as she found herself clinging to the armrests with both arms, with her fists clenched. *Wow! That is thought provoking.*

I must ponder the ramifications of not " hating half of the human race." That could totally transform my life. Oh my God, the hour is done, and I must run. "Thanks, Doc. See you in a couple of months."

As she said this, they both stood, shook hands, and walked to the door. She walked through the door as he held it open for her. She stepped through the reception room out onto the brick sidewalk. The sun still shone brightly and the cloud of puffy white still drifted across the sky, which was striped with the jet streams of the departing and arriving airplanes at National Airport. She raised her head to look at the sky better.

How beautiful! I think the next time that I see Dr. Lieberman, I will tell him that I'd like to belong to an astronomy club. With that fascinating and enthralling thought, she started heading down Connecticut Avenue to the Farragut West metro station, making her way past the homeless men and women who proliferated throughout the city. She always kept $10 in change to be dispensed if she thought one or more of them wanted something to eat or drink. *There,* she thought, *but for the grace of God go I.*

Part 3

Serendipity: Or, Back from the Edge

48

When We Were Sure

$\mathcal{E}$ILEEN AND MAUDIE WERE TALKING ON THE PHONE LATE IN SEP-tember 1999. "Eileen, Dr. Roland Eberhard is taking a group of people on a pilgrimage to the Holy Land in December. The highlight of the trip is to take place on Christmas Eve, looking out over Shepherd's Field and over Bethlehem. Would you like to go?" Maudie was excited about the prospect of going on this trip, which is one that had never in their wildest dreams occurred to either of them.

"Well, gee, Maudie, I don't know about this. How much does it cost?"

"The trip costs about $2,500, which includes airfare from Chicago's O'Hare International Airport."

For some years, Eileen had deviated from the straight and narrow path, as had Maudie. They both knew they needed a shot of spirituality.

"Okay, Maudie, let me call my brother Charles and see if he will lend me the money, as I am broke as usual."

"Yeah. Okay, Eileen, but make it fast. The seats are filling up quickly as this is the December before the new millennium. As usual, there are segments of society predicting the end of the world—at least life as we know it. If that is so, then you and I need to be rebaptized so that we will be sure where we'll spend eternity . . . if, in fact, this is the end." This was quite an unusually long speech for Maudie, normally a woman of few words.

"Goodness, Maudie, this is serious. Matthew is in Guam, but I will call him right away to see if he has some money to spare for me."

"Okay, but do not dally or dither. Just do it!" Maudie hung up the phone. Eileen sat in front of the phone, bemused, contemplating a trip to the Holy Land. *Wow! A pilgrimage and an opportunity to make sure that we are "saved." An occasion not to be passed up.* She immediately picked up the phone and called Matthew in Guam. When he answered, she explained that she really, really needed the money, and she promised to pay him back with interest.

"Sure, Eileen, I will lend you the money, and if I don't get home before you leave, have a good time. I myself am having a great time in Guam. I've learned to scuba dive and have also fallen in love."

"You mean it, Matthew? You've fallen in love? Tell me more," she exclaimed. Matthew usually did not discuss women with her, so she knew this was serious.

"I call her the 'dragon lady'." Eileen could hear his smirk over the phone line traversing the thousands of miles of land and ocean separating them. "She is Vietnamese and owns and runs a karaoke bar in Guam," he continued.

"Why do you call her the 'dragon lady,'" enquired Eileen, who was consumed with curiosity.

He replied with awe in his voice, "When I first met her, she was wearing a red satin dress with a dragon painted on it in gold."

"Oh!" Eileen answered, stupefied. This did not sound like her brother's usual girlfriends. But if the "dragon lady" made him happy, who was she to be censorious.

"Enjoy your stay in Guam, Matthew," she said as she hung up the phone. CLICK, CLICK . . . no more connection.

With the utmost haste, she called Maudie to tell her the good news.

December—three months later—they were staying in a kibbutz on the shore of the Sea of Galilee. They were ecstatic. Usually the world was overrun by tourists, but the State Department had issued a warning about the hazards of traveling in Israel at the time, so many people canceled their trips. Eileen and Maudie and their tour group had Israel to themselves.

Israel was divine. Maudie was blown away by the rocks scattered over the land. She was in heaven, being a geologist. Both of them could understand why it was called the Holy Land—beloved by God, and sacred to Jews, Muslims, and Christians.

They were there for two weeks. The highlight of the tour was to be the vigil overlooking Shepherd's Field on Christmas Eve, but for the two of them their opportunity for being rebaptized was foremost on their minds. Maudie was a little reluctant, but Eileen was insistent. After all, who could resist being submerged totally in the Jordan?

On December 19, 1999, after traveling all over the Sea of Galilee and visiting the spots frequented by Christ and his followers, they arrived at Yardent, a baptismal site on the Jordan. It was a beautiful day with a blue sky, and the sun sparkling down, causing them to feel peaceful and at ease with the world.

"Ladies and gentlemen," said the tour guide, Ari, a part-time guide and a physicist, "here is your chance. You can either be completely submerged or sprinkled. There will be two ministers—one is Dutch Reformed and the other is Presbyterian (USA)." A great deal of clapping occurred. As this bus was occupied mainly by Australians, except for

Eileen and Maudie, there was a loud chorus of "Right on mate!"

"Okay," he continued, "line up for your robe and towel."

"Come on Maudie," Eileen said as she paid for her towel and robe. "Don't chicken out now. Not after we've come so far."

"All right," Maudie replied as she also reached for her towel and robe, handing over her money to the attendant.

"By the way, Maudie, if I were you I would put on a bathing suit under your robe. They're rather sheer."

"Why, Eileen. How clever of you . That would never have occurred to me." Everyone on the bus had decided to participate, and there was a general air of festivity. They stood around or sat on the stone wall on the stone terrace overlooking the river, waiting and watching. There must have been at least one hundred people milling around waiting to be submerged or sprinkled. Excitement filled the air. Time sped by as Eileen and Maudie sat on the wall. The sun was warm, and the water sparkled. It was a sparkly brown instead of a sparkly blue. As they looked around, they noticed that everyone appeared to be happy as they emerged from the river, heading back to the bathhouse.

At last it was their turn. Maudie said, "Eileen, you go first."

"Fine," said Eileen as she stepped into the water, first a toe, then a knee, then a leg, and finally all of her up to the shoulders. The water was cold, which was to be expected as it was the middle of December. Eileen splashed up to where the two ministers were standing in the water. They had been standing in the cold water for several hours, and they were shivering.

"What is your name, young lady," said the Presbyterian.

"My name is Eileen," she said, wondering if the water was polluted. "Hold your nose," said the Dutch Reformed minister.

Eileen held her nose. Suddenly, she heard the Dutch Reformed minister say, "Eileen, I baptize you in the name of the Father, the Son, and the Holy Ghost . . ." then, under the water; her head was under the water. It was cold. It seemed like centuries before Eileen bobbed to the surface. Maudie, who was next in line said, "Well, what do you think?"

"I feel great. Now I don't have to worry anymore about anything."

Eileen waited for Maudie to resurface. When she did, Eileen noticed that she was grinning from ear to ear. They were both thankful for their bathing suits, as the robes were not only sheer but also transparent.

They traipsed back to the bathhouse and changed into their tourist clothes. "Come on Maudie, let's get some coffee," said Eileen as they left the baptismal site and headed to the coffee bar.

That was the happiest day of their lives . . . the Day They Were Sure. . . .

BOOK II

Eileen Meets
Robert Green

Prologue

EILEEN LOOKED DOWN AT THE PAPER BEFORE HER ON THE TABLE. The pen was still clutched in her right hand. With her left hand, she swept her fingers across her dry, red eyes—she was finished. Her book was complete. It was ended. She gave a sigh of relief and an equally big sigh of pleasure. It had taken her five years to complete it.

She laid her head on her arms, which were crossed on the table . . . *Mercy, Lord, Mercy* . . . that will be the title of this book. She closed her eyes . . . *I think I shall rest* . . . she closed down her conscious mind and drifted out into her land of dreams—a land more real to her than anything in the real world.

> "WOOF! WOOF!
> "WOOF! WOOF! WOOF! . . ."
> *PLOP . . . PLOP*
> *She did drop*

Right in the middle of a yard
Next to a man playing a fiddle

"Where am I?
Where am I?"
She did cry
She was also wondering why . . .

Why, it seems I have been transported
Through my dreams . . .
I seem to be entering
A proper, colonial house
Why, there is a cat chasing a mouse.
There is a rocking chair
Which on a rug doth sit
In the back corner
Where it doth fit.
The colors hooked thereunto
Are of many shades and many a hue . . .
Red, purple, green, gold, and blue.
In the shape of a ship
Traveling at a good clip!
If the waters get too horrendous
Over it will flip!
Over it will flip!
Its flag is flying merrily
Not the least bit scarily

"Why, oh why,"
Must we sigh deeply and die?
Yes! Yes! I wonder why.

So full of hope!
I hope to cope

Not to mope, you dope!

"WOOF! WOOF!
WOOF! WOOF! WOOF!"

1

Eileen Lands at Liberty Hall

*W*HERE AM I? WHAT AM I DOING IN THIS STRANGE HOUSE?" EX-claimed Eileen as she picked herself up off the floor where she had landed in a heap, her dress all tangled around her. She dusted herself off and looked around at the unusual surroundings, listening to the sound of a fiddle playing and the musician singing several verses of "Old Joe Clark." "Wahu, Wahu, where are you?"

> WOOF, WOOF
> WOOF, WOOF, WOOF!
> ARF, ARF,
> ARF, ARF, ARF, . . .

was the reply. . . .

Eileen looked in the direction of the barks and saw both Wahu and a strange-looking dog. It was a borzoi. Eileen had seen one for the first

time at the dog show that she and her friend, Jay, had attended the previous week in Fredericksburg. The borzoi was a beautiful, beautiful dog.
She was brown and white, as opposed to Wahu's black and white coloring. *Where did she come from?* wondered Eileen, who was not sure
whether or not the new dog and Wahu were on friendly terms. The borzoi stopped her barking and sauntered over to where Eileen was standing
and draped herself around Eileen's knees, gazing soulfully into the
human female's blue eyes. This encounter was a perfect example of the
old adage, love at first sight. "Why, you're the dog I met at the dog show
that Jay and I went to. Your name is Yahu! Yes, your name is Yahu!" The
dog looked up and barked at Eileen in agreement.

Once again Eileen was puzzled. Why is the dog here? In fact, where
is here?

Once again, Wahu was growling. "Oh shut up, Wahu!" she said as
she once again patted the Borzoi's head.

Arf, Arf,

Arf, Arf, Arf . . .

"You're a beautiful dog, Yahu, but don't forget that I also love
Wahu," said Eileen who was stunned by this moment of sheer enlight-
enment. "Why, Yahu has accepted me as her favorite human. Now I have
two dogs! My mother will have a fit."

As she was dusting herself off and contemplating her situation, a
man approached her. His face was red with anger. He was dressed in the
attire common to the upper class landed gentry of the early eighteenth
century. "Who are you?" yelled the man. He was positively livid. "Why
are you dressed in your underwear? Where are your clothes? You cannot
stand around at my party in your underwear."

"My underwear! This is one of Alf Wonderly's most exquisite summer creations!" She was shocked that anyone would think that her beautiful silver silk slip dress was underwear. With it she was wearing her
Matisse platform sandals with her silver butterfly pendent hanging from

her gold collar, a gorgeous pair of dangly silver earrings, and her gold silk shoulder bag. Her ensemble was complete and most appealing to her eyes. She had chosen it especially for her riverboat trip on which her brother, Charles, was sending her and her mother, Mrs. Gordon. He expected Eileen to get inspiration for a new series of paintings she was hoping to start. She had been short on inspiration lately, and he was hoping that this trip would perk up her brain, which had gone stale.

"Who *are* you?" growled Eileen, who was angry at being greeted in such an unmannerly manner. Then she took a second glance and exclaimed in a shaky voice, "Robert Green—Robert Green! You are my great-great-great-great-great-etc.-grandfather. The painting on the wall of you and my great-great-great-great-great-etc.-grandmother, Eleanor, is the same as the one my maternal grandmother, Mrs. Roberts, left me when she went to the great beyond. It sits on the chest of drawers in my bedroom. I would know you and Eleanor anywhere. My grandmother, Mrs. Roberts—whose mother was a Green—died having despaired of my ever getting married and having children. This is puzzling because I know that you came to the USA around 1710."

Mr. Green looked perplexed, as he kept muttering "Great-great-great-great-great-etc.-granddaughter. . . ."

Eileen once again shook her head in disbelief, and said, "Where am I? Better yet, *when* am I?"

"It is the year 1724. This is my farm, Liberty Hall, in Virginia. Who are those dogs?"

"They are Yahu, whom I just found, and Wahu, whom I picked up in Hawaii . . . I don't understand . . .

TING-A-LING . . .

TING-A-LING . . .

"My cell phone!" Eileen reached into her gold silk purse and grabbed the ringing phone. She raised it to her ear, and a robotic voice said, "Eileen, you have traveled back through time instead of forward.

You are now in the year 1724."

"1724!? Who is this speaking?"

"I am the computer. The bubbles are hidden in the grove of trees behind the privy. You have three days before you must be home for your trip to Costa Rica. When you are ready for your return trip, punch the numbers 1942* on the keypad, and lay your head on your arms, like you are going to sleep. I must go now. . . ."

"Now I understand," she said, shaking her head in bewilderment. Robert Green approached closer to get a look at the silver cell phone.

"Granddad! I have time-traveled in my dreams. We are in an alternate state of reality.

He looked her up and down and said, "Whatever are you talking about? I must admit, though, that you look like a Green, especially with that red hair."

At this moment, up walked Mrs. Green, who reached out her arms, and gave Eileen a great big bear hug. "Mr. Green, her grandmother, Annie Eliza Green, told me that Eileen would be visiting us this summer, and hopefully she will stay for a while." Eileen smiled and gave Mrs. Green a return hug.

The two dogs started howling again as a black and white border collie walked toward the small group of humans. The collie snarled at Yahu and Wahu, who were jumping up and down around the newcomer. "This is Scot," said Mr. Green as he affectionately rubbed the border collie's ears.

By now, more people in colonial duds had gathered in the great hall. The fiddler was again playing and singing the plaintive ballad, "Where Have You Been, Lord Randall, My Son?" Eileen recognized the ballad because she and her musical group, the Blue Ridge Chamber Ensemble, played it at their gigs, which were few and far between. She looked around at the picnic that was occurring on the lawn. 1942* . . . I must remember that . . . please, dear God in Heaven, help me to understand time travel through dreams, and alternate states of reality. . . .

"Eileen, that is a beautiful dress you are wearing, although it is a bit skimpy. Why don't you come with me and meet everyone? I particularly love your shoes." Mrs. Green placed her arm on Eileen's and started guiding her to the refreshment table for a glass of white wine . . . a party. . . .

Wahu, Yahu, and Scot, who had become the best of friends as a result of their brief acquaintance, followed. They were hoping for a treat.

As they made their way to the refreshment table, Eileen thought about the paintings of Mr. and Mrs. Green. They most definitely were the ones that Mrs. Roberts had willed Eileen upon her demise. Yes, I have traveled backwards through time. I vaguely remember the Bubble Machine coming to pick me up last night when I laid my head on my arms, after finishing my book *Mercy, Lord, Mercy* . . .

"Eileen, what do you mean by 'alternate reality?' We have never heard of such a thing . . . what do you mean?"

"Gosh, I have no idea. It just popped into my mind. I think we are experiencing it."

The fiddler continued fiddling and the guests starting dancing on the lawn and in the great hall.

"Oh great! I want to dance!"

The stars twinkled down through the dark night sky. Lanterns cast a mysterious glow, and the fireflies flickered on and off. Eileen and her two dogs had been accepted at Liberty Hall . . .

the festivities continued . . .

the stars continued twinkling . . .

the fiddler continued singing and fiddling. . . .

2

Coffee! Beautiful Coffee!

OOF! WOOF!

"WOOF, WOOF, WOOF!"

"Oh, my head! Oh, my head! Shut up, Wahu! My head! Oh, my head"

"Arf! Arf!

"Arf! Arf! Arf!"

"My teeth hurt! My eyes hurt! Shut up, Yahu! My whole body hurts!"

Eileen moaned and groaned, and tossed and turned as the sunlight filtered through the white cotton curtains fluttering in the breeze, which was coming into the room through the open windows. "Why do I feel so lousy?"

"Eileen, wake up! You must be dreaming," said a woman's voice—a familiar voice. "Wake up! It is time to get dressed for breakfast. It is a beautiful fall day and—"

"Coffee, I smell coffee! Hallelujah!" groaned Eileen as she slowly raised herself onto her elbows, peering around the room at the strange surroundings.

"Do you remember me, Eileen? From last night? Remember me? I am your great-great-great-etc.-grandmother, Eleanor. Do you remember meeting my husband, Robert, and me at the party last night? It seems that you traveled backwards in time and landed in the middle of our party as we were anticipating winning the Restitutionary War. Also, you drank one too many glasses of champagne. You certainly cannot drink much, and you do not handle your liquor well." As she said this she approached Eileen with a glass filled with golden liquid in her hand.

"Restitutionary War! What is that? You must mean the Revolutionary War. My mother traced her family back to your son, James, who fought in the Revolutionary War, in order to become a member of the DAR."

"Oh no! I have never heard of the Revolutionary War. But, come on—get dressed and come down to breakfast. Robert is entertaining several friends of his—military officers—and they are anxious to meet you. They can tell you about the Restitutionary War better than I can. Here are some clothes—more appropriate for this century. I have also tried to keep in mind your personal preferences, trying to accommodate your taste."

"Oh, all right! Do you have some dog food for Wahu and Yahu? They are hungry, and they are used to eating in the morning and in the evening. During the day they run around exploring and playing. That is why they are in such good shape." Eileen was looking over her new apparel with interest. She had seen pictures of colonial garb and thought it interesting.

"Do you have any aspirin or Advil. My head is splitting!" Eileen winced through her bloodshot eyes as the sun shone into the room, and the dogs barked for their breakfast.

"You mean for your hangover. No, I do not know what aspirin is, but here is a shot of whiskey, which just might help you."

Eileen grabbed the shot glass, threw back her head, said "Here goes," and tossed off her drink in one gulp. "Wow!" she said as tears appeared in her eyes.

The two dogs were looking at her anxiously. They were puzzled by her behavior and their new surroundings. As they sized up the situation they heard . . .

"ORR! ORR!
"ORR! ORR! ORR!"

It was Scot, who entered the room to see his two new friends. A tabby cat appeared on the scene, tailing Scot.

Eileen once again turned her attention to her new finery. "Gee, Eleanor, I have never worn so many clothes at one time, except in the most bitter days of the winter when I go out for a walk. But I will try them on for you." She slipped on a pair of black silk pantaloons, and pulled on over them a brown linen skirt—her grandparents were rich for their time. Then she put on a beautiful white linen blouse with collar and cuffs made of Belgian lace. Over these she put on a yellow apron-like garment and tied a red silk ribbon around her neck. It all went perfectly with her jewelry from the night before. To complete the outfit, Eleanor handed her a pair of black leather flats. Her look was complete.

Eleanor gave Eileen a good look and was pleased with her choice of clothes. "My goodness, Eileen! We certainly are good-looking women for our age! Especially when you consider how few women reach our age. Come on, Eileen! Are you feeling better after downing the whiskey? You look better, if I do say so myself." As she said this, she grabbed Eileen by the arm and directed her out of the bedroom, down the grand staircase, and into the room where the breakfast table was filled with the most divine foods, including pumpkin pie. Unfortunately, Eileen was not quite up to eating.

As she and Eleanor entered the room, Robert and his two distinguished guests rose to their feet and said, "Good morning, ladies."

Robert Green took Eileen's hand and said, "Eileen, I would like to present my two compatriots, General Lucius Oliver and Captain Jeremy Fields. We have just been planning our next campaign in the Restitutionary War—"

Eileen interrupted, "Tell me about the Restitutionary War. I have never heard of it." As she said this, one of the plantation slaves entered the room carrying a silver pot filled with steaming, aromatic coffee. The aroma from the coffee filled the room. It was the most divine smell. Beautiful, beautiful coffee! Another slave entered carrying a pot of tea.

"Would you like some tea, Eileen?" enquired Robert.

"No, but I could kill for some of that coffee!"

"Of course!" Robert directed the slave to pour a cup for his newly-found granddaughter.

"And some crème, please!" said Eileen, who was salivating at the thought of having some of the marvelous smelling brew.

"Would you care for sugar?"

"No, thank you," said Eileen as she was preparing her coffee to her taste. When the coffee looked perfect, Eileen raised the cup to her lips and took a dainty sip. "Ah!" A sigh of pleasure escaped her body. "Ah, divine!"

"Now," she said, returning her attention to war. "What is going on? Why are you at war, and with whom are you warring?"

"Coffee, Eileen. It is all about coffee. The English are determined that we drink their tea, and they are trying to cut off our supply lines to LoMumbia. We are determined to go down the Potowatomie River to New Orleans, as the English have blockaded our coastal ports. We are determined to join forces with General Walloby in order to increase our chances of defeating the English." As General Oliver finished his account of the war, he had another cup of coffee.

"Unfortunately, we are down to our last two pounds of coffee."

"You must be kidding! Why, that will only last a couple of days." Eileen took another sip and started thinking—her headache was gone. She was having her first thought of the day. "Okay, Robert, I have an idea: I am a stewardess and have a trip to Costa Rica on Saturday, and I could pick up, say, twelve pounds of coffee and two bottles of Café Rica liquor and bring these supplies back here, if I can actually transport myself back and forth through time."

"Stewardess? Costa Rica? I do not understand!" said Captain Fields.

"It's too complicated to go into now. Take my word for it! I can get twelve pounds and bring them back. And I have another idea! My brother, Charles, is a great canoeist and is used to living in the wilderness, and he can lead the trip down the Potowatomie River. Tell you what! You get together a bunch of canoes, and when I return, I will bring Charles with me, and we can start down the river toward New Orleans. We can't let the English win this war. We need coffee. I need coffee!"

The two officers looked confused by this conversation; but Robert had explained some of the situation to them; and they were desperate; and Eileen seemed positive; and . . . any port in a storm.

"Yes, yes," agreed the two military men, Robert Green, and Eleanor. "We will do it."

"Today is Wednesday. I will stay through Thursday and try to get back to the twenty-first century on Friday. Hopefully, I will be successful, and I will be able to also return next Wednesday with coffee, Café Rica liquor, and my brother Charles and his cat, CAT . . . and Wahu and Yahu . . . and down the river we'll go, and Eleanor must go also, as I will need to have a woman to talk to. We should have a great time. Are we in agreement?" Eileen turned to Eleanor, and said, "Gran, I will bring some proper canoeing clothing."

"We should have a great time," everyone sang out.

"*Vive la Café!*"

"*Vive la guerre!*"

3

Telemann and Raspberry Tea

*C*HIRP! CHIRP!
WOOF! WOOF!
ARF! ARF!
GRRR! GRRR!

The noise, oh, the noise. What is causing all the commotion? As she became conscious of all the noise, Eileen raised her head from her pillow, opened her eyes, and looked around at the strange surroundings. Oh yes, I remember. I'm at Liberty Hall, and the sound of the birds singing and the dogs barking are the accompaniment to the dulcet tones of a Baroque flute. My goodness, that is what I am learning to play—the Overture from the Suite in A Minor by Telemann. However, in all honesty, whoever is playing is better than me. Who can be playing so beautifully?

Eileen jumped out of bed, ran to the window, and looked around. The sun was shining over the windowsill. The darkness was leaving the sky . . . it was morning. Eileen hurriedly got cleaned up and dressed so that she could go downstairs and see who was playing the flute. This was even more important than having her first cup of coffee.

The dogs were bouncing up and down on the bed, telling her that they were hungry and wanted to take a long walk. "Just a minute! I will take care of you. Don't I always make sure you get fed and take you for a walk?"

Wahu, who understood Eileen the best, looked deep into her eyes and said "Woof!"

"Yes, Wahu, we will stroll around the premises, but first come with me. She grabbed Wahu in her arms and called for Yahu and Scot to follow—which they did in an orderly fashion. They, too, were enjoying the glorious music. They all tramped silently down the stairs and into the dining room, which doubled as a music room. It was Eleanor— the musician was Eleanor.

"Eleanor, you play so well," exclaimed Eileen. "And you have a real wooden Baroque flute. When I come back from my home and my time I will bring my flute, and we can play duets."

"Eileen, I did not know you also played the flute."

"Indeed I do. I have been taking lessons for ten years, and I started playing Telemann's Suite in A Minor last month. You, I must admit, play much better than I do."

"Coffee is served," said Anita, the dining hall slave and cook. "The gentlemen have gathered for breakfast and were hoping you would join them—so you all can make your plans for the trip down the Potowatomie River to New Orleans."

As they entered the parlor where the gentlemen were eating and drinking, Robert Green said, "Come on, Eileen! This is the last of our coffee, but since we are so pleased to have you as our guest, we are serving it for our breakfast before you return to your home this evening.

"Anita, please take the dogs for a walk, and serve them their breakfast on the porch."

Robert continued the conversation, "We hoped we could solidify our plans for our trip to New Orleans. General Walloby needs all of our help to win the battle being planned—Walloby's Rumble. Men, women and children from all of the colonies are gathering to help fight. We must win this war or we will all be slaves."

"Granddad, that is terrible, but you can count on me to help. I will take my trip to Costa Rica and pick up the twelve pounds of coffee and several bottles of Café Rica and hopefully be back here next Saturday— if all goes well. I fully intend to enlist the help of my brother, Charles. He is a skilled riverman, and I will talk him into leading our group to join General Walloby. He will also know how to join you in battle, as he was an enlisted man in our war in Vietman."

"Vietnam? Where is that?" enquired General Oliver with interest.

"Vietnam is in Asia, sort of in the same area as China. We engaged them in war during the 1960s and 1970s."

"Eileen, it is so interesting talking with you because you know of so many things we have never heard of. You must tell us how you intend to go to Costa Rica."

"As I told you, I am a stewardess for Universal Airlines, and I fly in airplanes, which were invented by Orville and Wilbur Wright. Airplanes are big machines that fly in the sky and carry passengers all over the world. I will try to bring some pictures back with me when I return."

Just then, Eleanor interrupted the conversation and said, "Tell me about your mother, Catherine. I understand she married a Gordon. Is that an old Virginia family? I certainly hope she did not marry a Yankee!"

"Eleanor, the Gordons are an established Virginia family. He also was very good-looking."

At that moment the three dogs entered the room, followed by the tabby cat. They all looked sleek, well fed, and satisfied.

"Anyway," continued Eileen once again changing the subject, "if you can provide the canoes, Charles can tell you what we need to carry with us. But you need to give me some idea of how many days the trip will take and approximately how many people will be in the group."

"It should not take more than two weeks, if the weather holds. We do, however, need to allow for the chance of Indians attacking us. They are hostile, but we should have enough experienced fighting men to pro-tect us," said General Oliver who had lit a pipe, even though it was early in the day. He continued speaking, "In addition to ourselves and our sol-diers, we should number twenty-five to thirty bodies."

DING, DONG!
DING, DONG! . . .

went the hall clock. . . .

"Sorry, ladies, but we must leave now. It is 9:00 A.M., and we must go to work. Although we must leave you, we look forward to your safe return," said Robert Green as he gave Eileen a quick hug.

Robert and his friends rose and left the room, having finished their coffee, and headed out to the barns and the stables. Eileen watched them as they departed, wondering if she would actually see them again. She was concerned whether or not she could control the Bubble Machine and not only return to her own time but also return back to Liberty Hall in time for Walloby's Rumble.

WOOF! WOOF!
ARF! ARF!
GRRR! GRRR!

Eleanor looked at the dogs and said, "Come on! Let us tour the gardens and the fabric room. Anita, why don't you join us?"

With that, the three women, the three dogs, and the tabby cat headed outdoors for their tour of the house and gardens. . . .

Anita joined them, and as they were touring the gardens, Eleanor told Eileen that Anita was their cook and in charge of the gardens and in charge of the textiles and all clothing made on the farm.

"Eleanor, thank you for the tour, and I have a wonderful idea. If it is all right with you and Anita, perhaps she would like to join us on the trip. Having a good cook would be a wonderful addition to our group. What do you say?"

Eleanor was thrilled with the idea, and Anita said, "Miss Eileen, I would love to go. I, too, love coffee and have no fond feelings for the British."

"Anita, you can just call me Eileen."

As the three women, the three dogs, and the tabby cat chattered away, they found themselves wandering through the flower and herb gardens. Most of the flowers were returning to the soil as it was early autumn. The dogs were excitedly chasing squirrels and rabbits and an occasional chipmunk. They continued inspecting the grounds, missing lunch. As the afternoon slipped away, Eileen became pensive. She must leave her new family and friends, and her dogs would miss Scot. It was, however, getting late in the afternoon, and she knew that she must leave before it became dark. She was new at piloting the Bubble Machine and she preferred that her first attempt would be in the daylight.

"Eileen, before you go, let us have tea. Anita makes wonderful raspberry tea, and we can have tea sandwiches."

"That's great! We can feed the dogs, and then I will say goodbye. I don't believe that the men will get back in time to see them once again."

Eleanor and Eileen headed back to the house, and Anita headed to the kitchen to make the tea. Eileen went to her room to change back into her own clothes that were more appropriate for the return to the twentieth century.

Eileen joined Eleanor and Anita for a repast of raspberry tea, cucumber sandwiches, and ham biscuits. The time had finally come to leave . . . "Here goes!" said Eileen, who nervously took the cell phone from her purse, and punched in the password which the Bubble Machine had given her . . . 1942*. . . .

TING-A-LING
TING-A-LING

Then a metallic voice ... "This is the Bubble. It is time to return to the future and your home. You must pick up the bottle of bubbles in the grove behind the house. Then you and Wahu and Yahu must return to the dining room and sit down at the dining table and rest your heads on your hands—or in the case of the dogs, on their paws. You blow the bubbles through the large silver needle. You close your eyes...."

"Yes, yes! I understand," murmured Eileen as she ran to the grove of trees. There on the ground was a glass jar filled with beautiful iridescent liquid and by it was a large silver needle. She picked them up and returned to her friends and the dogs.

"Come, Wahu! Come, Yahu! Say goodbye to Scot, and tell him that we hope to return next Saturday."

The dogs bade Scot farewell and joined Eileen at the table in the dining room.

"Sit, Wahu! Sit, Yahu! We must leave now!" As she said this, she stuck the silver needle into the beautiful liquid in the glass jar and blew. They all rested their heads and closed their eyes. Above them hovered a silver cloud ... slowly, slowly sparkling ... as it enveloped them ... POOF!

They were gone.

"Where are they?" said Anita, with a puzzled expression on her face. She felt quite peculiar with these strange goings-on.

"I do not know, Anita. I hope Eileen knows what she is doing. This is all so mysterious. I hope she comes back and brings her flute, so that we can play Telemann."

4

Where Are We?

OLD . . . COLD . . . COLD . . .
Iridescent colors shimmering
Iridescent colors glimmering
Twinkling, twinkling
Tumbling thru' the
Darkening air
Wondering, "Where?"

"Where are we?" Eileen moaned as the three beings felt the world
slip away . . . away . . . away. . . .

"Where are we?" the two dogs asked each other. They were dizzy.
It was dark and cold and slippery. Suddenly Eileen yelled, "Ouch!"

The darkness receded, leaving them in a puddle on the ground,
legs and arms and heads and tails all in a muddle. Eileen noticed that

she was frantically holding onto the bottle of bubbles and the silver needle. She looked up and exclaimed, "We have landed in Charles's garden. There is the ceramic turtle I gave him for Christmas, and there is his concrete Buddha. There is Charles, mowing his lawn. Look, he's seen us." As she said this she stood up and walked towards her brother, followed by the two dogs who noticed a gray cat with a white chest following Charles. Her fur was twitching and she was hissing. She could not help it—*Dogs are so stupid*, she thought as she approached the two surprised canines.

Charles approached his sister and said, "Why were you lying on the ground? What's going on here, and when did you get the dogs?"

"Charles, you won't believe what has happened to us. But I might have to explain later as I think I need to get ready for my trip to San Jose, Costa Rica. What time is it, and even more to the point, what day is it?" She brushed the dirt, twigs, and grass off of her silver slip dress. She was glad it was still in good condition even though it had traveled with her through time and space in her dream.

"Your trip is later this evening, so explain yourself. Where have you been? Ma and I have been sick with worry."

"Charles! I traveled back to the time of the Restitutionary War!"

"The what?" exclaimed Charles as he shook his head in bewilderment. Sometimes Eileen confused even him.

By now the two dogs and CAT were conversing amongst themselves. They had ascertained they were siblings, as their master and mistress were brother and sister. CAT was the most perturbed, but she realized that civility was called for. *At least the two dogs are good-looking and seem intelligent for dogs.* She was a little concerned about Wahu, who claimed that he was from Hawaii and had met Eileen when she was first sick. This puzzled CAT, but she would figure it all out in good time.

As the dogs and CAT were getting to know each other, Eileen was explaining the situation to Charles, who found the whole problem very absorbing. "Eileen, do you mean to tell me that you expect me to accompany you into the past when you get back from San Jose and that I am to make plans and determine the provisions needed to lead a party of thirty colonists down the Potowatomie River in canoes, which party includes our great-great-great-great-etc.-grandfather and grandmother, Robert and Eleanor Green?"

"Yes, Charles. I promised them that you were a wonderful riverman and could lead them all down the river in safety. You know you love river trips, and traveling through time in my dream will be most challenging and edifying."

"And Charles, while you are getting ready for the adventure, I'll bring back coffee and Café Rica for the trip."

"Well, Eileen, I guess if I have three days to get ready, I'd better get on the ball. Oh, by the way, I must renew my prescription for my asthma inhaler. We can't leave until I have that with me. Is that clear?" Charles was envisioning the trip in his mind's eye and found the prospect quite appealing.

"And Charles," exclaimed Eileen, "CAT is welcome on the trip. She will have the company of Wahu, Yahu, Tabby Cat, and Scot, our grandparent's border collie. They should get along famously."

"Eileen," interrupted Charles, "you need to get ready for your trip this evening.

Here is $100 for the coffee, and another $20 for the Café Rica," he said as he took some money out of his pocket.

"Thanks, Charles. How did you know I was short on cash?" puzzled Eileen who was intrigued with his powers of perception.

"You're always broke! Here, take the cash and run along. I need to finish mowing the lawn, and you need to straighten up for your trip. Tell Ma that Wahu and Yahu can stay with me and CAT while you are on your trip. 'Bye—"

The airplane . . . fifteen hours later . . . zooming through the sky where it would fly through the darkened night . . . no land in sight! It was stormy! Rain was crashing against the hull! Eileen, who was tired, went into the cockpit to take a break and rest her weary feet. She was strapped into her seat on the Airbus, a French airplane. She could not figure why Universal Airlines had invested in French planes, but then, there was no accounting for the tastes of pen-pushers.

"Eileen, look at the radar screen! Watch the storm!" said George, the copilot.

Eileen looked and yelled in surprise, "It is really spooky up here, flying through a major storm. Do you think we will make it to San Jose in one piece?"

"Sure," said Captain Logan, an experienced and over-optimistic pilot. "Watch me maneuver us through those two sets of clouds. It should be exciting, so enjoy the experience."

Eileen watched the ghostly forms of the storm on the radar screen glowing eerily green in the darkened cockpit. She was intrigued. Everything about planes and the sky fascinated her. Slowly, slowly the airplane was guided by the captain through a break in the storm clouds—sort of like going through a pass in the mountains. Finally, they were safely through the pass. Eileen said, "Thanks for letting me stay here and watch, but I had better get back to the cabin."

"Sure, Eileen! Could you bring George and me two cups of coffee with créme and two sugars?"

"Certainly! Back in a flash!" She straightened her navy blue dress, patted her hair, put her shoes back on her weary feet, opened the cockpit door, and sauntered out into the darkened cabin. She went directly to the galley, made a fresh pot of coffee, and returned to the cockpit with coffee for her crew several minutes later.

"Twenty minutes to landing! Prepare the cabin! It may be bumpy on descent! See you on the ground!" said George and Captain Logan as they thankfully took the coffee from Eileen. They needed to be alert for landing the plane at the airport.

The plane descended through the turbulent air and landed at the

San Jose Airport shortly after midnight. Then! . . . to the hotel . . . to bed . . . wired . . . tired . . . to sleep . . . 'til morning . . . through an earthquake . . . 'til morning . . . to the mall after breakfast. . . .

The Mercado Supermarket was open at 10:00 A.M. Eileen was there as the doors opened. Julio, the night manager, had accompanied her so as to help her carry her supplies back to the hotel. Eileen said, "Wait here, Julio! I will only be about twenty minutes." As she said this, she jumped out of the van and headed for the coffee section of the busy market. *There's the coffee! Beautiful, beautiful coffee!* She grinned from ear to ear as she placed twelve bags of coffee into her shopping cart.

She then headed for the liquor section where she picked up three bottles of Café Rica. She was thankful for Charles for giving her the extra money, so she bought one bottle of the dark, coffee-flavored, yummy liquor just for him.

She went through the checkout line with her supplies, and found Julio. He brought the hotel van to the front of the supermarket. They loaded up and headed back to the hotel, always under the watchful eyes of the armed guards on the roof of the market.

After her trip to the market, she took her favorite walk past the cows and horses and chickens and mangy yellow dogs, beyond the American Embassy. She loved to look at the mountains, and she admired the scary golden cows with their long horns. Although she was frightened of them, they had never charged her, so she was beginning to feel safer around them.

As the day started to darken, Eileen went to her room and dressed for dinner, which she was sharing with Julio. She had told him about her experiences lately. He was concerned for her safety. He, unlike most people, believed in things like time travel. As they dined on sea bass and beans and rice, he told her that he would pray for her safety and that the coffee would refresh the colonists. As they were talking, the band broke into some Latin music. Eileen and Julio sat back contentedly and listened to the beautiful music . . . sipping their wine . . . watching the dancers mamboing away to the haunting melodies . . . the sounds of the music reverberated through her brain . . . throughout her sleepless night . . . throughout her trip back from Costa Rica to Mexico City to Washington, DC.

She remembered Julio's last words to her as she left the hotel in the early hours of the morning . . . "Eileen, you don't need cosmetic surgery. . . ."

5

In the Sky, Clouds Passing By

*R*AINING, RAINING, RAINING . . . THE NEXT MORNING, THE CREW made their way by van to the airport. *Oh dear, it'll be bumpy, and I hate turbulence,* thought Eileen as she anticipated taking off into the stormy heavens. Although she had flown for many years, she had always been a nervous flyer when it came to turbulence.

The rest of her flying partners were nodding off in the early dark hours of the morning. They had partied hard the previous night and thought that a few extra hours of shut-eye would help improve their level of alertness. Arriving at the airport, they hurried through security so they could make their way to the Duty Free Shoppe. Eileen had loaded up on coffee and Café Rica, so she skipped duty free and made her way to the concession stand for her morning cup of java, which was splendid.

Finally, everyone was on board. The airplane took off into the bumpy firmament, rising up through the turbulence and into the dark, sullen clouds! At last the blue sky appeared at about 25,000 feet. It was a gorgeous sight—puffy white clouds skittering across the sky, blanketing the earth. Nothing to be seen except the horizon in the distance.

Golly, thought Eileen, who never tired of the sight of looking down into the clouds, *it's like being lost in space.* She realized that the cockpit crew knew where they were, so she relaxed. *Thank heaven for radar.* Breakfast was served, and the plane and crew and passengers headed for Mexico City. . . .

Later that morning after the breakfast service, Eileen was talking to her friend, Lulu Lee, telling her about the trip to the past. Lulu Lee had known Eileen for a long time and knew a tremendously overactive imagination when she encountered one.

"Eileen, are you absolutely sure that you traveled into the past?"

"Yes, Lulu Lee! That is why I bought all the coffee at the Mercado grocery store. I am taking it back with me after this trip. Charles and I are planning to leave on Tuesday. I have twenty-eight days of vacation and probably won't see you again until around Christmas. Charles is leading a party of around thirty people down the Potowatomie River to New Orleans and we are going to make our last stand there against the British. We all want to be free to drink the beverage of our choice. My great-great-great-great-etc.-grandparents, Robert and Eleanor, will be along with us. I am so excited! I have been bored lately, and this adventure has really perked me up."

"You mean there will be a real battle!" exclaimed Lulu Lee tossing her curly blond locks.

"Yes, Lulu Lee, I am going to be a scout since I don't know anything about fighting, but I am good at prowling around and finding out stuff."

"Wow! On your next trip can I go with you? I'm getting a little tired of domestic bliss myself. Although I look like a complete priss, as do you, I crave excitement, and marriage has its definitely dull moments."

"Sure! When Charles and I return—after, I am sure, winning our war—I'll make plans with Eleanor to arrange something special for the two of us. That is, of course, if I'm still able to travel back and forth through time. My bubble has a mind of its own."

Many hours later, they landed at Dulles International Airport and made their way through customs and into their cars in the employee parking lot. "Eileen, I wish you success in your battle, and tell Eleanor to start planning an adventure for you and me."

"Sure, thing, Lulu Lee," said Eileen as she unlocked her car, got in, and hit the road, accompanied by the dulcet tones of Jean Pierre Rampal, in her mind the greatest flutist of all time. . . .

"Yahu, wake up! I think she's home. I heard her car," said Wahu, as he woke up from a deep sleep.

"Wahu, I was having a wonderful dream. Why did you wake me?" said the confused Yahu, who was still partially lost in her dream.

"She's home! She's home! Now we can get prepared for our next adventure through her dreams."

"Oh yeah! We're heading back to Liberty Hall. We should remind Eileen to take a two-week supply of dog bones for us, and I am sure that CAT would like a supply of catnip and some Tuna Toasties."

"Come on! She's getting out of the car." The two dogs got up and bounded downstairs, heading for the backdoor and barking excitedly. "Mrs. Gordon, let us out! Mrs. Gordon, let us out!"

Mrs. Gordon, who was watching Julia Child and Jacques Pepin preparing dishes on their afternoon cooking show on TV, reluctantly got up from her black leather recliner. She knew she would get no peace and quiet until the dogs were let out the kitchen door to see their beloved mistress.

ARF, ARF
ARF, ARF, ARF
WOOF, WOOF
WOOF, WOOF, WOOF

Eileen stepped out of her car—a purple Gremlin—and onto the driveway, saw the two happy dogs, and gave them each a big hug. "Come here, Wahu! Come here Yahu! Let me say 'Hi' to Mom and then we'll go to Charles's house, and we will say 'Hi' to him and CAT," she said as she gave each of her two dogs a dog bone that she had brought from Costa Rica.

They went down the yard, across the road to her brother's beautiful little brick house. He was home and said, "I have made all the plans and have my inhaler. Tomorrow we must go to Appalachian Outfitters or L. L. Bean and get our clothes and supplies. I thought we would leave around 9:30 A.M. so as to miss the worst of the rush hour traffic."

At just that moment CAT appeared, dragging a mouse she had been playing with. *I think it's dead*, she thought. *I must have batted it too hard. Oh well, there are plenty more where that one came from* . . . CAT dropped the mouse and made a great big stretch from her neck to her tail. She gracefully walked over to Charles and gleefully wrapped herself around his left leg. *Good grief! Must I put up with those obnoxious dogs? I guess so, as they are going back to the time of the Restitutionary War with us. They really are not as awful as I sometimes think.*

The two dogs bounded over to CAT. "Hi, CAT," they said in unison. "We told Eileen to prepare a grocery bag full of catnip and Tuna Toasties for you for on the river."

"Thanks, guys! I appreciate your thoughtfulness! Let's go listen to Pop and Eileen."

"Charles, I told Mom where we're going, and she gave me some photographs to take to Eleanor and Robert. She thought that they might like to see pictures of their descendents. I have my flute, my pills, and a gorgeous pair of red leather high-heeled shoes for Eleanor. Let's leave the day after tomorrow, after we have completed our shopping and are packed."

The following day was the magical day when Charles would accompany CAT, Wahu, Yahu, and Eileen into the past. He was quite excited. Both he and his sister had picked out really good warm wool clothes and special goodies for everyone. The party of two humans, three animals, and supplies were gathered in a circle in Charles's backyard. Mrs. Gordon had brought some Texas sheet cake for them to take on their trip back to their ancestors. Eileen took the silver needle and bottle of bubbles out of her purse and dialed 1942* on her cell phone.

"Hello, this is Bubble!"

"We're ready!"

"Great!" said the melodious, mechanical voice. "Now blow the bubbles through the silver needle, and close your eyes."

Eileen slipped the silver needle into the bottle of iridescent bubbles, placed it in front of her lips, and blew. . . .

POOF! . . . a great big pink bubble encircled them . . . POOF! . . . they were gone!

Where?

Not a care!

POOF! . . .

6

Feverfew and You

I T WAS A WARM DAY IN LATE OCTOBER—A BEAUTIFUL INDIAN SUM-
mer day. It would not be long before the frost came and everything
started hibernating for the winter. The butterflies were flitting around,
filling the air with their spirit and color. The grasshoppers were hopping
around just for the fun of it. The sun was shining, filling the air with the
last heat of summer. Into this tranquil garden stepped a beautiful black
woman, a slave. It was Anita. She was walking slowly, seemingly preoccupied with some ponderous thought—some heavy thought that
caused her back to be bent.

What could it be? Ah, yes, a migraine headache. She slowly stepped
through the garden until she came to a lovely daisy-like white flower, a
feverfew that somehow had lived past July. Anita always gathered the
feverfew in July and dried it for use when she and Eleanor had their

mind-piercing headaches. She was ecstatic that there was still a live fever-few. She reached down and plucked several leaves and placed them in her mouth and started chewing.

Although at this time there were not many remedies for headaches, she was glad for this modest little plant that dated back to the time of the Romans. It had been shipped to Liberty Hall several years before and now was growing as a wildflower.

Ah! How I wish Eileen would return with some coffee. That always seems to help a little. Gingerly, she lowered herself onto the wooden bench in the garden. Everyone from the big house had gone hunting and for a picnic. She and the other four slaves had the afternoon to do as they pleased. She chewed and thought, *I know that I am treated well, but I should not be a slave. God did not intend that for his people.* Anita had very specific ideas about what did and did not please God. She knew that she liked music, and she had a beautiful voice, although untrained. She also knew how to read and write and do her numbers because Eleanor needed her help in running the farm and had seen to it that Anita had a rudimentary education.

The farm was lovely and isolated. Eleanor had been quite lonely and became aware that Anita, like herself, was intelligent and courageous. The two had developed a great friendship, but still Anita would love to be a free woman—free to go where she chose and marry whomever she pleased.

She realized that this sort of thinking was futile and led to depression. She heard a rustling noise and looked up from her reverie. She saw a solitary white man approaching. He had not seen her, but he sensed her presence. As he raised his head he saw Anita. He said, "Hello! May I sit with you?"

Anita was shocked by this informality. *Why would he want to sit with me?* she wondered. Captain Jeremy Fields—for in fact he was the solitary man—sensed her consternation, but he was desperately lonely and wanted company. He had lost his wife and child in childbirth the previous year. He was a gentleman and missed the company of an intelligent and compassionate woman. On this enchanted afternoon he noticed how beautiful Anita was. He wanted her company.

Anita recognized a kindred soul when she encountered one, and she replied with a shy smile, "Why yes, Captain Fields, I would like for you to join me."

Jeremy rearranged his jacket and scarf and sat down on the wooden bench beside the black slave. They sat there quietly enjoying the warm air and the birds warbling songs of thanks for the mild day and their daily ration of worms. . . .

When . . .

"Good grief, Charles! Get off my leg. You'll break it."

"Aw, shut up, Eileen. Must you always be thinking of yourself? Has it ever occurred to you that I might've broken my arm? Where are we?"

Eileen and Charles struggled to get up. The two dogs and CAT were all tangled up, and everyone was screeching and howling and barking and making a lot of noise.

"Eileen, where are we?" Charles repeated himself. "Is this Liberty Hall? Did we arrive in the past—to our great-great-great-great-etc.-grandparents' home?"

Eileen sat up straight, rubbing her aching leg. "Yes, Charles, we're behind the stables. Where is everyone?" She looked around then turned back to her brother. "Are our supplies all here and accounted for?"

Charles stood up, brushed the straw and dirt off of his new L. L. Bean woodsman clothes. He glanced at the animals, the bags of supplies, and food. "Yes, Eileen. Everything's here and seems to be in good condition. Are you hurt?" As he said this, he saw a black woman and a white man running toward them.

Eileen saw the two people at the same time and screamed, "Anita, we made it back. How is everything and everyone doing? We brought the coffee. As soon as possible, we'll make a pot for everyone. We have to be stingy, but just this once we'll splurge."

"Hallelujah!" screamed Anita. "My head is splitting and sometimes coffee helps."

Jeremy was standing still, somewhat confused. He did not understand Eileen and her story. Also, who was the man with her and the gray cat?

"Jeremy," said Eileen, "this is my brother, Charles. Remember I said that I would return with him to lead us down the river. Do you believe that I have traveled through time with him to help you win the Restitutionary War?"

"I don't understand, but you do seem real and so do the others." Jeremy turned to face Charles and extended his hand which Charles grabbed and pumped up and down. "Welcome. We need all of the help we can get for our trip down to New Orleans to help General Walloby."

"Nice to meet you Jeremy. This is strange to me, too."

Anita walked over to the dogs and CAT, who were gazing intently toward the stable, from where they saw a black and white border collie, Scot, and orange Tabby Cat, advancing slowly and stealthily. Scot and Tabby Cat were not easily shocked, but the appearance of Wahu, Yahu, and CAT out of thin air puzzled them.

CAT approached in a dignified way and said, "Who are you?" to Tabby Cat.

"I live here! Who are you?" hissed Tabby Cat, who was feeling the need to protect his territory. Besides which, this strange gray female cat was ruffling his fur.

Scot was standing still and thinking, *I believe Yahu and Wahu are back.* He advanced. "Hi!" said Scot. Yahu and Wahu raced up to talk to him. They liked Scot.

Anita finally had regained her wits. She turned to Jeremy and said, "Jeremy, could you go to the slave quarters and get Old Joseph? Tell him that Eileen has returned and we must celebrate when the others return from their picnic. We need him and the other musicians to perform during dinner. Tell them there will be a cup of coffee for everyone."

"Sure, Anita," said Jeremy who by now, like Anita and Scot, had regained his composure. He ran off to get the musicians lined up for the party. He knew that Anita was a good party organizer. His soul had been revived. He was happy.

Several hours later . . .

The sun had gone down just before the picnickers returned to find Charles and Eileen sitting on the front steps, each sipping a glass of peach brandy, looking cool, calm, and collected.

Robert and Eleanor hurried to the steps and hugged Eileen. "Granddad! This is your Great-great-great-great-etc.-grandson Charles. He's going to lead us on our great adventure down the Potowatomie River. And now, can we eat? It's been a long day, and we're hungry."

7

The Evening Continues

ℰVENING
     Falls, falls,
          falls
Merriment echoing
   through the halls
Horses neighing
   in the stalls
Evening,
   cool, cool
      Evening falls. . . .

"Drat!" exclaimed Jeremy, total disgust in his voice. "I fold. I'm out of this game. I've lost too much money."

"Too bad, Jeremy! I have a full house!" chuckled Charles as he placed his hands on all the money on the table and swept it into his waiting pockets.

The General, Robert, Jeremy, and Charles had finished a rousing game of poker, which they had been playing since after dinner. The fireplace was ablaze with the fire that Anita had started to take the chill off of the cool night air.

Everyone was sated after having their fill of Anita's lovely dinner. She had prepared a Brunswick stew using the rabbits that Robert and the general had shot while hunting during the afternoon. She had also baked a loaf of whole grain bread, and for dessert she had prepared fried apples.

Now she was removing the remnants of the dinner. Through the rooms floated the lilting melody of "Lord Randal, My Son," which was being played as a duet by Eleanor and Eileen on their flutes. Eileen had improved a lot over the years but was not nearly as good as Eleanor. Anita looked at the two ladies playing the flutes and wistfully sang the words to the mournful ballad under her breath.

Eleanor glanced at Anita, saw her softly singing and said, "Anita, why don't you join us and sing. You have such a lovely voice."

Anita gave a sigh of pleasure and walked over to where her friends were playing in front of the fire. The three musicians began their rendition of the old melody, the two flutes accompanied by the vocalist. Silence fell over the room. The fire flickered and danced and crackled. The three dogs were stretched out in front of the fireplace, peaceably taking an evening snooze. CAT and Tabby Cat were also lazing before the fire, dreaming of the mice they were going to eat the next day. Their claws were stretching and retracting as they dreamt of pouncing on their prey.

Eileen looked at them, all so peaceful. *I really wish that CAT didn't take so much pleasure in killing mice.* Nevertheless, she realized that was the way of cats, and she decided not to dwell on the subject.

While all of this was taking place, the men were enjoying a leisurely cigar, a cup of coffee, and some Café Rica. "Robert, now that Eileen and Charles are here, when will we begin our trip down the river?" the General asked. He was to lead the party in battle, but Charles was to lead the expedition down the river to New Orleans.

Robert turned to Charles, who was beginning to nod off. "Charles, there will only be seven of us in the party, instead of the original thirty. The others got worried about the weather turning bad. Since no one knew when or if you would get here, they decided to leave without us. We will meet up with the others in New Orleans."

"That's fine," said Charles. "Jeremy, Anita, and Tabby Cat can man the flatboat with our supplies. Robert, Eleanor, and Scot can paddle in one canoe; the General will go by himself; I will canoe with CAT; and Eileen will be in one canoe with Yahu and Wahu. I will make up a list of supplies for each boat."

Robert rejoined the conversation. "We must spend the day in church tomorrow. We could load up on Monday and then leave on Tuesday, if that suits you, Charles." Jeremy was being quiet as he flicked an ash that had just alighted on his powder blue wool vest.

"That's that!" said Charles, "but I think I'll skip church. I'm an agnostic."

"Sorry, Grandson. We all go to church. It is the law, and besides, we need prayer from the other neighbors for the well-being of our battle and the well-being of our souls."

"Oh, okay, but Eileen and I don't know how to ride horses; so do we walk? I hate walking," groused Charles as he finished off his Café Rica.

"We will have Thomas drive you two in the wagon."

"Great!" said Eileen who had been following the conversation between the men. That was one reason she had trouble playing the flute. She always got distracted, and her attention wavered from her playing. "Let's go to bed. Anita is recovering from a headache. I gave her some of my pills, but she needs to rest. Besides, all of us are tired and have very busy days before us."

By now all of the musicians had stopped playing, and Eleanor was putting out the candles and the oil lamps.

"Everyone! Time for bed!"

The grandfather clock in the hall chimed midnight. The hoot owl, who had just awakened, gave two loud hoots, and the cats and dogs quietly snored.

The humans all left the downstairs rooms and headed for their respective beds . . .

> Deeper night falls
> Throughout the halls and stalls
> Throughout the halls and stalls
> Deeper night falls. . . .

8

Hoot! Hoot! Livening up the Night!

*H*OOT! HOOT! HOOT! LIVENING UP THE EVENING NIGHT . . . AN-
nouncing the advent of evening! . . .

Eileen tossed and turned. It was about 3:00 A.M. She could not
seem to sleep . . . she was restlessly reliving her transportation from her
time to past time. *Time is very confusing,* she thought. *It seems to me that
they are both real, but how can that be?* She gazed into the fireplace, where
the last embers of the once-blazing fire were still shimmering. The flames
were lovely, sparkly, and dancing, and they emitted a small amount of
heat— enough to dissipate the chill in the room from the late October
night.

Wahu and Yahu were also thinking about their recent trip through
the kaleidoscopic range of colors that accompanied them on their trip
to the present past.

"Why us?" they said each to the other. "Why us?" Yahu, who was less insightful, whined, "Why us? We're just normal dogs, don't you think, Wahu?"

"Are you nuts?" barked Wahu. "Why, I'm from Hawaii, and I used to wander all over the lava fields . . . walking with Madame Pele, who thought that in order to be in the modern times, she needed a purebred dog. So she got a Weimaraner, and sent me off to be with Eileen. Madame Pele knew that Eileen needed me and would provide me with an interesting and profoundly entertaining home and life. Although, to be completely truthful, I was not prepared for time-travel through dreams. In fact, where are my dreams now when I need them?" Wahu unconsciously wagged his tail, and it was done in a most thoughtful manner.

"Shut up, Wahu," snapped Eileen who was disturbed by the dogs' chatter.

"Eileen is grumpy, isn't she?" asked Yahu, who did not know her new mistress as well as Wahu. In addition, Yahu was not used to the supernatural. She was a twenty-first century dog and did not believe in time-travel, except when she was watching Porthos, Captain Archer's dog, on *Star Trek*.

"Okay, Eileen, keep your knickers out of a twist," snarled Wahu, who was sleepy, tired, and generally befuddled. By now the fire had lowered itself, and the moon was dropping behind the horizon into the early morning sky.

Suddenly . . . birdsong! . . . a whippoorwill! . . . outside Eileen's window. . . .

Oh my gosh, it's time to get up; but first I must read Matthew 6. It always helps me when I'm anxious. As this thought lodged in her mind, she pulled her large-print King James version of the Bible out of her small tote bag. She quickly turned to her favorite chapter and began to read aloud, both for herself and for the dogs. The words were soothing, and quickly the three inhabitants of the room quieted down. They once again felt secure.

"Look, look," yelped Yahu, "the sun! The morning has come. The sun is rising. It's time for breakfast and a walk. Come on Eileen, time to get up." The two dogs jumped onto Eileen and began nudging her to the side of the bed. At that moment there was a gentle tapping at the door.

"Miss Eileen, it's Anita. I have some coffee and a breakfast snack for you."

"Come in, Anita," said Eileen who was beginning to salivate at the wonderful aroma of the Costa Rican coffee. As she spoke, the door opened and Anita stepped into the room, carrying a tray with two biscuits, strawberry preserves, and a silver pot of coffee. On the tray was also a beautiful porcelain pot of crème. The smell was enchanting.

Eileen walked over to the little table sitting at the side of the room and sat down. "What time are we leaving for church?"

"We are all leaving at 8:00 A.M. I have already taken coffee to your brother and CAT, and they told me they would be ready, although I don't believe they are happy to be going to church for the whole day. Anyway, it looks to be a lovely day, and I have prepared a ham and some biscuits and a pound cake to take for the supper between the services. Miss Eleanor is going to wear the red satin shoes you brought her after the first service. She thinks they are a little flamboyant but believes that the times are so perilous and ominous that folks will be cheered by their sheer frivolity. Enjoy your breakfast." Saying this, she set the tray down, opened the curtains, then withdrew through the open door.

Eileen ate breakfast and then started to worry about what to wear. Eleanor had told her she was welcome to anything in the trunk. Eileen walked over to the gorgeous cedar chest at the foot of the four-poster bed. She removed the brass candlestick and daintily opened the lid . . .

> The smell of cedar
> Wafting thru' the air . . .
> "Clothes, glorious clothes!
> Please have not a care . . . for
> Here you will surely find
> Something to wear."

"My God!" barked Wahu, "the trunk talked to Eileen, and she didn't even hear it."

"Wahu," said the trunk, "you see, Eileen is only a human, and they are not tuned into existential conversations such as the one we are—"

". . . Ooh! Lovely!" rang out Eileen's voice. "I don't know what to choose. Obviously something to chase away the blues! Oh, gosh, what shall I choose? . . ."

She looked deep into the trunk. Lo and behold! A tan skirt with a cream-colored petticoat, *which will be perfect with my 2BFree silk hoodie with the bronze-colored sequins outlining butterflies and flowers.*

"Perfect! I will wear my black leather boots. I will be perfectly dressed, following my three main rules of fashion:

1. Do I love it? Yes!
2. Is it flattering? Yes!
3. Is it appropriate for the time and place? Yes!"

Then, she put on her antique Russian silver and turquoise drop earrings and her twenty-dollar watch. "Spectacular! Splendid, if I do say so myself!" giggled Eileen, as she preened in front of the full-length mirror—for those times, an absolute extravagance.

After one final look, she headed for the stairs, wanting to see all of her new friends and new and old family. The dogs bounded after her. After all, they needed to take their morning constitutional and then have their breakfast. They were both dogs of habit. . . .

> Do they eat?
> Do they drink?
> Do they stop flying along?
> Do they sing a song?
> > Flying, flying, flying
> > Along! . . .

Thought flickered in shades of pink bordered by silver with just a touch of green. That was to liven things up. The spiral spiraled again and then—FLASH—as quickly as it had come, thought was gone. Never to be resurrected. . . . Eileen proceeded down the stairs. "Sallying forth before I morph into an iridescent beam or so it would seem . . . morph of course . . . I have done it before while leaving thru' an open door 'What for? . . .' so that I can see he who guides and leads me thru' eternity . . . an iridescent beam . . . iridescent . . . an iridescent streak of light piercing the darkness of the night . . . an iridescent streak of light piercing the stillness of the night . . . piercing the night . . ."

Down,

    Down,

        Down . . .

           HOOT! HOOT!

9

Descending into the Pit . . .

HELP! HELP! HELP!
Falling in her mind
Falling into the flames,
Flickering
Dancing
Higher, higher!
Help! Help! My brain is tingling under my scalp!
The nonexistent hairs on her arms were standing straight up . . .
The flames flickering
Higher, higher . . .
Help! Help! My brain is tingling under my scalp!

"Eileen, snap out of it . . . why are you yelling? You're in church . . . shut up." Charles was shaking her and everyone in the church was staring, wondering, "What is wrong with that crazy redhead? Is she nuts?"

Robert started shaking his great-great-great-great-etc.-granddaughter. "Eileen, wake up. You are having a bad dream. You fell asleep in church." Eileen jerked one more time and her eyes snapped open, eyes filled with fear.

"Where am I?" she cried, her voice shaking and tears falling down her face, slithering down her cheeks and onto her chin.

"Eileen, you were having a nightmare. What were you thinking?" Robert had grabbed one arm and Charles the other. They dragged her down the aisle, heading for the door, leaving the congregation staring as Eileen wobbled between her two relatives.

Once outside, the cool breezes blowing, her hairs still standing straight up, Eileen said, "Granddad, I remember what upset me so. I know what is so wrong. My pastor at home, Reverend McCall, is telling us about a series of sermons by the Puritan minister, Jonathan Edwards, and my mind flashed back to one of the sermons, 'Sinners in the Hands of an Angry God.'"

"What was it about the sermon that it could upset you so much?" inquired Robert, perplexed.

Eileen's eyes glazed over. She responded in a deep, robotic voice, "The ground split open, fire and flames jumped up. Thou wilt perish in the eternal flames of hell, thou wilt spend eternity in the flames of . . ."

"That's enough, Eileen. Perhaps you had better just sit out here until church is over. I know Charles would rather be outdoors than inside listening to a sermon. You two go over to the wagon and get some elderberry wine or tea. You both have had enough religion for today."

Eileen stopped shaking as Robert let go of her arm. "Sure, Granddad, if you say so. Just wait until I return to the future and tell my minister, Reverend McCall, about my extraordinary out-of-mind experience."

Charles let go of her other arm and headed for the wagon where the lunch food was stashed. He stood still, momentarily looking around at the scene laid out before him.

The wagon rested peacefully under a great oak tree, there before the first colonists came to Virginia. Its limbs were graceful, full of the last leaves of the fall, swaying gently in the breeze. In the distance he could see the beautiful old Anglican church that his great-great-great-great-etc.-grandparents helped to build. He admired the peaceful scene for a minute, hoping to return here if his party survived their battle in New Orleans. Looking around, he reached into the hamper for two glasses. Pouring tea into each glass, he returned to where Eileen was sitting, gazing at the lovely vista. Charles sat down beside her and said, "Here, Sis, drink up." As he said this, he reached into his side pocket and removed a flask filled with whiskey, which he carried for medicinal purposes. He poured a shot into the glass of tea. "Here, Sis, I think this is just what you need."

Eileen, who liked a nip or two on special occasions, grabbed the glass filled with tea and the fiery liquid and gulped it down. It went slithering down her throat, settling in her stomach, causing her to cough, and turning her face bright red.

"Eileen, why'd you think you were falling into the fiery pit? Since you and Maudie were baptized in the Jordan River in Israel you've known that you were saved. Remember that you believe in predestination. I thought old-timey Presbyterians who were saved didn't have such awful thoughts." Tossing back his head as he was saying this to his sister, he polished off his drink.

The dogs—Wahu, Yahu, and Scot—joined Eileen and Charles, who looked around for CAT and saw that she was playfully batting back and forth a little gray field mouse. CAT, happy, was feeling frisky. Playing with mice filled her with joy. Her tail twitched, her whiskers twitched, and her claws were out. Charles never tried to interfere when she played. He thought that he understood CAT's essential nature. He had no desire to change her . . . she was perfect.

The fear in Eileen's eyes disappeared. She was feeling good again. The sun's rays shown down, warming their backs and limbs. Breezes ruffled the leaves remaining on the trees . . . Indian summer . . . winter around the corner . . . the service was over . . . the congregation streaming out into the yard . . . time for lunch.

Robert and Jeremy joined Charles in order to make plans for their trip down river to New Orleans that was to begin on Tuesday. Anita and Eleanor gathered up Eileen. They knew she couldn't cook, but she could set a good table and was completely at home serving meals to hungry guests.

Anita, lifting down the picnic baskets, looked quickly and shyly in the direction of Jeremy. Her heart gave a thump. She wished she was not a slave . . . *if only I was free.*

She liked the color of her skin and thought her face quite lovely . . . *if only I was free.*

She placed the picnic baskets on the wooden tables along with food brought by the others. A feast by any standard.

Spread out on the tables was Brunswick stew; ham biscuits; fried chicken, which had been fried in lard; cucumbers and onions in vinegar; fresh vegetables cut into chunks; apples and hunks of fresh cheese; pound cakes; fruit pies; tea; and coffee, which had been prepared over an open fire—a wondrous feast.

Charles, who always liked to eat, left off planning his great adventure and, along with Robert and Jeremy, headed for the picnic tables. They were young, with healthy appetites. The other guests milled around, impatient to eat. They had all come from farms up to ten miles away, traveling all morning, then exchanging news and gossip, and finally sitting through the church service. Yes, hungry. They were all hungry.

Eileen was happily serving lunch, ladling up the Brunswick stew, made with rabbits that Robert had shot the previous day. Wielding a sharp knife, she cut the cornbread into squares and passed out the tea, unsweetened and sweetened.

Eleanor called all the animals and offered them lunch. CAT, her tail swishing back and forth, refused Eleanor's offer as she greedily swallowed the last of her mouse. Tabby Cat said, "Come on CAT, let's find a mouse for me. I'm hungry." The two scampered off to go hunting.

The preacher joined the party, fascinated by what Eileen had said about the Puritan preacher, Jonathan Edwards, who would be publishing his controversial sermon in several more years.

The sun was shining, slowly beginning its descent into the western sky. Clouds drifted about, fleecy and white with silvery-gray underbellies. The breeze was picking up some coolness.

"Eileen," yelled Eleanor across the yard, "get out our flutes, and we'll play for everyone."

"Sure thing, Eleanor," Eileen yelled back, as she wiped her hands on the yellow apron to dry them. She sauntered back to the wagon to get the two flutes. She assembled them and took one to Eleanor. They called for Anita to join them because she had such a lovely voice, and they loved for her to accompany them. As people finished eating, they assembled near the musicians, sat down, pulling out their flasks and pipes. The preacher looked the other way, and when no one was looking he reached into his jacket, brought out his flask, and took a nip. Sighing contentedly he joined his parishioners. . . .

As the afternoon shadows lengthened, music drifted through the air—"Lord Randall" or "Old Joe Clark"—the two flutes and singer joined by two violins, a recorder, and three guitars. Squirrels hopped around, chased by the cats and dogs . . . mockingbirds dive-bombing, trying to hit the cats. . . .

All thought of hellfire and damnation disappeared from Eileen's mind. The flute bobbed up and down as the music filled her soul. Her feet, clad in her beautiful brown suede boots, tapped in time to the music. Her coral dangly earrings danced merrily, keeping the beat. Just for a minute her attention was diverted by thoughts of clothes . . . *Damn! I look good*, she thought. Then she forgot about clothes and got lost in the music. Anita's beautiful voice soared across the churchyard. Eleanor was bobbing to the rhythm, attired in the new red satin shoes with silver buckles that Eileen had brought to her from Paris . . . from the future.

The music continued. The evening star appeared off in the western sky. The dropping temperature chilled everyone, and they reached for their jackets. They began to prepare for their long journeys home as night was approaching. Time for the Sunday gathering to end. Time to pack up and head home.

Eileen and Charles hopped onto the wagon alongside Anita, who was driving. Mounting their horses, Eleanor, Robert, and Jeremy pranced down the road, heading away from the church. There was a confusion of voices saying goodbyes and calling children and pets. Evening was coming . . . the party was over. All news had been shared.

Everyone wished the Greens and visitors good luck in their journey down the Potowatomie on Tuesday . . . the journey leading to the final battle of the Restitutionary War.

Good luck, Robert

Good luck, everyone

Godspeed. . . .

10

The Carnivorous Mushrooms

*E*EK!
   A shriek!
   A scream . . .
   My dream . . .
   Step out of the dream . . .

Eileen jerked upright and pulled her wits together. Putting on her jacket over her pajamas, she picked up her flashlight and tiptoed out of her room and down the stairs. It was dark. CREAK, CREAK, CREAK went the stairs. She aimed the light around her as she stepped out of the central hall and out onto the porch—down the steps—onto the lawn.

It was a damp and mysterious night. Looking up to the heavens she saw the Red Planet shining through the mist, vaguely, but she would know Mars no matter what the atmospheric conditions. *Mars, that's Mars,* thought Eileen. It twinkled softly, beckoning her to come. Then, suddenly it was obscured by a cloud skittering across the firmament. Mars was obliterated from her vision. She returned to the present and headed for her original destination: the river and the boats that they would be boarding in just a few hours, after breakfast.

The night was quiet, no noise from the happy revelers from the going-away party held the previous evening. *Too much partying*, thought Eileen as she remembered the festivities. Everyone was excited about embarking on their trip down the river. Too much hard cider and wine. Eileen didn't drink much because liquor did not mix well with her schizophrenia pills . . . even in her dreams. . . . Eileen rubbed her hands across her forehead. Even in her dreams Eileen was schizophrenic . . . down to the very core of her being.

SQUISH! CRUNCH!

She looked down! At her feet, which had obliterated a mushroom. *Gracious! There are mushrooms everywhere . . .*

> Mushrooms . . .
> come out
> After the rain
> When the sky is gray
> Full of wet
> Oh, so pretty,
> they get.
>
> Caps of white
> Caps of brown
> They also get an olive hue
> Woohoo!
>
> Stalks so thin
> Have nutrients within
> Flavors lodged within

Eileen contemplated, in a Zen-like frame of mind, what she saw below her on the ground: myriads of beautiful mushrooms. It made her hungry just to look at them . . .

> Waking up from a deep, deep sleep
> Into my nostrils there did creep
> The aroma, subtle . . .
> Gobble, gobble!
>
> Misty gray, the dawning day
> Misty white, waiting for the light
> Of the sun whose rays pour down
> Wilting the mushrooms
> Springing from the ground.
>
> For those less timorous than me
> What a dinner there will be.
> Portobello, such a fellow
> Causes my teeth to clack
> While gobbling it down the back
> Of my throat . . .

Continuing her meandering down to the river, she considered the more esoteric aspects of mushrooms . . . such as . . .

> Giant mushrooms
> Popped up from the grass.
> They took a bite as I went past.
> They chewed and chewed with all
> Of their might.
> Chewing mushrooms!
> Out of sight!
>
> They chewed and chewed on my socks
> They spit out the remains on the rocks.

They chewed through my boots
And chewed through my flesh
What an incredible
Inedible
Mess!
An incredible, inedible mess!

A dream. It's only a dream . . . Eileen cried in her dream. *Mushrooms don't eat humans. Humans eat mushrooms. . . .*

There is a moral here.
From mushrooms you must stay clear.
Or you will be gobbled up, I fear. . .
This was my dream!
Remember!
To be repeated in December.

Eileen took a deep breath, closed her eyes and sighed. *Out of my dream. I must get out of my dream . . .* she stepped into the next layer of reality, the real world . . . at least "real" in relation to the dream in her dream. . . . A walnut fell from the high branches of the walnut tree. It hit Eileen upside the head. "Ouch! That hurts!" Eileen rubbed her hands together, massaging her head where the nut had hit her. The evening breeze was causing the tree limbs to sway, and the nuts were falling all around . . . fall for sure.

She, in a semi-trance, made her way back across the lawn, back into the house, and up to her room . . . the gloom dissipated by the rays of her flashlight . . . back into her room. Anita was there and had placed a tea tray on the little table against the wall.

"Hi, Eileen! Where have you been? Everyone is stirring, and I thought you would like a cup of tea before we all gather together for breakfast."

"Sounds great, Anita. I think I was dreamwalking. I squashed a mushroom, then its friends bit me. It hurt, but I don't think it was a real experience."

"Well, Eileen, you will be pleased to know that I went out before it was light and picked some mushrooms which I am making into omelets."

"Sounds great! We all need to get our strength up for our trip down river. I must get dressed." Saying this, she headed for the wardrobe and started to look for something to wear that would be appropriate for a river trip, as the weather was getting cold.

Anita was dying to see what Eileen would wear. She started poking in the fireplace, stalling for time so that she might catch a glimpse of Eileen's choice of attire.

Eileen, while getting dressed, realized that she did not have many clothes. Her wool skirt was not appropriate, so she chose Ralph Lauren blue jeans with silver studs along the seams running down the sides of her legs. With it she wore black sneakers and her red boiled wool jacket over a black cashmere sweater, chosen for warmth. On her head she placed her black wool beret, with the white cats painted on it, straight from a jazzy boutique in Paris. Dangling from her ears hung her silver and turquoise earrings. She tucked a pair of red leather gloves in her pockets.

Anita was fascinated. She had never seen such clothes. The style was beyond exciting. She herself only had two skirts, three tops and one coat. She would love to wear trousers, but for now that was out of the question. But she would make a pattern and when they returned from New Orleans—and there was no doubt in her mind that they would win the war and return safely to Liberty Hall—she would make a pair of trousers for Eleanor and a pair for herself. Finally, she had to get back to work. She headed for the door, having drawn the curtains. "See you downstairs, Eileen."

Eileen, sipping the tea and musing, answered, "I'll be down in ten minutes, Anita."

Ten minutes later, Eileen joined her new friends and family, who were gathered around the breakfast table. Charles was having a ball. "Everything is ready, Granddad. I even included catnip for the cats and dog bones for Scot, Wahu, and Yahu. The canoes are in tip-top condition, and everything is securely packed in them and on the flatboat."

He extended his hands towards the flames in the fireplace. "It's going to be chilly going down the river." Having never transported through dreams and time before, he was fascinated by all that was happening. He was excited about the trip that he was to lead down the Potowatomie.

The dogs and cats were excited, their whiskers twitching, and their tails wagging.

It was going to be a great adventure. They knew there would be lots of squirrels, rabbits, and fish to torment, perhaps even to eat.

Pancakes and strawberry syrup, mushroom omelets, aromatic coffee—intoxicating fumes wafting through the house, out into the yard. There was also apple cobbler. It was a veritable feast, the last one to be enjoyed at Liberty Hall for a long time.

At last, breakfast was completed. Anita cleared the table and the men gathered for a puff on their pipes. After several leisurely puffs, Robert went outdoors to give last minute instructions to his slaves about tending the farm while his party was on their great adventure.

At last! No more delays. The party of six adventurers gathered at the canoes and flatboat. They boarded, gave a shove, and were out onto the river. The sun burned through the fog, lighting up the river. The chilly breeze blew, churning up the water and forming whitecaps.

"Goodbye!" waved Robert and Eleanor and Scot who followed Charles and CAT onto the river, followed by Jeremy and Anita on the flat boat with Tabby Cat, and last but not least, Eileen with Wahu and Yahu . . . the great adventure continued . . . down the river to their fates. . . .

In the back of Eileen's mind ran a refrain . . .

> The mushrooms so free
> Want to make omelets
> Out of we . . .
> Want to make omelets
> Out of we . . .
> Out of we . . .
> Out of we . . .

11

A Dip in the Drink

*F*LOATING . . . FLOATING . . . FLOATING . . .
Cruising . . . cruising . . . cruising. . . .

They had left Liberty Hall and were settling into the rhythm of the river. In her mind's eye, Eileen looked down the river, sensing Indian dugouts, manned each with forty warriors erupting out from behind an island, chasing the canoes, hoping to get some fresh scalps as they had not had any new ones since the last party of colonists had been attacked while canoeing down the river, hoping to reach General Walloby in time to participate in the final battle of the Restitutionary War, hoping for a victory—loosening them from the tyranny of Great Britain and her efforts to foist only tea on the colonists, who wanted coffee.

Eileen, Anita, and Eleanor were the only three ladies in the party. Eileen was by herself in her canoe, accompanied by Wahu and Yahu, who were behaving themselves admirably and were enjoying the ride down the river. Anita was on the flatboat filled with food and extra supplies that they all would need on their jaunt down the wide, wide river. Eleanor and her dog, Scot, were paddling and talking with her husband, Robert.

The Potowatomie was calm. It sparkled from the sun's rays bouncing off of the surface of the waves. The riverbank unfolded like a giant mural before their eyes. The trees were shades of green with a soupcon of yellow and blue just to keep things interesting. There were logs all over the banks. Floating down the river, they presented everpresent danger to the canoes and their occupants.

The sky was a gorgeous shade of blue. It flashed with rays of turquoise and lapis lazuli. The clouds were puffy—white and silver and gray—drifting along, keeping time with Eileen and her party made up of humans, dogs, and cats.

What to eat? Thank God for Anita and Charles. Charles was a gourmet on the river, and Anita was a superb cook for large groups. Best of all, there was coffee—enough for two weeks, if they were careful. They had decided to only give General Walloby two pounds of the precious beans. They also decided only to save one bottle of the Café Rica with which they would toast to victory. They knew—it was a foregone conclusion—that they would be victorious. Thanks to God, who desired that his people be free. Free to worship and to work joyously and to enjoy their coffee, which he had developed for his human's pleasure.

Eileen continued musing. *Wow! There must be a hurricane down near the Gulf of Mexico. Perhaps that would explain the torrential rain that has just exploded on the river.* As she pondered this, the heavens thundered, and noise exploded over the entire area. Lightning flashed across the sky. Waves were pounding against her canoe, causing its occupants to be a little concerned for their safety. *Oh dear, I hope we won't be electrocuted.*

Charles was also worrying, but he was more concerned about their dinner and supplies being lost if the canoes and flatboat should be torn apart in the turbulent waters. CAT sat on her seat in the front of the canoe, horrified that she might get her fur wet. When she agreed to come on the trip, getting caught in cold torrential rain had not been part of the plan. The birch bark canoes were not as sturdy and well balanced as her pop's Olde Town. *Oh well, that old tabby cat is not complaining and I refuse to be bested by a tomcat. The dogs also are greeting this turbulence with cool and equanimity. Therefore, I too, will be cool.*

Eileen was sitting in her canoe, paddling along, wondering about the rain and the swift current that seemed to have gotten out of her control. *Wow! No radio, no TV, no newspapers, no telephones. No one knows where we are and probably don't care.* She looked into the darkening sky and saw a bald eagle soaring near the treetops. It was mighty and impressive. She had only seen two other eagles soaring up a mountain draft in Idaho when she was young.

"Hi, ho, down the river we go," she sang out with a loud voice. The water splashed back and forth, pushed this way and that by the wind and pouring rain, with white caps racing towards the canoe.

Oh dear! I've gotten behind the rest of the party. Charles has been nagging me for years to read the river and keep up with everyone. I have been daydreaming. Oh my God! I've drifted close to a tree fallen in the river, and the current is pushing me quickly toward that tree fallen into the river. I distinctly remember Charles telling me, "Eileen, never get caught in a tree." Eileen started paddling with all of her might, but she was inexorably being swept to the tree. "Oh dear! I'll try to get out into the current caused by that little river to my left entering the Potowatomie," she yelled above the noise of the storm to her two dogs.

Paddle, paddle, paddle . . . all to no avail. She was not strong enough to get out of the current. Suddenly she was hanging onto a tree limb, one among many extending into the river, blocking her passage. She frantically held onto the branch, trying not to capsize. Wahu and Yahu had jumped into the water, and they swam to shore.

Suddenly, as she was about to drown, a hand pulled her out of the water back onto land. There was a fire and shot of whiskey.

She looked again at the fire. Some wonderful smelling food was cooking. She was too hungry to care what he was fixing, and, in fact, it smelled yummy. "What is cooking?" she inquired. She was ravenous.

"Rabbit! I shot it shortly before I found you in the river," said Elias, who was also hungry. He had not eaten since early morning. Eileen knew it was important that men eat regularly. She knew that they liked to eat a lot, and she was not sure that a tiny little rabbit would be enough . . .

Elias was cooking . . .

Eileen was thinking . . .

Ripple, ripple goes the stream
Merrily burbling
In a dream.
Flowing this way and then that
Wondering lazily where it is at.

Algae up and tip their hat
To the busy beaver who is fat
Creatively building a dam
Where the little fishes swam
At the entrance to the river
Where the little beavers shiver
At the entrance to the river.

When lo, and behold
In an elk skin hide
Elias the trapper sneakily strides
Hoping for a pelt or two
Then his day's work would be through.

Back to the stream in the sparkling sun.
Wondering merrily, "Where next will I run,
Providing a place for the beaver to work.
Busily, busily! they do not shirk . . . work

Ripple, ripple
Fast, then slow
Wondering, wondering
Which way to go
Which way to go
First fast, then slow
Wondering, wondering
Which way to go.

The graceful deer
Who comes to drink
Never considers that Elias might slink
Up and hide behind a tree
With his Kentucky longrifle
Propped on his knee.

So crafty
So crafty . . .
A good shot to the head!
A most perfect shot.
That deer is dead.
With a steady hand
And a steady arm
He pulls the trigger
The damage is done.
For just a second
The stream is in shock
As it tumbles over a rock.
Then once again it flows along
Forgetting quickly
That the deer is gone.

The law of nature
Cruel it seems . . .

"Survival of the fittest"
Seems awfully mean.
As the stream forgets
And burbles on
No longer aware the deer is gone.

12

Happily Honking

*B*RR! IT'S COLD," MURMURED ELIAS TO HIMSELF, AS HE PULLED the fur cap over his ears, pulled on his gloves, looked at the sky, and watched the Canada geese flying in formation, wings flapping, happily honking as loudly as they could. They were heading south to escape from the intense cold of the more northern areas of the New World. "Brr!" said Elias as he watched the golden and red and orange and pink leaves flutter to the ground, shaken from the trees by the breeze which was increasing in intensity as the temperature began to drop.

He stopped watching the geese and concentrated his attention on the woman sleeping on the ground. He heard a solitary squawk and once again looked at the sky, where he saw a solitary goose flying overhead, having fallen behind his friends. "He needs to hurry up, or he will be left behind."

Smoke rose from the campfire, drifting into the afternoon air. The fire provided a little warmth on the cool day. He reached into his deer-skin pants pocket and pulled out his prized pipe. After tamping some tobacco into the bowl, he reached for a stick lying on the ground, and stuck it into the fire. The small blaze was then used to light the pipe. He puffed deeply and sighed. He settled himself comfortably on his log, to do some serious thinking . . . thinking about the strange woman he had rescued.

Eileen was restlessly tossing and turning, knocked out from imbibing the strong liquor. She could not handle hard liquor well. Her red hair was glued to her scalp, still wet from her dump in the river. It was straight and unattractive, but she was oblivious to her appearance in her dreams. More leaves drifted down from the trees, causing the earth to look as though it was carpeted with a beautiful rug of the highest quality.

Elias thoughtfully puffed some more. He looked at the restless sleeping woman. He wondered aloud, "Where is she from?" He frowned, as he was puzzled by the strange bag he had found in her canoe. He had never seen material like it. It was hard and shiny and totally unlike any material he had ever seen. And her hair . . . he had never seen such a red-orange color . . . and her earrings . . . and her strange apparel . . . "Where are they from? I have been around a lot of the world and have seen many women with colored hair, but never anything like hers." He contemplated the late afternoon sun, glowing softly orange-red in the sky . . . "Sort of like her hair." He pondered these questions for the duration of his pipe. "She is different." He poked at the fire, trying to restore the dying flame. It needed some more wood. "Where are those dogs?"

Eileen yelled, "Where am I?" and sat bolt upright. Still not fully conscious, she looked at the deerskin clothed man stirring around in the fire, and said "Who are you?" She had completely forgotten that this was the man she had fallen in love with at first sight.

"Remember me? Elias Witherstone? I fished you out of the river, and I gave you some lunch and liquor. You passed out. At least your color is better, and you have stopped shaking."

Eileen tossed her head back and forth, trying to dislodge the migraine that had settled behind her left eye. "Whiskey! It always gives me a headache," she muttered to her rescuer. She was now fully aware of her surroundings, and of the frontiersman sitting on the log across the fire from where she was lying on the ground, wrapped in her Indian blanket from Santa Fe. It was red and blue and yellow and black—gorgeous. "Have you seen my dogs?" she inquired in a slightly worried tone of voice.

Elias puffed again on his pipe, and said, " Why, yes. They went running off downriver, to look for your party." He threw another piece of wood on the fire. "Where are you going?" asked Elias, who was curious about the activities of his new friend. He had not seen people for several months, and he was thrilled to have company.

Eileen looked thoughtfully at Elias, and said, "My group and I are going to New Orleans to participate in the final battle of the Restitutionary War. We're going to join up with General Walloby, who is the leader of the colonial forces."

"What a coincidence! That is where I am headed. Perhaps if your party finds you, I can join up with you. I would certainly enjoy your company. Care for a smoke?" Saying this, he handed the pipe to Eileen who did not usually smoke. She took a puff, however, and promptly went into a coughing jag.

"Sorry! I don't seem able to handle either liquor or tobacco. I would enjoy some wine, though; but I guess that is asking too much . . . to expect Pinot Grigio on the river. . . ." The smoke drifted upwards and they sat quietly in companionable silence. . . .

They heard voices, coming from downriver. "Hello! Eileen! Do you hear us? Where are you?" The dogs were howling and barking.

"Elias," said Eileen, "it's my brother and great-great-great-great-etc.-grandparents."

"Here," she yelled. "Here!" she yelled again, jumping up and down and screaming. The two dogs came bounding to her, barking as loudly as they could. The dogs came to the open fire, wagging their tails and joyfully bounding up and down, happy to once again be with Eileen and the strange man.

Up the river came Charles, Robert, and Eleanor. Elias noticed one man was dressed strangely like the woman he had rescued. They saw Eileen, and Charles yelled, "Are you okay?"

Elias got up from his log and walked towards the three strangers, extending his hand in friendship. Eileen greeted everyone, patted the dogs, and introduced Elias to her family. She told them about her adventure, and everyone was glad to meet the man who had helped her.

The sun was sinking into the West. It was getting really cold. Elias said to Charles, "Would it be possible for me to join up with your party? I am an excellent hunter, and feel that I would be a good addition to your group. I have my own canoe and supplies and will not be a bother."

"Let him join us, Charles. He's loads of fun, although sometimes rather somber."

"All right. We could use another fighter," agreed Charles.

Robert and Eleanor stepped forward and said, "Thank you for saving Eileen. We expect you are puzzled by her and Charles. It is hard to explain, but she is apparently able to transport herself, Charles, the two dogs, and some supplies through dreams, traveling in time. We know it sounds crazy, but they are from the future."

"You are nuts! There is no such thing!" Elias was so shocked that he dropped his prized pipe. Bending down to retrieve it, he stammered, "You are nuts! There is no such thing."

"Oh, yes there is," lamented Charles in a huffy voice. Trappers were peculiar, not his choice for a companion on the river. Charles was squeamish, due to a faulty liver, which had accumulated rust and occasional dust from the musty beer—a fearsome brew. Quite intoxicating! . . . Charles reached into the pocket of his L. L. Bean wool jacket and withdrew a slightly warm beer. He tipped his head back and took a slug. Beer trickled, then plummeted down his gullet. Robert and Eleanor sat quietly, gazing into the fire, contemplating why they were here. Elias was packing his gear back into his canoe.

He also was getting Eileen's canoe repacked. He was happy to have some traveling companions. As he thought about his new friends, he thought that perhaps it was true that they were from the future. That is the only way he could make sense of the materials and clothes he had seen.

Eileen sauntered to the edge of the river, watched Elias and spoke up. "Elias, I'm a flight attendant for Universal Airlines. Early in the twentieth century, Orville and Wilbur Wright invented the airplane. It is a machine that flies through the sky. I have spent years of my life in the air, flying over oceans and continents. If I am able to once again return to the future after the battle, I will try to return to this time with some pictures of planes. They are beautiful."

Elias was puzzled. But he returned his attention to the canoes and the trip down the river. He said to Charles, "We had better get going as it will be dark shortly, and we have to go about one mile, which shouldn't take long. You paddle your sister's boat, I will paddle mine, and the others can walk.

"Sure," said Charles as he pulled a large flashlight out of his bag. He flashed it on and startled Elias once again.

By now Eileen had thoroughly dried out, and her hair was also dry. She was relatively warm and was admiring the beautiful sunset. Soon it would be dark, and her party would be united for the evening. She salivated, thinking about the dinner that Jeremy and Anita would prepare. She was hoping for some ham or turkey—some protein. She needed something with substance. She once again walked over to Elias's canoe and said, "See you at the camp. You can then meet the others."

Elias regarded her again, stepped into his canoe, picked up his paddles, and said, "See you shortly. Be careful walking in the dark." He quietly paddled out into the current flowing swiftly down river. Charles followed closely behind.

Eileen, Robert, Eleanor, and the two dogs extinguished the fire, watched after the canoes that had gone on downriver, and started walking back to their camp.

Geese were still flying overhead through the sky, honking merrily. Were they, too, going to New Orleans? The sun was gone. Eileen turned on her large flashlight. The three humans and two dogs walked quietly, munching on some beef jerky. They were hungry. Life on the river worked up an appetite.

13

Slither, Slither, Our Hearts Aquiver

SLITHER, SLITHER
Slither, slither
Crawling, crawling
Hither, thither
Our hearts aquiver,
Also our livers

Crawling, crawling along
The birds above
Break into song
We are Zak and Mac
Of the tribe Jacawampum
Why are we here?
Why have we come?
And who are those persons

Sitting on the log
Could it be they are drinking grog?

Elias and Eileen were sitting on the log, discussing dream travel, and Elias's need to venture into the twenty-first century with Eileen and Charles, where he could see for himself firsthand the wonders of the sky: airplanes and spacecraft. Elias, with a look of wonder said, "I have never heard of such things. Do you really think that I can transport forward in time with you?"

Eileen thoughtfully gazed into the flickering flames. She raised her eyes and looked deeply into the handsome Elias's black eyes. "Well, Elias, I think that if I'm careful, I can transport you, if you'd like to go with me. Where would you like to go?"

Elias, who had been pondering this question said, "I think I need to return to the twenty-first century and see these wonders of which you are so enamored. Do you think Charles would mind?"

"Oh, no! I'm sure Charles finds you most interesting."

The two young people both gazed deeply into the dancing flames, leaping heavenward in the cold late afternoon by the river flowing downwards to New Orleans.

"Oh, look Elias! Twinkling above! It's Mars!"

"Why, so it is. I always know Mars because it is the only planet that twinkles. Let's go to Mars, Eileen. That would be a great adventure. You know, I believe you are the only person I have ever known who knows that Mars twinkles. Everyone says that the planet only glows. But we know better."

They raised their eyes to the softly twinkling planet, and each gave a great sigh. As they sat by the fire on the log, they could hear softly the dulcet tones of Anita's beautiful soprano voice, accompanied by Jeremy playing the guitar . . . "Where have you been Lord Randall, my son? Where have you been, my pretty young one? . . ."

Charles was down by the river cleaning the freshly caught fish for their evening dinner. Charles was quite the gourmet on the river. Elias had discovered that Eileen couldn't cook. He couldn't conceive of a woman not cooking, and he was disappointed. "Like Charles, I, too, am a great cook on the river. I had to learn because if I didn't cook, I didn't eat," he informed Eileen, who shook her head in wonder. Slowly the aroma of coffee filled the air around the campsite, drifting here and there as the wind dictated.

"Nobody knows the trouble I've seen, nobody knows but Jesus. . . ." Anita's beautiful voice was belting out the classic spiritual, in C major because Jeremy had only begun to play several months before the river trip, and it was easy to play in C.

The animals gathered around Charles, who was still cleaning the trout. Eleanor was stooping beside him as she prepared two squirrels and three rabbits, which she was going to put into a Brunswick stew. Charles and Anita had also made some sourdough bread. This was new to Anita, but being an experimental cook, she was always ready to learn new recipes and techniques of cooking. Charles had brought the starter through Eileen's dream journey, because he always carried sourdough starter on river trips.

"Do you know if we will be on the river for Thanksgiving two weeks from now?" enquired Eleanor as she slowly stirred the freshly cleaned meat into the stew.

Charles stood up slowly. He had finished cleaning the fish, and his knees were killing him. He had arthritis and was worried that he would not be able to canoe much longer. "I don't know, Eleanor. No one seems to be sure how many miles we'll have to cover. But if we're on the river at Thanksgiving, maybe we can catch a wild turkey or a deer."

The three dogs howled and the two cats growled along with Anita and Jeremy. They had just been fed some fish by Charles, and they were happy, trying to keep to the beat and in tune.

Mars twinkled down. Eileen and Elias were fascinated. Although Edgar Rice Burroughs had not been alive in the 1700s to write his Martian series, Eileen told Elias the story of John Carter, Dejah Thoris, and

Woola. Elias was an intelligent man and an adventurer. Often at night in the wilderness, he had sat on a log, as he was doing now, with pipe in hand, quietly smoking, and contemplating the wonder of Mars hanging in the heavens above him, shimmering in a red haze.

Eileen had always been mesmerized by the Red Planet. She was convinced that Edgar Rice Burroughs was ahead of his time, and although his characters were not "real" in the sense that most of humanity considered real, to her mind and in her dreams they were more real than anyone she knew. Although they did not have physical bodies, they were real in spirit. As she was pondering, Elias got up from the fire and quietly walked to his canoe and extracted a leather-bound box, which he carried back to the fire. He handed her the box. She opened it and was surprised to see a small oval painting of a beautiful young woman holding a small boy in her arms.

"Who is she, and who is the small boy?" enquired Eileen as she looked at Elias, hoping he was not married.

Elias quietly replied, "The young woman was my wife, and that was my son. We were living in London when there was a smallpox epidemic. They both contracted smallpox and died. I was unable to help them. No one could help."

Elias looked at the redhead sitting next to him, and he asked, "Eileen, are you married?"

She replied, "No, Elias. I suffer from a serious mental disease—some people would say that I am still crazy. I never could feel right about getting married. Marriage is restrictive. I have a somewhat shaky psyche." Saying this, she reached into her pocket and brought out a small plastic bottle with yellow pills. The conversation was making her nervous, so she popped one of the pretty yellow pills into her mouth and quickly swallowed it. Eileen always got nervous at the mention of marriage.

Elias saw that she was getting agitated, so he said, "Let's not talk anymore." So they sat in companionable silence and thought about planes and space travel.

As the evening progressed and as Elias thought about Eileen, he was convinced in his deepest being that she and her brother Charles were absolutely authentic: they had traveled back in time through a dream. All of a sudden, Wahu sat bolt upright and growled . . . and growled . . . and growled. He smelled strange humans. "What's up, Wahu?" enquired Yahu in a soft voice.

"I think we have visitors. Be quiet, but we must alert Elias and Eileen. The rest of the campers are too far away to be of help right now." As they said this, they had walked to the edge of the campsite where they saw two red-skinned humans crawling along the ground toward Elias and Eileen.

WOOF, WOOF

WOOF, WOOF, WOOF

ARF, ARF

ARF, ARF, ARF

Elias jumped to his feet. He had heard a twig break, and he heard the two dogs growl. "Quiet, Eileen. I think we have company." He eased forward toward the bushes. He saw two dark figures. Grabbing his Kentucky longrifle, he yelled, "Who goes there? Show yourselves or I will shoot."

The two figures eased themselves into the area by the fire. They stood up. "Indians! Indians, Eileen! Be prepared to run when I give the command." He grabbed Eileen's hand and dragged her away from the two advancing Indians. The one in front extended his hand toward Elias and said, "How!"

Elias, keeping his rifle aimed steadily at the two intruders said, "Howdy! Who are you and what do you want?"

"I am Zak and this is my brother Mac. We are the sons of the chief of the Jacawampum tribe, camped across the river. Our father smelled coffee and sent us to investigate. We love coffee and were excited at the prospect of having a cup. We mean no harm." He and his brother brushed leaves, dirt, and grass from off of their beautiful leather breeches.

"I've never heard of the Jacawampum. How is it you speak such good English?"

Mac spoke up, "Well, mister, our father believed that we as a tribe needed to be assimilated into the prevailing culture. He realized that the future was with the white man, so he sent us to the College of William and Mary, where we studied English and modern philosophy. Zak got As, and I got Cs. I am not a good scholar."

"Why," exclaimed Eileen in an amazed voice, "that's where Elias and I went to school. I studied art and dance, but I do not know what Elias studied."

The dogs crept up to the Indians and checked them out. They did not sense hostility, so they wagged their tails as the Indians petted their ears. Elias relaxed. He realized that Wahu and Yahu were good judges of character. "You smelled rightly," he said as he extended his hand. "The young lady brought some coffee when she left her home. You are welcome to have a cup."

"Thank you very much. It is exciting—the thought of having coffee. We haven't had any since we graduated from college two years ago. We hate the English for blockading the coast, preventing ships from bringing in coffee."

Eileen, still holding Elias's hand, said, "Come on! You are welcome to share dinner with us, followed by a tasty cup of black coffee. We do not have crème. Coffee is precious, but to be shared."

Zak and Mac were elated at their good luck. They grabbed their bows and arrows from the ground. The four people and two dogs headed over to where the coffee was brewing, their noses twitching at the prospect of a good cup of coffee.

"Eileen," said Elias, "do you think that we can transport coffee to Mars when we go, even as you and Charles transported it here? It would seem that it would be more difficult to get it and us through limitless space."

"Who knows? Elias, we can but try. We can but try."

14

Several Hours Earlier

TOM TOM AND ZUSETTE SAT IN FRONT OF THEIR CAMPFIRE, WON-
dering where Mac and Zak were and whether they would be coming back.

"I know it was dangerous to send them to check out the white man
and woman. I hope that they will be okay," said Tom Tom to his wife,
Zusette of the long black pigtail.

"Oh, Tom Tom, don't be such a worrywart. Mac and Zak are perfectly able to take care of themselves. I just hope that they discover the
source of the coffee that we smelled drifting across the river." Saying this,
she started to add more wood to the fire, which shot up in an effort to
reach the heavens.

Tom Tom and Zusette were cold, although they were both clad in
deer skins from tunics to leggings and in Zusette's case, a fringe shirt.

The beading on their clothing was gorgeous as Zusette was an incredible artist, and she had made beautiful designs of the planets and stars on Tom Tom's jacket and beautiful daisies on her jacket: blue, white, yellow, red, and green beads, bought on one of their trips to Williamsburg to see the boys at the College of William and Mary.

Tom Tom was rearranging the feathers in his headband. They were lonely . . . just the two of them . . . no boys.

Again came the faint aroma of coffee, drifting across the river. Zusette was roasting rabbits on a spit over the campfire to be eaten with some fry bread, a recipe she had learned from Flying Fish, her grandmother. It was a particularly good fry bread, flavored with garlic.

Tom Tom smelled the coffee once again and realized that he was hungry. They had been on the river all day and had not had lunch. "Hurry up Zusette. I am starving. How about you?"

"Well, Tom Tom. I guess I'm in need of a little sustenance, but I try not to think about it as we have a long way to go and not many surplus supplies. I know we won't starve because you are a good hunter, and I am good at grabbing fish in the river. In fact, tomorrow night why don't we have some fried fish?"

"Sounds good!" said Tom Tom as he walked from the fire. Meandering away, he noticed how cold it had become. He headed to the river, singing somberly, "I am a poor wayfaring stranger. . . ." His rich baritone floated upward toward the celestial sphere. The birds, squirrels, groundhogs, foxes, and deer strained to hear the beloved words of a lonely pilgrim on his journey toward his heavenly home.

Zusette poured water from the river into the iron pot, listening to her husband's beautiful voice, bringing the water to a boil.

"Hey Zusette, do you want Earl Grey or Darjeeling?" He dug into the bag of teas, bringing out two boxes, filled with either the Earl Grey or the Darjeeling.

The night owl hooted, and the evening star twinkled off in the low western sky. Several fish flashed silver as they leapt out of the river, feeling frisky in the cold water. The owl considered fish for dinner, but decided that he wanted field mice, or perhaps a baby fox.

"Ah, the intricacies of the food chain," mused Zusette as she admired the beautiful evening sky. Her reverie was brought to an abrupt halt by the far-off barking of dogs. "Where can they be?" she wondered as she placed dough in a pan to be fried.

Meanwhile, back at the canoes, Tom Tom brought out two wool blankets that he hoped would keep them warm during the coldness of the night.

He walked back to the campsite and threw the two blankets onto the ground next to the log on which they had been sitting earlier.

The owl hooted. "Dinner! Ah, it's dinnertime. If some mice don't show up soon, I will probably go hungry tonight." As he said this he peered through the impending gloom and "*Voilà!* There are two mice. One will suffice, but I hate to break up families." He flapped his wings and rolled back his eyes. . .

"Help me God! To catch those mice
I know that killing isn't nice,
but still, two mice should suffice.
I will catch them, yes I will!
Here I go, in for the kill."

He flapped his wings and gave a mighty lift into the air. . .

"I want those mice.
I do not care!
Two for dinner will suffice
I'm not a hog!
I will use the fog!
As a cover, as I hover
Above their heads
They are almost dead."

Saying this, he dived swiftly toward the mice who had not been paying attention to their surroundings.

Swoop! Swoop! He grabbed them up in his talons and giggled happily. He rose up, thinking, *They are awfully heavy. I hope I make it back to my limb.* He made a valiant effort, flapping his wings mightily. He landed on his limb, dinner in tow. He opened his beak and popped the two mice into his mouth. His stomach stopped growling because it knew that within ten to twenty minutes it would no longer be hungry.

Zusette and Tom Tom once again gathered by the flames flickering in the darkening evening, putting out just a tiny bit of warmth. Dinner was ready . . . rabbits roasted, fry bread with garlic, and Earl Grey tea; and after dinner a peace pipe . . .

> Pipe of Peace we welcome you
> Into our lungs at night
> Persuade our brains
> To not be strained
> And to do all things right.
> The smoke it climbs away up high
> Captivating the mice who have to die
> To provide dinner to the owl, the winner
> Oh, pipe of peace, we welcome you
> We love your smoke, we really do.
> We love your smoke, we really do.

15

Where Are My Pills?

EILEEN TOSSED AND TURNED ON HER BLANKET ON THE COLD, cold ground . . . on the hard, hard ground. Sleep eluded her as she gazed thoughtfully at the nighttime sky full of blazing stars, twinkling and winkling through the deep dark universe. She was especially fascinated by the mystical planet, the War Planet, Mars. . . .

Toss, toss. . . .

Turn, turn. . . .

Like a pig on a spit . . . roasting slowly in the fire, getting ready for dinner. Anita had gone hunting and found a large brown pig roaming through the woods. *Wonderful! Dinner should be glorious!* she thought as she slit the pig's throat and watched the blood gushing out onto the forest floor, staining the fallen leaves; a dark red stain ever spreading out from the dead pig. Anita was elated and grabbed the pig's legs, tugging it back to camp.

Still, Eileen was having a bad night. *I think that I'll take another pill. They usually help me to sleep.* She shook the bottle . . . nothing much . . . SHAKE, SHAKE . . . nothing much. Opening the bottle, she found that there were only two pills left—yellow . . . a pretty shade of yellow.

"Oh dear! I must return to the year 2008 and visit my doctor. I forgot! My appointment is for today. I certainly hope that the Bubble Machine still works, or I am in deep doo-doo." Saying this, she leapt to her feet and hastily put on her clothes. She saw in the misty early morning fog a canoe skittering across the river. "It must be Mac and Zak going to get their parents to come join us. Oh dear, it is 4:00 A.M. My appointment is at 10:00. I must hurry."

She padded over to where Charles was peacefully asleep, his head propped up on a log and the blanket covering every part of his body, except for his head. She gently shook his shoulders and whispered, "Charles, wake up. It's important."

Charles, who was in the middle of a good dream about canoeing down the Yukon in Alaska, was startled out of his deep sleep. He jerked upright, his hands reaching for his gun. Then he realized that it was only Eileen. "Why did you wake me up?" he whined, unhappy to be awakened out of such a good nighttime reverie.

"Charles, I have to return to my doctor's office today. I'm nearly out of pills, and even though we're in a dream, I still need my pills. So I must hurry, as my appointment is this morning at 10:00. I need to leave. Tell Zak and Mac that I will see them when I return—tonight, I hope.

"What are you two mumbling about? I heard you say that you were leaving. Where are you going?" groused Elias, who had materialized out of nowhere. He was the strong, silent type. Realizing that she should tell Elias the truth, Eileen spoke quietly to him so as not to wake the rest of the sleeping party. She told him about her schizophrenia.

"Schizophrenia! . . . What is that?" Elias mumbled as the sun was slowly cutting through the early morning fog, leaving a layer of dew to coat the riverside and forest floor. He shook his head. Definitely his new friend, Eileen, was not like other women he had known. Best to humor her.

"Elias, I must return to my doctor's office." Eileen was nervous from spilling the beans to her new friend. She was unsure whether he would still like her.

"Well then, I will go with you. It is not safe for women to travel in this strange future that you talk about. Also, I am curious to see for myself the wonders of which you speak. So no discussion, for I am going with you." Elias dropped down on a log and started stirring the fire, placing a pot of coffee on to brew.

"Elias, you're not dressed so well for the twenty-first century. People will think we are strange."

"Since when did you care what people think of the way you dress?" Elias stirred the fire again, and the small blaze sprang to life, providing light and a small amount of warmth.

Hearing a strange noise, the three companions turned from the fire and looked toward the forest, where they saw Anita dragging her newly slain pig. "Good morning, everyone," said Anita, who was glad to see the fire. "I got a pig for dinner. We should have a feast."

By now, Jeremy, Robert, and Eleanor had been aroused by all of the noise and commotion. The dogs and cats barked and meowed and stretched luxuriously. They all took a walk and returned to join the humans.

Robert said, "Good morning! We heard you say that you are leaving for the future."

"Yes, Granddad, I'm nearly out of my pills, so I'm going to keep my doctor's appointment. It is this morning. Elias is going with me. We hope to get to Washington, DC, on time. Then we hope to return in time for the roasted pig dinner and to meet Tom Tom and Zusette."

Meanwhile, Anita and Eleanor had started preparing grits and bacon for breakfast . . . just a touch of honey. Charles said, "Eileen, be sure to get some bags of coffee and bring back some dog and cat food with you."

"Elias," said Eileen, who was hurriedly fixing her hair, "there is no guarantee that we will get there and back. So far, everything has worked okay, but you never know. . . ."

"That is okay, Eileen, but wherever we end up, it will be better for you if I am along." After saying this, he stood up and shook his coonskin cap and placed it on his head. He reached down for a cup and poured himself some coffee. The smell of cooking bacon and coffee wafted through the frigid morning air.

"Oh dear," said Eileen, "it's nearly 7:00 A.M. We must get going." Wahu and Yahu were sitting beside her. They had decided to accompany her and Elias.

"Time to go!" Eileen and Elias and the two dogs stood quietly in a circle, and Eileen held up her communicator. She dialed 1942* . . . the bubble speaks. It's low, sonorous voice burbled into the air . . . "Who is with you?"

Eileen said, "Just me, Elias, and the two dogs. We need to get to Dupont Circle in Washington, DC. We need to return tonight after my appointment in time, we hope, for a cooked pig dinner."

"Okay," intoned the invisible bubble. "Grab hands and tails! POOF! Away we go! . . ."

Spiraling, spiraling . . .

Through the cold, damp air . . .

Black with sprinkles of twinkles . . .

Spiraling, spiraling . . . then, PLOP!

Onto Connecticut Avenue, bustling with traffic, . . . buses barreling by, cars, bicycles, and cop cars . . . constant turmoil!

The visitors from dreamland stood up and straightened their clothes. They checked on the dogs and looked around.

"Elias, this is the way I live," said Eileen as they narrowly avoided being hit by a bus as they crossed the street. Nobody noticed the four strange beings. "That," said Eileen, "is probably because they're only noticing themselves." Quickly they marched up the street to R Street. They passed the Starbucks coffeehouse. "Elias, would you like to stay here with the dogs and have a cup of coffee?"

"No, I want to meet your doctor." So they passed on to the next house, to the old brick building where Eileen had spent many countless hours over the years. Elias and the two dogs joined Eileen as she went into the building for her appointment. They all sat in his waiting room. . . .

Then he appears

She says . . .

> Dr. Goldberg, you are my friend
> So I will tell you where I have been
> My friends came with me at nine o'clock
> I told them they could meet my doc

He says . . .

> Tell me, missy, about your life
> Have you been dealing well with strife?
> Have you been taking your pills
> Which protect you from many ills?
> Yes indeedy, your pills.
> They were devised for people like you
> To help you get through
> The rough spots on the roads
> Which you share with squirrels and toads.
> Here is your prescription, fill it, dear!
> It is good for another year.

"Now, let's talk."

16

Later That Afternoon

ELIAS SAT PEACEFULLY IN THE CHAIR AT STARBUCKS' OUTDOOR café. He had put his coonskin cap on the table in front of him. He had noticed that it was drawing attention to himself, which attention he did not want. He was trying to adjust to his surroundings that he never in his wildest dreams had imagined. The coffee he was drinking was bold and hot. He was happy. The sun was drifting lazily toward the western horizon as he was getting worried about Eileen. Several cups of coffee had made him a little twitchy. "Where is she? She said that she would not be gone long."

Eileen, meanwhile, was deeply involved in conversation with Dr. Goldberg, her new doctor—scintillating conversation. "Miss Gordon, what you are telling me is incredible. Do you truly think that you have been transporting back and forth in time through your dreams? It is, you will admit, hard to believe. Normally I would think that you were having a relapse, but you seem perfectly normal for you. Tell me more!"

"Dr. Goldberg, if you'd like, I can get Elias, or we could join him. He is drinking coffee at Starbucks. We could go to him there. He might be intimidated talking to you in your office. Come on, let's go." Saying this, Eileen jumped to her feet, grabbed Dr. Goldberg's hand, pulling him swiftly to his feet. "Come on!"

The two of them went downstairs to tell the receptionist where they would be. She was surprised, as this was unusual behavior for him. "Certainly, doctor. If anyone calls, I'll tell them that you will be back in an hour." She looked at her computer.

"If we are later than 5:00 P.M., close the office and lock the door. I have my key to get back in." So Eileen and the doc walked out of his building into the cool fall weather, which was invigorating after being in the office. Traffic was honking and careening through the streets. Eileen and Dr. Goldberg strolled to Starbucks and saw Elias quietly drinking coffee and watching the pedestrians and the cars and buses wheeling by. He was astounded. "Am I dreaming, or have I certainly landed in the future?"

"Elias," said Eileen as she approached his table, "this is my doctor. He is having difficulty believing that I have been in the eighteenth century and has come to meet you."

Dr. Goldberg extended his hand, and the two men shook hands. "Elias, I am Eileen's doctor, and she said that you are from 1724 and are a native Bostonian. I see that you have been creating quite a commotion by the deerskin clothes you are wearing and the knife in your boot."

"Nice to meet you, doctor. Yes, I met Eileen on the river. We were both heading to New Orleans to fight the last battle of the Restitutionary War. I have taken a liking to her and came into the future as her escort. I don't think it's proper for ladies to travel by themselves." He took another gulp of coffee after dunking his chocolate biscotti in the dark brew.

Eileen sat quietly, listening to the two men converse. "Here, Dr. Goldberg, I got you some tea with lemon and sugar. I got you a blackberry muffin." She set the food and drink in front of him. "I hope it will hold you over until dinner. Dr. Goldberg, do you believe me now that he is as 'real' as you or I? And like me, he was not suited to sitting, so he left Boston after his wife and child died and took off for Canada, where he lived as a trapper. I truly think that God intended us to meet. Don't you think he's grand?" Eileen was grinning from ear to ear, which astonished Dr. Goldberg, as he knew she was totally uninterested in the men that she knew.

"Dr. Goldberg, it's almost 5:00 P.M., and Elias and I must try to get back to the past and the river. Anita is fixing a festive dinner, and we said that we would try to attend. We are going to start down the river again in the morning. Everyone is hoping that we can safely transport back."

"Very well, Miss Gordon. Let me go to your transporting point. If you disappear from my sight, I will know that I haven't been dreaming. And before you go, take this three-month prescription for your pills and run over to the pharmacy to get it filled. I guess that if you are schizophrenic, you are that way no matter where you are in time and space. While you are getting the pills, Elias and I will go to Kramerbooks and get some food for you to take with you on your journey, in case you two don't make it back to the river. I see that Elias has stocked up on bags of coffee, so that problem has been taken care of. Hurry!"

"Thanks, doc. I will try to return in three months. I set up an appointment with your secretary. If I don't show up, it means that I am somewhere else in time. So I'll meet you two at Kramerbooks, and then Elias and I will attempt to return to the past."

"Okay," and the two men and two dogs headed down Connecticut Avenue to Kramerbooks.

Half an hour later . . .

Eileen had her pills, and she met the two men and two dogs at the bookstore. They had two bags of food and were having a grand time talking about psychiatry and the progress that had been made since the advent of medication and the science of the mind.

"Thank you, doc. It's 5:30 P.M., and we must hurry if we are to get back in time for dinner. We must leave."

The three of them plus the two dogs hurried to Dupont Circle and stood together. "Dr. Goldberg, you'd better step back, as we don't want to transport you, too."

"Okay. Good luck, and I hope to see you in three months!"

Elias and Eileen joined hands after Eileen had dialed 1942*. A deep voice said, "Elias and Eileen, hang on." There was a POOF of pink bubble, and Eileen and Elias and the two dogs shimmered before Dr. Goldberg's puzzled eyes. POOF! There was no one there anymore. They were gone.

He pinched himself and said, "I'll be damned! . . ." He walked slowly, in a speculative mood, back to his office, which was closed. He walked upstairs and went into his office. "Was I dreaming?" He looked down and there, on the floor by his chair, was Eileen's pashmina stole. She had forgotten it.

"I will give it to her in January—if she returns. At least I know that she was actually here." The telephone rang . . .

TING-A-LING . . .

TING-A-LING . . .

It was his wife. "Where are you? When are you coming home? Shall I hold dinner?" She sounded worried because he was never late for dinner. Was that because she was such a good cook?

"Yes, dear, I'm fine. I'm leaving the office now. I just had the most amazing experience. I'll tell you all about it when I get home. What's for dinner? . . ."

17

An Interruption in Flight

IGHT HAD FALLEN, AND THE BUBBLE WAS FLITTING THROUGH the night sky . . . back through generation after generation . . . back three hundred years . . . back in time . . . back through the cold, cold centuries. Eileen and Elias were discussing what he had seen and heard in the twenty-first century. It was hard to digest, for Eileen was also displaced . . . finding the eighteenth century as strange to her as Elias was finding the twenty-first century strange to him. . . .

"Eileen, you tell me that you are a flight attendant and work on 'airplanes' in the sky. That is hard for me to understand. Do you mean to tell me that you work in bubbles like we are on now?"

"Well, not exactly Elias. Planes are more like silver tubes with wings, and they carry many people—as passengers—from one place on the planet to another. Not back and forth through time, like we're doing now. But yes, they fly through the air like our bubble."

All of a sudden there was a thump, and the bubble spoke, "Hold on folks, the skies are turbulent tonight, and we are heading into a storm!" Then, out of nowhere appeared a small circular screen, a radar screen. Eileen and Elias were startled.

"What is that Eileen?" Eileen looked at the small green screen. There were green spots and dots and lines—too cool for words.

Eileen said in a low voice, one that was puzzled by all that was happening, "Elias, that is a radar screen and it will show us where we are, but it has never appeared before when I was being transported through time. Something is different."

"I am different. I am tired of being a bubble and have decided to be more of a small ship, a plane if you will," growled a deep voice totally unlike that of the former voice of the pink bubble.

"Wow, bubble!" said Eileen as she giggled and pointed to the screen. "Oh look Elias, we are heading for a break in the storm clouds. It looks as though our means of transportation is trying to maneuver through that break in the clouds. Elias was flabbergasted. Never in his wildest dreams had he experienced anything like this.

BUMP! THUMP! The machine bounced around, throwing the two passengers from one sidewall to the other. "Seatbelt, Eileen! Seatbelt, Elias!" Suddenly there were two seats and a cockpit window.

"Elias, the bubble has changed shape and we seem to be in an airplane of some sort—or maybe a spaceship. I hope this vehicle knows what it's doing." Eileen expelled her breath suddenly and experienced shortness of breath. She was afraid. For that matter, this fear was not unusual because turbulence always scared her. She finally gasped in some air, and turned her attention to her friend Elias, whose countenance had turned a ghastly shade of grayish white. His eyes were dilated. His hands were shaking, but he managed to fasten his seatbelt like Eileen had showed him.

"Where are we?" he gasped as sweat rolled down from his forehead into his eyes, causing tears to roll down his face.

"I don't know. The bubble has never been like this before, and I haven't a clue as to what is going on."

"I am evolving, kids," thundered the deep voice. "I am thinking of endeavoring to become a spaceship. Wow! That would be too cool. Then we could go to Mars!"

The top of the thermos was the only cup they had, so the two shared the coffee in the top and munched on the jerky, now silently enjoying the ride. Then, looking out of the cockpit window they noticed that they were heading down, down, down, approaching the forested land below, hovering over the silver streak of the swiftly flowing river.

"Fasten your seatbelts, we are landing."

A thump . . . silence . . . no motion; they looked out the window. They were beside the river. "Get out!" said the voice. "I will see you later."

They stepped through the wall and were on terra firma. They looked around. The machine was gone. They were alone in the forest, beside the silvery streak of river slithering silently along it's path. Where were they? Then they noticed to the south a column of smoke ascending into the evening sky. "It must be our friends, cooking dinner." Eileen looked at her watch; only ten minutes had passed in real time. Elias was once more in charge of events. He grabbed his knife in one hand and Eileen's hand in the other. They silently started walking along the river toward the smoke curling into the darkening sky. Silently they went on, both pondering their recent experiences . . . voices . . . barking of Wahu, Yahu, and Scot.

"Here we are!" yelled Eileen, thankful to hear once again the voices of the three dogs, her friends. The dogs came bounding and barking, wagging their tails, full of joy to once again see the two time travelers. They had been missed. Bounding and barking, they jumped up and down, howling at the top of their lungs.

CAT appeared, almost invisible, her grey fur blending into the deepening darkness approaching. Then, "Eileen, where are you?" It was Charles and Robert Green approaching, guns held at their sides.

"Here we are!" yelled Elias. "Everything is fine. It is good to see you!"

Hugs and handshakes! The four humans, three dogs, and one gray cat headed downriver to the campsite. Dinnertime.

18

Too-Ka-Moo-Ka

*T*HANKSGIVING ON THE RIVER—AH, YES—THE FESTIVAL OF
Thanksgiving granted to the early explorers and pioneers. It was
a misty morning: mist rising up from the surface of the water, looking
mysterious and spooky. It was cold, too, this early morning on the Potowatomie. Anita was paddling the raft down the river behind the others
in the party in their canoes and the one kayak. CAT was lazing on the
front of the raft, and Scot, Yahoo, Wahoo, and Tabby Cat were judi-
ciously spaced out among the canoes. Wahu was upset by this arrangement because he wanted to be with Eileen, but the kayak had no room
for him. So he sat, somewhat unhappily in the front of Elias's canoe,
which was cruising down the river alongside Eileen in her craft.

Zusette had pulled alongside Anita, and they were worriedly discussing what to serve for Thanksgiving dinner on the river. Would there be enough?

"Zusette, do you think we have enough beets and onions to make a salad? Eileen brought back from the future some extra virgin olive oil that she said was imported from Greece. Where is Greece?" said Anita.

"Well, Greece is in the southeastern part of Europe. My boys, Mac and Zak, told me about Greece, which they said was the cradle of culture and our approach to thinking. The boys went to college and learned all sorts of neat stuff," said Zusette, who was inordinately proud of her twin boys.

Eleanor and Robert, who were in the lead screamed back to the others, "Hurry up! Look what we've found." Everyone hurried until they reached Eleanor and Robert. There they saw a sign sticking up on the riverbank. It said:

Thanksgiving Dinner
At Too-Ka-Moo-Ka Campgrounds
Just follow the signs
Along the way
And they will show you
Where we play.
Dinner is served at half past four
Which gives us time
To catch more animals
To eat—a treat.

Charles was curious. He said, "Come on group, let's tie up our canoes, kayak, and raft under those trees around the turn in the river— they should be out of sight. Let's see what is going on at Too-Ka-Moo-Ka."

They all did as he said and secured their vessels, gathered the food they had left—not much, as they were only about a week away from

New Orleans and General Walloby's forces. Charles had been hoarding four bottles of champagne he had brought from the wine cellar at Liberty Hall. He and Eileen preferred it chilled, but there was no ice and no refrigerator—things which he and Eileen took for granted. He securely placed it in his backpack, picked up his rifle, and took off along the trail leading through the woods toward the campsite. It was about nine o'clock in the morning and the mist was gently lifting off the river, the Potowatomie, which river the whole party loved for it's beauty and the sheer adventure of it's flat water, class five rapids where they had to portage—extremely burdened by the raft—and the beauty of the waterfalls, lovely forests, and the cool clear bluish green water flowing along it's way.

Anita yelled, "Hey look. Some mushrooms like the ones we eat at home." She scurried off, she and Eileen and Eleanor and Zusette, to pick the mushrooms. "They will be great sautéed in the olive oil," said Eileen, proud of her newly acquired culinary skills. She was planning to write a cookbook once the war was over. She and Eleanor and Anita had discussed doing this as a joint venture. Although Eileen was new to the art of cooking, the other ladies were accomplished cooks and had decided to do the recipes and let Eileen illustrate it.

The dogs and cats made a great noise, telling everyone to be careful. They had flushed out a baby skunk. Utter stillness and quiet fell upon the group, which watched transfixed as the baby skunk crossed the path in front of them.

Then a loud, masculine voice reverberated through the woods, "Yo! Over here! Keep going along the path. You are almost here." Everyone noticed that the voice had a Scottish accent. "Here! Welcome! I am Reverend Angus McDonald, and this is my lovely wife, Flora. We are going to New Orleans to join forces with General Walloby, and we stopped here to celebrate Thanksgiving."

"Glad to meet you Reverend. I am Robert Green from Virginia, and these are my friends and traveling companions; we are also going to participate in the Restitutionary War. Let's celebrate together. We don't have much food, but we do have four bottles of the best French champagne, and an occasion like this calls for celebration."

Flora walked over to the ladies and said, "Angus caught a deer this morning, and we obtained some kale from the last Indian village that we passed. We traded a pound of coffee for it. There is enough for everyone."

Charles said, "We have some coffee. I'll go back to our boats and get it. We don't have much left, but we'll be glad to contribute a pound of our wonderful French roast."

The dogs and cats were excitedly meowing and barking, "What is there for us? We're hungry too."

"Don't worry. I brought some food with me. It is just for you. Don't worry. There is not much for everyone, but we won't go hungry. Look! I also brought some apples for dessert," said Eleanor. "Come on girls. Let's start preparing for the party." Saying this, she unloaded her backpack in which she was carrying flour for bread and a bottle of cognac. "We can each have a swig after dinner. You don't mind do you, Angus? I know you are a man of the cloth and might disapprove."

"Actually I am Presbyterian and have nothing against liquor in moderation. After all, our dear savior's first miracle was to change water into wine for a wedding celebration."

Meanwhile Robert, Tom Tom, and Jeremy started skinning and preparing the deer in preparation for roasting over the campfire. Zak and Mac had headed back to the river to catch some fish, since it was to be a course meal service.

Jeremy was thinking how lucky he was. Since he had come on the river trip, he had fallen in love—which he was not sure was a feeling that was reciprocated—and he had made unusual new friends. A Boston trapper, two people from the future, four Indians, two Scots, and miscellaneous cats and dogs. He came from a very sheltered, upper class life, but he was having the time of his life. If only he could win Anita's heart, which surprised him because she was of a different race and a slave to boot. He and Robert had discussed this problem and Robert had said to him, "When we get to New Orleans, I shall get a lawyer and emancipate her. She can make a living anywhere with her talents as a cook, weaver, gardener, and seamstress. Eleanor will miss her greatly, but Anita deserves to be free. It suits her spirit."

By now, several hours had passed. The men had begun roasting the deer. They were also preparing several fish that they had caught. The women were spreading blankets on the ground. There were no tables or chairs. Anita had gone back to the raft and procured dinner ware. The bread was baked, and the mushrooms were sautéing to perfection. The beet and onion salad and the kale were ready, and apples were ready for the feast.

Everyone gathered around the campfire—the dogs were excited by the smell of roasting meat, and even CAT and Tabby Cat were more excited than was usual for them, especially as they knew there was enough to go around for the entire party.

The sun was dipping into the western sky, and chill filled the air. "Dinner time," yelled Angus as he held up his Bible. "Before we eat I will read some scripture," which he did: the twenty-third psalm. Then everyone joined hands in a circle, and he said grace:

> Thank you God for the vegetables and meat
> Thank you God for the food we eat.
> Bless us as we go on our way
> For the rest of the week—every day.
> Amen.

Eileen said, "All right, let's dig in." She was in her element serving a sumptuous feast to her new friends and family. Besides the food and champagne and cognac, there was wonderful water from the spring she had found. Not only did they drink the wonderful cold water, but Eileen had chilled the champagne in the spring. The animals joined in the feast, and everyone had a wonderful repast, until at last it was time to return to the boats, along with Angus and Flora who had decided to join Eileen and company. They were all going to fight to get rid of the Brits and re-store the coffee trade.

Night fell! The moon lit up the night sky. Dark clouds drifted across the horizon. They were tired and full of the wonders of their feast. They all spread their bedrolls upon the cold, hard ground and fell asleep as the fire slowly burned down until there were only embers . . . and dark-ness settled all around. . . . And the river rolled on, its lullaby of gently flowing water filling their souls with quiet. . . .

19

The Assignment

"Yes, General Walloby, my party and I just reached New Orleans, and we want to help the war effort. I understand that you have been informed of my unusual story and that of my friends."

"I hear, young lady, that you are from the future and have a means of transporting yourself through time and space. That seems farfetched to me, but I am desperate at this time and am willing to accept help from wherever it comes." Saying this, he pulled out his pipe, lit it, and puffed it several times.

"Thank you for trusting in us. There is no guarantee that we will be able to escape. I don't know all of the capacities of my Bubble Machine, but we are willing to trust it if we can be of any help in preventing the deadly battle tomorrow." Saying this, Eileen stood up and shook her short red curls. They bobbed up and down, making the general and his aids dizzy.

Elias, breaking into the conversation said, "General Walloby, we have the best chance of getting through enemy lines, killing General Trent, and returning to our own camp and literally disappear."

"I understand and wonder if there is any way we can help." Once again General Walloby puffed deeply on his pipe. He was puzzled, and the pipe helped him appear in control of the situation, part of the reason he was the general in charge of his army.

"Well, a map would be nice." Said Elias.

At this time, a voice rang out yelling, "Come and get it, dinner is served!" It was Anita, a chef superb. The party joined her, prepared to enjoy what might well be their last meal. They all sat down. Elias whipped out his hunting knife and proceeded to sharpen it.

The sun was setting, and a cool night breeze was rustling the leaves in the trees.

The old hoot owl was looking down on them from his perch in the old tree. As Elias and Eileen looked up into the night sky, they saw hundreds of buzzards circling and many, many more perched on the tree branches. They were waiting for the great feast following the next day's battle. The rabbits, squirrels, and birds had all gone for cover. They didn't trust buzzards. Buzzards also were part of the ecosystem but they were carnivorous, and the other citizens of the forest didn't trust them.

Yahu, Wahu, and CAT jumped up and down and howled. "We will help," CAT purred. She walked up to Elias. He reached down and automatically patted her head.

Eileen was talking to Eleanor, Charles, and Robert. "Would you like to take a chance that we can get to Mars on the Bubble Machine with Elias and me after we complete our mission? We have never killed anyone before, but it's the only chance we have to prevent a full-scale massacre tomorrow."

Robert and Eleanor said to her, "Eileen, we have emancipated Anita, and she and Jeremy have been given money to help them go anywhere in the world. They have decided to stay in New Orleans. Anita is going to start a restaurant, and Jeremy is going to start a military academy for young boys. So we don't have to worry about them; the rest of our party plan on returning to their homes back up the river when the war is over."

Charles piped up and said, "I want to go with you. You know that I like adventure, and this looks to be a dandy!"

Eileen meanwhile had brought out her guitar and was singing "St. James Infirmary." She was good on the guitar. Elias had never heard the song, or the blues for that matter. But he loved it. He joined in singing.

When dinner was over—sausage, collard greens, and potatoes—the whole party got up and headed for the circle where they were to meet when the adventurers returned. Elias and Eileen asked for a prayer for their success, and everyone bowed their heads and prayed.

Then came Elias's booming voice, "It is time to leave. Come on Eileen." They bid everyone goodbye and slipped into the forest and disappeared . . .

> Quiet as a mouse
> In their dark clothes
> Invisible. . . .

20

The Potowatomie at Night

*W*HAT A SIGHT!
The Potowatomie at night!
Fireflies flicker through the trees,
Lighting enhanced by the evening breeze.
The moon shines down as bright as can be
Appearing speckled through the trees.

"Elias, we've done it. We are committed. It's do or die. Why, oh why, did we tell General Walloby that we would take out General Trent, the commander of the British forces down here in New Orleans? Now we are on our own, and I guess we should tell Robert and the others what we're doing."

"Yes, Eileen! We must leave New Orleans within the hour. It is growing dark, and we must accomplish our mission then. We must be back at camp before sunrise."

"Elias, I've never killed a man before. It's too horrible to contemplate, but if we don't do this, thousands will lose their lives."

"Come on, Eileen. Let's tell Robert, Charles, Eleanor, and Anita. We must tell them that if we are not back by sunrise, we failed and won't be returning."

As the two conspirators made their way back to camp, they both noticed that their hearts were beating wildly. Then, there in front of them was their campfire and their companions seated around it on logs and blankets on the ground, roasting venison steaks over the fire. The aroma of cooking flesh assaulted their nostrils. They walked up to the campfire and hailed their companions.

Robert got up and walked up to Elias. He noticed that both his descendant and her friend were agitated.

"What is the matter?" he asked as they both sat down.

Elias raised his head and said, "We have been ordered to kill General Trent so as to prevent a huge battle tomorrow."

"Yes, Robert, and we came to tell you that if we don't return by daybreak, we won't be coming back. And if we do come back, it will be necessary for Elias and me to use the Bubble Machine to carry us away from here. I don't know if the Bubble Machine can transport all of us, but we should be willing to try. I don't know yet where we'll go, but my biggest desire is to go to Mars."

"Mars! That will be quite an undertaking!" said Robert as he stood in front of them, holding Eleanor's hand. Charles stood up while chewing on a hunk of venison.

"Wow! That is so cool. I would love to go to Mars," said Charles, grinning from ear to ear.

"Well, it's time for us to go. Get the animals together and we'll all try to leave when we get back."

Yahoo, Wahu, and CAT jumped up and down and howled. "We are going, too. You need us. We can be scouts. We can be attack dogs. CAT can be lookout."

"Okay, guys, come on, but you'll have to be silent. No barking or yowling."

It was dark. The moon was shining down, but all of a sudden there was cloud cover. They were having difficulty seeing and being quiet all at the same time. The three animals were leading the way, and the two humans were tiptoeing quietly behind.

After about two hours, they saw light from enemy campfires blazing up into the dark night sky. " CAT, can you creep into the camp and find out which tent General Trent is in and how many guards there are?"

CAT looked straight ahead, flicked her whiskers back and forth, and started heading for the enemy camp. Yahoo and Wahu looked back and forth and also headed for the campfires. They went quietly but confidently. They had been around humans enough to know that they would never be suspected of nefarious behavior.

After about fifteen minutes they had figured out where the enemy general was quartered, and they reported back to Elias and Eileen. "Come on, follow us," said the three animals.

"Come on Eileen, stay near me and we will kill General Trent," said Elias as he slid his sharpened hunting knife from it's sheath. Eileen was shaking from head to toe, but she gamely followed Elias. They started crawling to the general's tent. As Elias neared the tent, he noticed that one of the guards was snoozing on his watch. Elias crept up on the sleeping guard and stabbed him. Then he cut a hole in the tent, and he and Eileen entered and saw the general asleep on his cot. Quickly Elias stabbed him in the heart.

> A drop of blood fell on the floor
> It was followed by quite a few more.
> The sound of a knife
> FLICK, FLICK, FLICK
> A man fell down

Quick, quick, quick
Silently he lay there on the floor
Silently out the blood did pour
As he lay there on the floor.

The other surreptitiously looked around
Then directed his gaze to the ground
Bright, bright red was the blood
Quietly staining the Persian rug.

"Elias, Elias." Eileen screamed
"Is this happening, is this a dream?"

Elias came dashing
His knife flashing
Blood dripping down his face

"I tell you Eileen, this is not the time or place
To fall in two
We have lots that we must do."

She quieted down and looked around
The body was still, lying on the ground.
"Come on Elias, let's get out of here
Or we'll be in trouble, that is clear."

They left the tent, very intent
After removing their prints
They did not intend to leave any hints.

Yes, the deed was done, and all of the five—humans and critters—
quickly started running. Someone noticed the dead guard and went into
the tent where they found General Trent dead on the floor. A great cry
went up, and after being told the general was dead but still warm, the
soldiers started crashing through the trees on the trail of the killing party.

The clouds lifted, and Elias and Eileen and the animals could see where they were running. Their lives were at stake. The soldiers were only about twenty minutes behind, and they knew that they were in grave danger. Finally they saw their campground and their companions standing by the campfire with their weapons and equipment at their feet. They yelled to Elias and Eileen to hurry. Scot was excitedly jumping up and down.

He was sorry that he had not been part of the animal contingent, but he was quite old and could not have kept up.

Eileen hurried up, followed by Elias. "Quick, everyone, stand by me in a circle.

Let's all pray that the Bubble Machine can transport us all, hopefully to Mars."

They stood in a circle and Eileen held firmly onto her communicator, and dialed 1942*. All of a sudden a deep male voice said, "Hold on. Here we go." The oncoming soldiers saw the party in a circle, and then in a POOF they were gone. The soldiers heard a deep voice saying "Ho, ho, ho, off we go!"

Then as they stood there in amazement, their mouths hanging open, they heard a laughing female voice cry out, "In God we trust, it's Mars or bust! . . ."

BOOK III

In God We Trust, It's Mars or Bust!

Prologue

"WAKE UP! WAKE UP! WAKE UP!" BOOMED A DEEP MASCULINE voice. "We're off to Mars, I hope."

Eileen roused herself and looked around. She recognized the surroundings. It was like the first class cabin of the old DC-8, complete with galley, bathrooms, the lounge area with the table, and cockpit. Behind this area was the cabin, which was filled up with big boxes full of equipment.

Elias woke up at the same time and looked around at the unfamiliar space. He was astounded. Never in his wildest daydreams had he conjured up such a situation as he was now in. It was more complicated than the Bubble Machine and time travel, amazing as that was, transporting him and Eileen into the future and back to his colonial times . . .

1

Dinner on Board

Wow, Elias! This is different than the Bubble Machine. It's more like a spaceship!"

"Goodness, Eileen, you are right! In my wildest dreams I never imagined anything like this!"

Robert Green interjected with his most recent observation. "This ship has a water machine. It has a handle that says 'push me.' And I did, and water came gushing out into a cup made out of some strange material."

"Robert, that's plastic, which became available in the twentieth century." Eileen was gazing around the ship when all of a sudden came a booming voice . . .

"Well, folks, I am your spaceship that hopefully will get us all to Mars. I've never tried anything this ambitious, and I suggest that we all pray that we make it. You'll find food and drinks in the refrigerator that is in the galley."

Eileen perked up. After all, she was a flight attendant and totally knew her way around a galley. "Look what I've found . . . coffee! Where did that come from?"

She glanced at Charles who was looking at the radar screen in the cockpit. Charles replied, "I put some into my backpack because I knew that whatever happened we could all use a good, strong black cup of coffee."

Eleanor was looking through the refrigerator which surprised her because it was so cold. "Come on Eleanor, let's whip up some dinner and coffee."

"Right, Eileen!" Eleanor was puttering around the small space and discovered dishes and cooking utensils. "What do we use for a fire?"

Eileen agreed with Eleanor that they needed to whip up some grub. "Eleanor, the oven is a convection oven, and we need to adjust the dials so that we will get hot food. You turn the dial to the correct temperature and then turn it to 'on.'"

The men, meanwhile, had settled down at the lounge table with a deck of cards that Robert had found in his pocket. "Let's play a game of poker until dinner is ready." Charles laid a blanket on the lounge table. Elias picked up the cards with a big grin on his face and professionally shuffled them.

"Just think, Robert," mused Charles, "poker has survived down through the ages. What shall we use for money?"

Eileen piped up and said, "Look, in the box titled 'Entertainment.' There are some colored chips. Our machine has thought of everything."

"Folks," boomed the ship's voice, "settle down and try to relax. It's going to be a long trip unless I can figure how Einstein's theory of relativity works. Turn on the viewing screen. I have programmed the Rolling Stones' concert in Philadelphia back in the '80s. You all should enjoy it. I also programmed "Tumbling Dice," which I believe is appropriate for a game of poker."

"Yes, that is certainly appropriate," said Eileen who was having an attack of the giggles in the galley brought on by stress. She walked to the lounge table and told Elias that the Rolling Stones were a band popular in the last half of the twentieth century, her favorite band followed closely by the Beatles. Then BOOM, BOOM, BOOM—Charlie Watts on the drums, Keith Richards on the electric guitar, and Mick's wonderful voice filling the little spaceship.

Delicious scents wafting from the galley . . . organic beef and vegetables sautéing in garlic. Coffee was brewing, also filling the cabin with it's deep aroma . . .

The dogs and cats were beside themselves with joy. They loved to travel, and this mode of transportation was totally new to them. It was thrilling. They were ecstatic because Eileen had found some pet food. CAT's tail was swishing back and forth, and Tabby Cat was eating some nibbles. The three dogs were chomping down on chicken and gizzards complete with bones.

After displacing the card player—Elias being the winner and happy to be doing something familiar and which he was good at—Eleanor set the table and called everyone to dinner. After saying grace and thanking God that so far they were safe and thankful for the wonderful food, Eileen changed the music to the Baroque period, her very favorite. The beautiful music was relaxing. It provided a wonderful atmosphere for a gracious dining experience.

The ship's voice boomed once again, "Don't eat everything, and keep some water. What you see is what you get. I don't know when or if we get to Mars, and I don't know when you will find more food and water. Now look out the cockpit window."

They all finished dinner and headed for the cockpit. They looked out the window. It was black, black, black, with white pinpoints of stars, and straight ahead was a round red heavenly body. "Mars, Mars, Mars!" they all screamed in glee, "Oh, great planet of mystery."

The ship hurtled onward through the night, which looked just like day. The red dot and the white dots all gleamed and danced.

Then, to everyone's surprise, Eileen put a bottle of Benedictine and Brandy on the table. She had discovered it in the liquor drawer in the galley. There was a second bottle, but she decided to save that for later.

Elias pondered, "What is guiding this spaceship?"

Before her eyes closed in sleep, Eileen said in her most informed voice, "It's the automatic pilot. This ship is on automatic pilot."

Peace descended on the cabin. They all fell asleep sitting up at the lounge table, wondering in their dreams what the morrow would bring . . . what the future held. . . . Wahu was thinking, *How far I have come from Hawaii and Madame Pele. . . .*

The autopilot was thinking about his plans. *When and where in time will I arrive, with luck, on Mars? This is all so complicated compared to time travel and transporting via dreams. If I do get us to Mars, then I'll have to figure out how to get back to Earth so that I can refuel and restock the ship. . . .* The radar screen glowed in the dark with it's flickering lines lighting up the cabin. . . .

2

Day Arrives, But It Looks the Same

ILEEN AWOKE, FEELING STIFF AND UNCOMFORTABLE FROM SIT-
ting upright throughout the night. She crawled over Elias, who was
sound asleep. "I guess I'd better check and see what equipment we have."
So she quietly left the lounge area and passed the galley and bathroom
and stepped into the small cabin filled with boxes of equipment. She
was perplexed. There were boxes of stuff, one including three tents—
one for Eleanor and Robert, one for Elias and Charles, and one for
Eileen and the animals. There was a big box filled with several rifles,
three pistols, and five knives that were sharp as could be.

"You see," said the ship's voice, "I don't know what your surroundings will be like when we land, and I believe in being prepared. Go ahead
Eileen, look in the other boxes." The one labeled "Entertainment" attracted her immediately. There was a guitar, two bongos, and a flute.
There was also a Bible and some murder mysteries and a cookbook for
Eleanor. There was a gardening book for Robert and leather bones for
the animals.

As she was engrossed in looking through this box, she felt a tug at her pants leg. Looking down she saw that Wahu had joined her. She gave him a big hug, and he barked happily. He needed a quiet moment with Eileen all by himself.

"Hey, Wahu, we certainly have been leading an adventurous life lately. Ever since I joined forces with the bubble machine and the dream machine and now the spaceship, life has been most unpredictable. But I promise you that we will always be together.

Wahu wagged his tail and said, "Glad to hear that, Eileen."

Next she went to the box labeled "Clothes." There were spacesuits for all five of the humans and pressure helmets in case they were needed. Eileen was happy to see that the spacesuits were sleek and slimming. She always worried about looking fat. She noticed collars for the animals. Their instructions said to bark or meow three times, and stun beams would flash out and stun their adversaries. Sort of like a skunk surrounding itself with scent when cornered.

Wahu, Yahu, Scot, Tabby Cat, and CAT had all joined Eileen and were filled with curiosity as they looked into the box. Eileen fitted them with their collars and warned them to only use them if lives were in danger. They all agreed to be careful.

Wahu once again tugged on Eileen's pant leg. She looked at him, and he directed his gaze to a beautiful painting on the cabin wall. "Why, that's my painting, 'The Green Boys.' Whatever is it doing here?"

She was puzzled when the ship's voice said, "I picked this painting and several others either to decorate your environment or use for trade as money."

"Oh, thanks a lot," said Eileen, who wasn't sure that her paintings were of any value.

"Eileen, what are you doing?" said Elias who had joined her in the cabin. "What is that?" he said as he picked up a camera.

"Elias, that is a camera. It takes pictures. Charles is a good photographer, and that is intended for him to use for taking pictures of the land we are about to see. We might want to write a book about our adventures, and Charles will take pictures for the book."

Then Eileen saw a box labeled "Toiletries and First Aid." She was surprised at how thorough the ship had been. Looking through it, she saw a year's supply of her nutritional supplements for each member of the party. There were her magic pills for headaches and a year's supply of pills for her schizophrenia. A great load was immediately lifted from her mind. There were alcohol and antibiotics and bandages. "Hallelujah, we are prepared for whatever happens." There were even razors in case the men wanted to shave. And deodorant, which to twenty-first century citizens was an absolute must-have.

And to her absolute amazement she saw five bicycles. Normally this would have worried her because she wasn't much in the way of a cyclist, but she could see the need for them. Each bicycle had a backpack and a small cart to carry an animal.

There were sunglasses and reading glasses. There were toothpaste and toothbrushes.

Then . . . BUMP!

The ship's voice said "Hold on! We have come close to being sucked into a black hole. Hang on! Sit down and fasten your seat belts."

Elias and Eileen scrambled back to the lounge and clambered into their seats and buckled up.

Horrible bump! Horrible turbulence!

Eileen hated turbulence and had turned white. Charles had turned white. They recognized there was a problem, but Eleanor, Robert, and Elias were totally unprepared. They raised the window shades and looked out. The heavens were jumping up and down. The animals all hid under the table. It was crowded there with ten legs and five animals, but since they were all in this together they grinned and bore it.

Then, a terrible lurch!

And . . .

Then stillness.

They looked out the windows and saw that the sky was still. The ship's voice said "We are safe. I managed to get away from the black hole, but it was touch and go. Just relax."

Everyone drew a deep breath. Relaxing required more concentration.

Elias said "We need some music. How about the Rolling Stones. I like them. I want to learn to play the guitar like that fellow, Keith Richards. . . .

BANG, TWANG, YELL . . .
All is well . . .
All is well. . . .

3

Late at Night

L
ATE . . .
Late at night
The flight
Was cruising on
The Black Hole was gone
Gone—along

"What is this I am thinking, restlessly turning in the chair, while the others are sound asleep. Where will we land? Will we land?" Eileen reached down and gently patted Wahu's ears. The other animals were asleep, as well as their humans.

"Whatever happens, Eileen, I will be by your side," said Wahu in a low yip.

"We will always be together.

Right then, Elias stepped out of the cockpit. He had been learning to fly. Amazingly, he had taken to piloting effortlessly. His years of being in a canoe, canoeing over much of North America, had instilled in him a wonderful ability to steer any mode of transportation. He was looking forward to driving a car like the ones he had seen when he and Eileen had visited her shrink in the early twenty-first century. He walked over to the table and whispered to Eileen to join him in the cabin as everyone in the lounge was asleep. CAT meowed gently and whacked Wahu's left ear.

Eileen and Elias and the two animals walked, or rather, tiptoed out of the lounge, stopping at the galley for some treats and the remaining B&B. There was still some left from dinner because they had planned to discuss their adventures later that night and finish it off. Eileen looked out the left window and shrieked, "Elias, we're in the year 2012—in fact it's June fifth."

"How do you know that?" asked Elias, who never ceased to be amazed at the things his new friend said.

"Well, if you look out the window you will see Venus passing across the face of the sun between the sun and Earth. That configuration will not be seen for another hundred years."

"Wow! That is fascinating. I have never seen such a thing." They raised their glasses and saluted each other. Elias continued, "I was talking to the ship, and it said that we should make an attempt to land tomorrow afternoon—early. It cannot tell us too much, but it has been listening to the modulator-translator and has found that there is a war going on, called the Trillium War. Trillium is like our coffee. It appears to be much like the Restitutionary War, which we just ended before we fled Earth. It seems this is a warrior planet and I hope we fit in. The ship is not sure where we will land, but it thinks it can land us near the Midianite camp. It thinks the Midianites will be friendlier to us than the Ridianites. The modulator-translator has copied out some maps of the area on the computer's printer. The nearest city should be about fifty miles away. I also printed out a basic dictionary of the Midianite language. You are on your own where it concerns grammar.

"The ship also said to tell us and our traveling companions that it must return to Earth to restock itself and also to get your prescriptions for your pills renewed. It will need a written authorization from you to authorize Dr. Goldberg to renew the pills. . . ."

. . . Eileen rubbed her left eye. "Oh no, not a migraine." That meant she needed to take three gel caps of Advil for Migraine. That was the only thing that had ever helped her when she had a migraine.

Yahu, in true borzoi fashion, sauntered into the cabin. She had taken a special liking to Elias, and he returned her affection. "ARF, ARF, I missed you. Please remember that you are special to me and we need to stay together."

Elias looked carefully at Eileen, who had turned a strange color, brought on by the headache. He sympathized as he, too, got migraines, especially after he lost his family in England to smallpox during one of the epidemics. Eileen told him that smallpox had been nearly eradicated in America by the twentieth century. Neither she nor Charles was especially fond of pills and vaccines, but sometimes they were invaluable. Elias, Eleanor, and Robert were used to herbal remedies, and also they had strong constitutions. They thought that Eileen was somewhat prissy, but she was game to try new ways with them. One shining example was that she had given up her afternoon coffee for tea—"go-along-to-get-along." Elias thought that she was somewhat fragile but had a brave heart, so he didn't mind too much, as a brave heart was more important to him. . . .

Yes, he admired a brave heart, which started many an adventure that somehow she had survived and was still alive—in fact, did thrive. The love of being alive the five and the animals did share. No matter where the ship should land, as the ship planned. . . .

The ship bounced up and down, and the plates all clattered onto the floor; cups spilled, and utensils flew! What to do? The ship was trying to stay out of black holes—they were situated everywhere in the black night sky. Between the turbulence and migraine, Eileen had turned white, and sweat formed on her forehead and slid over her eyes, down past her nose and onto the rug. The others did not have headaches but were valiantly trying not to throw up onto the carpet. The animals had once again huddled beneath the lounge table.

"Look," thundered the ship, "there is Mars! It is nighttime and you can see the two moons. We should be there in time for us to land in the afternoon. You can set up camp before dark."

"Thanks for the information," said Elias who was so excited he was shaking. Eileen had fainted, and Wahu was sitting on her stomach. He thought the warmth and the touch of a living being would make her come around. It really bothered Wahu that she had difficulties. He had been very fond of Madame Pele, but he truly loved Eileen, who was not so temperamental.

He thought back to the days of fire being thrown into the sky, lava spilling down the ground on the mountain side—it did slide. He padded about, did sing and shout. It was so much fun when the dark obscured the sun. Pele—Madame—with her flaming clothes, wandering where the lava flows. Yes, it had been great knowing Madame Pele but he had gone on to new adventures. Off to a new planet, a red planet, wondering if he would once again see volcanoes erupting, throwing lava into the sky.

Eileen moaned and laboriously managed to sit up. "Where am I?" she asked.

Elias said, "You're not dead." He gave her a big hug, and every one of the people and the animals welcomed her back to their world. She had slipped away, slipped away, slipped away. . . .

"Finish your B&B," said Elias as he handed her the unfinished glass of B&B. . . .

4

Time to Sleep Again

*E*VERYONE HAD NODDED OFF. THE TIME-TRAVELING HAD BEEN overly stimulating, and everyone needed rest. Eileen, though, could not sleep. She had had a relapse and lost track of who she was and where she was. Everything was spooky to her except for Wahu, who knew that she was in trouble, and he was sticking close to her. He knew that something strange was going to happen and he needed to be close by.

Elias couldn't sleep as he sat next to the window. He was overstimulated. Like Wahu, he was concerned about Eileen. They had grown to be great pals, and he instinctively knew that something was brewing. Since his wife and child had died in London, he had been lonely. Eileen was the first person to break through his shell. He had grown to love her, as he knew that she loved him. He knew she would bolt if she thought their relationship through to a logical conclusion. Something, however, was wrong with her, and he had no idea how to help. Finally, being restless, he went to the cockpit to talk with the ship's computer. He liked to look out the window. The universe was lovely, although dangerous. Yahu joined him. Yahu felt about him like Wahu felt about Eileen, like CAT felt about Charles, and Tabby Cat and Scot felt about Eleanor and Robert Green.

The ship was still trying to figure out their estimated time of arrival, but its mathematical skills were limited. It told Elias about the Viking landers, and the latest lander named Curiosity and how Curiosity was heading for Mars about the same time as his crew, and the ship's computer thought that they would all be landing about the same time. They needed to land away from cities as they would need to acclimate themselves to the atmosphere and the gravity. Both were less than what they were used to. There was still a little food and water left, but it was imperative that they find both.

The ship's computer was telling Elias how to assemble the bikes for everyone and their baskets for the animals and for whatever tools and supplies they had—especially their iPads, which would allow them to stay in touch if they should become separated. The reconfigured batteries were good for one hundred hours. Elias sat there quietly listening. He was confused and concerned and reached into his backpack and pulled out his well-worn Bible. He did this everyday, especially when he was troubled. Right now he wanted to thank God for the wonderful experiences he and his new companions were sharing and to ask for guidance on their adventures.

Eileen, meanwhile, tossed and turned while she tried to return to the present. She was lost in time—back in Hawaii and meeting Wahu. He, himself, was still sitting next to her. Keeping watch. He was hoping that she would recover soon. Charles was sleeping on the floor with CAT sitting on his chest, counting his breaths. He had loaded all of the guns and sharpened the knives. He was prepared for whatever would happen.

Robert and Eleanor were asleep at the lounge table along with Scot and Tabby Cat.

Back in the cockpit, the ship's computer told Elias to get some sleep as it would be a full day in the morning and he would need all his wits about him; so he laid down with Yahu. Quiet reigned as the night sky whizzed by. . . .

Morning . . . everyone awoke and had a cup of coffee. They had one bag left to celebrate their successful landing and their first night on Mars. After coffee, they noticed the sun at a great distance away. The landscape of Mars was reddish and rocky.

"Get to your seats and fasten your seatbelts!" yelled the computer. "We are about to land." All of a sudden there was a great lurch. They were descending through the thin atmosphere. The ship wobbled greatly.

They were amazed to see the surface of this mysterious planet. It approached rapidly. Eileen looked dazed. Everyone was worried. She grabbed Elias's hand for comfort. She yelled over the sound of the engines, "Elias, I'm afraid something is going to happen to me. I wanted to tell you that you mean the world to me. I thank God that I got to meet you."

Wahu looked at the other animals and said to them, "Take care of your humans. They need you. . . ." Suddenly, the ship turned upside down, and everyone's blood rushed to their heads. They heard a loud noise and the ship's computer yelled, "It's a blue hole. Watch out!"

Then a great blue hole opened up under Eileen's body. She grabbed Wahu to her chest, and yelled, "I don't know where I'm going," and then . . . she and Wahu vanished.

Elias grabbed Yahu and slipped into the tail end of the blue hole. Where he and Yahu and Eileen and Wahu were going he hadn't a clue, but he knew that they would be together . . . somewhere, sometime, today. . .

5

Being in a Funk

"WE'RE SUNK, WAHU! WHERE ARE WE?" EILEEN LOOKED around. She was clutching Wahu to her chest with all her might. She knew that, no matter what happened, she needed to be with Wahu. They understood each other and had ever since they met in Hilo when Wahu approached her one night at the lagoon where she was sitting on the rocks, watching the lava from the volcano shoot up into the night air. Madame Pele had been throwing a fit, and lava was gushing everywhere. Lava leapt into the dark night. Wahu was out walking with Madame Pele when he noticed a sad soul sitting by herself, feeling forlorn and generally out of sorts. Wahu knew that Eileen's sad soul needed him.

"Hi," he said.

"Hi," she said.

They bonded as soul met soul.

"Can I explore with you from now on?" he inquired.

"Yes, it would please me greatly if we traveled together," she answered.

So they became the best of friends—forever. But now it was time to get back to the present, or wherever they were in the time continuum. Wahu tugged gently at her sleeve to bring her back to where they were. As he tugged gently, Eileen regathered her wits and concentrated, trying to figure out where they were. "Where are we, Wahu?

"As far as I can tell, we have jumped into a 'blue' hole, and we have landed in this strange room, sitting on this marble bench. Side by side!" Eileen was watching the room whirl around and around in lavender circles. Stars jumped up and down, distracting her from her concentration. She started thinking. "Wahu, I think we made a mistake by leaving our friends and family. I especially miss Elias. I wish I knew how to get back to Mars."

Wahu thought and thought and suddenly had an insight. "Eileen, I feel in my bones that Yahu and Elias are on our trail. Yahu will find us no matter where we are, and she will bring Elias with her. So, don't get discouraged."

They both sat there and watched the world whirl by their bench. The colors were mesmerizing to their eyes. All of a sudden they heard . . . "ARF. ARF. ARF."

"WOOF, WOOF, WOOF" went Wahu. "We're in a blue room. Keep on looking!"

Then, CRASH and BANG. Into the blue room with the dancing balloons and stars crashed Elias and Yahu. "We've found you," yelled Elias, and Yahu jumped up and down with joy, thrilled to be reunited with her new friends. Elias grabbed Eileen and gave her a huge bear-hug and said, "Hi, kid. I missed you. However, we must get back to our ship and friends. Remember, you have always wanted to go to Mars. Now is your opportunity. I brought my compass and iPad so that we can get in touch with everyone. Just before I jumped into the blue hole, I had a moment's conversation with the ship's computer, and it told me to keep my eyes open and when a 'pink' hole came into our range, we all were to jump in, and hopefully it will spit us up on Mars. Then we will have to find the others. It is the only way I know to get back to 'reality.'"

The four of them sat, waiting for a pink hole. They didn't appear often, but for some reason one had decided to stop for them. After sitting quietly thinking for a long time in the quiet, all of a sudden they heard a loud noise, and the earth rumbled and shook around them. "Grab Wahu!" Elias grabbed Yahu with one hand, and he grabbed Eileen's hand with his other. Then there appeared a "blue" hole that quickly turned pink. It grew large enough for all four of the living souls to jump in.

It screeched, "Jump!" The four of them jumped and started whirling round and round as they were dragged into the tumbling pink hole. They jumped together with a prayer . . . but to where? . . .

CPSIA information can be obtained at www.ICGtesting.com
Printed in the USA
LVOW02s0344260813

349594LV00015B/24/P

9 781887 730327